Accidentally Perfect

ALSO BY ELIZABETH STEVENS

unvamped
Netherfield Prep
No More Maybes
the Trouble with Hate is…

Accidentally Perfect

Elizabeth Stevens

SLEEPING DRAGON BOOKS
ADELAIDE

Sleeping Dragon Books

Accidentally Perfect
by Elizabeth Stevens

Print ISBN: 978-0648264859
Digital ISBN: 978-0648264842

Cover art by: Izzie Duffield

Copyright 2018 Elizabeth Stevens

Worldwide Electronic & Digital Rights
Worldwide English Language Print Rights

For Andy,
who never gives up on me.

Contents

Chapter One 1
Chapter Two 14
Chapter Three 26
Chapter Four 38
Chapter Five 50
Chapter Six 67
Chapter Seven 81
Chapter Eight 94
Chapter Nine 105
Chapter Ten 123
Chapter E l even 141
Chapter Twelve 154
Chapter Thirteen 164
Chapter Fourteen 176
Chapter Fifteen 188
Chapter Sixteen 199
Chapter Seventeen 211
Chapter Eighteen 224
Chapter Nineteen 236
Chapter Twenty 249
Chapter Twenty-One 268
Chapter Twenty-Two 279
Chapter Twenty-Three 289
Chapter Twenty-Four 299
Chapter Twenty-Five 311
Chapter Twenty-Six 323
Chapter Twenty-Seven 339
Chapter Twenty-Eight 347
Chapter Twenty-Nine 356
Chapter Thirty 365
Chapter Thirty-One 375
Thanks 387
About the Author 388

Chapter One
There goes the Neighbourhood.

Hadley covered my ears and glared at Tucker. "Don't say things like that in front of the young and innocent," she chastised and I waved her away.

"Hads," I grumbled as I shoved her hands off me and Tucker laughed.

"Of course. My bad," he said. "We couldn't possibly allow Piper to know about," he leant forwards, his hazel eyes shining, and whispered scandalously, "sex."

Hadley put an arm around me and I gave them a friendly smile as they laughed. Because what else was I going to do? I was the innocent, virginal, sweet little Piper Barlow and my friends had decided I shouldn't be in any rush to change myself. So they did what they called protecting me and I was plenty happy to let them.

Hadley looked at Tucker pointedly. "This is why a certain someone would be perf–"

A commotion to our right heralded Roman Lombardi staggering out of a classroom and I turned to watch Mr Dunbridge follow him. Both of them wore a scowl, although Roman's had a hint of amused defiance about it.

As usual, Roman's dark brown hair – shorter at the sides but longer on top – hung into his eyes, his shirt was half untucked, his tie was loose, and he carried his skateboard in one hand, his other hand a fist.

"I'm serious this time, Roman," the School's vice principal said as he pointed at the resident underachiever. "I catch you with it during class again and you'll get more than detention."

Roman held his hand up and the lighter in it flared to life. "What, this?" he asked, full of an innocence even I knew was completely fake. "This tiny little thing, Dunbridge? What *do* you think I'll get up to?"

"Do you enjoy spending Friday afternoons in my company, Roman?"

That amused defiance played at Roman's lips, but his eyes were hard and a muscle twitched in his jaw. "They're the highlight of my week, *sir*."

Mr Dunbridge sighed. "Well, consider this Friday something to look forward to."

Roman gave him the most condescendingly mocking bow. "With pleasure, *sir*." Again, he spat the word with a healthy amount of contempt.

"Get out of my sight before I kick you out, Roman," Mr Dunbridge pointed down the hallway, clearly at the end of his tether.

"Oh, you've tried that three times already, Dunbridge. And, where did that get you?" Roman sneered.

Mr Dunbridge's lip curled like he was trying to control a snarl. "Get out of here before I forget to care who your father is."

Roman's lip twitched but it wasn't pleasant. "Oh, but it's so much easier not to care, sir. Trust me, I'd know." He threw Mr Dunbridge a completely insincere smile and whirled on his heel.

As he passed the three of us, he gave us a once over with the laziest unimpressed expression as his eyes raked us up and down. We watched him stalk out of the building as he reached into his blazer pocket.

Mr Dunbridge threw us a terse grimace masquerading as a smile before he went back into the classroom and closed the door.

Tucker snorted and Hadley smiled.

"Well, I was just thinking we hadn't had nearly enough Roman drama this week," Hadley commented.

Tucker smirked. "I heard Shayla's still a lovely burnt orange under something like five layers of makeup."

I hid a smile.

The week before, Roman and his mates had broken into the girls' locker room and replaced all of Shayla and her clones' moisturisers with the darkest shade of tanning lotion. I might not have liked Shayla and the idea of her being orange might have been humorous, but even that failed to detract from the fact that anyone could be the next target of one of their pranks.

"Leave poor Shayla be," Hadley said with a grin.

"Oh, come on. She deserved it, at least."

"That's beside the point. How would you like to be orange?"

Tucker smiled to me. "I'm pretty sure I could pull off orange."

"You'd look like an oompa loompa."

"I'd make a better oompa loompa than Shayla. She's far too grumpy." He pouted playfully.

Hadley giggled. "Not funny."

"Very funny. Maybe we should convince them to put Nair in the shampoo next time?"

"Stop it!" Hadley said as she covered her mouth with her hand.

"Piper, tell her. Shayla wouldn't look anything like an angry Dwayne Johnson if she was bald, would she?"

I managed to control my smile, but Hadley responded before I could open my mouth.

"Don't corrupt her, you arse." She batted Tucker's arm.

Tucker held his hands up in defence. "I'm not doing anything of the sort. I just asked Piper's opinion."

"And she won't dignify your question with an answer because she's far too polite to even think such horrid things."

Actually, there were plenty of impolite things I could say about Shayla and the way she looked down on the rest of us regardless of whether people liked her or not. But, I wouldn't.

"Unlike you," Tucker pointed out.

Hadley nodded. "Someone has to make up for it."

Tucker laughed. "Oh, so you're only rude because Piper's lovely?"

Hadley nodded and they seemed to start heading for the doors as though we'd made a unilateral decision to move. I hurried after them after a heartbeat.

"Yes."

"Bullshit."

"Excuse me, I'm a lady."

Hadley wasn't a lady, but I wasn't going to remind her in front of Tucker. Not that he needed reminding.

"Are you? My bad, I hadn't noticed."

They laughed as we walked outside and Celeste came bounding up to us, her honey-blonde ponytail bouncing right along with the rest of her.

"There you are!" she said with a smile as she and Hadley joined arms and Hadley absently waved for mine.

I slipped my arm into hers as we meandered along in much the same way we had since Year One.

4

"Tucker, man!" Craig called and I looked over to see him standing with Mason and Simon.

I felt my cheeks heat and I practically hid behind Hadley.

"I'll see you *ladies* later," Tucker teased before he jogged off, catching the football Simon threw him.

"Hey Mason!" Hadley waved enthusiastically as she elbowed me. "Oh, Piper! It's Mason!" she said loud enough for him to hear.

"Leave it," I hissed and Hadley giggled.

"He'd be perfect, babes. Ease you in, look after you, be a proper gentleman."

I rolled my eyes, but I kept it to myself. "No one knows if he likes me or not. You're making assumptions because he smiles at me sometimes."

"He stares at you *all* the time," Celeste said.

"Like someone else we know," Hadley elbowed me again and I repaid the favour as my eyes jerked up.

Roman was over the other side of the oval where he and his mates usually were at Lunch. He was facing us, but nothing about that actually suggested he was looking at me.

"No one else looks at me."

"Firstly, lots of people look at you. Secondly, Roman certainly does look at you."

"God, I wish he looked at me," Celeste sighed.

"No, you don't," I muttered.

"Me, too." Hadley grabbed my arm with her other hand as we walked towards the bleachers. "Are you sure you've never spoken to him?"

I nodded. "I haven't talked to him any more than either of you."

"That is *not* what his eyes say."

"Eyes don't talk, Hads."

We all stopped and watched him for a moment as he and his mates goofed around doing whatever it was they did to entertain themselves. That was until some girl I only knew by sight approached him. You could feel the ice from the other side of the oval as he completely shut her down. Behind him, Steve and Jake doubled up in laughter before Rio gave Roman their weird handshake and the girl hurried away obviously upset.

"Roman Lombardi's eyes talk, Pipe. Oh, how they talk."

Did it not matter that we'd literally just watched him shit all over a girl he'd no doubt hooked up with over the weekend? That we'd just witnessed the infamous Roman Brush-Off, complete with insults from his friends? That she was the third girl in as many weeks that we'd seen, let alone the however many we didn't?

"It's about the only part of him that does," I grumbled.

"That's not true. We just heard him speaking."

"We heard him antagonising the vice principal, not quite the same thing."

"Oh, what did he do now?" Celeste asked excitedly.

Hadley recounted the incident in the hallway while Celeste gasped animatedly in all the right places.

I, meanwhile, snuck a look at Roman across the oval as we all sat down. It was true, we had just heard him talking. But, just about the only time anyone heard the sarcastic, gravelly notes of Roman's voice was when he was riling up the establishment. Otherwise, he just walked around with a look on his face like someone had pissed in his lemonade.

Although, I suspected it had been a while since Roman had drunk lemonade. At least judging by the last time he'd been arrested for public drunkenness.

6

My headphones were blaring in my ears so I didn't notice white twin cab ute until it was careening past me. I paused, my heart pounding in my chest. Then, before I kept on, I moved closer to the shoulder of the road.

I breathed deeply, trying to calm my heart. Except, the fright had sent it into a pattern it knew too well and I felt the usual shortness of breath and the antsy feeling in my fingers set in.

I shook out my hands as I walked, focussing on the song in my ears and the steps of my feet. I didn't really hear the lyrics. I didn't really hear the tune. I just focussed on counting the beat.

By the time I turned into the driveway, my heartbeat was back to normal and I remembered how to smile. That was until I noticed a mighty similar big white twin cab in the driveway next to ours, and Roman Lombardi was reaching into the tray and pulling out a cardboard box.

I frowned and blinked in confusion.

I knew the house had sold. Mum had told me the house had sold and there was a 'SOLD' sticker plastered across a 'For Sale' sign no one but the Barlows saw unless they'd come specifically looking.

Roman looked up as though he could sense me standing there and my heart thudded again along with a sick, sinking feeling in my stomach. My skin felt itchy the way it often did when he looked at me. I had that urge to get away from him, but my feet refused to move.

"Love, can you find the kitchen things?" a voice called from inside the house.

"I've got it," he called back, only half-looking to the house as though he couldn't take his eyes from me either.

The split second our gazes weren't locked was all it took to break whatever spell I'd fallen under. I pulled my phone out of my pocket as I tore my eyes from him and hurried inside.

Hadley picked up on the third ring. "What?"

"SOS!" I hissed as I closed the front door, pulling myself up on tip toes to sneak a look through the window.

"What?" she asked. "Are you okay?"

"NO!" I snapped, ducking down as though anyone could see me.

I heard Hadley laugh. "Okay, so it's not that bad. What is it? Did Mason ask you out on the way home and you need date outfit advice?"

I rolled my eyes. "No," I huffed. "The new neighbours have moved in."

"Oh! Tell me he's like twenty-five, rides a Harley and set you on fire with one look!" she squealed.

"Stop reading those books, Hadley," I ordered. "They are giving you a *completely* unrealistic view of the world."

"Okay. So he's thirteen, gawky braces, and he stuck his hands down his pants when he saw you?"

"Ew. I'm putting you on a timeout. Until you're eighty."

Hadley giggled. "You still haven't got to this oh-so-threatening SOS. Who moved in?"

"Roman Lombardi," I whispered and there was silence on the other side of the phone.

Just as I was about to ask her if she was still there, she screamed. Loud and excitable and right in my ear. I dropped my phone and fumbled to pick it back up again as I yelled her name.

8

"Honey, that you?" Mum called from the kitchen and I stood up, surprised.

"Uh, yeah."

"Oh, good. Hey, listen," she appeared at the door and I could tell she'd been cooking by the smudge on her cheek and the mess on her apron, "I invited Carmen over for dinner tonight."

I swallowed and nodded. "Carmen?"

"Lombardi, hon. You know. She's just bought the place next door and I invited her and the kids over."

Kids? Had Paris come home?

"Honey?" Mum sighed, humorously exasperated.

I jumped as my phone went off and I realised Hadley had hung up on me in frustration and was calling me back. I held a hand up to Mum and nodded.

"Sure, dinner. Good. Uh, Hads…" I said absently as I pointed to my phone then ran up the stairs.

"Leave me hanging, why don't you?" Hadley yelled in my ear as I rushed over to my window and stared out it.

"Sorry. Hads, he's unpacking cars. And, Mum just–"

"I heard. Oh my God, babes. Opportunity knocks!"

"Hadley," I warned.

"Piper?" Her voice was sugary sweet.

"Shut up," I snapped.

"But, he's just there, waiting for you to–"

"Hadley. Shut. Up," I repeated.

"Babes–"

"I'm going away now and I'm not speaking to you until tomorrow," I informed her.

"No! Pipe!"

"Tomorrow! Bye," I yelled after I'd pulled the phone from my ear, my eyes glued to the house next door, and I hung up on her.

I got changed and spent a couple of hours sitting in my window seat pretending I was reading my English book when I was actually watching the movement next door.

Somehow I must have actually got sucked into my book because the next thing I knew, I was jumping in surprise when the doorbell rang.

"Honey!" Dad called and I smoothed my shirt as I stood up, not sure why I should feel so nervous that Roman was standing at my door.

"Coming!"

I mean, Roman and I had been at school together for something like ten years. Sure, we hadn't talked to each other outside the vague requirements of a couple of shared classes over the years. And, sure the guy was trouble. But, honestly that was no reason to be nervous.

I took a deep breath and went downstairs to see Mum talking to a woman I recognised well as someone Mum socialised with from her book club.

And I'd stressed for no reason, because…

"No Roman?" Mum asked her.

Carmen shook her head. "Uh, no."

Carmen's expression suggested she was telling Mum a whole lot more and Mum's expression suggested she understood that whole lot more. I looked between them as Mum gave Carmen a smile before turning to me.

"Carmen, you remember Piper?" she asked, motioning me over and I wandered towards them.

The woman with the thick curly brown hair and the nicest light brown eyes I'd ever seen smiled at me warmly.

"I do, although you've grown up a lot," she replied and I smiled.

"Hi. It has been a while."

"I think it was the Year Eight play, maybe?"

I nodded. "Probably, yeah." I huffed a laugh, "Wow, I'd almost forgotten about that."

"You were wonderful."

I shook my head. "Not so much."

"You were very enthusiastic. That counts for a lot."

I laughed. "That's a good word for it."

"Carmen! Good to see you!" Dad cried as he came out to the hallway, wiping his hands on a tea towel.

"Matt, you too. Bree wasn't sure you were going to be home in time."

"I got out of my meeting. Come through. Come through. It's good to have you over. Bree just mentioned the setback. But, no Roman?"

Mum gave him an exasperated look and an apology crossed his face. Mum led us through to the living room.

"Oh, no. It's fine," Carmen brushed it off. "He'll be in bed by sun up."

"Wine, Carmen?" Dad asked and we were obviously skipping over any more talk of Roman.

"Thanks, yes."

"We have one of those whites?" Mum offered and Carmen smiled.

"Perfect."

Dad headed over into the kitchen while Mum and Carmen talked about things I had no idea about and they were obviously used to talking about together. I wondered if that was what Hadley and I looked like when we sat on that very couch and giggled.

11

Once Dad came back with a bottle and glasses – and a Coke for me – we both sat and watched them talking. I lay my head on Dad's shoulder and answered every now and then if conversation was directed to me.

Just as Dad got up to check the dinner, the doorbell rang again.

"I've got it," I said as I hopped up.

"You've got her well-trained," Carmen teased.

"Only in front of company," I replied with a laugh as I pulled the door open.

My laugh died as I took in the scene in front of me.

Roman Lombardi was standing on our doorstep, his arms behind his back, with two police officers flanking him. There was a cut on his lip that hadn't been there earlier and a bruise forming on his left cheekbone. His face was set, that muscle in his jaw twitching. He stared me down, full of anger.

"We're looking for Mrs Lombardi?" one of the police officers said and I pulled my eyes off Roman to look at her.

"Uh, sure. I'll just... Carmen?" I called, my eyes drifting to Roman again.

The laughter from the living room stopped and Mum followed Carmen to the hallway. Carmen's easy smile dropped as she took in the sight, then she sighed like she thought she was an idiot for expecting any better.

"I'm so sorry, Officer Daniels," she said as she stepped forward. "What was it this time?"

"Fighting. Mr Lombardi dealt with it."

"Couldn't possibly embarrass the old man again," Roman snarled.

Carmen shot Roman a look that quite clearly told him to shut up.

"What? He'll pay my bail but not for the house? It's not fucking–"

"Thank you for bringing him home," Carmen said loudly, cutting him off.

Officer Daniels nodded and took some keys off her belt. As she reached behind Roman, I realised she was undoing handcuffs.

As he stretched his arms out and rubbed his wrists, he flicked his hair out of his eyes. "Just in time for dinner."

Carmen huffed, said thank you to the police officers again before they left and turned to Mum with an apologetic smile. "I should get him home."

"Oh, are you sure? There's plenty."

Carmen shook her head. "Thanks, Bree. But, I think it's best if we…"

Mum nodded, her eyes full of sympathy. "Of course. No problems."

"Thank you for the wine. We should finish this sometime."

"When you're all settled." Mum smiled.

Carmen nodded.

"It was good to see you Roman," Mum said, but he only glared at her and gave her a slight nod.

"Night," Carmen said as she took hold of Roman's arm, barely coming up to his shoulder.

When I looked up to his face, I found him staring at me. Those deep black holes of eyes raked down my body and back up. His face remained stony as he sucked his teeth and let his mum pull him home.

Chapter Two
Perfection and the Douche.

It had been almost three weeks since Roman and his mum had moved in next door.

I'd spent the first week trying to get Hadley over the fact Roman had moved next door to me. I'd spent the next week trying to get her over the fact that we caught the same bus to and from school on the days he bothered to show up. I'd spent the third telling her there was no way I was going to be taking advantage of his proximity. I'd spent the whole time reminding her that it was not swoon-worthy that he'd shown up at my door beaten and bruised and brooding bloody murder.

And, I was starting to think she'd finally accepted it as fact and we could move on with our lives.

Hadley popped a bubble. "Remind me again why I'm wasting my Free here?" she asked, her caramel skin and the highlights in her dark brown curls shining in the sun.

"Because," I answered, "Mason suggested he wanted me to come to his lesson and you wanted to perve on the other boys."

I smiled as Mason waved and bowed to me from the field.

Mason was – in the eyes of every girl at school – pure perfection. He had light brown hair that he would flick out of his deep blue eyes like Prince Charming. With his almost six-foot height and definite six pack, kids either wanted to be him or be with him. But, none of that went to his head; he was nothing but nice and kind to everyone.

Hadley snorted. "Well, that does sound like me. But…" I could tell that something else had caught her eye. I watched her dip her sunglasses and bite her lip. "I've seen something *far* more to my taste…"

Unable to supress a grin, I followed her gaze and saw Roman and a couple of his stoner friends wandering past the bleachers. Roman had his trademark skateboard in one hand and a cigarette in his other. He was everything Mason wasn't; right down to his almost black hair and those eyes like two black holes. And, of course he was probably something ridiculous like at least six-foot-five. He was conceited, obnoxious, annoying, rude, and all that detracted massively from the unequivocal fact that he was gorgeous.

Or he would have been, if he wasn't such a douchebag.

Mason Carter was not a douchebag. As if anyone even needed a reminder, Mason Carter was just at that moment busy checking one of his classmates was okay after he'd been knocked over.

Hadley sighed dramatically. "Shame he only has eyes for someone else."

"Who does what now?" I asked, chewing on my finger as I watched Mason run around the field.

"That is *not* helping," Hadley commented and I looked over at her.

"What's not?"

Hadley sighed again and looked at me like I was a poor, unfortunate albeit lovable idiot. "Piper, you cannot suck your finger while a guy is already undressing you with his eyes."

My eyes darted to Roman – not that they had any reason to. The corner of his mouth twitched as he looked at me and my finger popped out of my mouth. I pulled my eyes away from Roman and back to Mason.

"I wasn't sucking on anything," I muttered, feeling my cheeks go red.

Hadley snorted. "Well, while you're busy denying the fact that you remain Roman Lombardi's Everest–"

"I am not his anything."

"He's been eyeing you for years."

"He's done nothing of the sort." *Much.*

"And, it's only got worse since he moved next door."

"There is nothing to get worse." *Really.*

"Regardless. While you're living comfortably in denial, do you want to maybe send him my way?"

"Sure Hads," I scoffed. "I'll get right on that. Next time Roman asks me out on a proper date like a normal guy, I'll let him down easy with the knowledge that your legs are just waiting to part for him."

She smacked me on the leg with a chuckle. "Again, sounds like me. But, maybe not lead with the 'my best friend's an epic slut just waiting to bang the hottest guy in school' thing."

"You really think he's the hottest guy in school?" I asked, not for the first time and I knew it wouldn't be the last.

"Objectively, hell yes. Are you going to tell me you don't? I mean, those eyes, Pipe. Come on! That man makes you wet just looking at someone else!"

Laughing, my eyes fell on Roman again, who was still standing at the bottom of the bleachers with his friends. He looked up at me expectantly as though my express purpose for looking at him had been to exchange a 'hello'. But, I couldn't look at him for long. I never could. There was something in his eyes when he looked at me. I didn't know what it was and I didn't have to be close enough to see it to know it was there, but it sent a shiver up my spine and made me antsy. It had been there before he moved house and it had only intensified since.

"No," I said, my laugh dying a little as I wriggled on the cold seat. "You've been reading too many trashy romance novels *again*. The only effect he has on me is repulsion. That *boy* is heinous. It's like he's the guy version of you, but just *so* much worse!"

Hadley snorted. "Wow, thanks. Stellar compliment." She smacked my leg again. "Finger out of mouth." I did as I was told. "I swear I can see Roman's boner from here."

I choked on an inconveniently placed glob of spit. "Stop already!" I spluttered. "Roman doesn't want me. He just likes the rumours that he sneaks into my house at night for wild sex."

"If only you weren't a virgin," she huffed. "Trust you to live in one of the two houses in the boondocks with Roman Lombardi…" She sighed.

"Firstly," I pointed at her, "I don't live *with* him. Secondly, it's hardly my fault his family moved into the house near mine."

"Next to yours. Next. To. Yours. And, you can be sure – if it was me – I'd be banging that on the regular."

"You'd get sick of no strings at some point, Hads. You talk a good game, but you'll want commitment one day and we all know Roman isn't that guy. He's not your John Cusack."

Hadley slid me a look. "Oh, but Mason *is* your John Cusack!" she cooed.

Now, I smacked her. "Shut up. Mason's very nice, but there's nothing there."

"Piper, he's all over you. Just give him some time to work up the courage, why not?"

"Boys like Mason don't need courage. They've got girls just begging to go out with them."

"No, men like Roman and Tucker don't need courage. Men like Mason are nice and genuine and sweet and don't want their hearts stomped all over."

"You keep insisting on calling them men. They're not men."

"If you tell me you're waiting for a real man, honey, I feel it's my duty as your best friend to tell you that not all of us have a John Cusack waiting for us. Some of us might need to settle for the Mason Carters of the world."

I smiled. "Like that would be such a hardship."

"See, you *like* him!" Hadley nudged me with her shoulder.

I laughed, very aware of keeping my finger out of my mouth. "He's fine, I guess."

"He's fine?" She pointed at him on the field below us. "He's nearly six-foot of lean muscle, who can't take his eyes off you. And, I'll bet he fucks like a pro. Not as good as Roman, I'll wager… But, beggars can't be choosers, I suppose," she sighed sarcastically and I ignored what I knew was little more than vulgar bluster.

But, ugh, why did my eyes slide back to Roman again?

He was busy pulling tricks on his board like a complete idiot. Mason may have been pure, lean muscle from years of sports training, but Roman's body was no less amazing. Objectively speaking, of course. He had a mastery over his body and the way he did those stupid tricks–

No!

What the hell was wrong with me?

18

"Okay. Purely objectively, Roman is…beautiful," I muttered, annoyed with myself.

Hadley laughed out loud and Roman turned to us, which made me quickly look back to Mason.

"Admitting it doesn't make you anything less than a woman with eyes, Piper. Don't be ashamed because you've got eyes. Go on, say it a little louder. You might like it."

I smiled and felt my cheeks flush again. "No. Thanks. You have at it."

She cleared her throat, smoothed her hair and stood up. I grabbed at her school skirt, but she resisted my pull. "Roman Lombardi is beautiful!" she yelled, her arms spreading wide. Then, she blew him a kiss!

I saw Roman was looking up at us with that intense stare just before I buried my face in my lap to hide my incredible embarrassment for the girl I loved so dearly. She laughed loudly as I felt her fall back down next to me and we dissolved into giggles. Between the ensuing mayhem, I saw Roman kept a watchful eye on us and Mason likewise didn't stop swinging glances my way.

The thing I hated about living in what Hadley considered the boondocks was that the bus didn't travel all the way to said boondocks. It stopped at the end of the long road that ran down to the boondocks and then it was a fifteen to twenty minute walk home.

This, on its own, wasn't terrible. The walk was good for me but it was a time when I lived in my head for a bit too long. So, I usually put my headphones on and listened to my music as tried not to think too much. It wasn't ideal when it was raining, but that was life.

The thing that made it terrible was Roman's insistence on catching the bus as well – even though he had a car! – and the annoying way he either skated around or walked with me.

For the last three weeks, I'd ignored him quite successfully. But that day, he wore this infuriatingly knowing smirk and I could tell he wanted to say something. I pulled my headphones off and glared at him, blinking against the slight drizzle.

"What?"

"So… Hadley thinks I'm gorgeous?"

I rolled my eyes. "Yes," is of course what I said because I had an inability to come up with decent lies or excuses on the fly and it was easier to just placate him.

He chuckled roughly. "Sweet. She need my number?"

I opened my mouth to say something that I expected would be quite scathing. But instead of saying it, I snapped my mouth shut and kept walking. That only served to make him laugh harder.

"See Barlow, the great thing about you is that you don't have a spine," he teased as he rode literal lazy circles around me.

I bristled. But, that lack of a spine showed itself far more obviously by my lack of response. I pulled my blazer around myself and crossed my arms.

"Why don't you drive to school? You have a car."

"Incredible powers of observation there, Barlow."

"Shut up, Lombardi," I muttered.

"Was that almost an insult?"

I sighed as it started raining more heavily. "At least one of us could be warm and dry…" I said to myself.

"While I appreciate you caring for my health, Barlow, I

couldn't possibly let you walk home alone by yourself. I'm far too much of a gentleman."

I gave him a look that told him exactly what I thought of that without having to put it into words.

"You seem particularly sour today. Has Carter *still* not asked you out?"

What did Roman know about Mason asking me out or not?

I glared at him some more. If that flash of lightning I caught from the corner of my eye had hit him, I don't think I would have minded all that much.

"Seriously, the guy either has no balls or he's playing you. If it was me, I'd have asked you out weeks ago."

"If you actually ever did do that, I'm supposed to let you down gently by telling you Hadley's waiting."

He paused. "Huh. I'll keep that in mind. But," he hurried to catch up with me, "that doesn't explain this funk you seem to be in."

"Who says I'm in a funk?" I asked, shifting my bag on my shoulder.

The most annoying thing was, he wasn't wrong; I was in a funk. It had nothing to do with the fact Mason hadn't actually asked me out yet despite the rumours swirling; like I'd told Hadley, I wasn't sure there was actually anything there. But, I didn't know what the funk was about. Sometimes, I was just in a funk and that was all there was to it. Not that I was going to tell Roman that, though.

"I say you're in a funk," he answered simply.

"And you're an authority now?"

He only chuckled aggravatingly.

"I'm not in a funk," I said, but my expression was as sour as he was claiming I was.

"Prove it. Give me one of those infamous Piper Barlow smiles."

I glared at him.

"Hmm…close, but no."

"You could be home by now." Which would be totally preferable to me.

"Come on, Barlow. Give me a smile."

"I'm fine. Thanks," I answered with as close to sarcasm as I got with anyone but Hadley.

He pulled ahead of me and I actually thought that he'd given up and was just going home. Then he pulled a trick, didn't land it, and ended up on his arse in a puddle, looking up at me expectantly.

I bit my lip to suppress a laugh but the answering humour in his eyes made me smile despite myself.

"There it is!" He pointed at me, totally victorious.

"You fell off your board. Of course I was going to laugh at you," I huffed, trying hard not to smile and failing spectacularly.

I instinctively held my hands out to help him up and he took them with one hand as he picked his board up with the other.

"Fell off. Sat in a puddle. Much of a muchness." He flicked his wet hair out of his eyes and looked at me with that characteristic Roman Lombardi intensity. "The result was as expected."

I looked down and kept walking. "Roman Lombardi isn't the kind of guy to fall off his skateboard to make someone else smile…"

He walked beside me at my pace. "Isn't he?"

I'd snorted and said "no" before I could stop myself.

He laughed. "Then, it must have been an accident."

"Must have," I said softly.

Once again, I couldn't look at him. Roman wasn't the kind of guy who would do anything to make someone feel better; the fact that he spent so much time at school pulling pranks on people proved the opposite. But here he was, heavily implying he'd fallen off his board because he knew that would make me smile.

But actually, I had to admit it wasn't the first time he'd done something similar in the last three weeks.

Never where anyone else would see him, of course. That wasn't his style. It was only along this stretch of road.

He'd make some quip that never failed to make me smile or did something to make himself look stupid. And he'd never outright said he was trying to make me feel better, but it was one of the things that made me feel antsy and weird around him because it seemed so out of character for him.

I lost all ability to be intelligent the same way I did around Mason, but Roman annoyed me and confused me. At school, on Main Street, at parties, he was the town bad boy. But on this stretch of road, when it was just the two of us, he acted like there might have been more.

His little stunt *had* brought me a little bit out of my funk and I appreciated the fact that he didn't feel the need to talk as we continued walking.

Sometimes, he chattered incessantly whether I had my headphones on or not. And, sometimes he just seemed content to wander along beside me in an almost companionable silence, like today.

Although, today he wasn't quite silent.

As we walked along, I realised he was humming. He had a nice voice – as much as you can tell when someone hums – and I thought I recognised the song. I stopped as he got to a bit I totally recognised and I blinked at him in surprise. He either didn't notice or didn't care because he kept walking and I hurried to keep up.

23

Yep, he was humming 'Waking up in Vegas'.

That made me snort.

And when he got to the chorus, he surprised me totally by breaking full into song. Even a pretty decent singing voice couldn't stop me laughing out loud. He slid a questioning look at me as though there was nothing weird going on until he got to 'why am I wearing your class ring?' and looked at me like he was truly asking me.

I couldn't stop laughing as he continued. Apart from a small head-bop, he kept walking as though everything were normal until he got to the chorus again and he added a little extra swagger into his walk.

Finally, he was done and I had tears escaping I was laughing so hard. He walked in silence, his expression completely deadpan, while I tried in vain to compose myself. Finally, I managed it.

"Speaking from experience?" I asked.

He nodded solemnly. "Definitely. The hangover was real. He was a perfect gentleman, though. The annulment was quick and easy. We still exchange Christmas cards."

That set me off again and he slid me a wry glance, looking very pleased with himself.

"I'll see you tomorrow, Barlow," he said as we got to his house.

I nodded and waved. "Sure. Perhaps you can regale me with another Katy Perry classic on the way to school?"

"You take that to your grave, Barlow!" he said, his face stern, but his eyes full of humour.

I crossed my heart. "Of course."

He shook his head with a smile threatening, slid me one more look as he bit his lip, and disappeared inside. I walked the bit further to my house, still laughing and wondering what the hell was wrong with Roman Lombardi.

I stopped as I wondered what the hell was wrong with me to be laughing at something Roman had done. Laughing like it was okay that he was making me laugh. When it so wasn't because Roman was a player and I was in no way interested if he was actually looking at me the way Hadley kept trying to tell me he was.

I was so busy telling myself I was not going to be Roman's next conquest that I didn't even realise until later that night that he'd brought me completely out of my funk…

Chapter Three
Lazily Ambling Turtles, Hads!

Unsurprisingly, Roman hadn't been anywhere in sight when I'd left the house that morning. So, I'd had an oddly lonely walk to school.

But, it was surprising just how lonely you could still be even though you were surrounded by people.

And I wasn't even craving anyone particular's company, I just had some moments when I was surrounded by my friends that I still felt alone. It was weird and irrational, so I didn't tell anyone. I just pretended everything was okay. It was like those times when I just felt crappy; sometimes it just was and sometimes it wasn't. When it was, I smiled and laughed and told myself it would pass. Sometimes it passed faster than others. Sometimes it was harder to pretend than others. But, it did always pass.

Anyway, the point of that segue was that Recess on Thursday was one of those times. Term was over the next day and I had two weeks stretching in front of me where I could just have a break from people if I wanted. Because sometimes you needed that. Sometimes, you just needed downtime where you didn't have to pretend everything was okay and it didn't matter if it wasn't.

So, there I was at Recess – already over my surprising but minor disappointment that Roman hadn't been singing at me first thing in the morning – and talking with Hadley and Celeste on the bleachers.

"Mason's coming," Celeste squealed at me and I looked up to see him heading towards us.

Like all things Mason did, he didn't do it by half. He was striding towards us purposefully, his eyes locked on me.

The blonde, semi-bombshell who didn't look orange anymore that was Shayla Green grabbed his arm as he passed. "Hey Mason!" she said, her tone full of meaning.

To Mason's credit, his eyes didn't leave my face as he smiled politely. "Hi, Shayla. How are you?"

"Fine. You coming to the party tomorrow night?"

One of Mason's eyebrows rose in my direction. "Don't know. Depends what Piper's up to."

Shayla threw me a heated glare, flicked her hair and rallied like a pro. "Well if *Piper's* busy, I'll be around."

Mason nodded. "I'll let Craig know."

He missed Shayla's face turn red as he was still looking at me. He pulled his arm from her hands gently before she had a chance to say anything more and kept walking towards me. He jogged effortlessly up the bleachers and stopped a couple of rows below us, a huge smile on his face.

"Hey," he said suavely and I bit my lip.

"Hi."

"How are you?"

"Fine. You?"

He nodded. "Good."

I looked down to try to hide my shy smile.

"So, about that party tomorrow…" he started and sounded a little awkward.

27

I looked up and shook my head. "Oh! No, it's fine. Your flight's on Saturday morning, isn't it?"

He looked more relieved than I was sure he needed to as he nodded. "Yeah, nine-ish." He ran a casual hand through his hair and I was sure every girl watching just sighed. "And we still need to get to Adelaide. I don't think my parents will be too keen on me going to a party the night before." He smiled an apology.

I shook my head. "No, that's totally understandable."

Why were we talking like we'd be going together otherwise? Had I missed the part of dating where you don't actually get asked out anymore? Had he asked me out and I'd missed it? Even worse, had I said yes and not just completely missed it but not even realised?

He grinned. "Sweet. Well, I – uh – told Tucker I'd meet him. So, I'll see you later, yeah?"

I nodded. "Sure," I said, realising I had my finger in my mouth again and pulling it out quickly.

Mason bowed his head to Hadley and Celeste and jogged back down the bleachers.

"Why didn't you tell me my finger was in my mouth again?" I hissed at Hadley, forcing a smile for Mason as he turned and waved at us.

"Oh, no. You can suck your finger as much as you like around him." She flicked her curls out of her face and took a sip from my Coke.

I blinked. "What? Why?"

"Because," Celeste said, "he wants you. But he's shy about it, so he needs encouraging."

"And Roman needs *dis*couraging," Hadley added.

"Oh, this again?" I huffed. "Roman isn't...couraged enough to need discouraging." Before she continued, I remembered what he'd said the day before. "He did ask if you needed his number though."

"What? When?"

"On the way home last night. I told him I was supposed to let him down by offering up you and he asked."

"Wait. Why were you letting Roman down?" Celeste asked scandalously.

I rolled my eyes. "It was a hypothetical. He was being a douche about Mason. Anyway, I told him you didn't actually."

Hadley huffed. "Trust you to ruin my chance at the best sex of my life."

"You don't know that," I answered.

She shrugged. "I won't now." She grinned. "Mason's watching you again."

I looked down and saw him with his mates. They jostled him and teased him – probably for the fact that he was staring at me – but it didn't seem to deter him.

I tucked my hair behind my ear and looked down with a smile.

"Why can't a guy look at me like that?"

"Honestly, it's worse than Tormund and Brienne. It's disgusting, really." Hadley snorted, but I saw she was smiling at me encouragingly.

And that was the thing about Mason Carter; he had girls literally hanging off him, begging for his attention. But, unlike some guys – see Roman for example A – it didn't go to his head. In fact, he barely seemed to notice. He was only concerned with the girl he was interested in.

We saw it with Kristen before, during and even a little after they'd dated. We saw it with Amy before that. And with Nikki before that. And whichever other girls had come before her. None of his exes ever had a bad word to say about him and, likewise, he only had good things to say about them. We had no idea who dumped who in any situation and it all seemed totally amicable.

To a certain degree, it seemed awfully unlikely. But, Mason was just that nice a guy that it was believable.

And, every day was a testament to how damned nice Mason Carter was.

Every time we saw each other in the corridor, he smiled at me like I was the only one in the room. He'd stare at me in class to the point where even teachers teased him for not paying attention. He'd stop to talk to me. He'd hold doors open for me. He just made me feel ridiculously special. Every time I saw him, I'd be smiling and blushing and I barely knew what I was saying. He turned me into a blithering idiot, but my chest warmed and I didn't hate it.

Lunch passed and he still hadn't asked me out. A part of me assumed it made sense what with him going to Europe for the next couple of weeks with his parents; what's the point of asking me out then going away? Another part of me wondered if he was actually going to get around to asking. Maybe everyone had the wrong end of the stick and we were just good friends.

When did dating get so difficult? Or, was it just me?

Some kids at school went on one date – or didn't even get that far – and they just seemed to know that they were going together, officially boyfriend-girlfriend. Other kids went on a couple of dates with the same person and it was just understood it was just two people hanging out, with or without kissing – or more – involved. I was at a loss as to how you were supposed to know which was which. Everyone else seemed on the same wavelength as their crush or whatever.

Everyone, except me.

I felt like a complete weirdo. But, who was I supposed to talk to about that sort of thing?

Friday, and still nothing from Mason.

But, my thoughts from the day before placated me.

Then I wondered, why placated?

I mean, I liked Mason – anyone with a brain did – and there was something enticing about the idea of him asking me out. But if I was honest, I wasn't super upset he hadn't. It was more the waiting and wondering that was annoying me. Either way, it seemed like a good idea that he didn't ask me out before he left for Europe. But, I would have liked some indication of whether he was going to when he got back.

I shifted my bag on my shoulder as I wandered down the hallway at the end of the day. I tried to work my way around my feelings while Roman was busy exasperating teachers with his refusal to apply himself, if the yelled "That's another F, Roman. You're smarter than this!" from one of the classrooms in the hallway was anything to go by.

Honestly, I was just feeling overwhelmed and all over the place with this Mason stuff. But I had two weeks to work it out, so that was going to–

"Piper!" Mason jogged up beside me and I smiled as I looked down.

"Hey. All packed and ready?"

He chuckled. "Yeah, I think so. Mum's been on me all week to make sure I've been packing. And, she's washing constantly so we don't forget anything. It's total mayhem, but I think it'll be all good in the end."

I nodded. "Sweet."

We walked in silence for a few minutes, then he blurted, "So, I mean, is it okay if I email you?"

I blinked in surprise for a second. "Uh, yeah. Of course. I'd love to hear what you're up to."

I shot him a look and found him grinning; calm, confident, hot. "Cool."

"Oi, Carter!"

We both looked up and saw Tucker waving at him as he hung out of his old Vitara.

"Uh, I'd better go. Tucker said he'd drop me home."

"Sure, no worries. Uh, have a good flight, yeah?"

He smiled and nodded. There was a moment of tension, then he hugged me quickly.

"Have a good holiday. I'll miss you."

"Yeah, you too. Have a great time," I answered as he let go.

He grinned again, nodded once and jogged over to Tucker's car.

"Ugh, nothing?" Hadley asked as she walked up behind me.

"Was there supposed to be something?" I asked.

She shrugged. "I would have thought so by now. Are you not…"

"Not what?" I asked when she didn't elaborate.

She shrugged again. "I don't know. I mean, you're not giving him the wrong idea, are you? Like, you're letting him know you're interested?"

I shrugged. "I don't know. What's the universal sign for interest? Is it blushing and being weird and awkward? If so, I'm doing great."

She laughed. "I think that's one of them." She ran her hand over her curls. "It's weird. I would have thought he'd have made a move by now."

"Has he actually said anything about liking me? Or, are we just making huge assumptions here?" I asked, looking at her.

She spared me an exasperated look. "He doesn't need to say anything. It's obvious how he feels."

I frowned. "Is it though?"

She nodded. "Yes. Look, everyone knows that you've got to take it slow with Piper Barlow."

I frowned. "Really?"

"Yes," Hadley replied, matter-of-fact. "No 'wham bam thank you ma'am' with you. Guys know they have to ease into it, be gentle."

My frown deepened. "Why is that again?"

"Because you're sweet and innocent and decent guys don't want to scare you off."

I sighed. "Well, maybe I should stop wasting my time with decent guys. Then, I might see *some* action before I die."

"You don't mean that," Hadley scoffed.

I did. But, we both knew how awkward I got around nice boys like Mason – let alone the Roman Lombardis of the world. I knew neither of us could actually picture me chasing after any guys, decent or otherwise. I just didn't get flirting.

"Yeah, but there's slow and there's *slow*, Hads."

"Just let him woo you!"

I snorted. "At this rate, a turtle lazily ambling in my direction would get to me faster than Mason! Without even meaning to."

She flicked her hair over her shoulder with a wry smile.

"Regardless. Party tonight?"

I sighed. "I guess."

"How are you getting there?"

"I'll ask Mum for the car, I guess."

"Shame we're not better friends with Roman. He could drive you."

I snorted. "If we were better friends with Roman you'd have ruined it because you'd have screwed him senseless, broken his heart and moved onto someone else. So, we wouldn't be friends anymore and I'd still not have a ride to the party."

Hadley huffed a laugh. "Yeah? Who's to say I'd be the one who did the breaking? Roman Lombardi is more likely to break my heart than I am his."

"I guess. But, still my lack of ride is still not solved unless I drive myself."

"Did I hear my name?" Roman asked and Hadley threw me a wicked grin.

But, it was a glare she turned on him. "No."

"If it's a ride you're after, ladies, I'd be more than happy to accommodate." He oozed dark charm and Hadley held her own quite successfully.

"I'm sure."

Roman looked between us, his black holes of eyes searching. "My...*ride*...suits two just as easily as one."

"Ugh," Hadley sighed. "Because that's *just* what I've been missing in my life."

Roman's eyes ran up and down her body slowly. "I live to serve, gorgeous."

"Well, go and serve it somewhere else."

"Barlow?" he asked, looking at me.

I blinked and looked between them in panic. "What?"

"Shall I, as Hadley suggests, go and serve it somewhere else?"

I looked between them again, hoping I wouldn't actually have to be involved.

Hadley always did this; she was rude and scathing to him, yet professed an ingrained desire to get in his pants. How she was going to achieve that when she just acted like a dick, I don't know. Maybe that's why I was sweet, innocent Piper Barlow and she was…well, *the* Hadley Reynolds; there was obviously some (read, many) nuance to flirting and dating that I was missing.

"I…don't mind. You do whatever you want, Lombardi." I turned to Hadley. "I need to get to the bus before it leaves or I have the pleasure of a half hour wait. I'll see you tonight."

She hugged me quickly. "If he offers to drive, say yes!" she whispered in my ear.

When I pulled away from her, I frowned. "Sure."

She grinned and I shook my head as I wandered off.

"Oi, Barlow! Wait up!" Roman called.

"Because she wants the likes of you chasing her!" Hadley called.

"Everyone wants the likes of me chasing them, Miss Reynolds," he called back, his tone dripping innuendo I could almost feel landing on my skin.

I jumped onto the bus and found a seat I hoped would keep Roman away from me. But, no dice. He sat in front of me, tucking his skateboard behind his head and leaning against the window.

I surreptitiously looked at him, but he noticed and his eyebrow rose slightly in humoured question. I rolled my eyes and slid down into my seat.

"I assume Hadley's looking for a ride tonight?"

Not the kind you're offering. "I'm driving."

He leant over the back of his seat toward me. "Are you now?"

"Yes."

"And, do you plan on driving all holidays? Or, just tonight? Perhaps hoping some nice boy will offer tonight and you'll be set up for the next two weeks?"

I looked up at him through my eyelashes. "Everyone else lives on the other side of town. I'm quite capable of driving."

"I don't live on the other side of town. Anymore."

"I'm sure you'll have your own schedule to stick to. And, I wouldn't dream of getting in your way."

"My way?"

I looked up at him again, finding those dark eyes watching me carefully between strands of equally dark hair. I had the sudden urge to get off the bus and run away; away from the way he seemed to see right through me. I hated running, but I'd do almost anything to get rid of my fidgetiness. I looked down again and made do with rearranging in my seat.

Everyone knew Roman Lombardi hooked up with at least one girl at every party or he left to go find one. I was not getting myself into the situation where I was going to need to rely on him for a ride; no doubt I'd want to leave way too early and he'd be off using my ride as a motel room. Not that I could say any of that out loud.

"I'll be fine. Thanks."

"Ah, you have someone else in mind."

I looked up sharply.

"Carter will be devastated," he sighed, his eyes shining with humour even as the rest of his face was hard.

I rolled my eyes again and sat back in my seat. I wasn't planning on going to any of the other parties anyway. Make one appearance and I was sure I could get away with skiving on the rest if I felt like it.

"I'm driving myself."

"Tonight, yes."

Ugh, why was he such a douche?

"Then you'll meet a lovely fella who'll offer to drive you to the rest and Carter will be all but forgotten. See, you take me up on my offer and you're just preserving yourself for Carter. You could say I'm doing him a favour."

"I could say a lot of things," I muttered.

He scoffed. "Yeah, but you won't. Because you're darling little Piper Barlow, never with a bad word to say to anyone."

I glared at him and found his eyes shining brighter and a hint of a smile at his lips.

Problem was, he wasn't entirely wrong.

As in, he was completely right.

I shook my head, pulled on my headphones and did my best to ignore him for the rest of the trip.

What is it about Bad Boys?

The music thumped and the bonfire soared into the starlit sky over the field. I watched my breath puff out of my mouth as I snuggled into my jacket further and nibbled on the edge of my cup.

I'd spaced out a little as Hadley was raving about Roman again and I was swaying to the beat of the slightly techno mix I didn't know the name of in the hopes of warming up a little. The first real Winter Holidays party tended to be colder than you expected; every year without fail, we never learnt.

Hadley whacked me and I looked up. "What?" I asked.

"Don't you think?"

I sighed. "Don't I think what, Hads?"

"That he's as *smooth* as they come."

I glared at her over the rim of my cup. "No."

"Oh, come on!" she whined. "This afternoon? You weren't the least bit tempted?"

"No." Because I hadn't been.

"What planet do you come from?" Hadley asked me as though she were disgusted or about to dissect me.

"The one where I don't want to be strung along and treated like God knows how many girls before me. The one where I don't find it attractive for a guy to be sporting bruises or– Case in point…"

I pointed over at Roman where he'd just pushed a guy and they were getting in each other's faces. I expected a fight, but Rio pulled Roman off the other guy who deflated a little as he watched how eager Roman was to keep at it. Rumour suggested only an idiot got into a fight with Roman Lombardi because he was the one who emerged victorious every time. Every. Time.

"Sorry, Hads. But, that just seems like too much trouble to me. And, I mean… Don't you want more from a guy than a nice face and maybe a decent hook up? I bet there is nothing going on in his head."

"He's like every bad boy out of every book or movie you've ever watched," she said earnestly. "Who cares what's going on in his head!"

"You need to stop reading those books and watching those movies, babes. I've told you before. It's unhealthy."

"You're the one who got me caught up on Patrick Thingy and Chase…what's his name?"

"Verona and Hammond," I replied without thinking because I'd seen *10 Things I Hate About You* and *Drive Me Crazy* probably twenty too many times and still couldn't get enough of them.

Mum and I had watched all those 80s and 90s Rom-Coms as I grew up and I'd never stopped loving them. I'd even looked for ones Mum might have missed and given Hadley and Celeste a heavy appreciation for most of them – or, at least the hot guys in them. And the older I got, the more I loved John Cusack in particular. His characters were sweet and adorable and just the perfect romance hero.

"Why do you remember these things?" Hadley asked me.

I threw her as cocky a grin as I ever got. "Because I'm loyal to the men I love."

She shook her head at me before looking back to Roman. "Well, I'm quite loyal to getting in those perfectly-fitting jeans," she said as she titled her head to supposedly get a better view of his arse.

And yes, it was not lost on me that he was still objectively attractive in jeans that tucked into black boots and a dark jacket that might have even been leather. Sometimes he did the canvas shoes, jeans and either t-shirt over long-sleeved top or t-shirt under the open button-up shirt combination. Sometimes he did the sneakers, chinos and baggy jumper combination. And sometimes, like just then, he looked like he'd walked out of one of Hadley's dirty romance books and was about to whisk you away on his motorcycle.

My not unflattering assessment of him only annoyed me further.

"Well if you stopped being such a dick to him, maybe he'd let you in those…jeans."

"What is up with you? Even this weird – is it even passive-aggressive? – display is rather aggressive for you."

I shook my shoulders and glared at Roman's back. "Nothing."

"Piper," she said in her 'I brook no argument' tone.

I huffed. "He's just so…infuriating!"

Hadley snorted. "That is the least flattering thing I've ever heard you say about anything."

I threw her a look. "He's just…"

"Gorgeous, mysterious, dark, brooding, fulfils your wildest fantasies?"

"I was going to say a vain, cocky, womanising arsehole. But, sure."

Except for those times when he seemed to try – and succeeded, let's be honest – to make me laugh. Except for those times he looked at me like he was capable of sincerity. Except for those times when I wasn't entirely sure if he was seriously interested or just looking to play me like every other girl. He'd become a walking contradiction all because he'd moved into the house next door and it annoyed the hell out of me.

I wriggled again, feeling that antsy, itchy feeling creeping along my skin.

"Three weeks of him following you home like a lost puppy and you're already sick of him?" she laughed.

"He doesn't follow me home like a lost puppy."

"I'd let him follow me home like a lost puppy."

"Well, why don't you go and tell him that? I'm sure his motorised motel room is stocked and ready for you."

"His what? You know what, I don't want to know," she giggled. "I get he's not your type, babes. But that arse, though?"

"What's so appealing about the bad boy?"

"Need I remind you how much you gushed about Patrick Thingy?"

"Verona," I muttered as Roman's eyes caught mine and I clenched my teeth around my cup. "And, fine. But, bad boys in real life? Hads, it's clichéd and I'll bet it's not as fun as we're made to believe."

"Well, the girl with a John Cusack would say that."

"I don't actually have a John Cusack, Hads…"

"Yeah no, but you do. Because Mason's perfect for you. He's kind, he's sweet, he'll go at your pace. A proper gentleman." She nodded curtly as though pleased with herself and I told myself Roman and I weren't staring each other down.

"A proper gentleman who *might* ask me out before I die of old age," I grumbled.

41

"Babes, you'll be safe with him," she said like a mum who knows best.

I knew she didn't mean to be patronising. Years of knowing her told me she didn't mean to be patronising. But, that spineless part of me that Roman seemed so fond of poking wanted to ask why I needed to be safe with anyone. I mean, safe sounded good. But not the way Hadley said it, like I was incapable of keeping myself safe. I didn't need to be babied. I knew it was done out of love, but really!

I huffed and stretched my neck as Roman finally looked away from me to look at Rio.

"Rio's cute in his own way…" Hadley mused.

"Oh, yeah. He's got that Loki thing going for him," Celeste giggled as she bumped into us.

"And what sort of time do you call this?" Hadley mock-chastised.

Celeste giggled some more. "Marty and I…" she petered off and Hadley cheered. "And, he was very eager."

"Was he now?" Hadley asked, waiting for more information.

"Marty's got a serious case of roving hands," Celeste said with a wink.

"Is it just me, or does it feel like guys are less obsessed with getting hand jobs or blow jobs than we've been led to believe?" Hadley asked.

"What do you mean?" Celeste snorted.

"Well, you hook up with a guy and his first instinct seems to be to get his hands in your pants, rather than yours in his. Don't you find that?"

Before they launched into their theories as to why that might be, I knew it was my cue to sidle over to the esky and see if I could find another soft drink.

The girl who'd stumbled on the way to third base had no place in that conversation. She had nothing to offer and really didn't feel like hanging around as she knew her best friends were either pitying her or sheltering her.

So as they giggled over whatever it was that Celeste had just been getting up to with Marty and why guys seemed less concerned with your hands down their pants, I took a few inconspicuous steps backwards, then spun and headed for the eskies. I avoided the eyes of anyone, hoping they'd think I was on a toilet mission or something and leave me alone.

Next to Hadley and Celeste – hell, even Tucker at a stretch – I could keep the anxiety at bay enough to look normal. But away from them, I really didn't want to find myself in an unexpected conversation.

Luckily, I didn't find myself in any unexpected conversations. Unluckily, I did find myself over-hearing some unexpected conversation.

"Yeah, nah. I've had Jess," I heard Roman's voice and I looked around surreptitiously.

"Any good?" Rio asked.

Roman shrugged. "Depends what you want."

"Well, what did she offer?"

"Everything. Until I went for it and she freaked out."

Rio snorted. "Fucking prude."

Roman shrugged again and his lip twitched like he was not saying something. "Her hand job's decent."

"Compared to Britt's?"

"Fuck, you know Britt's is the best."

"Shame she won't touch you with a fucking pole anymore."

Roman huffed in what was almost a laugh. "Nah, that's all good, mate. Plenty of girls willing. I'm not averse to a little bit of teaching if they're up for it."

"You willing to risk leading them on?"

"They know what they're signing up for."

"Dude, you're not the one they cry to when you're done with them." I couldn't tell if Rio was annoyed by that or not.

"Aw, you don't want my sloppy seconds, mate?" Roman asked him almost teasingly.

Rio chuckled. "Mate, they don't want me after they've tasted you. That's why I have to get to them first."

Suddenly, Rio looked at me like he knew I'd been eavesdropping and threw me a wink. My cheeks went bright red and I quickly looked in every direction but them in the most obvious way possible. But for some reason, my eyes found their way back to the boys and I saw Roman watching me with that unnecessary interest.

My stomach squirmed in a way I was worried wasn't entirely unpleasant and I felt myself frown in annoyance.

Roman was not going to get to me. He could make me laugh, he could look at me like…I didn't even know what that was. But, I wasn't falling for it. He was a player and, whether he'd decided I was his Everest or not, I was not giving him any reason to think he could conquer me.

Finally remembering why I'd even wandered over to the eskies, I hunted around for another drink. I would have liked a beer, but since I was driving I was going to stick to soft drink. Responsibility and the law aside, I was a lightweight.

"Barlow," the low voice slid over me unexpectedly and I jumped.

"Lombardi," I answered sullenly, giving him as good a once over as he was giving me.

I couldn't remember where the whole calling each other by our last names had come from. But, I couldn't really remember ever saying anything different to his face. Was that weird?

"You're lucky Carter's not here. You're not inspiring anything in that getup."

I blinked at him, not quite understanding but getting enough of an idea. I heard a noise and looked over to see stupid Shayla snorting before she walked away.

My face flushed some more and I cleared my throat. "We're not all on a mission to get laid."

His eyes scanned behind me and the corner of his lips quirked. "Shame that."

I was getting more confused by the second.

"You look kinda funky, there Barlow."

"Being insulted tends to do that to a girl."

All humour left his face as he looked me over. "Looks aren't all that…inspires…"

I huffed and was annoyed enough with him that I was completely honest. "I'm sure that sentence makes more sense when you know what that means."

Disgusted with myself that I'd let him get under my skin, I turned away. But, he caught my arm gently.

"Inspired, Barlow. As in inspiring a hard on. You with me?"

I looked at him and I had the annoying feeling his eyes were softening as he looked at me. *Actually interested? Playing me?*

"I understand you. I'm certainly not *with* you."

I watched as the fire highlighted the humour returning to his eyes. "Like I said, looks aren't all that inspire."

45

He searched my face for a second and walked away, leaving me with goose bumps trailing over my skin and my breath a little short. Had he just meant what it sounded like? Surely not. Roman didn't do… Well, anything that was more than a passing hook up.

To be insinuating I was…inspiring and it wasn't only my looks? He had to be playing me. There was no other reason. Hadley was right and I was some sort of Everest he'd decided to conquer and he was just smooth enough to know exactly how to get under my skin. That had to be it. But, why the hell was Roman Lombardi trying to play me *now*?

I'd heard that the more you were around someone the more inclined you were to like them. But, it's not like we were forced together. The guy could drive to school and we could go back to the same level of interaction we'd had for a decade.

So, maybe he wasn't playing me? The guy hadn't been wrong; all evidence indicated there was a line a mile long of girls who were willing to hook up with him. Surely that was all he needed to satisfy whatever reason he did it.

So, what was with that comment?

"Ugh!" I grunted as I made my way back to Hadley and Celeste. Nothing about him was making sense anymore and it was messing with my head.

"And, where have you been?" Hadley accused as I almost tripped on a clump of grass.

"Discovering that Britt's hand job is the best."

"Beg pardon?" Celeste choked on her drink.

"Roman and Rio were talking. I had the misfortune of overhearing them."

"I thought I saw someone standing awfully close to you. What did the sex-god extraordinaire want?"

"More of Britt's hand jobs, probably."

Hadley and Celeste both snorted, "Someone jealous?"

I glared at them both. "Yes. Hold me back before I can't possibly deny my passion any longer," I mono-toned.

"What did he actually want?"

"To tell me I'm apparently uninspiring."

"He's obviously being mean to hide his raging inspiration." Hadley failed to contain her giggles.

"I don't think you need to know anything about his raging inspirations, babes. Say it with me, now. Un. Healthy."

"What do you think Roman would do on a first date?" Celeste sighed, clearly in fantasy-land. I loved her, but she had this idea that every guy was secretly perfect boyfriend material. If Roman was ever going to be boyfriend material, it was only going to be in Celeste's mind.

Hadley and I shared a knowing look.

"He'll fuck you senseless, leave you craving more, and never speak to you again," Hadley replied matter-of-fact.

"See? Not worth it," I said.

"Totally worth it," Hadley disagreed.

"Oh my God!" a girl who we sometimes hung out with giggled as she sort of careened into our semi-circle.

"Tanya, hi," Hadley trilled.

Tanya giggled some more. "Erin's throwing herself at Roman!"

I frowned, but it was Celeste who voiced the reason for my frown.

"Hasn't she already had a shot with him?"

"Yep. But, apparently once isn't enough," Tanya answered.

"It never is, is it," I mumbled sarcastically.

We looked over and saw Roman and Rio were standing closer

47

to us than I'd have expected.

I couldn't hear their words, but Erin looked rather flirty as she flicked her hair and popped her hip. Roman looked at Rio and shrugged. He took Erin's hand and pulled her to him. He kissed her in a way that made your stomach flutter and your cheeks heat.

When he pulled away from her, he looked Erin over like she was nothing as he took a drag of his cigarette. Less than nothing. If that girl had got ice the other day, Erin was getting…whatever the hell was colder than ice. Roman's gaze could have cut diamond.

Roman shrugged lazily, his eyes found mine as he blew smoke up, and he and Rio walked away totally cavalierly.

"Ouch," Hadley winced.

"I've got it," Tanya said, suddenly sober.

It was one thing to joke Erin was going to be given that Roman Brush-Off. But, when it actually happens?

"And, you want to be one of those?" I asked Hadley.

"I'm not stupid enough to expect a repeat performance."

Yeah, but wasn't she? My best friend acted tough, but I was pretty sure that when it came down to it she was as wrapped up in the idea of the romance hero as I was.

By no means was I waiting to be swept off my feet. I didn't want any knights in shining armour. I didn't expect any princes. As nice as knights and princes sounded, I knew it was just a fantasy.

But, I liked the idea of the guy who proved himself through his loyalty and his friendship, through a connection you shared. I liked the idea that he expected me to prove myself too, because I wanted a guy who wanted more than just a pretty face with a preference for his brand of crazy.

I wanted what I'd come to think of as a John Cusack level of perfection, as much as Hadley teased me for it.

It was the kind of perfection that you can only find with that one other special person.

That one person who really got you and you're the only one who really got them.

I didn't really think that was too much to ask.

Was it?

We didn't see Roman or Rio for the rest of the night, so we managed to find other topics of conversation and I stopped wondering what was going on with him lately.

Hadley was leaving me the next day too for the next week and planned to sleep all day in the car, so we made the most of the night. I pulled my head out of my arse enough to act like the upbeat, happy girl who didn't have a care in the world. I put on the smile, no matter how much I kept checking the time on my phone and wanting to just curl up in bed with some John Cusack and a hot Milo.

I was the perfect Piper, the happy Piper.

Chapter Five
Katie Morris and the Cooties.

The sky was blessedly clear as I stared up at the stars and took a deep breath. Something about a clear winter night always calmed me.

With Hadley now in Melbourne visiting family and Mason on his way to Europe, little Piper Barlow had faded into the background and people went on without me. Sometimes, it bugged me. But, most of the time it gave me that much needed downtime. My parents expected me to be in the middle of the social scene, so I could stay out all night at the lake at the bottom of the hill behind our house all holidays if I wanted and just lie on my blanket and watch the stars.

And, that was my plan.

Because, no one came to the lake in winter; the bonfire parties were all in the fields on the other side of town. And, the first Saturday of the holidays was going to be no exception.

The one exception, of course proved itself when a huge car parked just above where I was lying.

The headlights were blinding even from behind me, so why I sat up and turned around to glare at them, I'm not sure. But, I was well blind by the time they were switched off and I blinked the spots out of my eyes furiously.

I turned back to the lake and stared at it as though my fierce concentration on the blotchy water would make whoever it was go away.

"Well, well, Barlow. A pleasant surprise," the familiar voice said and my skin had that weird feeling.

I really should have recognised that stupid Holden Colorado; I'd seen it every day in the driveway next door for the last three weeks.

"Wish I could say the same, Lombardi."

He dropped beside me and I glared at him, not that I could see much more than splodges still. Mind you, that did improve him somewhat.

"Do you mind?" I asked.

He shrugged. "Not particularly." I could see his splotchy silhouette as he flicked his dark hair out of his face and looked towards the lake.

The moon reflected in the water and the breeze was still. The whole thing was beautiful, but it was now just ruined by the wanker beside me. I wriggled, drawing my knees to my chest and wrapping my arms around them.

"I'd have thought you had better things to do than sit out here by yourself," he said after a while, picking up a stone and skimming it across the surface.

"Because I'm a loser now?" I snapped without thinking.

He huffed. "No. Trust you to take everything I say as an insult."

"I could have gone if I'd wanted."

"Of course you could have. It's not like I'm there either."

"Were you even invited?"

"*I* don't need to be invited, Barlow."

That was true.

51

"No, you just show up where you're not wanted like…" I stopped myself as my cheeks flamed; I was so not the girl who just insulted people. I hated confrontations, especially unfriendly ones. But, Roman had a way of getting under my skin and making my mouth run away without my brain.

He made a sound that might have been laughter. "No, don't stop now. Like what?"

"Nothing," I mumbled.

"No. I'm genuinely interested in hearing this scathing quip from you, Barlow."

"Nothing," I assured him.

"Come on, have a backbone. For once, say what's on that tantalising mind of yours."

"Nothing's on my perfectly normal mind," I huffed.

"Do I need to break out the Katy Perry?"

I hid my laugh. "No."

"Go on, then. Tell me what you really think of me. Or, I'll—"

"Like some venereal disease, all right? You just show up where you're not wanted like some venereal disease." My cheeks burned as I shoved them in my knees.

Plus, it wasn't at all true; if Roman was at a party, it was considered a success. Because for some reason Roman's apparent approval by appearance was the bar for considering a party cool. And everyone wanted their party to be cool.

He only laughed, which went to prove how badarse I *really* was. "Well, I feel honoured to be torn down by the girl who's chosen to sit on the shore of a lake by herself instead of being seen at tonight's *it* party."

"So, now it's a bad thing I don't go to all the raging bonfires and get drunk every night?" I wasn't really sure what I was actually

52

saying, but it was out now.

He slid a cocked eyebrow at me, as though telling me we both knew I'd made no real sense, and shook his head. "On the contrary, I have a new-found respect for you now."

I wanted to take that as some kind of insult. But, there was nothing but sincerity in his tone, which only served to confuse me about him more. Roman didn't respect anyone. Let alone me.

"Right, because that makes sense," was all my stupid brain could come up with.

He chuckled and skimmed another stone. I watched it skip five times across the water as though it were terribly important, because then I could almost pretend he wasn't there.

"It's just refreshing to know you're not a complete popular dick," he said.

I looked at him, flabbergasted. "This from the guy voted most likely to nail and bail."

He grinned and I told myself I was unaffected by it. I mean, a hot guy can smile at you and you're allowed to appreciate it. It doesn't mean you're attracted to him.

"That title was aptly awarded, true." He nodded.

I scoffed. "I'm surprised you even know the word 'apt'."

He laughed. "I'm not as stupid as I look, Barlow."

"No, I imagine not. Very few people could actually be as stupid as you look." It was delivered seamlessly, but my cheeks heated.

"Ouch," he chuckled. "Kudos on the insult. But, I'd be more offended if I didn't see the way you look at me."

Why did he have to be quite so…relaxed? Roman was a guy who didn't care about anything. He didn't care what people thought of him; he was him and he was perfectly comfortable as people judged him or looked down on him. He went through life with his

53

lazy indifference on his face and everything bounced off him, leaving him completely unaffected.

"I don't look at you like anything," I said, pulling my mind away from where his smirk led it and telling myself I wasn't lying.

"Sure you don't."

"I don't."

"Barlow, you don't need to be embarrassed that you like the way I look."

"I might be if I did."

He only chuckled and juggled the stone in his hand.

"Why are you here anyway? Don't you have other people to do on a Saturday night than come down to the lake by your lonesome?"

He skimmed the stone damned perfectly. "I suddenly found myself in need of some peace and quiet. My house is *very* loud all of a sudden. And you know, sometimes a meaningless fuck just doesn't do it for you."

I blinked and hid a smile. "No. I wouldn't know."

"'Course you wouldn't." Again, I couldn't get a read on his tone.

"What is that supposed to mean?" But, I was apparently insulted by something that shouldn't have been an insult.

He shrugged and leant back on his hands. "Only that I imagine you have far better taste than to fuck just whatever comes along."

"You know, Lombardi… Coming from you, I'm not sure if that's a compliment or an insult."

He raked his hand through his hair. "No, me either."

I laughed at that. I couldn't not. We caught each other's eye and he looked slightly less dour than usual. When I finally stopped, I looked at him for a moment.

I was torn between finding a polite way out of sitting on the lakeshore with Roman and finding out what catalyst completely broke his usual patterns.

"What do you mean your house is loud?" I heard myself ask.

He sighed and helped himself to lying down on my blanket. "You remember my sister?"

I nodded and after a few moments lay next to him. "Yeah, she was nice as far as I recall."

He chuckled, but it was humourless. "Yeah, about as nice as syphilis."

"Well, you'd know."

He snorted. "Right, either way. So you remember she was pregnant before she left?"

I thought back, trying to remember what Paris had been like before she'd left – yep, Roman and Paris, how would you be? – but there wasn't a huge amount there.

"Maybe?" I shrugged.

"Yeah, well she was. Had a little girl. That little girl, as sweet as she is, was dropped on Mum's doorstep a few weeks ago. Paris decided she wanted to travel and her daughter starting school was the perfect time to unload her and do just that. We moved, my sister pissed off, and now that little girl lives with us. So, I'm here in lieu of playing uncle."

I wondered if this niece was the other 'kid' Mum had referred to the day they moved in. I certainly hadn't seen any evidence of Paris… Not that I could remember seeing a little girl either. Maybe she was a very recent addition?

"Oh, do girls' panties not drop like they used to, the idea of a little girl hanging around you?" I teased. Although, I had to say, the idea of a little girl traipsing after Roman actually made him slightly more appealing to me.

He laughed, but it was humourless. "Very funny. Excuse me if I don't feel like dropping trou with the knowledge of what it leads to following me around the house incessantly."

I was trying to ignore that incessant niggling in my mind that Roman wasn't the guy I'd thought he was after that statement. So, I settled for teasing him.

"Oh, has Roman suddenly got a conscience?"

"You're cute like this, you know?" His voice was full of sarcasm.

I snorted very unattractively. "Sorry. But, I see you dealing with your problems in one of two ways. You fuck or you drink. I really don't see a third option."

"Firstly, I have never heard you say 'fuck' before. And secondly, you're looking at that third option right now."

"Yeah," I snorted. "Because you're totally not dreaming of getting in my pants."

"Oh, I never said that. Any man with eyes is dreaming about getting in *your* pants, Barlow," he answered, completely matter-of-fact. "And, any guy who tells you otherwise is full of shit. Your precious Carter included. But, it is a massive dampener to the inspiration when you keep remembering that sex leads to pregnancy. I came here with nothing but peace and quiet on my mind. I didn't even know you were here."

The sincerity with which he said that hit me like a sledgehammer and I didn't know what to address first. Maybe he wasn't so unaffected after all.

"I can…go…?" I offered softly.

He shifted so his head was right next to mine. "Nah, I don't mind my peace and quiet being invaded by you." He paused.

"You're like…peace personified."

"Isn't that just another way of saying I'm boring?"

He huffed another humourless laugh. "No, Barlow. It's a compliment." He sighed. "Lying here with you… It's like I can relax, but I don't have to be alone. Fuck, don't make me explain it. I'll just sound like some nancy wanker."

My chest fluttered, but I couldn't decide if it was because he could have been mistaken for being sweet or because that mistaken sweetness was turning my opinion of him on its head. Again, I had the urge to get out of there super-fast. But, I couldn't move and I had this insane sense of comfort.

So, I didn't look for an excuse to leave and we lay for a while in silence.

I just stared at the stars, drawing patterns and counting dots of light. I tried to empty out my brain, settle the manic humming it seemed to have like background noise; always on, always draining. Roman didn't seem to feel the need to talk either and strangely I didn't feel any weirdness lying next to the town's resident underachiever in the dark. We just lay, quiet. But finally, I had to break it.

"Lombardi?"

"Yeah?"

"What's she like?"

"What's who like?"

"Your niece."

He sighed and laced his hands under his head. "Fuck, I don't know. She's adorable – all dark curls and bright blue eyes. But, she's a handful. She's barely five and she's smarter than the lot of us. Swear to God, she's just full of questions. It's 'Uncie Roman' this and 'Uncie Roman' that. Drives me up the fucking wall."

Despite the way his voice softened with something strangely akin to fondness, that made me laugh. I tried to hold back my laughter, but I failed epically.

"What?" he asked incredulously.

"She calls you 'Uncie Roman'?"

"What's so wrong with that?" He sounded legitimately offended that I found that anything less than fantastic.

"Nothing," I laughed, trying to picture bad boy Roman Lombardi as 'Uncie' anything. "Nothing at all. Just kind of ruins your image a little, don't you think?"

"You know what, Barlow? I'm starting to regret telling you anything."

For some reason I didn't like that idea, even if he didn't sound completely serious and I had no reason to feel that way. "Okay, I'm sorry. All kinds of serious now…"

"Really?" I didn't blame the note of teasing scepticism in his voice.

I snorted. "No, but I'll do my best. Tell me more about her."

He chuckled. "Fine. Look, I don't know, okay? It feels fucking too much like having my own kid for comfort, you know?"

"Not really."

"I thought you were going to be helpful?"

"I don't think that was part of the deal, Lombardi."

"Fair point," he conceded then sighed heavily.

"How's your mum handling it?"

"Not well. She pretty much leaves it to me."

"Sorry about that."

"Eh, there's only so much she can do while she's working to support the three of us. Maddy's all right really. I just need a break sometimes, you know?"

There was something about lying in the dark on the shore of the lake that made it easy to forget this was the Roman I'd known for years. It didn't feel weird airing dirty laundry or listening to him talk about things I knew he'd never say any other time. Hell, I doubted I'd ever listen any other time.

"Barlow?"

"Lombardi?"

"What are you doing out here?"

I sighed. "Like you said, peace and quiet."

"You okay?"

There was something in the way he asked that that was nothing like the way other people asked it. It was at the same time a totally off-hand comment, but also an incredibly sincere question; like he was genuinely happy to listen, but also respected I might not want to answer. It took me off-guard for a second.

But again, that lying in the dark on the lakeshore, just the two of us, gave me a sense of security. There was a sense of trust that caused conflict in me. This was Roman, the guy who sneered at everyone, the guy who even traded punches with his closest friend. So when I opened my mouth and I found the truth coming out, I prayed I wasn't making a terrible mistake.

"Are you ever surrounded by people and you still feel alone?"

"Huh…" He paused. "I've never really thought about it. Why? Do you?"

I stared at the stars, glad we weren't looking at each other. "More often than I used to."

He was silent a while and I thought he was going to say something rude or teasing, something typically Roman. But, he surprised me.

"Is that why you bailed on the party tonight?"

I took a deep breath. "Sometimes it's easier to be alone without a whole bunch of people around. You know? Less effort."

"Less effort how?" he asked, like he was genuinely interested and something twitched in me.

"I don't know. Like I don't have to pretend everything's okay. It gets tiring after a while."

"So, don't pretend."

I scoffed and sat up. "Yeah, because people would accept that Piper Barlow had issues."

"What does that make me, then?"

I looked back down at him and saw him staring at me intently, like he was actually listening, like maybe he actually cared. Who would have thought that Roman Lombardi was capable of sympathy? My chest did that flutter thing again and I felt like my whole brain was turning itself inside out as it tried to decide if it needed to change its mind about him or not.

"Just because you haven't actually voiced your disbelief out loud, doesn't mean you don't think I'm whining unnecessarily. I'm just waiting for the African orphan speech. Hell, you've got real issues with your niece. What right do I have to complain I feel a little down or a little alone sometimes?"

He snorted. "Firstly, that's bullshit." He sat up and his shoulder accidentally bumped mine. "No one else's experiences should invalidate your own feelings, Barlow."

"I have no reason for it–"

"So what? Feelings don't listen to reason. I am perfectly happy to accept Piper Barlow has issues and if you want to sit here and not talk about it, fine. You want to talk about it, fine. Let's just share the peace and quiet and feel a little less alone together."

I turned to look at him and found him looking out over the lake.

60

"You're perfectly happy to accept Piper Barlow has issues?" I asked slowly, trying to stay serious.

A slight grin spread across his face, but he nodded solemnly. "Yes. I'm very understanding that way."

"About my having issues?"

He still didn't look at me and that smile looked harder to fight. "Yes."

I looked over the lake as well and laughed. "Of course you are."

He skipped another stone and we sat together in companionable silence for a while longer.

Roman leant his elbows on his knees and stared at the lake. I kept sneaking looks at him, wondering if there was more to the enigma than everyone thought. Surely not. Surely the mysterious, arrogant, brooding Roman didn't have any hidden depths. I'd known him almost half my life just like I'd known most of the people my age in town – when you had one school to go to, you got to know people – and he'd never given me any reason to think he was anything more than what he seemed.

I jumped as my phone went off and I dragged my eyes from Roman's profile as I pulled it out of my pocket. It was a string of messages from Hadley; expressing her boredom, complaining about old people being old, telling me what she ate for dinner, that there'd been a hot guy at the petrol station outside Ballarat… The list went on and I figured she must have been super bored – or maybe only just found decent internet again – to be sending it all at once.

My fingers hovered over the keyboard for a moment before I just put my phone on silent and slid it back into my pocket.

"Don't let me keep you, Barlow," Roman said, his tone teasing like he assumed my phone was buzzing with steamy booty calls. I doubted he actually believed it though.

"It's just Hadley."

"Ah. And, what is Miss Reynolds up to tonight? Or should I ask who?"

I hid a smile as I rearranged my legs and looked at my hands in my lap. "She and her parents drove to Melbourne today to see her grandparents."

"So, her night will not compare to ours then." His tone was completely matter-of-fact, no hint of sarcasm.

I snorted. "I think even she would prefer to sit on a cold lakeshore with you than be stuck at her grandparents' house."

He looked at me sharply. "You're cold?"

I shrugged. "Not really." Although, the way I burrowed into my jumper probably didn't help convince him. It was as much the unfamiliar concern in his voice as the slight chill that had me burrowing, though.

"You can have my jacket." He started pulling it off and I put a hand on his arm to stop him, trying not to take it personally that maybe there was a sweet side to him.

"I'm fine, Lombardi. But, thanks."

His arms were still up, mid shuck. "You sure?"

I nodded. "You give me your jacket and I'll be overheating and you'll be freezing and I'll feel guilty."

He dropped his arms with a shrug. "Well. Can't have that."

"No."

"Much better that I'm comfortable and you're cold."

"I'm only a little cold. I'm fine."

"I'll tell you a secret, Barlow. I'm a little cold, too. So, I'm bloody glad you didn't take me up on it."

I scoffed. "Oh, was that you being a gentleman again?"

He rifled in his pockets and was then lighting a cigarette. "Can't be. I'm not a gentleman, remember?"

"I remember a lot of things about you."

He chuckled as he blew smoke straight up and leant back on one hand. "Yeah, like what?"

I grinned as something hit me. "I remember the time in Year Four when Katie Morris kissed you on the playground and you cried."

He spluttered smoke, sat up straighter and looked at me. "I what?"

"You cried and ran to Miss… Oh, what was her name?" I sighed in frustration.

"Miss Davies," he replied as though I'd asked him for the time.

"Ha! So you do remember."

He took another drag. "Not at all. I do not at all remember my first kiss on the playground and burying my face in Miss Davies skirts because I was petrified of girl cooties. No idea what you're talking about, Barlow."

I nodded. "Of course not."

"*Had* that happened, it still would not have been as embarrassing as the time you and Hadley did that God awful dance routine in Year Five." As he said it, I totally remembered it and a loud bark of laughter escaped me. That didn't deter him though. "I swear, I still have nightmares about it. The colours, the total cheesiness, not to mention the hair. What nancy arse band did you decide you were going to dance with?"

"Big Time Rush," I sniggered; we'd had costumes and everything and it had been…plainly awful. "We were going to go to the US and be their backup dancers, be on the show and be super famous."

"Shame about the fact you couldn't sing *or* dance."

I snorted again and buried my face in my knees. When I finally resurfaced, I saw him looking at me with humour playing at his lips.

"The point was we were having fun. Besides, you can accomplish anything with your best friend beside you."

"Ah, yes. The infamously inseparable duo of Piper and Hadley. Padley if you will. Or, perhaps Hadler?"

A completely undignified laugh escaped me and I leant on his arm as I laughed. "Not funny."

"Your guffawing would suggest otherwise."

I sat up and looked at him with my best stern face. But, the humour on his set me off again and he gave me a crooked smirk.

"So if Hadley wasn't in Melbourne, what would you two be up to tonight?" he asked as he looked back over the lake.

My smile fell and I dropped back onto the blanket. "She'd be at the party and I'd still be here."

He rearranged and lay down next to me. "You still wouldn't have gone?"

I shrugged and felt my shoulder bump his. "I doubt it. Put in one appearance, it's all good."

"And she would have just let you sit here alone, being lonely?"

I wriggled and found myself being honest again. "She wouldn't have had any reason not to go."

There was a very pregnant pause in which I could almost hear him thinking. "She doesn't know."

I breathed out heavily, rethinking the sense in being completely honest with him. "About what?"

I felt him laugh. "Oh no, you can't play that card now, Barlow. We're baring our souls here tonight."

I felt myself smile, even though I didn't know why I'd have any reason to feel happy about that. "Fine. No, she doesn't know I get a little…"

"Funky?" he offered with a slight tease to his voice.

I nudged him and he nudged me back. "Yeah. Funky."

"Why not?"

I looked up at the stars and wondered about that. "I don't know. I guess I don't want to worry her. I don't think she'll understand. I don't really want to have to explain myself to her when she doesn't get it but tries to. The idea of talking to her about it is almost more stressful than the feeling."

"Huh. I guess that makes sense."

"You either don't actually want to listen to my issues, or you don't need to ask about them because you already understand…" I petered off, waiting for him to pick up the thread of conversation.

"Could it be Barlow, that I do want to listen – that I understand just enough to sympathise – but that I also just don't want to push you further than you're willing to go?" he asked slowly, like he wasn't sure himself.

It felt like we were straying into far too serious territory, so I scoffed. "I doubt it. I'd say you were just bored."

"That must be it, then," he replied.

I heard the smile in his voice. It was much like his answer when we'd both known he'd fallen off his board to make me feel better the other day, but neither of us had seemed willing to admit it.

We lay and looked at the stars, chatting a little or just being until I decided I'd lain on the lakeshore with an undesirable companion for long enough.

Although, how undesirable was he now? I'd seen a whole new side of him that night, I'd felt a whole new comfort with him I never would have believed possible. I still wasn't sure if was advisable, but there was something about it that intrigued me. But intrigued or not, I refused to let myself hang out with him for too long.

Roman offered to drive me back up to the house and I let him. He gave me a gorgeously sincere smile before I climbed out of his car and I went inside to deal with the no doubt barrage of messages from Hadley.

Chapter Six

Uncompliments and Appropriate Fondling.

I was completely convinced that Roman wasn't going to be the kind of guy to mope two nights in a row. He didn't strike me as the kind of guy who'd let the consequences of sex get in the way for long. So I felt it was safe to wander down to the lake again on Sunday night, ready to have a mope on my own.

So of course, I was wrong.

Because anything you expect Roman Lombardi to do, you should really expect he'll do the opposite. His character may have been pretty consistent – until recently – but his behaviour was erratic. He had a speaker sitting on the shore a little behind him playing Nirvana and he stood skimming stones.

I watched him for a while, as his body turned and his arm flicked across his chest. He was wearing dark jeans and a hoody under his jacket, and I did take a minute to appreciate how nice his silhouette was. He leant his hands on his head when he ran out of stones and stared out at the lake like it had the answers to all his troubles, and it looked like he was feeling pretty troubled. Suddenly, my issues seemed insignificant.

I debated whether I wanted to run back up to my house and avoid him or see if I could find that weird sense of comfort around him again. It was decided for me when he turned as he went to pick up another stone and I swear he jumped.

"Fuck, Barlow!" he chuckled self-consciously.

"Hi." Why did I wave? Who knows? "Is this a private pity party, or can anyone join?"

He smirked a little, but something about his posture made him look really tense. "Depends. How are your issues on this fine night?" He sounded forcibly upbeat as he bent over and picked up a few more stones.

I smiled a little awkwardly and looked at my shoes while I spoke. "They're…issues. How's the niece?"

"She went to bed before she passed out from exhaustion tonight. So, that's something," he answered, looking at the stone he juggled. He sounded like *he* might pass out from exhaustion at any point.

I both liked and didn't like seeing him differently.

I nodded and stepped up beside him as he went back to skimming. "Yay," I offered somewhat weakly.

He huffed a laugh. "Yeah."

I spread my blanket out and sat down. He juggled that one last stone as he dropped beside me. We sat, not talking, and the music washed over us. I only vaguely recognised half the songs that played, but I didn't mind; they all seemed to mirror our moods perfectly. I could feel the tension radiating off him as he had a smoke and I wondered what vibe he got from me. But as we sat there, breathing became easier.

And sitting there, I realised I was glad he'd been there.

With Roman, even not talking, I didn't feel quite so alone. Like those times we walked home, it was almost like he just knew when I just needed to sit and be and he was perfectly happy to sit and be with me. I didn't know if he was feeling it, but I felt completely comfortable in a way I almost never did.

Not with Hadley, who always exuded anticipation or nervous energy. Not with my parents, around who I felt like I always had to be switched on to bubbly so they didn't worry. Not with Celeste, who always opened her mouth when there was a split second of silence.

I didn't feel the need to fill the void, to prepare for whatever crazy thing might come next, or pretend I was fine. I could relax, be myself, breathe easy. All the tension faded away.

It was both concerning and exciting.

During a song that I thought I recognised as Muse, he started singing softly, his hand running through his hair.

"You've got a nice voice," I said, both of us just staring at the lake.

He lay down and I followed suit.

"I didn't picture you as a singer."

He laughed, but it was still tense and humourless. "I don't tend to bring it out at school, true."

I smiled to myself. "You're different."

"What do you mean?"

"Well, at school you're all cool–"

"Aw, you think I'm cool?" he teased.

"Shut up," I replied with humour. "You're all cool and confident, and…" I was distracted as I caught the lyrics of the new song. "Sorry, is that guy singing about punani?"

He shook with silent laughter. "Yeah."

It was some kind of techno thing. "Huh. It's catchy."

He snorted and nudged me. "I'll teach you all the words later. Come on, you were telling me how great I am."

I scoffed. "Sure. No. But you… I don't know. I just didn't picture you outside that charming, cocky, with-it persona."

"Yeah, because you're nothing like that at school," he said sarcastically.

"What's that supposed to mean?"

I felt him shrug. "Because you're totally not the popular, cool girl with the perfect hair, the perfect grades, the perfect family, the perfect everything." He said it like fact; not judgemental, just fact.

I sighed. "Yeah, but am I really?"

"Well, no," he answered as though it was obvious. "Because you're more than just some teenage jerkoff's wet dream. Only just mind," he amended and I bumped him even though I was sure he was fifty percent teasing. He burst into laughter. "What?"

"Not cool!" I giggled.

"Why? You trying to tell me that you're oblivious to the effect you have on the male population in this town?"

I blinked and looked at him. "What effect?"

That sent him off harder. "Seriously? You ever wonder why everyone thinks you and Carter would be perfect together?"

That seemed like a really obvious question. Didn't it? "Uh, because he likes me?" I asked.

He scoffed. "Okay, I'll brush aside your *obvious* desire for him." I almost saw him roll his eyes. "It's because you're the same. He's you, you're him. You're both the idiotically popular, hot kids–"

"I'm not popular."

"You're not unpopular."

I blinked again. "What? What does that even mean?"

He continued like I hadn't spoken, "And, it would be a total travesty if the two of you didn't get married as soon as exams were over and have a million beautiful babies."

I grimaced. But, I wasn't sure if was the idea or hearing it from

Roman. "Please tell me you heard that somewhere. Because that just sounded heinous coming out of your mouth."

He laughed. "Thankfully, yes. I did hear that somewhere. Quite a lot of somewheres actually."

I ruminated for a few moments before I spoke again. "What do you think about it?"

"About what?"

"Me and Mason."

"Am I supposed to have an opinion?" He sounded surprised I'd bother asking and I looked over at him. "Seems to me that's your business."

I appreciated that, but it wasn't the answer I was looking for. "Humour me."

He turned his head to look at me and our noses almost touched. His eyes searched mine for a moment and I thought he might be about to kiss me. The moment became two and a stupid excited flutter rippled through me. But, then a look passed over his face and he looked up again. "Well, the town gossips aren't wrong. The two of you look good next to each other."

Somehow, that didn't make me feel better. "But?"

"Well, that doesn't necessarily set you up for a successful relationship, does it? And," I felt him shrug, "you could look just as good next to someone else."

I smiled and told myself he didn't mean what it sounded like. "Got any particular someone else in mind there?"

"'Course not," he replied, coyly. "I just think you'd look nice next to...other people."

His hand slid off his stomach and it fell next to mine. It was like one of those cheesy romance moments, but neither of us made a move.

I grinned. "Other people?"

"Other people," he agreed, sounding like he was holding back a smile of his own.

"And does this have anything to do with the totally bogus effect I supposedly have on the male population of our town?"

He laughed. "You can't be serious?"

"What? Why?"

"You can't seriously not realise, Barlow?"

"Let's for the time being assume so, Lombardi."

"You're very assertive suddenly."

"Shall I get back in my box?"

He huffed a laugh and sat up. "Fuck no, Barlow. Whatever you do, don't do that," he said, looking back at me with a devilish smirk. "Please, never do that. Not with me."

"You don't like me in my box?" I asked, pretending I was insulted.

I just saw his smile grow before he turned to look back over the lake as though I wasn't supposed to see it. "I like you fine in your box. If you really want back in your box, I won't stop you." He ran a hand over his chin. "But, I'm not nearly annoyed enough by your incessant yabbering to wish you back in it."

I grabbed his arm to pull myself to sitting. I almost didn't let go, but I finally did. "You prefer me out of my box?" I hedged.

He chuckled roughly. "I don't prefer you any way."

"Is that not the same as saying you don't like me?"

I was aiming for teasing, but the speed with which he turned to look at me with a frown on that aggravatingly handsome face made me think it passed over him. I could tell he was looking me over carefully, but I couldn't have told you what was going through his head. He was quiet for so long, the intensity radiating off him, that

72

I felt like I had to lighten the mood.

"You want to take a picture, Lombardi? It'll last longer."

The next thing I knew, a flash went off in my eyes and I was almost as blinded as the night before. I blinked, spluttering a laugh, and heard him chuckle roughly.

"I wasn't being serious!" I giggled.

"Well, you shouldn't offer things you aren't willing to give."

I was still blinking furiously, trying to clear the spots from my eyes. "It's less I was unwilling to give it and more I preferred to not be blind!"

"Oh, come on, Barlow. Think of the actual blind people in the world. I doubt they'll take kindly to your complaining."

I did my best to glare at him as I tried surreptitiously to pull my phone out of my pocket. As I whipped it up and touched the button to take a picture, I saw him smirk around the cigarette in his mouth as though he was totally expecting it. But, then he was complaining just as much.

"Okay. No. Fair. That is painful," he laughed and rubbed his eyes.

"Ah, revenge is sweet," I teased and he laughed again.

"You at least seem in a better mood now," he said as he rubbed his eyes again and shook his head.

"I was in a bad mood before?"

He shrugged. "You seemed kinda…funky."

"I wasn't the only one."

He nodded as he kept his eyes over the lake. "No, you weren't."

"You seem less…funky now."

"I am less funky now."

Ignoring the confusion at a seemingly new side to him that still hung around the edges of my mind, I cleared my throat. "Um…

Anything you want to talk about? Maddy's…okay?"

He shrugged again. "I'm not going to do you the disservice of telling you your life seems easy, Barlow. All I'll say is that you probably know life isn't always as simple as it can be made to look."

I nodded. "Fair enough."

It was a completely true statement. I knew for a fact that people thought my life was easy and I tried to keep it that way. I would never try to imply that my life was hard, but it never felt as simple as I tried to make people think it was.

The idea that Roman's life wasn't a simple as he seemed to make it look was still a revelation to me.

"If there's anything I've learnt, it's that no one's life is ever as simple as you think."

"Are you implying I have depths, Barlow?" he scoffed.

I pulled my knees to my chest and smiled into them, not sure if I believed it myself. "I wouldn't dare tarnish your reputation."

I felt him shrug. "In my experience, reputations are overrated."

"Shall I go back to school and tell everyone you like unicorns and keep fuzzy pink dice in your truck?"

He barked a laugh like it was totally unbidden. "Okay, you've made your point. You have the power, my queen. Please, for the love of all things I hold dear–"

"Your dick for one?" popped out before I could stop myself; something about Roman seemed to switch off my filter.

He turned to stare at me in complete shock, his cigarette hanging comically from his mouth. He blinked, grabbed his smoke and snuffed it out on the sand on his other side, all while keeping his eyes on me.

"Who the hell are you?" he huffed in surprise.

I felt my cheeks flame as I shoved my forehead into my knees. But, it wasn't shame. I was just a little embarrassed I'd so brazenly said what was on my mind. And a little embarrassed that Roman brought it out in me.

"Sorry," I mumbled into my legs.

Roman laughed. "Oh no. None of that bullshit, Barlow. That was nothing to apologise for."

"I shouldn't have said it," I breathed, still surprised I had.

"Try saying something else uncomplimentary about me," he said.

I snuck a look at him. "What?"

He nodded once. "Go on. What would you say to me if you were going to be completely honest with me?"

I looked over the lake and thought about it. "I don't... Nothing. I wouldn't say anything."

He laughed. "True. You and your lack of spine would probably not say anything. If we – for one second – pretend that you do have a spine, what would you say?"

I opened my mouth, then closed it and breathed heavily out of my nose. "You're not very complimentary, yourself," I pointed out, thinking I wasn't going to be the only one to break habits.

"You don't seem to like my compliments," he countered.

"I..." I looked at him again and found him watching me with interest. "You don't compliment me."

"Because you don't like it."

"Fine. You give me something complimentary and I'll give you something uncomplimentary."

He chuckled and lit another cigarette. I realised that maybe he wasn't quite as relaxed as he seemed; he smoked a fair amount, but I hadn't seen him smoke that much in such a short span of time.

Not that I was really in a good position to make comparisons, but it still seemed more than usual.

"All right. A proper compliment, hey?" He paused and I was pretty sure he was thinking, so I didn't interrupt. "All right. Your eyes look crazy beautiful when you get embarrassed giggly. That's the one time I see *you* these days."

I'd been going to tease him for how long it had taken. But, my brain stuttered to a halt. I had to admit, I wasn't sure how to take that. I needed so much more explanation for…just so much of that statement.

"I'm waiting on this uncompliment, Barlow."

"I'm going to need more before I let that pass as a compliment," I answered.

He huffed and lay back down. "In what way?"

I shrugged and leant my elbows on my knees. "Firstly, what's embarrassed giggly?"

His chuckle this time was lighter. "It's when you find something funny but embarrassing at the same time—"

"How often do *you* have cause to be embarrassed?" I scoffed.

"No, Barlow. It's unique to you. I mean, probably not like only you in the whole world. But, it's not a generic thing. You get like it when Hadley does something crazy—"

"Like when she called you beautiful the other day?" I offered, trying not to let it get to me that Roman obviously noticed things about me.

He laughed. "Yeah, like that. Like when I sing at you. And like those rare moments when you have a spine and say exactly what's on your mind. Then you flush this cute shade of pink, you give this gorgeous little smile and your eyes fucking shine, Piper. It's a beautiful thing to see, and it's one time you're really you."

Well, if anything was going to set my cheeks flushing, it would be something like that. I tried to take my mind off the weird fluttery feeling he'd just given me because, let's be real here, it was Roman Lombardi for crying out loud. Whether there were actually depths or not, he was still the guy that went through girls faster than I went through chocolate cake.

An uncompliment. The guy wanted an uncompliment. It would have to be something relatively real because otherwise it was just being mean for being mean's sake.

"I know you're totally flattered by my compliment, Barlow. But, I'm waiting on something scathing."

"You know, you are so not as good as you think you are. Just because you're demanding and smile nicely, doesn't actually make you adorable. I have no idea why girls fall over themselves for you. You're rude and obnoxious and seriously annoying." I realised what I'd said and turned to him. "No! What I meant was…"

He just stared up at me, his face stony.

"I mean, I'm sure you… I can see why…" I huffed a breath. "That is, you have… Of course you have…good… What?" I asked as he'd started laughing.

"Oh, and you were doing so well!" he cried, putting one arm behind his head. "Sure, it wasn't exactly original. But, it was unfiltered until the filter seemed to be stu…stu…stuttering back to life."

I shoved his leg playfully. "Shut up. There is nothing wrong with a filter, nothing wrong with civility and human decency."

"No, Barlow. I don't suppose there is. But, there is such a thing as simpering. It's a fine line to walk."

"I think you left the line behind a long time ago, Lombardi." I spread my arm out wide. "Like, you are now so far past the line –

out in the wilderness – that you'll never find your way back."

"Yeah, quite possibly. But, at least you'll never wonder what I'm really thinking."

"Don't pretend you care what I'm really thinking outside any entertainment I might give you."

"I'm hurt, Barlow! How could you think I didn't care?"

"Because you're Roman Lombardi, resident underachiever, obnoxious delinquent, trouble-maker, and horrible flirt."

He snorted. "Barlow, you insult me. I am a fantastic flirt, thank you."

I looked back at him and grinned. "Yes, I know. Hence, horrible."

He nodded. "Oh, I see. Horrible in the sense I do it a lot, rather than describing my ability."

I shook my head at his mockery. "Yes, Lombardi."

He sat up and bumped my shoulder with his. "Is that you admitting my flirting is fantastic?"

"That is me agreeing that we're on the same page with that you flirt…" I stopped, realising that any way I ended that sentence would be a compliment to his flirting. "I'll admit a lot of girls seem to think you're good at it."

"But, not you?" He sounded like he didn't believe me.

"I wasn't aware you actually tried to flirt with me. I'm not sure that mentioning you wanted to get into my pants one time counted as flirting. I assumed you were stating fact." I shrugged nonchalantly.

He snorted. "Well, I suppose that's not wrong."

"Of course, your being here instead of using said flirting skills could be a testament to the fact all those stories about your flirting are trumped up exaggeration?" I hedged.

"Is that what you think?"

I shrugged, thinking whatever this was it was weird behaviour. "I can only call it like I see it, Lombardi."

He scoffed. "Yeah, righto. I suppose Carter's full of witty flirtation."

I looked over the lake, my fingers finding my shoelace to play with. "Mason's sincere–"

"And, you think I'm not."

"I never said that."

"You were thinking it."

"I assume it based on how many girls you seem to get through."

"Just because I share, does not make me insincere."

"How sincere can you be when you move on right away?"

"I live in the moment, Barlow. Something I feel you need to learn more about."

"There will be no inappropriate touching or fondling, Lombardi."

"How about appropriate touching and fondling? I do a very good appropriate fondle."

I looked at him, incredulous, and the smile he threw me no matter how small was completely infectious.

"I can never tell when you're being serious or not."

"Really?" he asked.

His tone was still light, but his eyes had gone serious.

And, that was one problem. I'd lied; I somehow did know when Roman was being serious and when he wasn't. I knew what was intended as a joke to cheer me up, what was him being…well, Roman, and what was a combination of both.

"Really," I replied as I wriggled guiltily.

"All right, then." I was pretty sure he didn't believe me either.

Like the night before, we hung out for a little while longer, sometimes in companionable silence, sometimes with bits of conversation and laughs until he walked me back up to our houses and said goodnight.

Chapter Seven
Definitely Not a Date.

Monday saw me unusually antsy and I had no idea why until I was halfway through a text conversation with Hadley.

> **Hads:** *You seem distracted.*
>
> **Me:** *How can I seem distracted? We're texting.*
>
> **Hads:** *Yeah, but I know you. What have you been up to?*
>
> **Hads:** *Tell me you're talking to Mason!*

And, that was when I realised I was staring out the window and watching Roman seemingly trying to wrangle what I assumed was this niece. She looked utterly in her element, running backwards and forwards as he tried to grab her. He, meanwhile, looked totally fed up. I had never seen him look so *out* of his element.

And, I couldn't stop the way my brain was making me look at him differently. I distracted myself by replying to Hadley.

> **Me:** *No, sorry. Watching John Cusack.*

Which wasn't a complete lie, *High Fidelity* was on in the background.

> **Hads:** *Haha, I'll leave you to it then. Gran's calling anyway.*
>
> **Me:** *Okay, cya xx*
>
> **Hads:** *Much love babes xo*

I opened the window and watched Roman close his arms on empty air and yell in frustration.

"Mads! Come on!" I heard him call.

He stretched his neck and his gaze fell on me. He gave me a small smile hello, pointed at the tiny running person and shrugged. I bit my lip to hide a smile and shook my head with an apologetic shrug. His look told me he didn't think I was terribly helpful. I smiled and closed the window. He shrugged again incredulously and I held a finger up to tell him to hold on.

I jogged down the stairs and out the back door. By the time I stopped next to him, Maddy was running around at the bottom of their yard with her arms spread wide. Well, the bottom of the yard here constituting where the trees that surrounded the lake began.

"Is she a plane or a fairy?" I asked.

"No fucking clue."

"And you…?"

"She's fast, okay?" he huffed.

I looked at him with a smile. "I'm not judging."

"You so were. I saw you up there."

I coughed to cover a laugh. "Does she know what she's doing?"

"Do they ever?"

"Uncie Roman, look!" she giggled as she threw herself on the ground in something that was supposed to be a cartwheel and I almost erupted in laughter.

Roman huffed and reached into his pocket, but pulled it out empty. "Shut up."

I barely held in a snigger. "I didn't say anything."

"Shut up," he repeated.

"No, it's actually adorable."

"Yeah, of course it is," he muttered

"Did you see?" Maddy asked, hands on hips and glaring at him.

"I saw. It was great!" he called back, then threw me a look that simultaneously asked me if it was great or not and told me to keep my mouth shut at his enthusiasm.

"Don't ask me. I don't have small children in my life," I sniggered.

He growled, changing it to an awkward laugh as Maddy ran up to us. She frowned at me with the honesty only a small child can manage.

I hadn't really seen her around. In fact, I wasn't sure I'd really paid much attention to next door since they'd moved in unless I'd noticed Roman outside.

"Hi." I smiled.

"Who are you?"

"Uh, Piper." I pointed behind me. "I live next door."

Maddy looked between us and I saw the family resemblance. Finally, she smiled and held her hand out. "I'm Maddy."

I shook it because I'm polite and her confidence kind of scared me. "Nice to meet you. Roman…mentioned you."

"Are you Uncie Roman's girlfriend?"

I wasn't the only one who seemed to have an inconvenient piece of spit they choked on.

"Uh, no. But, we go to school together."

Maddy nodded. "I'm going to school next term."

I smiled. "That's pretty cool."

She shrugged. "Can you do cartwheels?"

I was a little taken aback by the change in topic, but I rallied. "Uh. Last I tried, I could."

"When did you try last?"

"Oh, good question. It was a while ago."

83

"Uncie Roman can't."

"Is that so?"

She nodded. "Will *you* help me? He's useless."

I looked at Roman and tried not to laugh. "I'm not at all surprised."

His eyes widened and the corner of his lip quirked, but he nodded in agreement.

"Well, I can't promise anything. But, I'll do my best."

Maddy grabbed my hand and pulled me to a clear spot on the lawn. "Okay, go!" she cried.

"Oh, now? Okay."

I tried to remember how to do a cartwheel. I'd done gymnastics for a while when I was younger, so I tried to remember what I'd done then.

I took a run up and launched, praying to any and all deities that I wasn't going to make an idiot of myself. My body just kind of took over and I managed one cartwheel and a sort of flip before I stumbled a little and (un)gracefully fell on my butt.

"Wow!" Maddy yelled and I rolled onto my stomach to look at her with a smile. "Teach me!"

She ran over and I spent the rest of the afternoon teaching – or, trying to teach – her how to cartwheel while Roman watched and was incredibly chatty and unhelpful. We'd made some progress by the time Roman's mum got home from work and she found us outside. I didn't notice she'd been standing there until I realised Roman was talking to her.

"She's been all right. How was work?" he asked. I saw him kiss her temple and take his arm off from around her shoulders.

"Fine. Same old," she answered.

Maddy looked up and broke into a grin. "Grandma!" she

giggled and ran over to latch onto her waist.

I stood awkwardly for a moment.

"Uh, Mum, you know Piper Barlow?"

She nodded and threw Roman a look like she wondered if he was on something. "Of course I know Piper." She gave me a conspiratorial smile. "How are you, dear?"

I smiled. "Fine, thanks, Carmen. How about you?"

Carmen gave me a smile that didn't reach her tired eyes. "Still going. Could you tell your mum that I will definitely bring that chicken recipe to book club this week? She's been on me for months about it." I nodded as she chuckled, then looked down at Maddy. "How about we wash up and get dinner on?"

"I'll help!" Maddy cried and hurried inside.

"Hands first!" Carmen called after her. "Thanks for that, Piper. You don't have to indulge her." She smiled at me kindly.

"Oh… For…? No, that's fine. I wasn't doing anything anyway. I had a good day."

Carmen looked between me and Roman and I saw him shift weirdly. I couldn't help but smile, or try to hide a smile. Carmen rose an eyebrow in my direction and I did smile at her then.

"Are you home tonight, Roman?" she asked slowly.

"For dinner." He wouldn't look at either of us.

"After that?"

He looked uncomfortable and I suddenly wondered what his mum thought he was up to when he was out all night. I mean, I didn't think she was an idiot. But, I wondered what went through her mind. No one at school knew exactly what he got up to. I couldn't imagine what Carmen thought, when he wasn't being brought home by the police obviously.

"I don't know yet."

"Oh, don't worry about me," I said to him, waving a hand weirdly. I wasn't sure if he didn't want to make plans in case we both found ourselves at the lake again, or so we would, or because I might expect it. Still, I probably could have phrased that differently.

Both Carmen and Roman looked at me in question.

"Oh," I chuckled. "I mean, Roman's been… We…" I cleared my throat and found semi-bullshit coming out, "That is, he was teaching me how to skip stones the last couple of nights and I'm terrible at it…"

Roman's eyebrow rose and I could see him fighting a smirk. Carmen's face softened considerably as she looked at me.

Well, that gives me some idea of what she thinks he's up to…

"He's been with you?" she asked me.

I nodded far too quickly. "Well, I mean… We didn't plan it. Just, we hung out at the lake the last couple of nights. Just chatting you know, and uh–"

"Skipping stones, listening to music," Roman finished, humour in his voice, and I nodded.

"Oh," Carmen smiled warmly. "Well, no. If you have plans, by all means…"

"I mean," I shrugged, my hands clasped in front of me awkwardly, "they're not set or anything."

"Whatever you want to do. Just let me know what you're up to."

"Grandma!" Maddy yelled impatiently from inside and Carmen smiled.

"Good to see you, Piper. Say hi to your parents for me."

"You too, Carmen! Will do," I called as she went inside.

"You know, she's going to think we're dating now," Roman

86

said.

I scoffed against that sudden weird feeling in my chest. "Yeah, because Roman Lombardi dates."

"I could date."

"Eh, could you though?"

"Okay. What counts as a date? I'll meet you down here at, what? Nine? We'll go down to the lake and I'll teach you how to skip stones if you really want?" he asked quickly.

I laughed. "I'll meet you at nine and you can even teach me to skip stones, but the word date will in no way be attached to any time we spend together. Ever. Okay?"

He looked through his hair at me with humour dancing in his eyes. "Thank fuck." And, I laughed again.

"Wow, took a load of convincing."

"I'll see you here at nine."

"Sure, Lombardi."

I watched him run inside and made my way back to my room to find a bunch of text messages from Hadley and Celeste and an email from Mason to deal with.

I jogged down the stairs a little before nine, dressed in my jeans and a warm jacket.

"Hiya sweetie," Dad said and Mum looked up at me.

"I'm just popping out for a bit, wandering down to the lake."

Mum and Dad looked at me like I was keeping a secret. I sort of felt like I was.

"By yourself?" Mum asked.

I opened my mouth. "Um... No...?"

"Are you sure?" Dad chuckled.

"I'm just hanging out, nothing special."

They both nodded like they thought whatever it was must be terribly important because of how not important I was trying to tell them it was.

"All right. Have a good time and keep warm."

I nodded. "Yep, will do."

I replied to a text from Hadley as I walked out of the house and shoved my keys in my pocket. Hadley had been on my case about Mason even more in the few days she'd been away than she had like the whole time leading up to it. Of course, there were plenty mentions as well of how I should give Roman a go over the holidays before Mason got back. In Hadley's mind; since she couldn't, one of us should and that left me. I hadn't mentioned I'd been hanging out with him, let alone anything that could lead her to think that there would be any hooking up with him.

"I'm about to run out of things to be gentlemanly about here, Barlow."

I looked up and saw Roman smirking at me as he looked me up and down. He dropped his cigarette butt on the ground and crushed it under his heel.

"And just what does that mean?"

"Well, you rugged up, so I won't need to offer you my jacket. I'm already walking you down to the lake – so, your safety's all good. If you're not careful, you'll be a completely independent young woman."

I scoffed and kept walking towards the lake, meaning he had to follow. "Gosh. Wouldn't want that, would we?"

"How would Carter come swooping in to save you if you were

88

all independent?"

I looked back at him for a moment as I picked my way over tree roots. "I don't need anyone swooping in to save me, thank you."

"Well, I'm all right with that. But, I highly doubt that he knows how to be anything but the chivalrous white knight."

"No one would ever confuse you for the chivalrous anything, Lombardi," I laughed. "Don't worry."

"I am very chivalrous in bed, thank you. I'm all about giving. I'm very gallant. Some have even called me a romantic."

"Had they been dropped on their heads as children?"

He didn't say anything, but I heard him clap. I stopped and turned to him with a wry smile.

"What?" I asked.

He gave me a bow, his arms thrown wide. "No stutter. Quick retort. Why Barlow, I think I've ruined you."

"Yeah, you wish," I snorted.

"No, that would be ravage. Totally different."

I stumbled on something on the ground, but he was there to catch me. We looked at each other for a moment, our noses close. My heart beat a little faster in anticipation, but he didn't make any moves.

"How do you just come out and say things like that?" I asked.

His eyes darted between mine. "I don't know, I just do. Some call it confidence, some call it arrogance, others call me dirty–"

"Yes, I'll bet a lot of people call you dirty and it's not always an insult."

He threw a split-second grin at me and my chest went all fluttery again. Then, he pulled us both to standing straight and let go of me, starting to move toward the lake again.

"Others call me passionate."

"I'll bet they're the same ones who think dirty is a compliment," I answered as I followed him, my eyes on the dark ground. "Passion. Dirt. I suppose it's all the same to you really."

I gasped as I ran into him and found him looking down at me. I would have said his eyes held a hint of humour, but it was just a little dark where we were standing.

"There's nothing dirty about passion, Piper. Nothing wrong with acting on mutual attraction. Passion and attraction isn't something you can help. It happens whether you want it to or not. You get to decide what you do with it, not anyone else."

To take my mind off the way he made my heart race, I argued, "And, what about all the girls you leave behind? What happens when you're out of passion for them?"

He shrugged. "How many girls do you hear wanting more from me, Barlow?"

"Every single one you've been with."

He blinked like that actually surprised him. But, I couldn't tell if it was me or the statement he was surprised by.

"Come on, don't pretend you have no idea. Don't tell me you thought you had your fun with them then they wandered off into the sunset completely fine."

"I wouldn't pretend anything of the sort. I just didn't expect you to be keeping tabs on my sex life."

Feeling annoyed and not knowing why, I shoved past him and kept walking. "It's a little hard not to keep tabs on your sex life when that's the majority of the gossip at school."

"Oh Barlow, anyone would think you cared!" he teased.

"Shut up."

We walked along in silence for a while. As we came towards the last few trees, he grabbed my arm gently.

"Look, I don't make a habit of telling anyone to expect more than what I'll give them, Barlow. If girls expect more after, it's because they've created whole fantasies in their heads. What you see is what you get with me. That they forget that and think they can change me is not my fault."

You could probably do something about that. Multiple somethings even… is not a thing I said out loud.

Instead I looked up at him, trying to figure him out. There was something beseeching in him, something that made me think he was being completely sincere. But, I wondered why the hell he'd feel the need to be sincere about something like that with me. It seemed a very un-Roman move in my opinion.

Sure, I'd love for him to turn around and tell me that all the stories were wrong, that really he was a decent guy. I wanted him to deny it all. I didn't need a reminder that the guy I'd been hanging out with went through girls like it was going out of fashion and he was completely unapologetic. On some level it bothered me. On another, I was pleased he was being honest with me. But, I just couldn't help feeling a little bothered by it deep down and that annoyed me because I shouldn't be bothered by that.

"I can't be changed, Piper…" he said slowly and I knew he believed it.

I nodded curtly. "*I* am well aware of that fact." Although, hadn't he seemed to have changed recently?

"And, yet you're still here."

I scoffed and hoped maybe my insides would stop twisting unpleasantly. "I don't know what you're expecting to happen here, Lombardi. But, I wasn't under the impression your inability to change would have any effect on my life. Far as I can tell, we're just two people having an extended pity party and you're supposed to be teaching me how to skip stones."

"You don't seem particularly funky tonight," he pointed out.

"Neither do you."

He ran a hand over his jaw. "Well, I had something to look forward to tonight."

Here the twisting turned to squirming. Then my heart beat erratically in the face of his complete suaveness. "If you have more important or exciting things – or people – to do tonight, I can skip stones by myself."

"I was talking about you, Barlow. For some reason, you calm me. You make me feel…settled. Wrestling Maddy into bed tonight was a piece of cake knowing I was going to be meeting up with you after. The fact I might get to laugh at you was just icing. Come on, then."

"Is this why girls expect more from you?" I asked and he stopped.

"What do you mean?"

"Well, I mean… What? You tell them not expect anything, then you pop out with things like that. I don't blame them for their expectations if you tell them things like that."

He huffed. "Yeah no. I don't make it a habit to talk to girls. The wordiest I get is telling them how I want it or them."

"So, what makes me different?"

"I'm not promising you anything either."

"Aren't you?" I asked, certainly feeling like there was a promise of something going on here.

He looked me over carefully. "No, Piper. I… I like hanging out with you. You're comforting," he said slowly. "But, I'm too broken to ever be good enough for you."

I wasn't sure what to respond to that, so I took a leaf out of his book and brushed it off. "Okay. Good. We're on the same page then."

He gave that humourless laugh. "Exactly. We feel better together. Let's not overthink it."

He headed towards the water and I took a moment to move after him as I was busy trying not to overthink it.

I couldn't deny it. Roman made it easier to breathe, easier to be me. No matter how anxious I was feeling, a few minutes with Roman and I had a respite from it all. It was absolute craziness and I'd deny it to anyone who asked. But, I also couldn't help the fact that it was becoming harder to deny I was drawn to more than just the settled feeling he gave me.

He looked back at me and sighed before coming back. He grabbed my hand and pulled me towards the water. "Lesson one, the closer to the water you are, the easier it is."

I laughed as I stopped thinking and waited to see what lesson two would be.

Chapter Eight
No Judgements. No Apologies.

Roman had done his best to try to teach me to skip stones on Monday night, but we'd eventually given up and just sat around chatting or in silence for a few hours. Tuesday, my stone skipping technique was still no good and I was practising when Roman's appearance was unexpected but not unwelcome.

"I didn't think you were coming. Thought you had better things to do tonight?" I asked. I didn't really care, but I *had* thought he was going to a mate's.

He shrugged. "I found myself here instead."

I nodded and yelled as my next stone just plummeted into the lake.

"It's fine, Barlow," he chuckled. "It just takes practise."

I sighed. "Yeah, it's not the stones. I mean, it's not helping. But…"

He nodded. "You want to talk about it?"

I shook my head. "There really isn't anything to talk about. I just feel shit."

"Yeah, fair enough. Pity party for two, yeah?"

I chuckled humourlessly.

"What?" he asked.

"I just never imagined, of all the people in my life, I could feel the most normal around you." Yep, I'd been going to deny it until my dying breath. But, with the appearance of Roman went my filter.

"I feel like that's *supposed* to be a compliment…?"

I gave him a smile. "It just never crossed my mind that I'd come here instead of all the parties we'd been invited to or instead of sitting in my room with my movies because just sitting with you, even saying nothing, I feel less alone than I do anywhere else at the moment. I guess I'm trying to say thank you."

"For what? I haven't done anything a decent human being shouldn't already be doing."

"A, you're talking about Mason now and that's hardly fair. And B, you're not supposed to be a decent human being, remember?"

He chuckled. "Oh yeah. I'd almost forgotten."

I laughed and tried another stone. Of course, it failed.

"Come here."

He stepped up behind me and put a hand on my waist while the other took hold of my wrist. Oddly, it didn't feel weird or awkward. I didn't even question it; I just took some comfort in the physical connection and let him get to his point.

He moved my arm back and forth. "Like this. Ready?"

"For what?"

"I'll move your arm and tell you when to let go."

I nodded. "Okay."

He moved my arm a couple of times again, then said "now" and I let go of the rock. It jumped twice before plonking into the water.

My arms shot up into the air as I whooped. He laughed, wrapped his arms around my waist and spun me around. He finally let my feet down, but didn't let me go.

"See, told you that you could do it," he said, his lips close to my ear.

"Again!" I laughed, as I hugged his arms.

We went through the motions a few times and, more often than not, my stone skipped at least twice.

"Oh, watch out. I'll get better than you soon," I teased.

"You what?" he laughed.

"Yep, the student becomes the master." I brushed off my shoulders mock-arrogantly and he laughed out loud; a pure, happy sound I don't think I'd heard from him ever. It was more than just sincere, it was beautiful.

"Yeah, we'll see about that," he said as he tickled me.

I giggled helplessly while I tried to pant, "Uncle".

"I think you'll find it's pronounced 'uncie'," he said deadpan.

That set me off further. I took a deep breath and finally got out "okay, okay, Uncie Roman!" through laughing.

He let go of me, but I was so busy laughing that my legs almost gave out. He just got his arms around me as we collapsed onto the ground, setting us off again. Once we'd finally calmed down, we just lay there, perfectly content where we'd fallen – arms and legs everywhere.

"No music tonight?" I asked.

"Didn't want to interrupt your pity party."

I smiled and picked up his hand. "I kind of like your music."

"Really?" His thumb ran over the back of my hand.

I nodded. "Yeah, seems…suitable."

"Huh," he chuckled and pulled his phone out of his pocket with the hand I wasn't holding.

Music washed over us and we lay in silence for a bit.

"Barlow?"

"Hm?"

"What are your plans for next year?"

I was completely taken back by that question. "What?"

"I mean, you don't have to tell me or anything. I just wondered."

I shifted my head slightly where it lay on his arm. "No. I... Um, well uni in Adelaide I guess."

I hated thinking about it because moving out of home, and leaving my friends and family, and everything else involved seemed hugely scary, and I couldn't really deal with it. Mum had already started the excited planning, but all it served to do was give me anxiety and a headache.

I felt him nod. "Fair enough."

I didn't say anything, just did my usual staring up at the sky. Not that I could see the stars that night because it was cloudy. There was a blotch of white where the moon was trying to peek through, but the rest was grey.

Finally, I heard him ask, "You okay?"

I nodded. "Uh, yeah. I just... Sorry," I sighed.

"What for?"

I shrugged and sat up, my legs still over one of his. "You don't want to hear all my unnecessary, inexplicable shit, Lombardi."

"How about a new rule?"

I looked back at him and found him watching me, his hands behind his head. "New rule?"

He nodded. "Yeah. We don't apologise."

"We don't...?"

He nodded again. "Yeah. You just *be*, Barlow, and I'll accept you as is. You never have to apologise to me for anything. You want to be in a shit? Be in a shit and I'll take you as you are. You want to be ridiculously, annoyingly happy? I'll take that, too –

97

although I reserve the right to tease you a little. You can't or don't want to talk? No judgements. No apologies, Piper. We just be ourselves."

I was in danger of forgetting everything I thought I knew about Roman Lombardi before the holidays. I didn't let it show.

"Just be ourselves?"

"Yep."

"No apologies?"

"Yep."

I sighed, thinking it over. I lay back down next to him and he put his arm back under my head. "Okay, Roman. No judgements. No apologies. I won't expect you to be anything but you, and you likewise. We are who we are in the moment and that just is," I said, testing out how it sounded.

I felt him nod again. "Exactly."

"Huh… Okay."

He chuckled. "If I ask you what you want to do at uni, is that going to bring on some more funk?"

I smiled. "I think I want to do teaching."

"What years?"

"Primary."

"Really?"

"Yeah, I've always liked kids."

"Even after yesterday with Maddy?"

I snorted. "Okay, I may be rethinking it," I teased. "Why? What are you doing next year?"

"Haven't you heard the teachers at school?"

That shouldn't have brought a smile to my face. "I've heard Mr Dunbridge tell everyone you're going nowhere fast."

"Well, he's not wrong."

"I'm sure that's not true."

"Don't tell me you've forgotten who I am, Barlow."

My smile fell. "No. I haven't forgotten. I'm just not quite as convinced as I once was that you're a total write off."

"You're the only one, then. Trust me, Dunbridge isn't wrong."

I had no evidence to mount an argument, so I said, "Well, you must still have an idea what you'll be busy doing on the road to nowhere?"

He sighed. "Well, Dad wants me to move to the city with him and his new wife. Mum simultaneously wants me to go to uni and stay with her forever. So, you know…" He shrugged. "I expect I'll get a terrible ATAR and bludge until Mum makes me get a job or gets sick of me."

"Where does your dad live?"

"Sydney."

I nodded. "Do you see him much?"

"Nope."

"Sorry, if you–"

His arm wrapped around my shoulder and gave me a slight squeeze. "No apologies, Barlow."

I chuckled. "Okay. If you don't want to talk about it, that's fine."

"Eh, there's just not much to talk about. He gives me money in lieu of love and expects me to worship him."

"He's rich then?"

His laugh was humourless. "Like fuck. How else do I have my car? He gives me an allowance and if I need more I just ask him. Mum, annoyingly, won't let me help out with the mortgage. Dad pays the minimum, but he could do so much more. Still no matter how much I try, she won't let me." He sighed. "Something about it

99

not being a kid's job."

"She loves you."

"She does."

Mum and Carmen weren't best friends or anything, but they travelled in the same circles – it was a small town among small towns, so there weren't that many circles – and they obviously got along so I knew of her pretty well. And after getting to know Roman, I'd started to think that it wasn't just maternal instinct that made her love her son so much.

Silence fell again and I tapped my foot along to the music even though it wasn't something I knew. I'd opened my mouth to ask him something when rain just started pouring down. My eyes closed and I yelped.

I heard Roman laugh and felt him jump up. He grabbed my hands and pulled me to standing where I smacked into his chest and he had to catch me before I fell again. I opened my eyes, squinting against the rain and saw him looking down at me with a smile.

"You scream like a girl, Barlow." But, I knew he was only teasing.

"Yeah, and I'm sure you scream like a *real man*," I huffed and he laughed.

We just stood and looked at each other for a moment and I almost forgot it was raining. The air around us seemed warm and I liked what I saw in his eyes; they were softer than usual, something about him not just the cocky, womanising arsehole. Then, lightning flashed and I fully remembered who he was and where we were.

I pulled away gently and bent to pick up the blanket.

"Here." He took it from me, grabbed my hand and pulled me after him towards our houses.

I would have pulled my hand from his, but I slipped once and his hand was the only thing that kept me standing.

We finally ducked under my back veranda and he shook his wet hair from his face with a gorgeous smile on his face.

"I enjoyed tonight, Barlow," he said.

I nodded. "I surprisingly don't hate spending time with you, Lombardi."

He grinned. "Maybe it won't be raining tomorrow night."

"Yeah, maybe."

"I guess I might see you then."

"You might."

His eyes were still warm and full of nothing but trouble now, but I still felt the most comfortable that I had with another person in a long time.

"Night, Piper."

"Night, Roman."

We stood awkwardly for a moment, then I ducked my head and went inside. Before I closed the curtains behind me, I looked back at him and wondered again where the Roman I thought I knew was.

But then, maybe he was still the Roman he'd always been and I was just seeing him differently, seeing a little more of him. Just like I was still Piper with him, just a version of me I didn't show the world.

"Hey, sweetie," Mum said and I turned to find her pouring hot water into a mug. "Was that Roman I just saw?"

I blinked. "Uh, yes…"

She pursed her lips like she was trying not to smile. "I see."

"No. Nothing to see here!" I said far too quickly.

Mum did smile then. "Of course not."

"Nothing happened."

Mum looked me over. "Darling, when you walk into the house with a smile like that on your face after seeing a boy like Roman? I won't judge anything that happened as long as you were being sensible."

My cheeks flamed; the last thing I needed was for my parents to think I was…up to things with Roman. Although, my embarrassment at the idea probably solidified in her mind that we had been up to…things.

"No need. We skipped stones, listened to music, got rained on… You know, the usual." I chuckled self-deprecatingly.

Mum stirred her tea and nodded. "Of course, sweetie. Don't worry. I get it. Roman has that bad boy thing going for him, a little danger, and Mason's a different kind of boy."

There was a knowingly teasing look on her face that had me skip over the part about how it was apparently okay I was hanging out with Roman.

"Mason and I… Well, I don't know. I think I'm hoping he'll ask me out when he gets home?"

"Really?"

I nodded. "Yes. In fact, I should go and check if he's emailed again. And… And, reply to him if he has." Dear God, how could my own mother make me feel so nervous about literally nothing?

"I wouldn't mention Roman, darling. Keep *him* for your dreams tonight." She gave me a wink and swanned up to her bedroom.

I stood at the bottom of the stairs and didn't really know what to say or to think. My first thought was that Mum and Dad had had a couple more wines after dinner than usual. It didn't happen often, but she got super mellow when she drank a little. Like hippie mellow. Free love and tattoos and weed kind of mellow.

I shucked my jacket, realising that I was dripping all over the floor and ran up to my room. Thankfully, I didn't see Dad. But, Mum wasn't likely to have told Dad anything. Not when we'd just been doing what she called 'mother-daughter bonding'.

I pushed into my room and closed the door. I dropped my jacket over my desk chair and pulled off my jumper. Somehow, I found myself at my window and I didn't realise I was looking for Roman until I found him leaning against a tree. At least, I assumed the dark, person-shaped blob with the orange spark was Roman smoking as he leant against a tree.

The shadow gave me a wave and I waved back.

It wasn't until I closed my curtains and gone to pull my singlet off that I realised I'd pulled said singlet off with my jumper and had been standing in my window in nothing but a black bra. As my cheeks flamed and I turned on my laptop, I just had to hope he hadn't noticed.

I pulled on some warm pyjamas then enthusiastically read and replied to Mason's most recent email. I'd never really thought about Europe outside a vague notion that it would be nice to go one day. But, Mason made it sound amazing and the pictures were great.

I thought I'd fall asleep thinking about Europe. At the very least, I expected to be thinking about John Cusack in Europe – thanks to my latest movie choice, this time *America's Sweethearts*. But, I didn't. As I lay in bed, trying to sleep, all I could think about was Roman.

I even got out of bed and snuck a look out my curtains, but I didn't see him. I had a mad urge to get dressed and go down to the lake to see if he was there.

"That is ridiculous," I muttered to myself as I forced myself back into bed.

It might have been ridiculous. But, it might have been better than lying in bed awake for hours thinking about him. At least, it was one of the first nights in a long time that I wasn't stressed about not sleeping or just generally anxious.

I wasn't sure I liked that he had that effect on me, but it was preferable to the uncomfortable way the unnecessary anxiety sat in my chest.

Chapter Nine

Cigarettes, Sex, and Everest.

I just happened to look out my window on Wednesday night to see him standing next to his ute. There was a dark pile of something in the tray and a spark of orange at his hand.

I held up a hand to him with a smile, pulled my ugg boots on over my socks, headed downstairs, and opened the back door.

"Hey," I said as he jumped onto the porch.

"Hey."

"What's up?"

"Well… I've loaded the tray up with blankets and wondered if you wanted to go and watch the stars with me?"

"That almost sounds romantic," I pretended to chastise him.

He smirked, but his eyes were hard. "Yeah, or it sounds like it's been pouring rain all day and I don't want to sit on the wet lakeshore like a pussy."

"Okay, less romantic," I laughed, approving.

His eyes softened slightly. "You don't have to come. But, I thought you might like to hang out."

That stopped me in my tracks. "You okay?"

He looked behind me and shrugged nonchalantly. "Not really."

"You want some company though?"

There was that shrug again. "What can I say, Barlow? I feel

better when we're not saying anything."

I nodded, a little bubble of warmth growing in my chest. I knew what he meant and I was glad it wasn't all one-sided. "Okay, sounds good. Let me just leave Mum and Dad a note, yeah?"

He finally looked back at me and smiled. "Take all the time you want."

I paused for some unknown reason, then popped back inside to leave my parents a note saying I was out and safe, and would be back. I wasn't in my warmest clothes. But if he had blankets, I was sure I'd be fine.

I jumped back out the door and he looked down at me.

"Not changing?"

"Do I need to?" I asked, looking down at my shorts and knee-high ugg boots.

"Doesn't bother me."

"Oh, won't you keep me warm, Roman?" I teased and he chuckled as we got into the car.

"You just have to say the word, Piper, and I'll keep you warm *all* night long."

"Oh, and now you've ruined it!" I said sarcastically.

"I'm not apologising," he said as he started driving.

"Good. If you did, I'd be worried you got abducted by aliens or something."

He laughed that big, open laugh. "If I ever apologise, you'll know I'm being held hostage."

I giggled. "That will definitely be your tell."

"And yours?"

I looked over at him as he navigated through the trees. "My what?"

"Your tell? For if you ever get abducted." He shot me a quick glance before he went back to concentrating.

"Um…" I thought about it. "'I hate John Cusack'."

"Well I don't love him, but that seems a bit harsh, Barlow. What did he ever do to you?"

I laughed. "No, that'd be my tell."

"John Cusack?"

I nodded. "Yep."

"Okay. Well, Carter will be devastated."

I smiled as he threw the car in park and jumped out of the cab, and I followed suit. "Oh, Mason knows about my love for John."

"He's a better man than me, then."

"I get the impression you don't know who John Cusack is…"

"Oh, what gave it away?" His face popped up over the tray and I grinned at him and shook my head.

He walked around the back of the ute and beckoned for me to join him. He pulled the tailgate down and turned to me. When he'd been holding his hands out for a while, I looked down at them in confusion.

"Do you want a hand up, or not so much?" he asked.

I looked back at him and finally got what he was asking. I nodded and he put his hands on my waist and lifted me up onto the back. We froze for a moment, him standing between my legs, his hands on my waist. A flutter ran through me and my skin broke out into goose bumps.

I couldn't see wonderfully since he'd just turned the headlights off and my eyes weren't used to the moonlight yet, but I was glad of that. I wasn't entirely convinced of what I'd see in his eyes if I could see them properly. But that antsy feeling was back, if slightly different than before. I smiled and shuffled backwards.

He pulled himself up into the back with ease, sending my

imagination into overdrive as I watched his body move and eliciting a whole bunch of weird feelings in me that I ignored furiously.

He lay down, then looked at me. "You okay?"

"I should be asking you that, surely?"

He shrugged and held up the blankets for me to wriggle under them next to him.

"Do you want to talk about it?" I asked.

"I want to not talk about it."

"Okay." I said with a nod and we lay there in the dark, snuggled side-by-side under his blankets.

Eventually, he was the one who broke the companionable silence.

"Barlow?"

"Lombardi?"

"You ever feel like just everything's going to shit, no matter what you do?"

I did. More than I would have liked. "Yeah, I guess…"

"Like, you're just going along in life and you get thrown a curveball and you have to re-evaluate everything."

I found his hand and held it. I felt him tense for a second, then he gave my hand a small squeeze.

"Do you want to talk about that?"

"I don't know. It's just this feeling I have. I haven't really worked out what it goes with yet."

"Is it Maddy?"

I felt him shrug. "I don't think so. I'm getting used to her. As much as I'd get used to any kid in my life."

For some reason, that surprised me.

"You don't want kids?"

He scoffed. "You think I'd be a good dad?"

"That's not what I asked."

I felt him shift and turned to find him looking at me, his head propped up on his hand.

"There's a difference, you know," I said, searching his eyes. "You can still want them even if you think you won't be any good at it."

He dropped onto his back again and stared up. "First, I'd need to work out how to be with someone long enough. You don't just have kids without thinking of the consequences. They deserve better than that."

I nodded and lay my head on his shoulder. "Yeah. But, so do you."

He scoffed. "Is that a compliment?"

I nudged him. "I'm serious. You can want something even if you think you're not good enough or it's not good for you."

"Because you'd have experience with that." His voice sounded rough and annoyed.

"Well, maybe not as much as some. But, enough to get the concept."

"Fine. Give me an example, then."

"Right, well… Chocolate, right? I could look at a huge chocolate cake and decide that I want to eat all of it. But, I also know I shouldn't because otherwise I'd be sick or get fat or whatever. Plus, I have never done anything in my life that deserves the reward a whole chocolate cake."

"Is this thing you have for chocolate cake something that should make Carter jealous… Or?"

"Very cute. Like my love for John, Mason is well aware of my love for chocolate cake."

"And, this is all Johns and all chocolate cakes, or just certain ones?"

"One John and one chocolate cake. Mud cake. Dense and dark and moist– What?" I asked when he snorted.

"Nothing. I just can't with that word."

I smiled. "Moist isn't a dirty word, Roman."

He barked a laugh and his arm wrapped around me. "No, I don't suppose it is. Funny though, and gives a guy all sorts of ideas."

"Well, you can take those ideas and leave them in the gutter where they belong."

"Ah, Barlow. Any guy who told you he didn't get ideas around you has to be lying. But, I shall be a gentleman and keep them to myself."

"There goes that word again," I teased. "Anyone who told you they thought you could be a gentleman has to be lying. But as a lady, I won't go spreading it around."

I felt him shake his head with a laugh and he pulled me closer. "You think you're a lady, do you?"

"I do."

"How many ladies do you know who wear short shorts and ugg boots?"

"Lady Piper of Barlow was famous for them."

He laughed that pure happy laugh. "Of course she was."

"Caused a bit of a scandal at court, you understand. But, she was a trendsetter."

I couldn't be sure if he kissed my hair or not. "I'll bet she was. She seems happy at least."

"She is."

"Heard a lot from Carter, then? He regaling you with tales of his travels?"

"He is actually." I know I didn't imagine the way Roman tensed. "But, it's the resident underachiever actually who seems to have this weird habit of de-funking me."

Roman relaxed, but like it cost him some effort.

"Not that I'd tell him. What with that being stupid nancy words and all."

"No, 'course. He wouldn't appreciate it anyway, I'd bet. Too stupid."

I nodded. "That is what I hear."

We fell into a companionable silence again and I realised my hand had reached up for his around my shoulder. But, he didn't pull it away so I made no move to draw attention to it.

I felt him moving and wondered if he was uncomfortable. But when I smelled smoke, I realised he'd just been shuffling in his pockets.

"I could have moved," I offered.

"You could have."

"You just had to ask."

"Maybe I didn't want to disturb your peace and quiet."

"That doesn't sound like you."

He chuckled. "Doesn't much, does it."

"Well, you just have to ask next time."

"I like you exactly the way you are, Barlow. If I asked you to move for a sec, you might think I don't want you lying on me. Then, where would I be?"

I didn't have to hide my smile because I didn't think he'd be able to see it. The warmth in my chest I was sure he couldn't see. "Well, now I know how you feel about that, I'll make sure to lie on you as often as possible."

"Good."

We lay in silence a little while longer, until he broke it.

"Barlow?"

"Hm?"

"You never seemed fussed by my smoking."

I shrugged. "Am I meant to be?"

"Most people are. Especially the non-smokers." He gasped mockingly. "Unless, you're a closet smoker!"

I giggled. "No. Not a closet smoker. I just don't think it's my business and it doesn't bother me. You want to smoke? Smoke."

"You're not judging the underage smoker? Wondering how I get them?"

"We don't judge, remember?"

"Seriously, Barlow?"

"What? Sure, it's not the greatest habit–"

"What did you think of it last week?"

"Nothing."

"Bullshit. Spine, please."

"Fine. That it was stupid and made you a total idiot," I replied.

"And, what made you change your mind?"

"I guess, deep down I didn't. But, you're you and you smoke." I shrugged. "So sure, it's inadvisable and probably illegal. But, it's not up to me to tell you what to do."

"I do try not to blow it your way."

"I figured as much."

And, it was true. I wondered if most of why it didn't bother me was because he seemed to try to be as thoughtful about it as he could. Naturally, he couldn't control wind direction, but he seemed to try. And, I appreciated that.

I rolled onto my side to look at him.

"What?" he asked.

"Nothing. I was just wondering why you were still here."

"Well, killing myself seems a little drastic and no matter how hard I try to put myself in dubious situations, I just seem unkillable."

"That is in incredibly poor taste, Roman," I said, forcing myself not to smile regardless of its poor taste.

He stubbed out his cigarette on the side of the tray and threw it over before he rolled onto his side towards me. "Why am I still where, Piper?" he asked with a wry smile.

"Here. Surely your booty calls miss you? Or, are you fitting them in around me?" I kept my eyes on his, seeing him easily now that my eyes had adjusted to the limited light.

"You make yourself sound like an obligation."

I readjusted so my head was leaning on the flat of my hand rather than my fist. "It hadn't crossed my mind until now."

His eyebrows narrowed. "Instead of me explaining myself, how about I just tell you I'm thinking of some choice nancy wanker words?"

"I don't like it any more than you."

The consternation left his face as it dropped into humoured shock. "Don't like it?"

I shrugged and tried to keep the smile from my face. "What's to like about the fact I find *you* easy to be around?"

"You could have sat in your room. I am quite adept at pity parties for one."

I leant towards him. "But, we're better at pity parties for two."

We stared into each other's eyes, my heart fluttering and my skin tingling. If one of us moved forward, then we'd kiss. For all his talk of wanting to get into my pants and how nice my eyes were, I knew I wasn't the sort of girl Roman liked to kiss. So, I didn't have anywhere near enough nerves to move forward. But, despite some serious heat sizzling off him, he didn't move forward either.

"There's something far more satisfying in making you feel better than moping alone, Barlow," he said, his voice low and rough. He blinked and cleared his throat as he dropped back on to his back, his arm behind his head. "Plus, who would I sing to?"

I smiled, keeping my eyes on his face. He turned to look at me, a frown on that face.

"What?" he asked. "If you're going to take another picture, warn me this time."

I shook my head. "No. One is plenty."

"On the contrary, Barlow. A phone full would never be enough."

"I do not need a phone full of pictures of *you*."

"Who says I was talking about your phone and my pictures?"

"I can think of only one use you'd have for any pictures of me, Lombardi. And one is plenty."

He snorted. "Maybe if I'd caught one of you at your window last night."

I sat up and looked at him, past caring that my cheeks were hot as hell. "What?"

He shrugged. "Barlow, the light was behind you, but there was enough. I never pegged you for the black bra type." He winked.

My cheeks flamed even more and I turned and stuck them against the blankets over my knees.

Roman chuckled. "Don't be embarrassed, please. I promise I only whipped it out to your photo once and I didn't even think about it after seeing you in your bra… Much. I didn't think about it much. Okay, I thought about it a lot. And, I might have whipped it out twice, but that's all. I wouldn't tarnish your good name more than that. Well, no. I would, but I won't…"

He petered off as I finally turned to look at him, really not sure how much of that speech had been designed to make me laugh and how much was true. He wore the most annoyingly sexy, innocent little smirk as he looked at me.

"Just how many times have you…whipped it out to…me?" I asked hesitantly.

"Lifetime or in the last week?" he replied, totally at ease.

Panicking, I frowned. "I don't know if I want to know."

"Uh, in the last week… It was only once. Before that, I honestly couldn't tell you."

I blinked. "What?"

He shrugged. "What? It's totally natural, Barlow. I'm deprived just at the moment and – to be fair – you've been adorable. Also to be fair, it wasn't intentionally to you. You just happened to be the last girl I was around. So, naturally you popped into my head."

"That makes a scary amount of sense. I'm not sure I can be annoyed by that."

His grin widened. "You'll understand us men folk, yet!"

I gave him an exasperated glare. "Men I understand. Dicks, less so."

"That's fair. We are pretty much separate entities."

I snorted. "Really?"

"Did your precious Carter not explain this to you already? What *have* you two been doing?"

"Not talking about our genitals."

"Well, we're actually only talking about mine. Which I feel is sexist and unfair…"

I snorted again. "Vaginas seem to be less trouble. I'm not really sure what I could tell you about that is remotely similar."

"Last time you masturbated to visions of me!" he said, totally cavalier.

I choked on an inconvenient piece of spit and turned to face the back of the tray. I don't think I'd ever felt my face flush that hard.

He laughed and sat up. "Come on, Barlow. You expect me to think you don't?" he asked. His lips that close to my ear sent goose bumps across my body.

Annoyingly, they weren't entirely unpleasant.

I cleared my throat. "No, I don't–"

"Piper…" he coaxed.

I shoved my face in my knees again. "Once or twice."

"Tell me that's to me. Because if that's in total, I might cry."

I laughed and couldn't help but look at him. Realising that the conversation was not actually as embarrassing as I was trying to make it, I flopped back onto my back. "Well, get your hanky ready, Roman."

Roman groaned as he dropped back beside me and nudged his arm under my head again. "That is seriously disheartening."

"Why? You got hot to the image of me in my black bra, touching myself as I thought of you?"

"Well, I didn't. But, I will now. Thanks." Oddly enough, he didn't seem thrilled by the idea. "Tell me, do you plan to be such a prude with your precious Carter?"

"Firstly, I'm not a prude. It's just so much work for so little reward–"

"Oh!" he crowed. "I see now. You're just not doing it right!"

"How would you know?"

"Because doing it right is not too much work for not enough reward. I'd be happy to educate you."

I snuggled into him. "I'll bet you would."

116

"In the interests of science and your health only."

I chuckled. "Of course."

"It should be exciting, not...whatever reaction this is."

"Bored indifference?"

"Yeah, that."

"And how often should I be doing it, Roman? How often do you count enough? Are you a one a day kind of guy?"

He sniggered. "Sometimes."

"Other times?"

"Three or four."

I rolled over too quickly and found myself half on top of him, but neither of us seemed to feel the need to move. "What?"

He shrugged and I could see he was fighting a smile. "What?"

"Three of four times a day?"

He gave me the quickest, far too adorable grin before it was gone again. "Sometimes." The arm that had been under my head wrapped around my waist and his lips were at my ear. "I'm a very good teacher, you know."

I laughed and he joined me as he let me go and I lay against his side. "You're a comedian you know," I said.

"All comedy comes from truth."

"A cocky comedian."

"Damn straight."

We both dissolved into laughter, holding onto each other until it finally subsided and I pulled back just enough to look him in the eyes.

"You seem less funky."

His smile was warm and his eyes were far too soft, but I couldn't stop looking at him. "I am less funky. Thank you."

I shrugged. "Nothing a decent human being would do."

"I thought we'd talked about this? Carter is a perfectly good human being."

I smirked. "Very cute."

"Oh, I know I am."

I shook my head. "You wish you were as cute as you think you are."

"You wish I wasn't as cute as you think I am."

I looked away, but didn't hide my agreeing smile quick enough.

"Don't worry, Barlow. I won't tell anyone you like the way I look."

"I thought we established the other night that I don't like the way you look?"

"Uh, no. I let you think I'd conceded. In reality, we both know you like the way I look. It's futile to refute it."

"Again, I'm surprised you know so many big words."

"You won't distract me this time, Barlow. Go on, own it."

"Why?"

I felt him shrug. "Sense of freedom. Humouring me. Relieving yourself of the truth. Take your pick."

"Fine. I *might* like the way you look."

His arm tightened around me momentarily. "See, that wasn't hard was it?"

"Just because you're attractive, doesn't mean you should expect people to fawn over you."

"Firstly, I don't expect people to fawn over me because very few people do. Do you know how many times I've been hauled to the police station just because the cops assume I've just done something bad by existing?"

"Can they do that?"

"It would appear they can. Secondly, you just admitted you

thought I was attractive."

"No, I was making a generalisation."

"A generalisation that includes you."

"It does not. How many times have you been arrested?"

"Eighteen. And, it does include you. Go on, Barlow. Try on some honesty for once."

I rolled over to look at him. "Eighteen?"

"Seven times actually charged. Hauled in for questioning a lot more."

As usual, I liked his honesty. But, I didn't know that I needed the reminder of the kind of guy he was outside those holidays.

"Would you be so forthcoming if I asked you how many girls you've hooked up with?"

His eyes narrowed like he was thinking. "Will that have any bearing on you admitting you think I'm hot?"

"For now, let's just assume I'm curious."

"Quid pro quo, Clarice."

"What do you want to know in return?"

"How many guys you've been with."

I felt my cheeks burn again. "Not nearly as many girls as you."

"All right, let's make it easier. How many guys have you kissed?"

I breathed in as I thought. "Five?"

"You don't sound so sure…" he teased.

I frowned. "Five."

He nodded. "I would guess I've been with…" He looked at me. "You really want to know, Barlow?"

I paused before I nodded, wondering if I did really want to know the number. But, what did it matter to me? Whatever we were doing here wasn't likely to last once school went back. Even without adding to Roman's notches, I was sure he'd get bored of me and I'd go back to pretending I was all right.

"Yes, I want to know."

He sucked on his lip for a second. "Close to thirty, I think."

Holy shit. "Now who doesn't sound sure?"

"I don't exactly keep a list or anything."

"And, this was kissing? Sex? What?"

He looked at me. "I don't have sex with all of them."

I rolled over onto my back and looked up at the stars.

"Barlow?"

"Lombardi?"

"To be fair, you knew I was a slut."

I chuckled and sat up. "I did."

He sat too, somehow encasing me with his body as he did so. He lent his arm on his bent knee by my right side and I could feel his other leg and arm behind me. I felt warm and secure, even though my insides were a tumult of opposing feelings.

"I can't apologise…"

I shook my head. "Firstly, I'd just think you'd been abducted. Secondly, what the hell do you have to apologise for?"

"Being a slut?"

"Why would you possibly have to apologise to *me* for that?" I asked.

"Because I was looking forward to hearing you admit you think I'm hot."

I turned at the humour in his voice and I couldn't help but smile. Our noses were close to touching, but again no one made a move forward.

So, yeah. I did think he was hot. Even subjectively, I thought he was hot. He'd been hot the week before. But whatever side of him he'd been showing me the last few days, it just made him more attractive. I was pretty sure I could admit it without losing anything.

"Of course I think you're hot, Roman. Anyone with eyes thinks you're gorgeous." I was starkly reminded of my conversation with Hadley the week before. "You are, objectively, beautiful and I am not ashamed to admit I am a woman with eyes."

He smiled softly. "Is that so?"

I nodded. "Hadley shouted it last week because she was trying to get me to admit it."

"You and Hadley were talking about me?"

"Yep."

"What sort of stuff?"

"Well she thinks I'm your Everest," I ticked them off on my fingers, "she expects Mason would fuck like a pro but you'd do it better, she thinks you're the hottest guy in school, says you make any girl wet just looking at another, and if she lived next door to you that she'd be banging you on the regular."

He smirked. "Really? And, I'm wasting my time here with you because…?" he teased.

"Very funny."

"What's an Everest?" he asked, nudging my nose with his.

I snorted, remembering Hadley's ridiculous theory. "You know, Mount Everest? Unscaleable and all that. She thinks I'm the one girl you want but can't have."

"And, that's funny?"

"It's absurd."

"Is it?"

I looked at him again, my chest getting all fluttery. "Isn't it?"

He shrugged. "Well, you're certainly the one girl I could never have." He paused, then went on in a much lighter tone. "Mind you, she's not wrong though."

My heart tripped over itself. "Not wrong about…?"

"I fuck far better than a pro."

I looked at him for a moment, wondering if he was being serious. Of course, he was. I couldn't help but laugh and he joined in.

I couldn't remember a time when I'd laughed so hard and so often as I had in the last few days with Roman Lombardi of all people.

Chapter Ten
hOw dO yOu fLiRt?

I pulled my clothes out of the washing machine and loaded the dryer up.

"Isn't John missing you?" I heard Mum ask with a chuckle.

I jumped and turned to face her. She'd obviously just walked in; she was still wearing her pencil skirt and suit jacket. I smiled at her.

"I'll get back to him. I just figured doing some washing might be helpful."

"Thanks, darling. It is helpful. Very unlike you, though..." Mum seemed waiting for me to explain something.

"What? Oh, no. I just had some pent up energy, felt like I should do something more than watch John all day and think about homework."

Mum nodded, but I was pretty sure she didn't believe me. "Has this got anything to do with the fact that you were humming when I walked in?"

I blinked. "Sorry?"

She smiled wider. "Humming. I haven't heard you sing or hum in years."

"Probably because I am the world's worst singer." I grinned.

"That never used to stop you and it shouldn't now." She ducked in and kissed my head before heading back out. "I'm going to go change. Back in a bit."

And she was right. I hadn't sung or hummed in… I couldn't even remember. Well actually, I sung in the shower now and then when I had a particularly annoying earworm. But, no one could hear me in there so I considered that safe. The fact I was unintentionally humming, well… It was a little south of odd.

I turned on the dryer and wandered out to the living room.

Dad wasn't home yet so I turned the kettle on to make Mum and me a cup of tea. As I got cups and tea bags out, I realised I was humming Katy Perry. I shook my head with a smile and suddenly wondered what Roman was up to.

Given the time, he was probably helping Carmen deal with Maddy and dinner.

"Why do you even know that?" I muttered to myself.

A week ago I would have had zero ideas what Roman was up to at any given time, even if I could physically see him. I would certainly never have assumed he was at home playing family duties. I'd have guessed he was out looking for his next notch or getting publically drunk and probably arrested for the nineteenth time.

I shouldn't know that, either.

As I was pouring milk into the cups, Mum walked back in pulling her hair up into a mess of a bun that made me proud.

"You all packed for Saturday?" I asked.

She laughed and pulled herself onto the barstool across the bench from me. "I think so. I mean, it's only a few days. I don't even know where we're going."

I grinned at her. "Dad is nothing if not a closet romantic."

"You know, don't you?" Mum asked as I passed her the cup. "Thanks."

I did know. I knew almost everything Dad had planned for their twentieth wedding anniversary getaway. But I'd also sworn to secrecy, so I couldn't tell her that. I gave her my best Roman-blank-stare impression.

"No. He didn't tell me anything."

"Lies!" Mum chuckled, then waved her hand. "Fine. You two lie to me then."

"It's called a surprise, actually. And, you'll find out in a few days!"

Her smile dropped and she looked at me. "You going to be okay here by yourself?"

I nodded. "Sure. The place is stocked. I'll even put your breakable trinkets away before I throw the raging party."

The corners of her eyes crinkled and she nodded. "Funny girl. Funny. But, I'm serious."

"So am I. If I need anything…" I'd been going to say Roman was next door, but that was ridiculous, "Carmen's next door and you know she'll fuss over me worse than Gramma on my birthday."

Mum smiled widely. "Oh, yes, *Carmen's* next door." She winked and I threw her some shade.

"She is."

"So is her son."

"I thought you were drunk the other night?"

"Oh, I was – don't drink, stay in school. But, don't think I don't remember you walking in here with a smile larger than I wore the day I had you."

My frown deepened. "You were in labour for hours. Like *hours*."

"And it was still one of the two best days of my life."

"Roman is *not* one of the best days of my life."

Mum shrugged. "No, 'course not."

"Okay, enough. We're just two people hanging out!" I chuckled.

"Of course. Mason's your John Cusack."

I nodded. "Mason's my John Cusack. Mason's lovely, he's nice, he's the romance."

"All right. I won't say any more about Roman then."

I looked at her. "Okay."

"Except to ask if you're seeing him tonight."

I rolled my eyes. "We don't make plans, Mum. We just…" I shrugged. "We sometimes find ourselves in the same vicinity."

Mum nodded slowly like she understood some unspoken words she read between the lines. "Of course. Simple. Easy. Playing it cool."

I crossed my arms and glared at her. "Mum, I love you. But, there is nothing to play here, cool or otherwise. We're at most friends. We just…live next to each other."

"Because of Mason."

I shook my head. "No, not because of Mason. Because Roman is not the kind of guy you look to for a relationship and he's barely capable of even friendship with Rio."

"Who's Rio?" Mum asked.

The only guy who's been brave enough to fight Roman at school in the last year or two.

I waved a hand as I turned to the kettle and turned it on again. "Some guy in our class. They hang out."

"And, they're not friends?"

"No, they are. It's just. I don't know. Roman's… Soon, he'll once again just be a guy I don't talk to, I'm sure."

"Honey…" Mum started. "You know, Carmen talks–"

But, I never got to ask what it was Carmen talked about because Dad's voice came from the front door loud and proud. "Daddy's home!"

Any mood I'd been feeling about our conversation dissipated as I shared a knowing smile with Mum.

"In here, babe!" she called to him.

He stuck his head into the kitchen and smiled at us. "There my girls are."

"How was your day?" I asked.

"Good. What are you two gossiping about?"

"Nothing," I answered quickly as Mum pretended to flick her hair back all cool and said, "Boys."

I groaned as Dad laughed. "Well, I know when I'm not wanted. I'll go and change and let you finish up."

"Thanks, babe!" Mum called happily as he walked out.

"No! Dad! It's fine… We're done…" I sighed, but he was gone.

Mum laughed and I shot her a look.

She held up her hands. "Don't worry, honey. Your Dad knows better than to even ask me later. Your secrets are safe with me."

"I don't have any secrets, Mum," I whined.

"Not even Mason?" she cooed, batting her eyelashes.

"No, trust me. Everyone knows about Mason."

"Ah, but does Mason?" she asked.

That question hit me.

Hadley had spent so much time telling me he liked me and that it was only a matter of time before he asked me out, that I'd just assumed that she *knew* somehow. Like he'd told her or something. Maybe she'd also been right in asking me if I was encouraging him enough. I'd thought so, but maybe not… Maybe Mason hadn't asked me out yet because I wasn't…flirty enough.

God, that didn't help.

I didn't know how to flirt any better.

hOw dO YoU fLiRt? I felt like that Spongebob Squarepants meme.

"Piper, honey?" Mum laughed.

"Uh, I think so…" I said slowly, my brain still having no idea how you flirted anymore.

I pictured Mason and… Nothing.

No witty quips. No knowledge of what to do with my eyes or my lips or my hands.

"Okay, well good. I hope it all goes according to plan."

I threw her a smile as I went through the motions of making another tea.

"Me, too."

"About Roman, though…" she said.

I turned to her with an exasperated glare. "What about Roman?"

"I don't know him very well. But, there are good stories about him as well as the bad ones."

I watched her carefully, not entirely sure I understood what she was getting at.

"So, who wants to hear about my day?" Dad asked as he came back in.

Mum and I shared a look I felt was heavier than the situation maybe called for. Then she turned to Dad with a big smile.

"I do!"

I'd got to a point where I had to tell myself I'd been hoping he was going to come, but that maybe he wasn't. I was annoyed with myself for expecting it and by how disappointed I was that he hadn't showed. But, that's really what I should have been expecting.

It's not like we'd made plans. But, he had asked 'see you tomorrow?' when he'd parked his truck in his driveway the night before and I'd said yes. What should I have expected after so much sex talk? He probably preferred to go and let off some steam rather than deal with my whiny arse again.

I wrapped my arms around myself and actually thought I'd just go back home and re-watch something like *10 Things I hate About You* instead of sitting there by myself on a Thursday night in the holidays. Then, I turned and saw him jogging over the rise, a smile growing on my face. Only, it wasn't the sight of him per se that had me smiling, but what was on his head.

He stopped in front of me and noticed my grin. "What?"

I held back a laugh. "What are you wearing?"

He looked up as though he could see it. "Maddy refused to let me out of the house unless I put it on. And turns out it's warm, so I decided not to take it off."

I covered my mouth so I didn't laugh out loud. The pink beanie sat on his head comically. It was obviously too small for him, and the idea that he'd worn it for Maddy was far too sweet for me to handle. So, I ignored that fact.

"It is very cold tonight," I agreed, failing to stifle my smile.

He nodded once. "It is." He was far better at keeping his composure than I was.

"I really should have brought my own."

"You should have."

"Although, some guys would offer theirs to a lady in need."

"Some would, true." He grinned ruefully.

"But, they'd be considered pussies."

"They would."

"Or even worse, gentleman."

"The horror."

"Some girls might just nick yours."

"They wouldn't dare," he gasped. "My niece forced this on me at toy-gun point!"

I snorted a laugh and went to snatch it from his head. I think I surprised us both when I managed to grab it. We both looked at it in my hand for a moment, then I saw the look in his eyes and I took off at a run. He chased after me and we laughed as we ran across the lakeshore.

"You bring that back, Barlow!" he laughed.

"I will not!" I giggled.

"Damn. You're faster than I expected."

I dodged out of his grasp far more nimbly than I'd have expected from me. "Or are you just slow, Lombardi?"

"I'll give you slow!" he chuckled. "Come back here!"

"No!" I squealed as I dodged him again and he laughed.

He finally caught up to me, his arm going around my waist, both of us breathing hard amidst laughter. I looked up at him and found his face was just there. My laughter half-died on my lips, but my smile grew.

His face was just so open and carefree and warm. And, the way he was looking at me made my heart stop for a moment before it started beating harder in my chest. My stomach fluttered and I felt weird. I found myself *wanting* him to kiss me, actually wondering what it would be like. Until I remembered it was Roman Lombardi, and I thought I'd gone mad.

But, it wasn't the first time I'd noticed us looking at each other like that in the last few days. We'd caught each other's eye now and then and there'd been a moment where one of us could have moved forward, but didn't. There had been a lot of moments and zero moving forward.

I wasn't sure if I was just not desirable enough for Roman Lombardi, or if perhaps whatever we had was actually something more. By no means did I think that we were falling for each other – that was a ridiculous notion – but maybe it was possible to really be friends with the guy.

"Piper…" he said slowly.

I held up the beanie between us like some sort of shield as my heart threatened to pound out of my chest – and it wouldn't have just been the running to blame. Except, if I wasn't falling for him, why did I get those flutters around him?

It was attraction, at most. Surely. Attraction and a new-found appreciation for the sweeter side of him.

"I believe you were looking for this."

He took it from me and pulled it onto my head, pulling it far enough that it went over my eyes. I grinned and pushed it up, noticing his arm was still around me and I still leant on him.

"I thought you were cold?" I asked.

He shrugged, flipped his hood onto his head, and wrapped his other arm around me. "I'm being a gentleman, don't ruin it." His voice was gruff, but with a note of teasing.

I contentedly rested my head against his chest as we just held each other for a bit. One of his hands fell down my back a little and I gave him a small squeeze. He dropped his nose to my ear and returned it.

Goose bumps skittered across my skin and I firmly chastised

the flutter in my stomach.

This was Roman Lombardi, for God's sake.

Stomach flutters and goose bumps weren't allowed.

It didn't matter that he was gorgeous.

It didn't matter that we'd spent every night for the last week together.

It didn't matter that I felt more comfortable not talking to him than I did gossiping with Hadley.

He wasn't interested.

And even if he was, I wasn't.

Was I?

I looked at him with a laugh as we lay in the back of his ute the next night. "No, not possible."

He smiled, our noses almost touching. His shoulder was warm under my neck. He nodded and threaded his fingers through mine.

"Yes. I think you'll find, yes."

I looked into his eyes, those deep brown pools that were, in actual fact, nothing like black holes. Even with only the moon for light, I could see them sparkle with warmth and something I didn't think I'd ever seen in them before. A shiver ran through me, but it wasn't the same as it used to be and the goose bumps on my skin were excitement, anticipation, desire.

We just looked at each other, no need to say anything, no need to do anything but just feel comfortable with each other. Our faces inched closer together and I had plenty of time to stop myself. But I didn't want to stop myself, not this time.

So, I let Roman Lombardi kiss me.

It was chaste and sweet and…

And…

After all the flirting and the banter of the last week, I didn't know how I felt about it.

It was like the beginnings of fireworks, but instead of soaring and bursting in brilliant points of colours, they just fizzled out mere meters off the ground. He felt stilted and stiff, like he just totally wasn't into it or something. I pulled away from him, untangled myself from the blankets and jumped out of the tray. Cold air hit my arms and legs, but I ignored it.

"Barlow?"

I turned back to him and opened my mouth, but had no idea what to say so I just snapped it shut and turned around again. I was annoyed by something but my brain was taking a little bit of time working out what it was all about. It hit me just as I felt his hand on my arm and I whirled back to face him.

"You!" I started and saw him blink in surprise.

Which wasn't surprising in itself; I don't think I'd ever yelled at him. I'd chastised him and teased him and snarked at him, but I'd never raised my voice at him. I'd been angry with him, but I'd never really acted angry with him. He probably didn't even know I had it in me to be so assertive. It was certainly a surprise to me.

"You of all people!" I snapped, pointing a finger at him. I stopped, feeling frustrated.

"Me what, Barlow?" he asked, hands up in defence.

"You! You weren't…" I took a deep breath. "Out of everyone, I thought you'd at least do me the curtesy of not treating poor little fragile Piper Barlow with kid gloves!"

He blinked again. "What? I don't even know what that

means…"

I sighed and threw my arms in the air. "Everyone thinks I'm so sweet and innocent. Like I'll break if you apply the tiniest bit of pressure. Like I have no idea what I want!"

"Barlow, you're acting crazy. I don't know what you're talking about."

"That kiss, Lombardi!" I snapped.

He shook his head. "What about it?"

"What the hell was that?"

His eyebrows drew together and his lips thinned. "Not usually the response I get."

"No, I doubt you kiss all the girls like you're not into it!" I said.

"Not into it?" he huffed a mirthless chuckle. "Not into it? Barlow, I've wanted to kiss you all fucking week! To say nothing of the years before that or the fact I want to do more than just kiss you. What the fuck is up with you?"

"So, was it just me? It was no good? I was no good?"

"What?" he asked. "Look, if you've got a problem with the way I kiss–"

"Of course I have a problem with it! I'd thought, out of everyone, you'd have kissed me like you meant it. It would have been fireworks and ruined me for every other guy–"

"Right, so you were just looking for the infamous Roman Lombardi experience?" His voice was full of sarcasm. "Well if you'd just said so a week ago we could have skipped all this feelings and hand-holding bullshit, and got down to business." He crossed his arms and glared at me.

"No, I don't want the Roman Lombardi experience! I wanted *you*, Roman. Whoever that is, I wanted you. I didn't want your reputation. I just wanted you to touch me like you wanted to, not like you were going to break me."

"I was trying to be a gentleman, Barlow! I know your reputation as well as you know mine, and I didn't want to push you."

"A gentleman? A gentleman! Jokes aside, no one who's ever met you would expect you to be a gentleman, Lombardi. I knew exactly what could happen if we kept hanging out. I'd like to think I'm a big enough girl to say no if you went too far."

"I didn't want you to have to say no!" he cried, annoyed and exasperated. "I'm sorry I was trying to make you feel comfortable with me. I was trying to exert some self-control!"

"Yes, because your goal in life is to make girls feel comfortable with you and you're well-known for your self-control. It's not fragile little Piper Barlow at all. I trusted that you – out of everyone in my life – wouldn't feel the need to *protect* me. That you'd be honest and real. What the hell is so wrong with losing control around me? What could possibly happen?"

He was suddenly right in front of me, staring down at me with those dark eyes, his hair hanging over his forehead and masking his face in shadow. That new shiver ran through me and I felt my stomach flutter. I'd never seen him look so intense, and he was known for his intensity.

Our clothes brushed lightly, but he didn't touch me.

Oh, but I wanted him to, though. At that moment, I couldn't remember ever wanting anything more.

The air felt charged around us and the hairs on the back on my neck stood on end.

"You really want to know what could possibly happen if I lost control around you, Barlow?" he asked, slowly and deliberately so there was no way I could misunderstand him. He certainly sounded like he was barely holding on to his self-control.

I licked my bottom lip and it caught in my teeth.

"Be sure about this. Because you drive me crazy, Piper. This week's been a serious test of my control." His voice shook like it was taking everything he had to keep himself together.

I was still pissed with him. So, maybe I nodded as much to taunt him as I really wanted to know. I'd barely nodded once when he'd pushed me against the cab of his ute, pulling my legs around his waist. As his lips crashed down on mine, rain poured down and thunder rumbled above us. He was hard against me and I was totally lost in everything about him for what felt like hours as he kissed me and it felt like I couldn't get close enough to him. Hands roamed, lips were bitten, and we rubbed against each other feverishly. Then, I felt his hand between us.

My eyes flew open and caught his as he pulled back slightly. Lightning burst over us and his gorgeous face flashed bright like it was the only thing in my world. He looked just as angry as I felt, but his dark eyes held more than I could fathom in that second and my heart constricted. We both breathed heavily and I nodded. He searched my eyes and I nodded again.

I took his face in my hands and pulled him back to me. He kissed me again, then my undies were pushed aside and he was sliding into me. I held onto him for dear life as he rocked my world in the least gentle way possible.

I barely registered the pain and discomfort as pleasure took over. I'd never finished that hard or that fast, and it put those two attempts at masturbation to shame. Even after hearing all the stories about him, I didn't expect the weird sense of passion or protectiveness that swirled through the anger of the moment.

As we both panted, still joined, I lifted my face to the rain and took a deep breath. "So…that…" I started. "That's what happens when you lose control?"

His face dipped into my neck and his breath against my skin made me shiver all over again. "Around you, apparently."

"What's that supposed to mean?"

I felt him shrug and he pulled back to look at me, still breathing hard. "I don't know what it is about you, Barlow. But, you do something to me." He paused and I felt him tense before he dropped his head onto my shoulder. "Fuck!"

"What?"

"What?" he chuckled, but there was no humour in it. "How about I was a completely irresponsible arsehole? Fuck, fuck, fuck!"

He pulled out of me and tucked himself back into his pants as he turned around.

"What are you...? Oh..." I breathed as it hit me. Panic surged for a moment, then I told myself to calm down. "I finished last week, I'm sure it's fine..."

He turned back to me for a second. "Are you on the pill?"

I shrugged. "I am. For...other things."

He was standing in front of me and took my hands in his. "I swear that is the first time that's happened. I've been safe every other time. I'm clean."

I nodded, feeling my face flush. "I trust you, Roman. It'll be fine."

He pulled me to him and held me close. "I'm sorry, Piper."

"I thought there were no apologies?"

"For this, there aren't enough."

"I get I'm no expert or anything, but do I get none of the blame?"

He huffed a laugh and kissed my hair. "No. No, you definitely don't."

"Why not?"

"Firstly, I have a perfectly good condom in my pocket. Secondly, it's completely up to me to make sure I take necessary steps to ensure I don't end up with unwanted consequences."

"So, should I not as well?" I appreciated the sentiment, but I did feel like this went both ways.

He shook his head and took my face in his hands. "You're responsible for what your body can do, sure. But, I'm responsible for mine. It doesn't matter how you make me feel, I shouldn't have let myself get carried away."

"We both got carried away…"

"Yeah, we did. But, you're not fertile every day of the year, are you? I don't expect you to be on the pill and I have no respect for guys who do. If we don't want a kid out of it, it's really not that difficult to be prepared. And a condom is seriously cheaper than alimony."

I looked at him. There was obviously something else going on that made him feel this way other than what seemed a very progressive view. Paris, perhaps? I didn't feel lectured at, rather he was trying to convey something that was really important to him.

"So…your fault?"

He gave me that smile. "Totally my fault."

"Not at all my fault?"

"Well, maybe like…twenty percent your fault." He gave me that sexy, teasing smirk. "You could have reminded me. But, I shouldn't have forgotten."

I nodded slowly. "I don't regret it."

"No?"

"No."

"Thank God." He pulled me close and kissed my hair.

So, that was how I lost my virginity; in the pouring rain, in a thunderstorm, against Roman Lombardi's ute, still clothed, completely bareback, while we were both totally pissed with each other for who knew exactly what reason.

It was by no means perfect.

In fact, if you'd asked me what I'd thought about that particular method of cherry popping before it occurred, I would have said it sounded like the worst possible way.

But, in reality, it was even better than fireworks.

Eventually, he pulled away from me and brushed my hair from my eyes. "You okay?"

I nodded. "I'm fine. I promise I'm fine."

And, I felt fine. Maybe a little tender and swollen, and my heart beat too quickly given I had no idea what was going to happen next (and my undies were in a serious need of a change…way to go movies never telling me about the mess after condom-less sex…). But, I did feel fine; I didn't feel violated or taken advantage of, I didn't feel embarrassed or ashamed. I felt fine. Normal. Relaxed. Happy even.

He tipped my chin to him and kissed me gently. It felt an awful lot like he was apologising.

"No apologies, Roman," I whispered against his lips.

He huffed a laughed and nudged my nose with his. "I'll take you back home."

He pulled away before I had a chance to answer and had pulled the car door open. He helped me in, giving me a soft smile before he closed the door.

When we got back to his driveway, he looked me over carefully. "You sure you're okay?"

"Why do I feel like you regret it, Roman?"

He shook his head. "My idiocy aside, I only regret it if I hurt you."

I smiled and leant over the centre console. "Not hurt."

His eyes lost that pinched look and he nodded. "Okay, good. I'd best let you get in and get warm."

I had a feeling that what had just happened was going to keep me warm for a while, but I didn't tell him that.

"I guess, yeah."

He jumped out his side and was at mine to help me out before I was halfway there.

"Night, Roman," I said, looking up at him.

He cupped my cheek and pressed a kiss to my lips. "Night, Piper."

As I walked back to my house, I could have sworn I heard something. When I turned back to look, I had a sneaking suspicion that he'd just kicked his tyre but was playing it cool. I bit my lip against a smile, gave him a wave – to which he gave me a curt nod – and headed inside to deal with the fact that condom-less sex creates a mess that isn't shy about dripping down the inside of your leg.

Chapter Eleven
Ballerina Roman meets John.

"Okay, okay! We're going and we love you!"

I laughed and waved as Dad drove away with Mum still trying to hang out the window. I'd been apprehensive about them going away for a whole week despite what I'd told her. But, now I was just glad it was going to give me some serious alone time to think about what I'd done.

Not that I thought I deserved to be punished or anything. I just wasn't sure I'd had time to process it or what it meant. Roman might have shown me there was another side to him, but what did sleeping together mean?

Neither Mum nor Dad had seemed to notice anything different about me that morning. So, that was good. I mean, are you supposed to look different after? Was that even a thing? I know books and movies tell you that you feel different, more adult or something. Personally, I couldn't say I felt older or wiser or better or…well, anything except unsure.

And I wasn't unsure about having done it. I was, though, now rather unsure about how first time sex was being depicted in movies compared to the reality. I was still a little tender, there was this sort of dull ache but it wasn't entirely uncomfortable.

And yes, I got the implication of the whole unsafe thing. But, I was on the pill and I took it every day – the doctor always said the pill was only ineffective if there was user error. So, I wasn't going to panic unless there seemed something to panic about, and it would be another few weeks before I'd have any idea anyway.

Obviously pregnancy wasn't the only concern, I know. And taking Roman at face value may have been a poor choice, but I trusted him when he said–

"Piper!"

I looked over and saw Carmen waving.

Of course, my initial thought was that she knew I'd lost my virginity to her degenerate son and she was going to think I was a slut. But, then sense took over and I realised I didn't care what she'd think if she found out because, even if he was done with me now, I wasn't just another one of those girls. I hadn't just fallen for him instantly and thrown away my morals; I'd got to know him and we'd just accidentally found ourselves…together.

"How are you, dear?" Carmen asked and I pulled my head out of my own arse long enough to smile at her.

"Good, thanks. How are you? How's Maddy?"

I wandered over to her as she answered, "I'm good, thank you. Glad it's the weekend. You kids should really enjoy your holidays while you have them! Maddy, poor love, has a bit of a sniffle. But, we'll see how she is when she wakes up. Poor thing sleeps like the dead when she's got a cold."

"Oh, well I hope she's feeling better soon."

"Thank you, love." She started pulling groceries out of the car.

"Do you want some help?"

Carmen looked up, surprised but in a good way. "If you don't mind? I think Roman's still asleep."

I smiled. "That wouldn't surprise me."

And no, I didn't think my sex skills were that amazing that I'd worn out Roman Lombardi. It just happened to barely be half ten in the middle of the school holidays. I was surprised I was awake to be honest.

I walked over to her car and took a bunch of the bags for her, then followed her to the back door.

"You didn't have to do this, Piper. Thank you again. Roman would usually. But, he's been so good about Maddy that I thought I'd give him a bit of respite. I knew he'd wake up if she did, so I took the time out to get the shopping done."

I nodded as I followed her to the kitchen. I hadn't been in their house before; it was really nice. It was bigger than ours, all open plan and modern chic. The judgemental arse in me would never have imagined Roman would have ever set foot in a place like this, let alone lived there.

"No worries. I imagine it's different having a little one in the house again."

Carmen chuckled. "It is. I thought I'd put that all behind me when Roman got all independent. It's sort of nice in a way, having a small one around. But, when you want that second glass of wine or to go out, you remember why you didn't have more kids."

I smiled at her. "I don't doubt that. Well, you let me know if I can do anything to help."

She looked at me like I was already doing so much. But, all she said was, "Can I get you a drink?"

"Uh, sure. Yes. Please." Let it not be said that little Piper Barlow forgot her manners even when flustered. Especially in the face of the mother of the guy she'd lost her virginity to the night before.

"Coffee?"

I nodded. "Perfect. Thanks."

"Wonderful. Take a seat, love."

I pulled myself onto one of the breakfast bar stools. She talked to me as she went around the kitchen, making coffee and putting the groceries away. I was firmly refused when I offered to help and Carmen just seemed happy to natter about Roman, Maddy, Paris, the gardening, anything.

Oddly, I didn't feel anything but comfortable. Carmen was funny and lovely and I tried hard to connect her with the guy who seemed to have written himself off. But, then I could hardly talk, could I? My life was supposed to be perfect, and I was still me. I just hid it while Roman seemed to prefer revelling in it.

"How's school going?" she finally asked, leaning over the kitchen bench towards me.

I swallowed my mouthful of coffee and nodded. "Uh, it's okay I think." I smiled. "Stress is mounting and teachers are simultaneously trying to make us work our arses off and stop us panicking at the same time."

Carmen grinned. "I can imagine. The pressures on you kids today. You know, when I was in Year Twelve, I took the Biology exam?"

I raised my eyebrow at her, wondering where this was going. "Really?"

She nodded. "I got a C. I didn't even take Biology."

I laughed. "That hardly seems fair."

Her smile was so much like Roman's. "I agree." She looked me over carefully for a minute in that calculating way mums have. "Have you seen Roman much this week?"

I licked my lip. "Uh, yeah. We've found ourselves at the lake every night actually."

She nodded. "I'm glad."

"Oh, we're not–"

"Oh love, I didn't think you were. My son isn't that type and you're much too smart. But, I'm glad he's been under a good influence. Rio's a sweet boy really, but he hides it under a mountain of pain, anger and poor choices. I think that's what drew them together in the first place, the two of them are the same." She paused and brightened. "You know, when Roman was Maddy's age, he was convinced he was going to be a ballerina?"

"No!" I gasped, trying hard not to laugh. But, I pictured Roman as he was now – all hard and muscular and broody – in those pink ballet outfits and I couldn't help it. "Tell me more."

And, she did.

Which is why I was in fits of laughter, tears streaming down my face, when a sleepy Roman walked into the kitchen in all states of confusion.

"Morning, love– Well, afternoon. Almost," Carmen chuckled as she turned the coffee machine on again.

"Barlow?" he asked, his voice rough from sleep.

I was going to extraordinary lengths to tell myself that I wasn't at all affected by the sight of him in nothing but tracksuit pants that left little to the imagination. His hair was messy from sleeping on it, his eyes unfocussed, and his voice thick and low.

It did nothing for me. Well, nothing more than physical. I was going to stop refusing to admit I was attracted to him. Because he was attractive. But, it went no deeper than the physical. It couldn't go deeper than the physical.

Roman was someone who I think I considered a friend and we happened to have had sex and now he was probably done with me.

That idea conflicted in me. On one hand, if he was done with me, then good because I didn't have to worry what came next. On the other, a part of me would miss his easy calm. So naturally, my brain totally overthought everything in that moment and the anxiety set in. I felt my heart flutter, my mouth went dry and my hands went hot.

"Lombardi, hi."

"What are you…?" he asked, looking between his mum and me in complete confusion. I could have seriously done without the dragging his hand through his hair thing.

"Uh, I should probably go," I chuckled nervously.

"Are you sure, love?" Carmen asked.

I nodded.

"Well, thank you for your help with the bags."

"Thank you, Carmen, for the coffee and the stories. Roman in a tutu is an image I will always treasure." I slid off the stool and headed for their back door. Carmen and I shared a humoured look while Roman glared in panic.

"Bye, love," Carmen called to me as Roman spat, "You did what?" at her.

"Oh, it's nothing. We were just…" I lost track of Carmen's voice as I closed the door behind me.

I grinned as I headed towards my house. It was magnified when I was almost to the back door and I heard Roman call my name.

"Piper!" And he didn't sound too happy.

I stopped and turned, taking one last moment to appreciate his body.

"Whatever she told you–"

"I take to my grave, Roman. I wouldn't dare ruin ballet-Roman by sharing him with anyone."

He glared at me. "Not funny."

"Hilarious."

The corner of his lip quirked, but he didn't give into it. "How are you?"

"Still fine."

His eyes slid down my body then back to my eyes. "Good. Good." He sucked his teeth like he was contemplating something.

"Seriously, Roman. I'm fine. No regrets, no concerns, I'm fine."

"If you wanted me to…" he started.

"To what?" I pressed.

He sighed. "If it would make you feel better, I'd be more than happy to go get you the morning after pill?"

My stomach fluttered and my cheeks heated. 'Uh… I think…" I cleared my throat. "Thanks. But, I think it'll be fine. I haven't missed any. So…"

"Are you sure? It was my bad. I'm not above taking responsibility for my actions."

How was I supposed to convince myself that any attraction I had to him was just physical when he said things like that? Over and over until I believed it was how.

I tucked some hair behind my ear. "I'm sure. Thank you, though. I appreciate it."

He looked at me like something was haunting him. But just as he opened his mouth, he was interrupted.

"Uncie Roman!" Maddy called, hanging out the door in a bright pink dressing gown.

"In a minute, Mads!" he called.

"But, Grandma said you'd make me pancakes!" She sounded like her nose was all blocked up and her voice was scratchy.

"Of course she did," he muttered.

"You'd best go," I said softly.

"Yeah, I'd best."

"See you later." I gave him a small wave.

"Yeah, catchya."

He looked at me like he wanted to say something else, but just ran his hand through his hair and jogged back to his house to pick Maddy up as she squealed in happiness.

Which didn't at all make me think entirely wrong things about him…

I checked my phone and saw the response from Hadley.

> **Hadley:** *Thank GOD we're coming home tomorrow!*
>
> **Me:** *It'll be good to have you home.*
>
> **Hadley:** *It'll be good to make you go out some more! Celeste told me you'd been skiving?????*
>
> **Me:** *lol, yeah a little. I've been busy.*
>
> **Hadley:** *Oh well. No excuse after tomorrow. Although Dad's told me we have to go to some dinner tomorrow. But, I'll see you first thing Monday?*
>
> **Me:** *As long as first thing is like 11?*
>
> **Hadley:** *Duh. I'll come over?*
>
> **Me:** *Sounds good.*
>
> **Hadley:** *Talk to you later xoxo*
>
> **Me:** *night babes xo*

I chucked my phone on charging, went back to the movie and snuggled down.

Just after I'd started the new one, something distracted me. There was a noise at my window, I was sure of it. I paused the movie and listened. Sure enough, there it was again. I crawled out of bed, pulled the window open, and looked down.

"Seriously?" I hissed.

Roman grinned up at me, juggling a pebble in his hand. "Hey."

"What are you doing?"

"Avoiding the screaming, flu-y five year old. What are you doing?"

"Having a John Cusack movie marathon."

"Seriously?" he hissed sceptically. "Lame!"

"That's rich coming from the guy running away from a five year old!"

He shrugged. "Yeah, true."

"Did you want something?" I asked.

He shrugged again. "I dunno. Thought you might like to hang out?"

I smiled. "John Cusack takes precedence over you and your five-year-old avoidance, sorry."

I saw him smile back. "Can I at least join you?"

"You're going to voluntarily watch John Cusack movies?"

"I have no idea who that is, remember."

"I'm having a Rom-Com binge, *comprende*?"

His nose scrunched adorably. "Still preferable to the whiny child at my house."

"Damn, it must be bad."

"Can I hang out with you or not?"

I crossed my arms. "What do you plan on doing if I say no?"

He looked around. "I will hang out down here and have a rollicking good time of which you will be terribly jealous."

I snorted. "Fine. I'll come down and let you in."

"What about your parents?"

"They're not home this week!"

He grinned, waggling his eyebrows suggestively. I shook my head before closing my window and heading downstairs. I opened the curtains to find him jumping up onto the veranda, still grinning. I opened the door and levelled a look on him.

"No funny business, mind," I said, mock-seriously.

"No, I wouldn't dare." He looked down. "What is *that*?"

"My nightie?" I asked, following his gaze down my body.

"Nightie. Right." He looked sceptical. "T-shirt not a more apt description?"

"Yeah, yeah. We know the word apt. Very clever," I muttered.

He laughed and followed my inviting arm inside. I closed and locked the door behind him and pulled the curtain.

"Drink?"

"What are you offering?"

"Whatever you want that I have. Beer, wine, soft drink? Dad has some spirits somewhere?"

"Beer, why not."

I padded to the fridge, him following close behind. I pulled a six-pack out of it and handed it to him. His eyebrow rose and I glared mockingly.

"You telling me you can't get through six?"

"You're going to make me drink alone?"

"Would it be the first time?"

He snorted. "No."

"Then, you'll be fine."

"Ah, but it's more fun to drink with someone."

"I might have *one*."

"One?"

"I guarantee if I have two, I'll be pissed," I answered, taking his hand and pulling him upstairs. "More than that, it's chaos."

"Yeah, I've heard Hadley talk about you when you're drunk. I'm quite looking forward to it." He chuckled.

"Oh, no! I'm not having any more than one."

"Sure you're not. What's the worst that can happen?"

"Oh, I don't know. You've apparently heard the stories about handsy, chatty Piper. I could get all lovey-dovey on your arse."

He chuckled as we walked into my room and he made an appreciative noise. "Yeah, lovey-dovey I suspect will be the least of my problems. Besides, we've already fucked. So really, how bad can it get?"

"Already fucked? That's a charming way of talking about you being granted the treasure of my virginity," I said sarcastically; I in no way thought it was all that great a treasure. I mean sort of special, but nothing like the books and movies go on about.

He pulled me around to face him and I noticed he'd put the beers down. His arms wrapped around my waist, his fingers lacing behind my back. He leant his head against mine and sighed.

"Yeah, I know. Are you okay, Barlow?"

I smiled and cupped his cheek. "It's not the way I thought it would happen. But I still don't regret it, if that's what you're asking."

"I…" He sighed heavily.

"What are you doing here, anyway? Showering my window with pebbles is hardly nailing and bailing behaviour."

He huffed a laugh. "Is it terrible that I wanted to spend time with you?"

I gasped sarcastically. "Even after you got everything you wanted?"

His smile was rueful. "Yeah, laugh it up."

"Oh, I will. Don't tell me you're looking for seconds, Lombardi?"

He looked up to the ceiling. "What if it's less seconds and more...I just enjoy your company?"

I decided not to tell him the feeling was mutual.

Instead, I pulled out of his arms, took his hand again, and led him back to the bed. "Come on. I just started this one so I'll go back to the beginning."

"What are we watching?"

"*Say Anything.*"

"It's already my favourite," he huffed sarcastically.

"Oh, something we have in common!" I teased.

"Yay," he offered weakly.

"You were the one who asked to join me. Suck it up."

He chuckled. "What's it about?"

"Why don't you shut up and find out?"

We sat back against the headboard of my bed and he popped two beers for us. I rewound and started it from the beginning. A few minutes in, he leant his head against mine.

"Thanks, Barlow."

"For what?"

"For not making a big deal out of this."

I leant into him. "You're the one making a big deal out of it, Lombardi, and ruining an excellent movie in the process."

He just chuckled and put his arm around my shoulders. I nestled against him and settled in for the ride.

Chapter Twelve
Sex and Vaginas and Stuff.

I woke up and wondered why I was lying against someone and their arm was over my waist. Inadvertently, I wriggled and felt that someone was very hard.

There was a familiar chuckle and I felt a kiss on my shoulder. "Morning, Barlow."

"I didn't peg you for a snuggler," I replied, aiming for flippant so I could ignore what Roman's deep morning voice did to me.

"Does it count as snuggling if all we did was watch movies and fall asleep?" There was a smile in his voice, but something nagged at me.

"Roman?"

I felt him tense. "Piper?"

"Is there… I mean… Why did…" I stopped since I was clearly getting nowhere fast and my cheeks had heated.

"You want to try that again?"

"The other night?"

"Yeah…?"

"Was it…bad…?"

He scoffed and rolled me over to face him as he leant over me. "Bad? Why would you ask if it was bad?"

I shrugged and really didn't want to look into his eyes. "I don't know. You just didn't…" I sighed, "Like it matters."

"It matters to me. What is it?"

"I don't know. I guess I just thought… After we'd done it once… You were in my bed… You'd want to do it again?"

He didn't say anything for a bit so I finally looked up and found him smiling at me. "Uh huh. Right. Well, I *was* trying to be considerate, it having been your first time and I wasn't exactly gentle. I figured you'd be sore and not exactly a 'go at it like rabbits' type."

"How do you just come out and say things like that?" I asked, once again completely astonished with how comfortable he was just talking about sex and vaginas and just all of it.

He shrugged and brushed a piece of hair off my face. "Because if you can't talk about sex, then you probably shouldn't be doing it. Besides, honesty is important. How else do you get satisfaction? Sexual partners aren't mind readers, you know. You have to be able to talk about this stuff. About what you want, what you like, and what you don't."

It was a fair enough philosophy, I guessed. But, maybe I was really the innocent little Piper my friends thought I was because the idea of talking about it felt…weird.

"Did you want to do it again?" he asked, his voice taking on a teasing tone that had me blushing like mad. He chuckled and nuzzled his nose under my ear. "Because you just have to say."

"I can't do that," I whispered like it would be some great scandal and I felt him laugh.

"You can if it's what you want."

"No." I shook my head. "I can't."

"It's me, Barlow. You can tell me anything and I won't judge you."

I took a deep breath and closed my eyes like that would give me some courage. "I want to have sex with you again, Roman." My cheeks felt tomato-red even before I'd barely started the sentence.

I felt him pull away and he laughed. "You're fucking adorable, you know that?"

My eyes flew open in panic. "Not *really* the response I was hoping for."

His eyes hooded and he licked his lip. "Relax, Barlow. I want to again, too. I haven't stopped thinking about you. But this time, we're doing it right."

"Right?"

He nodded and a wicked smirk lit his face before he was kissing me again. It wasn't hard and fast. It was slow, deliberate, but full of heat. I was already breathing heavily when he gently pulled me to sitting and ran his hands over my hips. A flash of panic ran through me but his calm smile grounded me.

"First, we get rid of this."

"I'm not wearing anything under this except undies…" I said, slowly.

"Even better." He winked and slowly lifted it off me.

I was sure I could have told him to stop at any point, and the heart hammering in my chest half-wanted to. But, the rest of me was more resolved in its desire. If having sex with Roman Lombardi the wrong way had been all at once amazing and unexpected, I wanted to know what doing it right felt like.

He dropped my nightie to the floor and ran a hand gently over my breast. I tingled as his thumb traced my skin and I broke out in goose bumps.

"You're beautiful, Piper," he said softly, looking in my eyes.

"They're lopsided."

"They're real and they're beautiful."

I flushed, but this time I wasn't embarrassed. This time, I was actually just finding it hard to reconcile the fact that a guy who saw as many girls naked as he probably did could look at me like that and I genuinely believed he thought I was beautiful.

He picked up my hand and directed it to the bottom of his t-shirt. I lifted it up and he helped me get it over his head. He snuck a quick kiss as I leant towards him and I smiled. I looked down and I was surprised a guy like that was wasting his time with me.

I'd seen Roman without his top on before, of course I had – just the afternoon before I had. Plus the boys at school went swimming in the summer and, just because Roman wasn't known for following social mores, didn't mean he didn't get hot like the rest of us. But, something about having him right here – in my bed, close enough to touch – was exhilarating.

His muscles twitched involuntarily under my touch and he huffed an almost embarrassed laugh. I thought he was going to move my hand, but he only lay his over mine for a second on his stomach before guiding me back down to the bed and nestling between my legs.

The other night, I'd noticed he felt large – *she says like she has any idea*. I mean I'd had him in me, it would have been hard not to notice. But having him up against me now, with still my undies and his boxers between us, he felt too big and the nerves set in again, making my stomach and chest flutter weirdly.

Roman kissed me to distraction – as if he could tell – and I relaxed against him as his kisses trailed over my cheek and down my neck. He didn't stop there; he moved down my body, over my breasts and down to my stomach. Gently, he slid my undies off and ran a finger between my legs. Then, something warm and wet replaced his finger and I realised his mouth was over me.

Once the shock was passed, I wasn't complaining though. Pleasure coiled in me and was close to release when he slid a finger inside me and that was all it took for me to cum. He pressed one more kiss to me before he moved back up my body.

"That was… Wow. That was wow," I panted and he smiled, those deep brown eyes shining warmth.

"I'm glad."

With an assertiveness I didn't know I possessed, my fingers found the top of his boxers and started pulling them down. He flashed me that wicked grin and helped me get them off him. Then, he reached over and grabbed something from his wallet on the bedside table. He ripped open the packet and held it out to me.

"Care to do the honours?" he asked with a wink.

I chuckled. "Oh, so we remembered this time?"

He shook his head with a wry smile. "Like I said, we're doing it right this time."

I nodded and took the condom from him. Looking down at his erection, I asked, "All right, how do I do this?"

"You want to use your mouth or your hand?"

Mouth? My gaze flew up, but I was fairly sure he was joking. I hoped he was joking.

"Check which way it rolls down." He showed me. "Like this. Then, put it on top and roll it down all the way."

I did as I was instructed and I had the distinct impression he was getting some enjoyment out of it, especially if his sharp inhalation was anything to go by. When he seemed happy it was on properly – though I have no idea how he could really tell – he guided me back down and kissed me, once again soft and deliberate and heated.

I could feel his tip pressing against me and I arched into him, all at once anxious and excited.

"You sure about this?" he asked as he kissed my neck.

I nodded. "I'm sure."

He pushed into me slowly. At one point, he paused and looked at me, care and concern marked on his face. "Still with me?"

I nodded again.

He smiled down at me, all reassuring warmth. "Just relax."

So, I did.

As he kissed me gently, his hand cupped my hip and pulled my leg higher around his hip. Whatever that did, he slid in easily. With one hand on my hip, the other found my hand and held it above my head as he started moving slowly and steadily.

If the other night had been fireworks, this was slow burning flames. When his lips weren't on me, he was looking down at me with such tenderness I found it hard to remember this was the same guy who'd apparently made his way through most of the school already. I could almost believe I was the only one in his universe.

Everything about it was steady and purposeful. It wasn't rushed, hurried or just some quick fuck. I felt – as corny as it sounds – worshipped, like it was the only place he wanted to be.

When my breath came shorter and I couldn't help the moan or two that escaped, he picked up the pace; still long thrusts, but faster. He felt incredible. I didn't know if he was just made that way or if he just knew where all the right buttons were. Maybe it was practise.

He was sucking on my neck, sending shots of pleasure through me when I felt my climax build again. I couldn't stop myself from moaning his name, but I put my mouth against his shoulder to try to muffle some of my noise.

As my orgasm rolled over me in building waves, he increased his pace further and it was just one jolt of pleasure after another until everything just felt tingly amazingness. I felt him tense and he ran his hand up my side. One arm held him up and the other cupped my face as he kissed me softly and thrust slowly.

We were both breathing heavily when we caught each other's eyes. I hadn't had a word for it the other night, or when he'd looked at me just then. But now, I think what I saw in his eyes when he looked at me was…a connection, an understanding, some message only I could decipher. But, it didn't need deciphering into words; it was a feeling. A feeling I was sure he saw answered in my eyes.

While I was thinking all this, he gave me the kind of grin you melt for. "Did you actually just bite me?"

My cheeks flamed and I buried my head in his shoulder. "Maybe. Sorry."

He laughed as he pulled out of me with a kiss to my forehead. "Fuck, no. Don't be sorry, you kinky bitch."

Embarrassed, I pulled the blankets over my head. I felt him get up, but he was back before I could even begin to think what he'd been doing. He got back into the bed beside me and pulled the blankets down far enough to look into my eyes.

"Sex has to be honest, remember? I'm not into that BDSM stuff, but I can handle you being a bit of a biter. Just maybe try not to break skin, yeah?"

"Oh, so you think this is going to happen again, do you?" I asked quite brazenly from behind the safety of my blanket mask.

He lay down and pulled me to him, putting his arm under my head. "If I had my way, I'd…" He stopped and I felt him tense.

I rolled to look at him, sliding my hand between my chin and his shoulder. "What?"

He looked quite purposefully out the window and not at me. "Well, of course I want to do it again. Considering I know your experience intimately, I have no problems telling you that you're just *fucking* amazing."

"That's not what you were going to say."

I giggled as he rolled on top of me.

"It's not just how tight you are, it's how you respond to me, Barlow. Hands down, you are my best fuck." His voice held that tone of mocking that I was starting to know meant – while the sentiment may have been mostly sincere – his words were meant tongue-in-cheek.

Smiling, I looked up at him. "Compliments will not distract me, Lombardi."

His face was settled in its usual lazy smirk, but his eyes looked troubled.

"Sex has to be honest remember?" I reminded him of his previous words.

He sighed and flopped back on the bed, his arm landing over his eyes. "Fine. I was going to say that if it was up to me, you'd be the only girl I fucked for the rest of my life."

A stupid flutter shifted in my chest just as I knew there was a 'but'. And, I knew what that 'but' was.

"But, you don't do forever." I finished for him.

He looked at me, frowned, then looked away. "Barlow, I–"

"It's fine, Lombardi," I said softly and it was. "Just like I knew what could happen if I kept hanging out with you, I knew what would happen after that. Once you're bored, you'll move on. I don't expect anything else from you."

He scoffed, but I didn't think he was annoyed with me. He sat up, leaning his elbows on his knees. "They all say that, until suddenly it's forgotten and they think they can change me."

"Roman…" I chastised and I sat up next to him when he finally looked at me. "This, here? There are no expectations, okay?" I cupped his cheek. "We've had fun, but that's all it is and I get that. I mean no offence, but you're hardly the guy I want to introduce to my parents as my boyfriend."

He huffed a laugh. "No. Carter is far more the right guy for that job."

I shrugged. "I don't know." I ignored the pointed, quizzical look he threw my way. "My point is, I know you're not. I know we've had a good time these holidays. Hell, I'd hazard to say we've got close. We've even had some legitimate moments. But aside from the whole sex thing, we can't be more than friends. And, I'm okay with that."

He looked at me sceptically. "You're really okay with that?"

I was okay with that. He'd told me numerous times that he wasn't the kind of guy who did more – I'd seen plenty of evidence to suggest he wasn't the kind of guy who did more – and I wasn't sure he was the kind of guy I wanted more with. I had come to like him, but if he didn't do more then I wasn't going to let myself fall for him and get my heart broken.

I nodded. "I mean, the idea that you'll probably sleep with other girls at the same time doesn't fill me with rainbows. But, I don't expect you to change who you are just because we've had…something…"

"Let me get this straight? Piper Barlow is willing to just have casual sex? With me?"

I snorted and lay down. "It's less that I'm willing to have casual sex with you and more I don't want to stop hanging out with you. If the sex happens, then the sex happens. If it doesn't…" I shrugged.

"I never thought I'd see the day."

"Yeah, me either."

And, I *was* surprised. But, I enjoyed Roman's company, as weird as it was to admit it. I really enjoyed his company and I really enjoyed having sex with him. Besides, it wasn't like this would last long. I still fully believed that we'd get back to school and things would go back to the way they always had. Although, maybe we'd still be friends of sorts.

"Well, fuck me!" he breathed.

"Yeah, I think I covered that one. Quite spectacularly if reviews are to be believed."

He spluttered a laugh. "Who the hell are you? And what have you done with Piper Barlow?"

I shrugged. "Apparently, a right fucking makes a girl less afraid to speak her mind."

He rolled on top of me with that pure, happy laugh and tickled me, making me giggle like an idiot.

Chapter Thirteen
Lies = Bad. Normal = Good.

Conveniently, it decided to rain all Sunday. So we stayed in my room and he actually agreed to watch whatever I chose. I was a terror and made him watch a bunch of Rom-Coms, but paid him back by making him a pasta bake he apparently loved and throwing in a few of John Cusack's non-Rom-Com movies for good measure.

We spent a crazy amount of time with each other over the next week. When Hadley wasn't in my ear or making me go shopping (thank God, she accepted my excuses to stay home at night), I was with Roman. Something held us together that neither of us seemed inclined to put into words. I wasn't sure if it was one or both of us feeling down, or the fact that he made me feel good, calm, relaxed, and sang at me far too often. But whatever it was, not putting it into words was fine by me.

During the day, we'd spend time with Maddy or just hang out while he did tricks on his board, I read or did homework, we played on our phones, channel surfed, I made him watch bad movies, or we ate complete junk and called it lunch. Nights were much the same with my parents away. He shared dinner with me some nights – sitting on the kitchen bench and being unhelpful, useless, funny, and annoying. Others he went home for as long as it took to get

Maddy to bed then came back in a mood and put his head in my lap while we watched TV.

There was no pressure to get physical, and we didn't always. Some days, we barely kissed. Others we couldn't seem to get enough of each other. Roman just seemed to know when I felt like it; his touch was never unwelcome, I never had to hurry myself up to get in the mood to match his libido or anything – not that I'd ever done anything I didn't want with anyone, but sometimes it took a bit of time to get in sync.

We laughed, we talked, we didn't talk. It was one of the best weeks of my life and there was zero pressure and zero expectations. Juggling Hadley and keeping Roman quiet when she rang was difficult at times. But, he seemed just as keen as me to keep whatever we had on the down-low; I noticed him gloss over his precise whereabouts on the few occasions he talked to his friends on the phone.

It wasn't until my parents got back on Friday night and Mum asked if I'd really been okay while they were gone that I realised I hadn't felt that overwhelming anxiety or funk for days. When I told Mum I felt good, I really meant it for the first time in what felt like a long time.

She and Dad monopolised my time as much as possible over the next few days, but Roman and I still managed to make some time for each other during those last few days of the holidays.

But, Tuesday it was back to school and I walked out my front door to find Roman, actually in his uniform, leaning against his car and puffing away on a cigarette.

"Oh, you're actually going to school today?" I quipped and he grinned.

He shook his head and avoided looking at me. "I thought maybe you might like to avoid the bus and I *was* going to offer to drive you. But, for that, I might just make you take the bus anyway."

I shrugged. "It's all the same to me. I'll see you at school, then,"

We caught each other's eye and he laughed. "Get in the car, Barlow."

"Bossy this morning."

His humour faded. "Sorry. Maddy was up all night last night in excitement and was a right terror this morning."

"I thought we didn't apologise?" I asked, meaning to be funny, but he obviously didn't take it that way.

He glared at me. "Do I apologise for apologising? Or, is that not allowed either?"

"Jesus, you're moody today!"

"I thought *that* was allowed."

I walked up to him and cupped his cheek. "You can be as cranky as you like, but it's going to make me worry about you. You want to talk about it, or you just want to be in a super foul mood?"

He blew smoke over my head and wouldn't look at me. "I just want to be in a super foul mood."

There were a few times I didn't like being so much shorter than him and this was one of those few times. He wouldn't look at me and I couldn't make him. So, I just nodded, pulled myself to tip toes, and kissed his cheek. As I pulled away, his arm went around me and he pulled me close. It was all the apology or gratitude I would ever need from him.

Funny how, after two weeks with someone, it was possible to know them so well. When others you've spent years with and feel like maybe you don't know them so well after all.

He kissed the top of my head as he pulled the door open and helped me into the cab. Still not looking at me, he shut the door and went around to the driver's side, having ditched his cigarette butt outside. We didn't talk. For the second time in the last two weeks, the tension sizzled between us like charged air. We all remember what happened last time, but I had no idea what was coming this time.

I hadn't told Hadley about any of the past two weeks. I'd wanted to keep it just mine. Besides, how do you tell your best friend that you did something that she would think was totally out of character? I didn't want her having a go at me and ruining something I'd enjoyed.

Had it been entirely sensible? No, not so much. Okay, probably not at all. Hanging out with the school's resident underachiever was probably on the bottom of my bright ideas list. Having sex with him was probably at the top of my dumb ideas list. But, it had been fun and I didn't regret a second of it. I *was* worried Hadley's – or anyone else's – reaction might make me, though.

Even so, as we pulled into the school carpark, the first bit of regret started gnawing at me. But, I knew I was just being stupid.

"You ready for this?" Roman asked, staring forwards.

"For what?"

"People are going to notice we drove to school together."

I laughed to try and break some of the tension. "Just thought of that, did you?"

He scoffed, an almost-smile breaking on his face. "I suppose you *did* think of it and decided it was irrelevant?"

I nodded. "Yeah, well. It makes sense. We live next door to each other, getting the bus is a bitch and it's winter."

He nodded almost subconsciously. He seemed to have changed in the last two weeks. There was still the lazy charmer in him, but between the laughter he was more brooding, sadder. I had a feeling

167

this was the real Roman Lombardi and I didn't know how I could help. But, I wanted to.

As if he could read my mind, he shook himself and gave me his patented cheeky smirk. "Let's do this, Barlow. Ready to cause a commotion?"

I grinned, for now shoving aside any concern I might have had for him. "Let's blow this popsicle stand, Lombardi."

"All you're missing is the sunnies, Barlow."

"I do like to be unaccommodating," I chuckled.

We gave each other one more smile, then dropped out of the car and went our separate ways. Of course, by the time I got to my locker, the whole school was talking about how little Piper Barlow had driven to school with sex-god Roman Lombardi.

"So, got any news?" Hadley appeared at my shoulder.

"Missed you, too," I said sarcastically, as though I hadn't only seen her on Friday.

"Yeah, yeah. I missed you. Pleasantries over. What's the goss?"

I rolled my eyes and closed my locker. "I was complaining about walking in the rain last term and Roman offered to drive us to school. There is nothing more to it than that."

I'd never lied to Hadley, not on purpose and not outright – I'd spent the last week skating over the truth and dangerously close to lying without ever actually lying. But, it came far too easily for my liking.

"Really? And he remembered two weeks later?"

I shrugged. "Guess he's not as stupid as he looks."

"S'pose not, then. I wonder how many girls he slept with over the holidays?" she mused wistfully – and I so knew what was on her mind – as we wandered to class.

"Who knows?" I didn't even want to begin to wonder.

"Well, him presumably."

I smiled and ducked my head as I caught Roman's eye in the hallway. "Presumably."

Roman and I awkwardly interacted for most of the day.

Well, I felt awkward.

He seemed to be going about his usual day in that nonchalant way I'd almost forgotten he had; eyeing off girls left, right and centre, skating down the corridors, smoking on the oval, avoiding class like the plague. We caught each other's eye now and then and I avoided the humour only noticeable in his eyes each time.

"I see Everest really didn't give in to any climbers while I was away," Hadley commented, harking back to our conversation the previous term, with a friendly elbow to the ribs.

And I shit you not, I jumped like the guiltiest person on the planet. But thank God, she didn't seem to notice.

"No, that I didn't. I told you last week I didn't."

"He's still after you something shocking. Fuck, I could only dream he was after me that badly."

I snuck a look at Roman as we walked into class and shook my head at him once. I wished I could believe her; but, Roman had had me. He didn't need to be after me. So, why then did Hadley think he still was? Had his behaviour not changed at all? Surely he wasn't such a great actor, it had to be that maybe I wasn't just another of his nail and bails? Not quite to the degree of the others anyway. I was surely still a novelty, but he'd get bored soon enough.

Not that it actually mattered to me.

Because it didn't. Because we were just friends who enjoyed each other's company and sometimes had sex. When he turned around and got bored of me, then it was going to be okay because it was inevitable and I didn't expect him to change for me. But, I was going to enjoy it while it lasted.

"He never was and he isn't. Leave it, Hads." I smiled as we sat down in our seats.

Despite being very near the classroom, Roman unsurprisingly didn't turn up for class.

It wasn't until I left the classroom for a short trip to the library that I saw him again.

Scanning shelves as I looked for the book I needed, I was pulled behind another shelf and a familiar pair of lips found mine. I let him kiss me for a moment, then I pushed him away gently.

"What are you doing?" I asked, smiling.

"I'm kissing you. Or, did you get hit on the head today?" He looked very concerned as he ran a hand over my hair.

I smiled and batted him. "This is weird behaviour for you, Lombardi."

"I missed your touch. So sue me." He shrugged and flicked his hair out of his eyes. But, I was pretty sure I saw through his nonchalant façade.

"Anyone would think you'd gone soft for me."

He frowned down at me. His presence was commanding, to say the least. It always was. Roman had a way of demanding your attention – his eyes were always fierce and intense, he radiated this combination of attraction and warning, and it didn't hurt that he was so tall – and my attention was certainly demanded.

"I was joking. Relax," I said, patting his chest.

He pulled away. "You want a ride home?"

I looked him over, wondering at his weirdness. "Well, I'd super appreciate it. But, I get if you've got other things to do."

He wouldn't look at me. "I don't have other things to do."

"Lombardi?"

"Barlow?"

"What is up with you today?"

His gaze flickered to me and away again. "Nothing. What's up with you?"

"Well, aside from me feeling super weirded out and feeling like Hadley's got some huge secret, nothing." I didn't feel like Hadley had a secret – if anyone had a secret, it was me – but I wanted to see if he was paying attention.

No surprise, he wasn't.

I pulled him to face me.

"What is going on?"

"What? Nothing?"

"Come on, Lombardi. Even for you, you're acting weird."

"I'm not acting weird. You are."

I rolled my eyes. "Sure." I shoved him out of my way and went back to my book search.

"How is Piper Barlow so okay with this?" he asked, following behind me.

"Okay with what?"

"With this. With us?"

"I wasn't aware there was an us."

"You know what I mean."

"What can I say? You've changed me."

"I don't know that I like that." He sounded legitimately displeased.

"Well, tough luck. What do you want here, Roman? I can either fawn all over you at school and make a fool of myself? Or, I can act like normal? Which I am. So…what do you want me to do?"

"Normal. Normal is good." But, his tone made it sound the opposite.

I sighed and turned back to face him. "Roman?"

His gaze flickered to me for a split second. "Piper?"

"What happened to honesty, huh?" I tried to get him to look at me again.

He shrugged away from me. "Fuck this," he muttered, raking a hand through his hair.

"All right. You want to be a dick, fine. If you need me when you're done, I'll be around."

He stepped in front of me and pressed me against the bookcase. "And, if I need you now?"

I smiled at him ruefully. "We're at school, Lombardi…"

"I'm aware of that, Barlow. What's your point?"

"We both know us being seen together hurts you more than it hurts me."

"How is that?"

"People will think Roman Lombardi's capable of dating."

He scoffed. "Of course, because innocent little Piper Barlow couldn't possibly be capable of not."

I knew what he was thinking; last term he was like everyone else and believed it, but now he knew I was certainly capable of not dating.

"People want to see good in you, they don't want to see bad in me. It's just how it is."

"People?"

"Girls," I conceded. "Girls want to see the good in you."

"And don't want to see the bad in you?" The corner of his lip quirked like it did when he was trying not to smile. "I didn't think they cared so much."

I bit my lip. "Well, some of them. But, most just won't like me being competition, I'm sure."

"For me or *Mason*?"

I frowned. "What's that supposed to mean?"

"Has he asked you out yet? Or, did he not find his sack in Europe?"

"What is up your arse today?"

He opened his mouth and I stopped him.

"If you say 'nothing', I will hit you. We don't lie to each other, Lombardi. That was the deal. We don't have to talk about it, we don't apologise for it, but we don't lie. Remember?"

He sighed. "I don't know, okay? I don't know." He dropped his forehead to mine.

I sympathised, really. But, now was not the time for this.

"I've got to get back to class. I'll see you later?"

"You don't want to be seen with me?" he asked, his tone dry. "Maybe a little bit of competition will light a fire under Carter's arse." His hand fell to my waist and he leant closer.

"Firstly, any guy who only wants me when there's competition isn't worth my time. Secondly, I don't care if we're seen together. I assumed you did."

Well, I sort of did. But, not for the reasons he'd assume. I wasn't embarrassed or ashamed I'd spent time with him or I'd slept with him. I was still worried people would spend hours berating me, making me doubt my decisions and just rain down on my parade. People finding out would ruin it, make me question him and myself, and the last thing I wanted was it being ruined. I wanted to keep feeling good about it, and about him.

"And, what if I only want you because there's competition?"

I snorted. "*You*, jealous of Mason? No, I don't think so."

He looked at me seriously. "And, if I was?"

I looked at him seriously back. "Last term or this term?"

"Does it matter?"

"Of course it does. Last term, your motivation is highly suspect. This term, you being jealous would actually be kind of cute."

"Cute?"

I nodded, looking into his eyes. They were warm even though his face was stony. "Like you and Maddy."

He grabbed me around the waist and I stifled a giggle against his shoulder.

"If you bite me again, Barlow, I may try to persuade you to ditch next lesson."

I found his eyes again and saw him smiling at me playfully. "Well, we couldn't have that." I gave him a peck on the lips and wriggled out of his arms. "I have to go. I'll see you later."

"So, I *can* see you around?"

"Lombardi, you can do whatever you want," I chuckled, walking away from him backwards.

"Kiss you on the oval?"

I grinned and checked no one was watching. "If you wanted to ruin your reputation, yes. But somehow, I don't think you will."

He looked genuinely surprised, but pleased. "Oh, you think you know me so well, Barlow? How's that?"

I grinned and gave him a wink. "Takes one to know one, Lombardi."

"That it does." He gave me a slow smile that warmed me up inside and out.

I ducked my head and hurried out of the library. When I skidded back into class, I had to force my face out of its ridiculous happy dance.

"Where's your book, Piper?" Mrs Carstone asked, pleasantly.

I looked up quickly and felt the blush. "Uh, they didn't have it…"

She smiled. "Ah, well. Maybe next time." She pointed to my seat and I collapsed into it.

Hadley leant over to me. "Run into Mason, did we?" she whispered.

I grinned, but didn't answer her.

Let her think what she wanted.

Chapter Fourteen
Not Asked Out. Twice.

Mason and Tucker had taken to sitting with Hadley, Celeste and me at Lunch. The rumour mill was furiously circling. If you believed everything you heard, Mason was going to ask me out any minute even though I'd secretly hooked up with Roman in the holidays but also couldn't have possibly because I didn't do that sort of thing and he was still talking to me so I must have been tutoring him or he was finally making a pass at Hadley through me.

My head spun just trying not to think about it.

Roman, of course, found it hilarious. But, he hadn't gone near me at school since Tuesday. We parted at his ute in the morning and may as well not have existed to each other except for the usual level of interaction prior to the holidays until the last bell went and I met him back there.

He went through school with his stony expression exuding defiance, being yelled at by teachers, and Thursday I saw him and Rio running away from the building just before the fire alarm went off and we got doused by the sprinklers.

It wasn't until Friday that I realised I hadn't felt alone with my friends all week. I'd been happy for the most part and, when I wasn't, hiding it wasn't so much of an effort. I'd just had the epiphany and that had put me in a good enough mood when Mason caught up to me in the hallway at the start of Lunch.

"Hey, Piper. I was wondering if we could talk?" he asked.

I nodded as I shuffled with books in my locker. "Yeah, sure. I just need to run to the bathroom. I'll catch up to you outside?"

"Uh, sure."

"Great. Thanks, Mason." I threw him a smile and dashed off. To be fair, it was only in hindsight that it occurred to me that he might have been about to ask me out and, in my defence, I had been desperate to go most of the previous lesson.

Either way, I was walking across the oval towards the group when Roman broke off from his friends and met me halfway. Absently, he put a hand on my stomach and ducked his head to my ear.

"Not causing trouble today?" I asked.

"Obviously not enough if you haven't heard about it," he answered ruefully, but his eyes were hard.

I smiled but was going to leave that where it was. "What's up?"

"I have to go pick up Maddy. But, I should be back by end of the day," he said softly.

I frowned at him. "She okay?"

"Yeah, I–" He shook his head. "I don't know. I think so, but who knows. Mum just said I needed to go get her because she can't get off work." He took a drag of the cigarette I'd become so used to I'd stopped even noticing the smell – funny how he smoked so much but never smelled like it. "There's a whole car seat thing and I need to go now."

"Are *you* okay?"

He turned his face to me. We looked at each other for a moment quite intently. Finally, he looked behind me again.

"No."

I nodded. "All right. Need anything?"

He shook his head. "Not now."

Even knowing Roman the way I did, I couldn't see anything explicitly sexual in that. It was the Roman equivalent of 'we'll talk later', only without the expectation that there'd be talking; we might just sit on the lakeshore and listen to music for a few hours.

"Okay. Well–"

"–I know where to find you," he finished for me. "I know." He sounded distracted, but not so much that he didn't sound somewhat heartened by the knowledge I was there for him.

He shifted and I knew he was about to walk away. I put a hand on his chest. "Roman?"

He looked down at me. There was nothing in his eyes but stress and concern and that muscle in his jaw was twitching. I never seemed to know how to help him, not like he seemed to know with me. He seemed to know when I needed to be quiet, when I needed to talk, to be distracted, to laugh. When it came to him? I felt like the worst of all friends.

"Piper?" he asked back.

I blinked. "I can get the bus if it's easier?"

He sighed and touched his forehead to mine for a split second. "No, it's fine. I could do with some decent company this afternoon." His hand tightened against my stomach for a moment, then he walked off.

I watched him for a moment, then shook my head and hurried over to the group. I plonked down onto the grass next to Hadley and crossed my legs, shoving my skirt between them so I didn't flash anyone.

"Uh. So, what was that about?" Hadley asked.

I jumped and looked up to find the conversation was on pause and they were all staring at me. "What?"

"That, with Roman?"

I looked behind me. "Oh, he has to…do something. Might not be here to take me home is all." I waved a hand. "It's fine." It was fine, wasn't it? I mean, I was allowed to be friends with people…

"Looked kind of cosy…" Hadley said, her voice full of implication and fishing for information.

I gave her a look that told her what I thought of that. "There is nothing cosy about him." Which wasn't strictly true, but she didn't need to know that. "Lombardi's not known for his adherence to boundaries, is he?" I smiled at her and turned it to Mason. "So, what did you want to talk to me about?"

Talk slowly resumed around us as Mason smiled at me. Those big blue eyes watched me carefully like I had secrets to give away. "I…uh," His eyes dropped and he fiddled with a piece of grass at his feet. "Well I mean, I don't want to be…" He cleared his throat. "I mean, you and Roman…?"

I blinked. "Oh my God, no." I chuckled self-consciously. "No, why would you…?"

He huffed a laugh, sounding as self-conscious as I did. "People talk." He shrugged. "I just… If you're not – uh – I was wondering if you wanted to go to *Lacey's* tonight?" I was just about to feel something about him finally asking me out when he kept talking. "Just, the others are going. And I thought it might be nice to, you know…as a group?"

Well, now I was going to feel less bad about declining.

"Yeah, no. Of course…"

"Sweet." He nodded.

"Oh, no!" I blurted and his face fell. "I mean, I'd like to, but I…have plans tonight. Sorry."

I felt bad that I'd disappointed him. Although, I couldn't say a part of me didn't enjoy his obvious disappointment. I know that sounds terribly sadistic, but at least it was a sign that he did actually like me.

But, he rallied well. "Oh. Well another time, then?"

I nodded. "I'd like that."

"Next weekend, maybe?"

"Maybe." I grinned.

He smiled, turned to Tucker, looked at me again, then started talking to Tucker. I felt Hadley nudge me none too gently.

"What?" I hissed, elbowing the offending elbow.

"You didn't tell me you were busy tonight?"

"So?"

"What are you doing?"

"Uh…babysitting," I said. I looked at her out of the corner of my eye and saw her looking sceptical.

"Babysitting?"

I nodded.

"Who the hell are you babysitting for?"

"Family friend," came out before I could stop it.

"How old?"

"Five."

She nodded. "Well, have fun." I knew how much fun she thought I'd be having.

I smiled. "I'm sure I will."

So, I'd successfully lied to Hadley again and she'd bought it again. My stomach twinged uncomfortably and a part of me wished I felt like I could tell her everything. But she'd either think there was more to Roman and I than there was or she'd be on my case about how there wasn't more to us. So lying seemed like the only choice at the time.

And, I guess it wasn't quite a lie; I'd sort of signed up for babysitting Roman. He wasn't five, but Maddy was. So, not too bad, really. As lies went…. Maybe…

I had a quick look for Roman's ute in the carpark after school and was almost surprised when I saw it. I wandered over and opened the passenger door.

"You know we should probably…" I stopped as I saw him put his finger to his lips and kick his head into the back seat.

I peered around the seat and saw Maddy asleep in her car seat.

"You didn't have to come back for me," I hissed.

He shrugged. "She's asleep anyway," he said quietly.

I rolled my eyes and clambered awkwardly into the car.

"You're not getting any better at that you know."

"Thanks. I hadn't noticed," I muttered as I went to pull the door closed and saw Hadley, Tucker and Mason waving at me.

My stomach did a weird sort of half flip-half shrivel, jump-plummet thing as I waved back and pulled the door closed.

"What were you shouting before?" he asked as he pulled out of the carpark.

"I don't know." I pulled my eyes from Mason, wondering at that weird feeling in my stomach.

"You okay, Barlow?"

I rested my head back on the seat and closed my eyes. "No."

I heard him chuckle, then felt him reach over to take my hand. I was surprised by the action, but I tried not to let it show.

"What's up?"

"At Lunch, Mason may or may not have asked me out."

I felt Roman's hand twitch like he was about to pull it back, but he didn't. "And what does that mean?" he asked slowly, almost as if he didn't want to know the answer.

I shrugged and turned a bit to face him. "I don't know. He asked me to go out tonight, but then clarified that everyone was going and it would be fun to hang out with the group."

"Right…" Roman's hand twitched again. He looked down for a second, squeezed my hand and pulled his away to change gears. "So?"

"Well, does that mean he's shy or he's not interested?"

Roman shrugged, turned the corner, changed gears again and took my hand back. "I don't know, Barlow."

"Well if you were going to ask me out, how would you do it?"

He slid me a humoured glance. "Barlow, if this is a sorry attempt to get me to ask you out–"

"If I wanted to date you, I'm woman enough to just ask you and risk being shut down, Lombardi. But, thanks," I huffed.

He supressed a smile. "Oh, you're woman enough all right."

I looked down to hide my smile, sneaking a look to make sure Maddy was still asleep. "So? You wouldn't want to hang out with all our friends on a date, would you?"

Roman sighed. "Are we being serious now?"

I looked at his profile for a moment before I replied. "Yes."

"Okay then." He shifted adorably in his seat like it was suddenly too big for him or something and put both hands on the steering wheel. He cleared his throat. "Aside from the serious fact that our friends seriously don't get along and I suspect not even a serious apocalypse would change that, seriously no."

I was stuck wondering if that had been a subtle John Cusack reference so I forgot what it was a 'no' to for a second. "No, what?"

"No, I wouldn't want to hang out with our friends on a date."

"What would you want to do?"

"What?"

"Say you were taking me out on this proverbial date, what would we do?"

"Again, not asking you out, Barlow," he chuckled.

I swatted him playfully. "I know. But… Pretend I'd asked you out! What would we do?"

"You asked me out? How would that go, then?" he teased.

"Oh, I don't know. I expect I'd say something like 'Roman?' and you'd say 'yes, Piper?'" I dropped my voice low and he laughed, then checked the mirror; but, Maddy was still asleep.

"Was that supposed to be me?"

I nodded. "Yes. Shush, I'm getting in the zone."

"Oh, I'm sorry."

"Not allowed. Now, shush. So, you'd say 'yes, Piper?' and I'd probably blush bright red and look at my shoes and say 'I know I said I'd never be one of those girls, but I broke my promise. We said no lies, so no lies, Roman. I think I'm falling in love with you and I want you to be that guy. I want to date you.' Right, so then–" I paused when I saw his face. "What?"

"You…" He shook his head and wriggled again. "Never mind. So, then what do I say?"

I looked out the side window. "Well, I imagine you'd say something like 'Piper, I've been in love with you this whole time but I've been too busy maintaining my mysteriously brooding, bad boy image to admit it.' Then I expect you'd fall to your knees at my feet and agree to date me."

183

He snorted and I turned to see him shaking his head. "Of course, I would."

"Well, what do you think you'd say then?"

He drummed his fingers on the steering wheel and I saw him steal a couple of glances from the corner of his eyes. He leant his elbow on the door while his hand held the steering wheel and rubbed his chin with his other hand.

"I think I'd be more likely to say something like 'Piper, I've never wanted to be that guy before. But even if you weren't that girl, I've found myself wanting to be that guy for you. You're beautiful, you're smart, you know how to make me smile, you make me happy without even trying, and your touch drives me wild. I fell in love with you, Piper, before I even really knew what love was, before I really knew you. Now, I know both far more intimately than I ever thought I could, and I would be honoured to date you'."

My cheeks had flamed burning heat, but I couldn't look away from him. I could only stare at him and blink. My chest constricted and my stomach cartwheeled. I opened my mouth a couple of times. But, nothing came out and I forced myself to look out the other window.

"Barlow?"

"Jesus, that was…something else, Lombardi," I breathed.

"Just because I'm not romantic doesn't mean I've failed to grasp the concept. Besides, you forced enough of those movies on me last week. I like to think I've picked up *something*."

I nodded. "Sure. Of course you would have."

"You okay?"

"Yeah, fine."

He pulled into his driveway. "You sure?"

I grabbed my bag and paused with my fingers on the door handle. "You caught me off-guard, Lombardi, that's all. No girl – no matter how smart – is going to be unaffected by you saying something like that."

Before he could say anything, I threw the door open and climbed out.

But, the bastard was quick as he was standing in front of me when I finally got both my feet on the ground without falling over and closed the door. He was looking at me in concern and… *Dear God, let that not be pity…*

"Barlow?" he said, his tone a warning.

"I am *fine*. Okay?" I made to push past him, but he stopped me.

"I know you're not stupid enough to fall for me…are you?"

"I like how that sounds awfully one-sided," I huffed.

Roman grimaced, then pulled the back door of the car open. "Maybe, Barlow, just maybe," he said softly as he got the sleeping Maddy out of her car seat. I watched her snuggle into him and it really wasn't helping the conversation. But, I knew he needed her as a shield, "that's because *I'm* not too stupid." He closed the door quietly and turned to me.

I looked at him, completely dumbfounded. "What?"

He smoothed Maddy's hair and stepped towards me. "Maybe I'm not too stupid and maybe it doesn't matter either way because we both know I will never be that guy, Piper. Even if I wanted to be – even if it was for *you* – I don't have it in me. Whatever this thing was, it was only ever lasting until Carter pulled his fuc–" He stopped himself, glanced at Maddy and sighed, "–his finger out and asked you out. It was a bit of fun, nothing more, and now it's over."

"Roman, I…"

I looked at him, not sure about anything anymore; if he'd had a

185

planned expiry for whatever we were doing this the whole time, how did that change things? I thought he'd enjoyed my company, but would he have got bored if he'd seen an end in sight? Probably not. Easy Piper Barlow next door was a guaranteed lay without any risk of commitment, and that was definitely not going anywhere. So, what if he'd actually already got bored and just hid it really well? He'd only have to stick it out a little longer and then I wouldn't be his problem…

I bit my lip and frowned. So many things were on the tip of my tongue. But, I didn't know what to start with and nothing was polite enough to step forward for me to say it.

"What time's your date?" he asked softly, cupping my cheek.

Not that it *was* a date.

"I…" I took a deep breath and looked at Maddy's shoe against his leg. "I told him I was busy…" I swung my face out of his hand.

"What? Why?"

"You were feeling shit and I said I'd be there. Foolishly, I thought you needed me tonight. So, I… Not that it was a date. But, no date." I rearranged my bag strap on my shoulder. "Bye, Roman. Tell Maddy I hope she feels better."

"Piper," he called in a harsh whisper, but I shook my head and ducked into my house as quickly as I could.

Of course I'd been stupid enough to think that Roman and I were friends. Friends with spectacular benefits, it's true. But, I'd honestly felt the most normal with him than I had in longer than I really remembered. There was no bullshit between us; we said exactly what we meant, what we felt – even if it didn't make sense to us at the time – and didn't have to worry the other one was going to look at them differently. I could be in a foul mood and he didn't care. Well, I mean, I thought he'd cared…as it were…but…

"Ugh, get over it, Piper," I muttered to myself as I threw my bag on my bedroom floor. I dropped onto my bed and sighed.

'It was a bit of fun, nothing more, and now it's over,' he'd said.

"Friendship included." *If we'd ever even really had that to begin with…*

I took a deep breath and told myself that wasn't tears that I felt threatening at the assumption that the time I'd been waiting for had come. Roman was moving on and I was going to keep telling myself it was okay.

Chapter Fifteen
That Sexy Wet Dog Smell.

I avoided everyone the whole weekend; it was just me, my blanket, some chocolate, and John. I avoided Hadley, Celeste and Mason by telling them I was sick. I avoided my parents much the same way. I avoided Roman by just simply telling him I didn't want to talk to him.

I'd been going to suggest we swap numbers on Friday afternoon, but I was glad I hadn't got that far now.

I was feeling as innocent and naïve as my friends thought I was. Stupid Piper had thought she and Roman Lombardi were friends and that it was going to be okay when he walked away. So really, the sense of betrayal sitting in my chest was my own damned fault.

I shouldn't have convinced myself that his friendship was less to me than it was, that I was fine with it being temporary. Just the same way I shouldn't have convinced myself that it was possible to be friends with him in the first place.

"Roman's waiting for you by his car," Mum said, poking her head around my doorway on Monday morning.

I tucked my hair behind my ear and busied myself so I didn't have to look at her. "Can you drive me to the bus stop this morning, please?"

"Piper, honey. Are you two fighting?"

"What?" I huffed an incredulous laugh.

"Well, the two of you have been spending a lot of time together lately and… Well, I just assumed…?"

Great, it seemed no amount of assuring her we were just friends had worked – although if we were never really friends, was I surprised? Carmen had probably told her how much time we'd spent together while she and Dad were away. I really wished they didn't go to book club together sometimes…

"You know what happens when you ass*ume*, Mum – you make an ass of Ume." I picked up my bag and pulled it over my shoulder. "And that's just rude."

She looked me over. "Honey, I won't pretend to remember what it was like when I was your age. But, boyfriends are hard work. Especially–"

"Whoa! Roman and I aren't dating, Mum– Weren't dating," I said quickly. "No dating."

Mum nodded, looking like she wasn't sure if she was relieved or not. I bristled on Roman's behalf, despite everything. "Okay, good. So, you can go to school with him, then." She popped into my room, kissed my hair and headed for downstairs. "See you tonight, honey!"

That doesn't mean we're not fighting.

I stood in my room for a minute, flabbergasted.

Until I heard Mum open the front door with a, "Morning, Roman. She's upstairs."

I grimaced and didn't even make it out of my room before he'd jogged up the stairs and was standing in front of me.

"Barlow–"

"Not now, okay?"

"Look, I'm sorry–"

"We don't apologise, Lombardi. Those are the rules."

"And when one of us is a fucking idiot and does something that needs to be apologised for?"

"That's the whole point! It's impossible for us to do anything to the other that could possibly need an apology. I don't expect you to be anything other than your true self with me and that's all you've ever been. No apologies."

As angry as I was that I'd let myself forget what he was really like, that was the deal and I was sticking with it. We weren't really friends? That wasn't Roman's fault; he shouldn't have to apologise that I'd thought I'd seen something in him that wasn't there.

"If that was true, you wouldn't have avoided me all weekend. So, I am sor–"

I pushed past him with a yell of frustration and pounded down the stairs.

I felt like something weird and uncomfortable had shifted between us and if he changed any of the rules on me now the whole thing was going to implode. I felt like I was going to implode. I felt like I was about to lose my grip on all rational thought.

God, I hadn't felt like that in so long. And, I had to get away before I did something even stupider than think I was friends with Roman.

"Piper!" he called, hurrying after me.

I didn't even bother closing my front door behind me (luckily, Roman did), I just stormed out and started heading for the bus stop. My face felt hot, but not from flushing. I felt itchy and antsy, the kind I hadn't felt in weeks. Even the chill in the air couldn't cool me down. Thunder rumbled in the distance and the grey skies seemed to mirror my mood like some cheesy movie.

I thought he'd given up, but I was proven wrong when he

grabbed my arm and pulled me to face him. His hands cupped my cheeks and he was kissing me. Out of pure habit, I leant into him for a second, then I pulled away and pushed against him.

"What was that?"

He looked confused. "What was what?"

"You don't just go around kissing people!"

That didn't help his confusion any.

"I'm not just here at your beck and call, Lombardi. Okay? I'm not just some booty call you can turn to when you don't have anything better or you're too lazy to go looking."

"I don't think– Where is this coming from?"

Joy, it started raining.

I huffed. "You can't just drop a bombshell on someone and think you haven't changed things."

Why *had* he come over that morning anyway?

"Is this because I said it was over?" he asked, looking up as though I'd failed to notice it was raining and maybe we should do something about it.

Of course, I'd noticed; I mentioned it just before. Fact is, I didn't care. All I could feel was a keen sense of loss and I was starting to blame him and his smooth, bad boy charm.

"Something that never started cannot – by definition – end, Lombardi."

"So, you *are* pissed I said it was over?" He threw his hands up. "I knew it. Look, we both knew what this was. I actually thought, out of both of us, you remembered better than I did!"

I bristled. "I *thought* I knew what this was! Turns out you were lying to me after all. Honesty my fucking arse! You're a piece of shit, Roman Lombardi. I wish I'd never insulted you!"

He scoffed. "You wish you'd never insulted me? Well, if that's not an insult to end all insults, I don't know what is."

"Fuck you, Roman!" I snapped. "You're the one who invaded my space, who insisted on making me laugh when I felt shit, who took it upon himself to worm his way into every facet of my holidays. I didn't ask to hang out with you. I was quite happy sitting at the lake by myself having some damned peace and quiet!"

"You were happier with me."

I growled. "Exactly, *I* was happier with *you*. You saw a convenient lay. I'm surprised you bothered after it took me so long to get with the program!"

It didn't bother me that I'd lost my virginity to a guy I wasn't madly in love with. I was fine with the fact it was just sex. But, I was annoyed that I'd thought the just sex had at least stemmed from friendship and mutual respect, and I'd been wrong.

He shook his head. "Hang on. What the fuck is this actually about? Because, as I recall, sex takes two and you were just as willing as me."

"Of course I was. I never said I wasn't. But, I was under the misguided assumption that we were friends!" I screamed, well past caring that my blazer now smelled like wet dog or that there was a slim chance someone could see or hear us.

"What?"

"You heard me. Perhaps it's a ridiculous notion for someone like you, but here stupid little Piper Barlow was thinking we were friends! Well, she's not so stupid anymore. Thank God Mason asked me out when he did and now you don't have to bother about me anymore! So, congratulations, Roman. You are free to roam greener, less boring, more open pastures!"

"You're fucking mental, you know that?" he sighed, shaking his head. He took a step towards me, but I stepped back. "Come here," he said roughly, grabbed my arm gently and pulled me to him.

But, he didn't try to kiss me. He just wrapped his arms around me and hugged me fiercely. He hugged me like he meant it. As usual, Roman Lombardi knew what I needed and was going to give it to me whether I wanted him to or not.

And, as usual, I couldn't not accept it.

Finally, after a bit of wanky hand-waving hesitation, I put my arms around him. He kissed my temple and lay his cheek on my head. A part of me hated how the antsy, itchy feeling dissipated in his embrace, even now.

"Okay. Now, do you want to talk about whatever the fuck this is actually about? Or are you going to let me drive you to school and we'll deal with it later?"

I felt like I should push him away, but I couldn't bring myself to do it. I rested my hands on his chest and didn't say anything because I thought I'd start crying if I opened my mouth.

"Piper. Come on, babe. If it's about that arsehole, Carter. He'll get to it, okay? I see the way he looks at you and I know he wants you. I shouldn't have kissed you, not when he'd asked you out. That wasn't fair of me. And I know we don't apologise, but I will apologise for that. Because, I was putting me first – not you – and there's no excuse for that."

I sighed and shook my head, burying my face in his jumper.

"You can't say things like that," I mumbled, feeling like I was holding onto his blazer lapels for dear life.

"Like what?" he asked.

"Like putting me first."

"Why not? Isn't that what friends do, Barlow?"

I sighed, but couldn't answer.

He pushed me to arm's length and crouched to look me in the eye. "Barlow?"

"So, we are friends then?"

"Why would you think we weren't?"

I huffed and turned away from him, waving my arms like an idiot. "Oh, I don't know. How about the whole fact that I'd assumed we'd had sex because we had…an emotional connection? And I'm not talking love or romance, or whatever other bullshit excuse you might pull out here. I'm talking about actual, proper friendship that just happened to lead to sex. Two people who were there for each other emotionally were there for each other physically. But what am I supposed to think, knowing you gave us an expiry date? An expiry date, Roman!"

"What? I never… Where are you getting this?"

"From you. You said it was over when Mason asked me out. So, what?" I flailed my arms in a wild shrug. "Mason asks me out and that's it? I lose your friendship? I have to choose between him and you?"

"Fuck! No," he sighed. "That's not what I meant. I just thought it was a little immoral for us to have sex after he asks you out."

"Well, duh. But, that means we can't even hang out?"

"No! I just assumed you'd be going on your date."

Not that it was a date.

"When you obviously needed me?"

"Well you weren't exactly there anyway, were you?"

"I assumed we were over!" I shouted, my voice heavy with sarcasm.

"Barlow, come on!" he yelled. "What do you actually think will happen when he asks you out for real, huh? You and I are still going to sit in your room and watch movies or lie in my truck and look at the stars? I don't really think your *boyfriend* is going to be okay with that."

"So in essence, I do have to choose. I say yes to Mason and I lose your friendship?"

"No, I'm always going to be here for you. But, the nature of our relationship is going to have to change. That's just how it is."

I didn't want to agree with him and I hated that he was the one thinking logically right now, but I had to admit he was right. What would it look like if Roman and I still did even the harmless things we did now?

"Fine," I spat. "But, that day hasn't come, okay? Whatever relationship I have with Mason is none of your goddamn business and you have no right to change *our* relationship unless you're unhappy with it! No other reason!" I sounded like a petulant child having a tantrum, but I was so past caring about anything except not losing Roman at that point. I was being irrational and weird, but I couldn't stop the feeling of impending doom.

He held his hands up in defeat and nodded. "Okay. We keep on keeping on until you give the word, Barlow."

I nodded, breathing heavily.

"Can I hug you now?" he asked slowly, taking a tentative step forward.

I opened my mouth, closed it and tried again. "I was just a total dick."

He shrugged. "Happens to the best of us. I was a dick first, so it wasn't entirely uncalled for." He took another step forward. "Can I hug you now?"

"Why?"

"You're still being a dick."

I stuck my tongue out at him and he caught me around the waist before I could dodge his arms. He kissed my neck and held me tightly.

"Are you going to stop being a dick now?" he asked.

"Are you?"

He chuckled and his breath tickled my neck pleasantly. "I might."

"I might not."

"I can live with that."

He picked me up around the middle and carried me to the car in a most undignified manner over his shoulder.

"Excuse you!" I yelled, smacking his back as I tried not to drop my bag.

"That feels awfully too close to an apology, Barlow."

"Lombardi, I'm serious! You can't just manhandle me!"

He put me down and took my face in his hands. He pouted at me and I had to admit it was somewhat adorable. "But, you're so tiny!"

"But, fierce!" I snapped, thumping him on the shoulder.

He grinned and I thought he was going to hug me again, but he just reached around and opened my door for me. "Get in loser, I'm driving."

I snorted so hard at him quoting *Mean Girls* that my loss of dignity before looked minor in comparison.

"Wow, I'm rubbing off on you," I chortled.

"Yeah, if only, Barlow."

I looked up at him and bit my lip. "Shame we have to get to school then."

"Oh, fuck. Don't do that. You're fucking evil." As if to prove his point, Roman rearranged his pants, picked me up by the waist and sat me in the car.

I rubbed my knee against his crotch and he glared at me.

"That's not funny. You know what he's like around you and I really don't feel like suffering through first lesson with a boner."

"Well, let me do something about that then…"

"I thought we had to get to school?" He looked up at my room. "By the time we get inside, get busy, get–"

"Who said anything about going inside?"

He looked back to me, his mouth parted like he'd been going to say something. Then, he frowned.

"What?" I asked, my insides plummeting a little.

"Sometimes, Barlow, I look at you now and I think I don't know who you are anymore. Then, I realise I've just had the privilege of seeing you come out of that fucking depressingly prudish shell." He put his foot on the running board. "Up and over then, love."

He winked and I sort of stood up as he pulled himself into the passenger seat. I straddled him as I reached into his front pocket for the condom. I put it between my teeth as my hands went to his belt.

It was quick, it was awkward, it was heated, but it was amazing.

He held me tight, lazily kissing my neck, before I got off him.

"You know, you're the only girl I've done in here."

"Sure I am," I laughed as I slid off him. I did love how he made that super disappointed noise whenever I did that, though.

"No lies, Barlow. Scout's honour. You're the only girl I've done in my car, on my car, against my car… Really, anything to do with my car."

I looked at him as we tidied up. "You weren't in the Scouts."

"It's a figure of speech, Barlow," he huffed sarcastically as he shifted into the driver's seat.

I sat down, pulled on my belt and fluffed out my hair in the visor mirror. Something stopped me in my tracks.

"You gave me a hicky!" I cried.

He snorted. "Yeah, my bad."

"You…" I muttered as I rifled in my bag for my scarf. "Just be lucky it's still cold enough for this."

He snorted again and started the car. "You love it."

Weirdly, I sort of did.

Chapter Sixteen

Hadley and the Roman-tic Dick Move.

Things were getting out of hand. Well, no. I was getting out of hand.

I couldn't believe I'd had sex with Roman in his ute when we were already late for school in broad daylight. It was like he'd said; I had no idea who I was anymore. I didn't know what was scarier; that I didn't recognise myself half the time, or I didn't hate who I'd become.

So when Hadley suggested we get some fish and chips after school and lounge at the park for a bit, I decided that was as good a time as any to get a touch of normalcy back in my life.

We were heading to class after Lunch when I realised I should tell Roman I wouldn't need a ride home.

"Lombardi!" I called back to him, following my friend backwards.

"Barlow?" he questioned as he looked up from his board, his face that indifferent laziness.

"You going to class, slacker?"

"What do you think, princess?"

I chuckled. "We're going to the park after school–"

"Kind of you to think of me. But alas, I have plans!"

I smirked at him. "Cute. No, I'm just not going to need a ride home."

"No worries. I'll see you in the morning!"

I waved, turned and hurried to catch up to the others. As we walked into the school building, I felt my phone vibrate. I pulled it out of my pocket and grinned at the picture I'd taken of Roman that second night at the lake.

> **Roman:** *Full disclosure, I didn't have plans – I do now. We still on for the C&B eating contest?*

We'd decided to finally settle the great 'who could stuff more Cheese and Bacon Balls in their mouth' debate, and we'd scheduled it for that night. We had also finally exchanged numbers, as if you couldn't tell.

> **Me:** *I don't know, I feel like you'll have an unfair advantage if I've just been stuffing myself full of chips…*
>
> **Roman:** *I'll stuff you ;)*

I snorted and put my phone away quickly.

"You right?" Hadley asked and I nodded.

"Yeah, just… Dad, you know."

She gave me a funny look – which I didn't blame if she knew who it had actually been and what he'd said – but she just nodded slowly as we took our seats.

The teacher looked around the room and I heard the mutter about yet another Roman no-show before she started checking out names off the roll.

After my phone went off a few more times I pulled it out.

> **Roman:** **sigh* fine, we'll reschedule the contest.*
>
> **Roman:** *But just so you know I was in fine*

form for this afternoon.

Roman: *[poop emoji]*

Roman: *[unicorn emoji]*

Roman: **double sigh* I won't even eat the packets we had ready... Happy?*

Me: **snort* How very chivalrous!*

Roman: *It seemed apt.*

Me: *One day, you're going to use that and get it wrong, and I will laugh SO hard!*

Roman: *Not possible. I totes know what it means.*

I sent him the GIF from *The Princess Bride* for good measure and shoved my phone back in my pocket. I ignored the incessant buzzing the whole way through class – a double, yay! – and pulled it out again as I followed Hadley to her car. I opened my message centre to find a bunch of random GIFs. There were some John Cusack ones, one with a dancing poop emoji, a couple of *Mean Girls* ones, and one with a pineapple. There was also a video of him stacking it on his skateboard captioned 'total accident' with a winking face.

Me: *You're a total weirdo.*

Roman: *Takes one to know one.*

"You quite right there?" Hadley asked with a smile as we pulled out of the car park.

"Fine, why?"

"You're very into your phone at the moment. I thought Mason was driving?"

"Oh. Yeah, I don't know–"

"I know he hasn't said anything yet, babes. But, give him some time. He's just being a gentleman."

There was that word again; gentleman. Honestly, I was starting to think the whole concept was overrated. How the hell had the world functioned when gentlemen were in charge?

"Hads, at this rate, I'm going to lose interest or entirely lack the ability to believe he's interested. We had the turtle talk like…five weeks ago! And, still nothing."

"Not nothing! He asked you to *Lacey's* last weekend."

"He suggested I tag along on the group outing. That's not exactly trying to shower me in love and affection."

Hadley sighed. "Okay. Well, maybe you need to be more encouraging?"

"Like what?" I asked. "We hug. I even started kissing his cheek! I blush like a pro every time he smiles at me and I laugh at all his jokes. What else can I do?"

I felt my cheeks heat and I hoped they hadn't gone pink as I remembered that I'd known exactly what to do with Roman. So, why didn't I know what to do with Mason?

"I dunno, babes," she said, pulling into a carpark between the park and the chip shop. "Let me think on it."

"Or, maybe he doesn't actually like me?"

"I feel like this is the preference for you?" Why did that seem to annoy *her*?

I shrugged. "Am I supposed to wait forever?"

"What other options do you have at the moment? I don't see anyone else lining up for your hand."

I looked down at my phone. "Yeah, I suppose," I lied.

Although, was it really a lie?

We got out of the car and traipsed into the chip shop to wait for the others. When we had our packages safely secured, we hurried back over to the park and sat around, eating and chatting.

Mason and the boys had invited a few other friends and they were kicking a football around. As usual, Mason grinned at me, but I found myself comparing him to Roman. Not in like a 'would Roman actually make a decent boyfriend kind of way' but more a 'how would I act if that was Roman' sort of way.

If it had been Roman, I would have winked at him and teased him when he missed the mark or dropped the ball. Roman would have probably picked me up and insisted I play. If Roman were the type to kick a football around. But, he wasn't. If he was the type to hang out anywhere public sober, he was the type to hang out at the skate park.

My eyes slid over to the skate park situated next to us and I smirked when a certain someone caught my eye and proceeded to fall off his board.

"Dude! You totally had that! What happened?" his mate, Steve, called.

"Dunno, man. Accident." He looked at me and I could picture the humour in his eyes even though he was a little too far away for me to see it properly.

I looked down to hide my laugh.

"Oh. My. God! He's following you," Hadley hissed and Celeste leant in to join in on the conversation.

"He's not following me," I sighed.

"He is!" Hadley smacked my leg like I wasn't already giving her my full attention. I waited expectantly for her to stop and continue. "That's why you're so paranoid about Mason!" She might have continued but she also kept hitting me.

I blinked as I grabbed her hand. "I'm what now?"

Hadley grinned like she'd discovered my big secret. And, for a second, I thought maybe she had. But, then she looked between

Mason and Roman. I followed her gaze and I don't think I'd ever actually made such an obvious comparison between the two of them.

I wasn't sure what conclusion I drew.

"You're worried Mason won't ask you out before Roman does. Then you'll have to decide between them. If Mason gets his act together, you'll have extra ammunition to say no to Roman."

I frowned at my best friend. "Firstly, there is *no* competition between the two of them. Secondly, I am perfectly capable of saying no to Roman Lombardi without going out with someone else."

Hadley waved away my 'excuses'. "Hey, Roman!"

"Yeah?" he replied as he lazily skated around. I'm sure it wasn't actually as easy as he made it look, though.

"Ask Piper out!"

Well, because that didn't cause a chain reaction of hilarious events.

Over at the skate park, Roman spun too quickly and legitimately fell off his board. Which meant he and it both slid down the ramp thing and wiped out Jake, dropping them both in a heap of confusion. That, in turn, set off Steve and Rio. One of whom fell down all on his own in a fit of laughter and the other joined the pileup.

On the grass, meanwhile, Mason looked at Hadley which meant he ran into Simon, and Marty crashed into the back of them both. The ball flew to the right where Craig and Henry raced to mark it, running into each other as they did so. And, Tucker just plain fell over in the middle of a clear zone, by himself, for good measure like the good sport he was.

"You see what you did there?" I asked with a sigh.

"I doubt any one woman has ever had such power…" Celeste gasped.

Roman and Mason both shot up from their respective piles almost comically. I was sure Roman thought there was some other game afoot; suspicion rippled over him. Mason, bless him, was just white.

"You want me to what, Miss Reynolds?" Roman asked, the slight panic on his face was novel.

"You scared, Roman?"

"Scared? No, sweetheart. More confused. What makes you think I want to go out with Barlow, there?" he asked. He managed to get back some composure as he picked up his board and climbed out of the bowl thing.

I had to force myself not to move when I saw he was limping. I think I was the only one who surreptitiously noticed the look he threw my way and I hoped my look of apology was only seen by him. I practically read his mind saying 'no apologies' before he turned back to Hadley.

"Humour me, skater boy," she replied, leaning back on the table we were sitting on and crossing her legs. "Ask Piper out."

He crooked an eyebrow at me, then looked behind him to Mason. When he turned back to me, I didn't like the shining look of resolve in his eyes. After our conversation of a couple of weeks ago – *God, no it was only last Friday* – I didn't want to know how thick Roman was going to layer it on.

"I didn't want to have to do this in front of everyone, Barlow. But, I guess there's very little choice now." Roman shrugged and, even I had to admit, he looked very sincere. The self-conscious rub of the back of his head helped and I forced my face and heart to stay neutral. He shrugged awkwardly and I thought this was almost better than the words he'd used the week before. "Do you want to go on a date with me some time?"

I made sure not to look at Mason to see his reaction – Hadley would have that covered, anyway – because that was a dick move. Mind you, the whole thing Hadley had orchestrated here was a dick move.

I smiled as sickly sweet at Roman as I could manage. "Not if you were the last human being on the planet, Lombardi."

"Ouch. That's pretty definitive, man," Rio said with a grin that didn't reach his eyes.

Roman smirked at me, his eyes full of humour. He pulled a cigarette out and stuck it in the corner of his mouth. "Thank, fuck. Now that's over with… Miss Hadley Reynolds!"

Hadley jumped beside me and I swear I felt her vibrating in excitement. "Yes?"

"Barlow tells me you guys need a ride on the weekend?"

Hadley sat up straighter and flicked her hair back. "We do."

"Sweet. Well, let me know if you find one. I need one, too."

With that, he gave her a sinfully sexy grin, dropped his board and skated back into the bowl. I coughed to cover my snort as I felt Hadley deflate beside me.

"Should have known better. No good, wanking…" she muttered and I laughed.

My eyes fell on Mason, whose arm was being plucked by Simon to get back to their game. I gave him a shy smile and found myself biting my lip. He threw one last look after Roman and back to me, a self-satisfied smile growing on his face.

"Is it just me, or does Mason have a little more pep in his step now?" Hadley asked with plenty of pep of her own. Seemed Mason wasn't the only self-satisfied one.

"That was a dick move, bitch," I laughed.

"I thought he was going to pass out," Celeste agreed.

"Which one?" I asked.

"Both," Celeste admitted.

"Well, maybe Mason'll get his arse into gear now he sees you're waiting on him," Hadley said. "That lip bite didn't hurt either. Throw him some more of that. Bit more smoulder in your eyes…"

Celeste joined her and I lost track of the ways in which I was supposed to lure Mason into asking me out because I was watching Roman. I wondered what it was about me that I seemed to have surrounded myself with people who thought Mason needed – as Roman put it – a fire lit under his arse. But like I'd said to Roman, I didn't want Mason asking me out because he thought there was competition. If he was going to ask me out, then I wanted him to ask me because he wanted me, not because he didn't want anyone else to have me.

And now, I'd put myself in a funk.

I hopped off the table and picked up my bag.

"I'm going to get the bus, bitches."

Celeste and Hadley moaned, but I wouldn't be deterred; I didn't want to be around people and I didn't really want Mason to ask me out after they were done because he thought I might change my mind about Roman – even though it had been a totally bogus ask out, but I guess only Roman and I knew that.

I hugged both my friends goodbye, slung on my headphones, and headed for the bus stop. I yelped when I felt an arm go around my shoulder and I smacked Roman for scaring me.

"Do you mind?" I asked, pulling off my headphones.

"Not particularly." Thankfully, he kept his arms to himself. He flicked his cigarette butt away.

"How's your ankle?" I asked.

"Fine."

"Good."

"I'll let you put your music on if you let me drive you home."

I stopped walking and looked up at him. "As loud as I want?"

He hung his head back and sighed dramatically. "Yes."

"All right." I headed for his ute.

"I liked that trick back there."

"Which one?" I asked.

"The one to help Carter find his sack."

"I swear that had nothing to do with me," I answered as I pulled my door open. "I think you broke Hadley's heart, though."

He grinned as we closed our doors in unison. "Tell her I'll drive you both on Saturday if it makes her happy."

"You? Go to a party and not drink?" I gasped as I plugged my iPod in.

He glared at the radio like it had betrayed him as he turned the car on and my music started, then glared at me.

"The things I fucking do for you," he sighed as he started the car properly, completely disgusted by my music tastes.

"Eh, you love me," I replied flippantly, looking out the side window.

"I certainly don't hate you."

"What a glowing review," I scoffed.

"Well, I'm hardly going to agree. What sort of message would that give you?"

I snorted. "Okay. I will give you this one chance to say *anything* to me. A totally off the cuff remark which I will take purely at face value." I slid him a look, interested to see what his response would

208

be.

"Okay. One thing. Each. Anything. Total face value. And, we never speak of it again?"

I nodded. "Sure."

"Okay."

"That's it?"

He grinned. "Shut up, I'm thinking."

"All right, take your time. You don't want to break anything."

He huffed a laugh. "Face value? Then, I do kind of love you."

I kept my gaze fixated out the window to hide the force of my smile at the knowledge our friendship really wasn't one-sided. Because I knew Roman Lombardi, and I knew that there was nothing romantic involved in that – it was like when I said it to Hadley or Celeste – so, I felt completely comfortable in my answer.

"I kind of love you, too."

"Oh, now that's just copying. Boo! Get your own material, Barlow," he teased, taking my hand. His tone was sarcastic, but his smile was sincere.

I laughed. "Fine. That not good enough for you? How's this; I love that… 'You say it best, when you say nothing at all'!" I sang along with the song. And, my voice was nowhere near as good as his – read; awful. But, my statement was no less true for the humour-value.

Roman laughed one of those pure laughs. "You're a total loon." He pulled my hand to his lips and kissed the back of it.

The song changed and I sang along in my head; I loved Tony Lee Scott's 'Take Me Away'.

Roman surprised me yet a-freaking-gain when he started singing along. And as far as I could tell, he got all the lyrics right. Even that line about the carrots…

"How the hell do you know that song?" I asked when it was finished, mouth agape.

He threw me a look and shrugged. "Dunno. What is it?"

"Um, a song so obscure I can't find it on YouTube, Soundcloud, iTunes, anywhere…"

"Spotify?"

"Nope."

"Radio?"

"Yeah, no."

He breathed out heavily. "Okay… So I have a legitimate right to be embarrassed?"

I shrugged. "I think I found it in a box of CDs your mum gave me that used to be Paris'. She probably played it a lot?"

He nodded. "Yeah, maybe."

"Or, now is the time you tell me you have a penchant for obscure love songs?"

He smirked. "Maybe I've been inspired."

I snorted. "Yeah, of course you have."

We shared a quick, humoured glance and laughed.

And that's just how it was with Roman; it was easy, it was simple, there was no second guessing, no wondering what I might have been doing right or wrong because I knew how to be. We just were.

Chapter Seventeen
More Than Two Beers Later.

The bonfire was raging and Hadley and I were dancing. I'd had a little bit much to drink, true. But, I didn't think I was completely wasted.

I knew Roman was watching me, cradling his soft drink can to his chest like some sort of bodyguard as he leant against a tree. Which, to be fair, I probably needed when I was mixing fire and alcohol.

Just as I looked back to him, I saw him push off the tree, stretch his neck, turn, and walk off through the trees. I was heading after him before I knew my feet were moving.

"Pipe, Mason's coming," I vaguely heard Hadley say.

I patted her arm. "Yeah, yeah. I'll be back in a second."

I hurried after Roman, wondering which way he'd gone. I stumbled a little on something in the dark and felt arms steady me.

"You right there, Barlow?"

I turned and gave him a big smile that he, for once, did not return. My face fell.

"What's up?"

He shrugged. "Just needed to stretch my legs."

I nodded and suddenly the motion was a little much. My hand flew to my stomach, but the nausea passed quickly and I looked back up at him.

"You're lovely, you know?" I said to him.

He gave a gruff huff and looked out over my head. "More than two beers, huh?"

"What?" I asked indignantly, pulling away from him, which was a poor choice as my legs did *not* want to behave themselves.

He caught me again, easily.

"That's how you respond to my niceties?" Although it did sound more like 'nice-titties'…

He smiled at me then. "Barlow, you're drunk as fuck. Do you want me to take you home?"

I grinned. "No! I'm having a good time for once!"

He laughed, "Are you sure?"

"Yes! Don't make me go," I whined.

"All right. Far be it for me to deny you anything you want, babe. Just ease off the alcohol, yeah?"

"You can't tell me what to do. You're not my mum," I grumbled.

He pushed some hair off my face and cupped my cheek. "No. I'm certainly not."

I frowned as I remembered something. "You were right, you know."

He looked like he expected whatever came out of my mouth next to be good. "I was right?"

I nodded. "I do like the way you look."

Even drunk, I could see he was trying not to smile. "What can I say? Takes one to know one, Barlow."

"But, I don't sleep with you because you're freaking gorgeous."

"You don't?"

I shook my head. "No."

"Why do you sleep with me, then?" he asked softly.

I looked into his eyes and it hit me just how much I felt for this guy. I mean not romantically, but everything else. He'd somehow burrowed into my very soul and I couldn't imagine my life without him in it anymore.

But, how do you put all that into words? Especially when those words would be what he considered nancy wanker words.

I lay my hand over his heart. "Because of what's in here."

His hand went over mine. "Barlow…" His voice was a tense warning.

Shaking my head, I clarified, "No, not like that. Because you don't expect me to be something I'm not and you're always there for me. Plus, you are like crazy good in bed!"

He laughed and hugged me tightly. "Right back at you, love."

I leant up to kiss him and was surprised when he pulled away.

"You're meant to be here courting Carter. Not off in the trees with me."

I frowned. "I–"

My words were cut off as I almost hurled. My hand flew to my mouth as I doubled over and I held a hand up to Roman to keep his damned mouth shut. Didn't stop him laughing though.

"Right. I'm taking you home." He took my arm gently and steered me back to the paddock. "Tucker, man!" he called out and Tucker turned with a quizzical look.

"Yeah?"

I wasn't surprised that Tucker was surprised; he and Roman weren't exactly friends.

"Barlow's had her limit, so I need to take her home. Are you okay to see Hadley home?" Roman asked and I noticed he was keeping a very stilted stance next to me.

Tucker looked at me, then back at Roman and nodded. "Sure, man. She okay?"

"She will be."

The boys did some sideways-five-fist-bump-thing and Roman steered me to where he'd parked his car. He bundled me in, avoiding all attempts I made to kiss him while I giggled drunkenly.

As we drove home, I reached my hand over to his leg. But, he stopped its progress to his crotch. He held my hand tightly, his eyes focussed on the road.

After pulling into his driveway, he shut off the car, jumped out and was there to help me out before I fell out. I giggled as I came up hard against him.

"Hi," I laughed.

He smiled, but I noticed he was still tense. His arms were around my waist and I slid my hands up his chest and around his neck. Before my lips found his, he turned his face slightly.

"What?" I asked.

"We're not..." He sighed. "We're not doing this now, Barlow."

"Not doing what?"

"We're not having sex."

I ran my hand over the very obvious bulge in his pants and looked up at him sceptically. "That's not what this tells me."

He scoffed and pulled my hand away. "Yeah, that's being vocal enough about this without you encouraging it, Barlow."

"So, what's the problem?"

"The problem is we're not doing this while you're drunk. Especially not when you're drunk and I'm stone cold sober."

"So what?"

"So, I..."

"No lies, Lombardi."

"I'm not doing anything that even has the potential to have you looking at me badly in the morning. We do this now and I would have to apologise, Piper. No matter what our rules are."

Even drunk, I heard something in his voice that made me pause. For whatever reason, something was important to him. I pulled away and nodded.

"Okay, Roman."

He sighed heavily and pulled me to him for a tight hug. I felt him kiss my hair and could have sworn he was shaking his head.

"You'll be right to get upstairs?"

I nodded. "Yep."

I pulled away from him and stumbled a little. With an exasperated sigh that was half a laugh, he picked me up and carried me to my back door.

"Keys?"

I shuffled in my pocket and pulled my keys out. Roman took them from me and opened the door. I giggled as he closed and locked the door behind us and he shushed me.

"Your parents will kill me if they find me in here, Barlow. Shut up!" he hissed.

I put my finger to my lips and nodded solemnly. He carried me upstairs and then swung me down at the landing. I guffawed a little and he cringed. I took a couple of steps towards my bedroom and heard a throat clear behind me.

Dad was standing behind us, an expectant look on his face.

"This is not what it looks like," Roman said quickly and I snorted. He threw me a glare and Dad looked at me in interest.

"It's fine, Dad–"

"Piper, go to your room, please…"

All hilarity I found in the moment was gone and I nodded as I walked to my bedroom. But, I wasn't quite so freaked out that I didn't press my ear against the door after I'd closed it behind me.

"So, Roman?" I heard Dad say.

"I just wanted to see her in safely, Matt."

"I appreciate that."

There was silence for a few moments.

"I'm not stupid enough to disrespect you in your own house," Roman said slowly.

Maybe not while they were home, I sniggered to myself.

"Bree said you'd been spending time together."

"We're friends."

"You're sober, aren't you, son?"

"I was driving Piper home."

Dad made a noise of agreement. "And, I believe you. You care about her."

"Like I said, we're friends."

"Friends?"

"Yeah, friends."

Dad chuckled. "In my day, men sacked up a little more, son."

"I'd like to say I don't know what you're talking about. But, Piper and I are just friends. No one's kidding themselves that I'm the sort of guy who can give her what she needs, let alone what she deserves…"

My heart hitched weirdly. I totally wasn't kidding myself that he was that guy, but I hated that he didn't think he was good enough for me. I really didn't think there was anything so great about me to warrant that.

I also didn't know why I saw Dad nodding thoughtfully in my mind's eye. "At least you're man enough to admit it."

"Why do I feel like that might not be a compliment, Matt?"

"Well, Roman, that may be because it might not have been."

"Other people's expectations are what get us into problems," Roman said slowly. "Piper and I are on the same page here. She knows me better than all you lot who've written me off." *Because you haven't written yourself off,* I thought, sarcastically. "She knows better than to expect anything more from me but she doesn't care. She doesn't need me to change."

"And, when she does?"

Roman sighed. "Your daughter is far too intelligent for that."

"You sound disappointed."

Roman paused. "I'm not disappointed. She's a wonderful young woman and I'm privileged to have her in my life. She's safe with me."

"I want to believe you, Roman–"

"I don't know what else I can say."

Dad huffed. "Problem is, son, you don't have to. You're a father's worst nightmare. You're the guy every father dreads the very thought of being anywhere near their daughter. And then, son… Well, then Piper's smiling again and you bring her home completely responsibly. I mean, I remember the night you were taken to the police station for being drunk and now…?"

"I'm a degenerate – not an idiot – and I said I'd look out for her."

"I'd normally expect more respect from a teenager. But, there's something oddly pleasant about your honesty."

I could visualise Roman shrugging, perhaps raking his hair out of his face. "Piper and I are honest. It's why it works. I can be me, she can be her, and we can be friends. That doesn't work without complete honesty."

"You're really not as stupid as you look, are you?"

"That's what Piper tells me."

Dad gave a rough noise of approval. "Go on in and say goodnight, son. She'll yell at us both once the headache's gone if I don't let you."

"Are you sure about that?"

"Just keep in mind that I'm right down the hall and I'm a light sleeper."

Roman huffed a laughed. "Yeah, I don't think that'll be a problem."

"You're a good man, Roman."

"I don't know about that."

I heard Dad chuckle, then the door was opening. I stumbled away from it and smiled at Roman.

"So in good news, I get to keep my nads tonight."

I giggled and he directed me towards the bed.

"Hang on, wait…"

He pulled me back to him and got me out of my jacket. I looked up at him and knew I had that stupid grin you wear when you're drunk. And – as was unexpectedly expected of Roman Lombardi – he grinned back at me, his eyes warm with humour.

"You right?" he asked, that smirk I somehow now knew so well playing at his lips.

I nodded. "Maybe."

He snorted. "Excellent. Stop wriggling."

"I'm not wriggling."

"You are."

Okay, seems I was. I was good and stood still.

His hands fell to my jeans button and I looked at him with interest.

"No funny business, Barlow," he said as he unbuttoned me.

"I wouldn't dream of it, Lombardi," I snickered.

"Yeah, well. I will be," he muttered. "Now, jeans off and get into bed. Where's your water bottle?"

I pointed to my desk as I clambered into bed and dropped under the covers.

Roman climbed onto the bed beside me and I snuggled up to him as best I could with him on top of the blankets and me under. He sat against my headboard and I put my head on his stomach.

"Ugh, I drank too much."

Roman chuckled and brushed hair off my face. "How do you figure?"

"The world only spins like this when I'm drunk," I grumbled into his shirt.

"You'll be fine." He leant down and kissed my temple. I felt him shift. "Look, I'd better go."

"No!" I scrunched a handful of his top in my fist. "Stay until the world stops spinning? Please!"

He huffed a soft laugh. "My world will keep spinning as long as you're in it, Barlow. So, I hope it never stops."

I smiled and felt all warm inside. "Lombardi?"

"Yeah?"

"Will you hold my hair back if I puke?"

"Hm... Do I get to tease you?"

I snorted. "I'd expect nothing less."

"Then, of course I will."

"Thanks."

I felt myself drifting off to sleep, then thought of something.

"Lombardi?"

"Barlow?"

"Thanks for being you."

"Likewise. Now, go to sleep."

I sniggered. "Okay, Mister Bossy."

"Night, Piper."

I snuggled further into him and his arm tightened around me.

"Night, Roman."

I woke up and my mouth felt fuzzy, much like my memory of how I'd got home the night before and what I assumed was a fair amount before that. Last thing I remembered was...dancing with Hadley next to the bonfire?

There was this stellar ache in my head and my stomach felt terrible.

And, there was a super annoying noise.

It was coming from my phone and I realised it was an alarm. Like loud screeching in my tired ears.

I groaned and picked up my phone, wondering why the hell an alarm I would never have set was going off. My eyes took a moment to adjust, but I saw writing on the screen. I blinked a few more times and couldn't help smiling when I finally registered what it said;

> *Because every good hangover starts with a rude awakening :P*

I swiped the alarm off and saw there was a new message from Roman and his hilarious yet somehow still flattering picture.

> **Roman:** *See you in the morning, you adorable drunk. And, don't think about deleting it! I have the original.*

I clicked on the picture to enlarge it and groaned. It was a selfie of the two of us presumably from the night before. I had my head on his chest and I was either passed out or asleep – probably passed out, even though I looked fairly respectable. Roman was smiling. But, it wasn't one of those sweet smiles you usually see on people in those sorts of pictures; he was totally paying me out.

So, I sent him a reply to his text with a bunch of stupid cat GIFs. That would learn him for A, taking a terribly incriminating picture, and B, being a dick by setting that annoying alarm.

I got a reply while I was still lying in bed and wondering if I'd have to visit the bathroom to no doubt gag up the incredible amount of nothing I felt like I had in my stomach.

> **Roman:** *So, you're alive.*
>
> **Me:** *I'm alive. I think.*

I added a couple more annoying GIFs for good measure.

> **Roman:** *I liked that one with the flamingo, though.*
>
> **Me:** *That's what you get for being a dick.*
>
> **Roman:** *Annoyed by you incessantly?*
>
> **Me:** *You love it.*
>
> **Roman:** *I do. Wouldn't have you any other way.*
>
> **Me:** *What happened last night? Did you bring me home?*
>
> **Roman:** *I did. I was a perfect gentleman.*

I snorted.

> **Me:** *Why don't I believe that?*
>
> **Roman:** *I'm hurt, Barlow! I was very respectable. You, on the other hand...*
>
> **Me:** *What's that supposed to mean!*

Roman: *You got a little handsy and giggly and you almost lost me my nads.*

Me: *How did I manage that?*

Roman: *You were noisy as fuck and woke your dad up.*

Me: *Oh, shit…*

Roman: *Eh, you'll be fine. We had some words, but it's fine.*

I sunk back into the pillows and groaned. The last thing I needed was Dad knowing Roman was in my room last night. I was about to reply when there was a knock on my door. I looked up and saw Dad poke his head around the door. I was fairly sure I was already incredibly pale; was it possible to get paler?

"Morning," he said, coming in. "How are you feeling?"

"Uh, fuzzy and gross…"

Dad sat on the end of my bed and looked at me intently.

"Sorry I got drunk…" I started, wondering how much trouble I was going to get in.

Dad shrugged. "You're almost eighteen, these things happen. And, you got home safe and not too late. Just don't make a habit of it."

I nodded slowly. "Uh, yeah… About–"

"It seems, maybe, there's more to Roman than meets the eyes, Pipe…" he mused.

I swallowed. "Um… We're just friends…"

Dad nodded. "I know."

"You don't have to worry. We're not… I mean, we just…"

God, I seriously hoped Roman and I hadn't had sex just after we'd woken my dad up. I felt my cheeks heat and hoped he didn't notice.

Dad looked at me with interest. "You know, darl, a few months ago I would have been more pleased by that than I am now." He stood, kissed my hair and started to leave. "Have a shower and I'll get some coffee on, yeah?"

I nodded dumbly and watched him leave.

What in the hell is the world coming to when my dad has anything positive to say about Roman Lombardi?

Chapter Eighteen
So, Yeah. I'm Friends with Roman.

On the way out to Recess, I walked past a classroom and stopped when I noticed Roman and Rio huddled around the teacher's computer. I paused, knowing I didn't *really* want to know what they were up to.

Just as I'd decided to move on without drawing attention to myself, Rio looked up.

"Oi, oi," he said with a salute and a sarcastic smirk.

Roman looked at him, then followed his gaze. When he saw me, the look of defiant contempt left his face and he almost smiled.

"Barlow." He nodded, then went back to whatever he was doing.

I swayed towards the door, but really didn't want to get involved. "Boys. Causing trouble, I assume?"

"Oh, you know us," Rio answered, smirking at me with something hard in his eyes. "On a mission to do the impossible. Mission Impossible Seven!" He grinned.

"And, what might that be?" I knew I'd regret asking.

"Getting Lombardi expelled, of course."

"Of course." I looked around the hallway, but there was no one heading in our direction. I leant on the doorframe and watched them. "And, what's your plan this time?"

"Lombardi's hacking the System Admin for back door access–" The boys both sniggered and fist-bumped. "And leaving a couple of sweet little Trojans behind as he goes."

I frowned. "And, that will do what?"

Rio shrugged. "Be a fucking nuisance."

"Oh, good. Because why be useful?"

Roman looked up at me and I saw a flicker of hesitation cross his face, then he was back to his nonchalant self. "Go on, Barlow. If we get caught, I don't want you involved."

"You soft for her, mate?" Rio teased, but he looked at me like he knew something I didn't.

"Soft isn't the word I'd use," Roman muttered as he threw me a wink.

If by some miracle Rio hadn't understood him, the way my cheeks flushed would have told him exactly what Roman meant. I cleared my throat awkwardly.

"I'm going to leave you two to it…"

Roman's fingers played across the keyboard, then he pushed away from the desk and strode over to me rather purposefully. He was all cool and assertive and had that commanding aura around him.

"What?" I asked him, my heart thumping.

A smirk played at his lips, but he had that lazily indifferent look in his eyes. He stopped in front of me, wound his arm around my waist and pulled me to him.

"Roman?" I warned him, sliding a look around the hallway.

"What? Bloke needs a good luck kiss before he goes on the lamb," he said, his voice low and sultry.

I swallowed and was seriously glad I didn't see this Roman often. This Roman wasn't the one I was used to in close proximity, though I'd seen it plenty from afar. This Roman, especially knowing the other one, was damned hard to resist.

I had one more look around the hallway, then reached up and kissed him. It might not have been long, but it was enough to send a thrill through me and made me wish we weren't at school. When I pulled away, he let me slip out of his arms. I looked at Rio and saw he was watching me carefully.

"Rio." I nodded to him and he gave me another salute as his eyes were hard. I looked to Roman as I started walking backwards. "Roman."

"Piper," he said slowly as he leant against the doorframe casually and crossed his arms.

He watched me walk away, exuding a heat I wanted to run to, and I had to turn or I thought I might combust. I hurried out of the building and made for my friends, trying to cool my cheeks.

"I missed you, Saturday," Mason said with a smile when he caught up to me just before I got to everyone else.

I nodded and told my heart to stop beating so fast. "Yeah, sorry. I…uh…" I chuckled awkwardly.

"Tucker might have mentioned something about it." Mason's smile grew more rueful.

I felt my cheeks warm just after I'd managed to get some control over them. I looked at the grass as I tucked my hair behind my ear.

"Uh, yeah," I laughed. "Not my finest moment. No tactical chunders required, though. That I know of…"

"Roman got you home okay?"

All right. What sort of question was that?

Was he just asking, or was he digging for information? Would Hadley bat her eyes and tell him she'd have preferred it to be him? Was this one of those flirting opportunities, or was I just meant to answer a question? Why did I need to make my way through five-thousand options and still not know what to do?

I swallowed and nodded again.

"Yep, all good. He saw me into the house then went off to do whatever it is he does on a Saturday night." I shrugged.

I didn't know how long Roman had been there or what he'd done after. I didn't even remember if we'd talked.

"Well, we certainly didn't see him again."

I was trying to get a read on Mason. He looked as calm and confident as usual, his face open and honest and just so damn charming. But, we were hovering next to weird territory here and I wasn't sure how to sidle the other way.

"Maybe he met up with Rio?"

Oh, I should not have said that like I knew Rio or anything about Roman's movements. From the look on Mason's face, he might have been thinking something along the same lines. Or, he might not.

"So, you're uh friends with him now, huh?" Mason scratched the back of his head. "Roman. I mean, he drives you to school, he drove you and Hads, and I've seen you two talking."

I licked my lip nervously. "I guess you could call us *friends*…?"

"But I mean, you hang out and stuff?"

I felt like this was going somewhere and I had no idea where. But, we were certainly not sidling in the preferable direction.

We spend hours together and sometimes it leads to sex, does that count? "Well, we chat a bit in the car I guess. And, we find ourselves in the same vicinity now and then. So, we talk…and hang a little… Sort of…"

Mason nodded.

Not sure what he might be thinking, I blurted, "I mean, what

Hadley did last week…" I huffed another awkward laugh. "That was just her being a dick. She's got this theory that Roman…" *Too much information!* "Anyway, he doesn't. I can guarantee that. He didn't even want to ask me out, he was just teasing Hads. Personally, I think…" I didn't know what I thought or where my brain had been planning to lead me with that opener, so I crashed to a halt.

"Think what?" Mason asked, totally interested.

An idea popped into my head and I don't know why I ran with it. "I personally think Roman was just stirring shit for Hads. She talks enough about how she'd…hook up with him. Roman probably thought it was funny to ask me out in front of her. What he thought that was going to do, I don't know. Maybe he thinks jealousy works well on getting people to make a move or something?"

"What do you think?" he asked.

"About what? Hads and Roman?"

"No, the jealousy thing."

I shrugged again and hoped my answer wasn't going to be too pointed. "I think if someone doesn't feel the need to make a move until there's a reason to be jealous, then maybe they weren't really feeling it after all."

Mason nodded slowly. "Makes sense, I guess. What does Roman think of your theory?"

I laughed just thinking about it. "He thinks lighting a fire under someone's arse is a legitimate seduction strategy."

"You guys talk about that stuff a lot?"

I nodded, then stopped myself. "Well, you know Roman and boundaries. If it's none of his business, he just has to know about it."

"I didn't even know you guys were friends."

I breathed out heavily. "Well, we weren't really. We just both happened to be at the lake during the holidays – you know, since he moved next door and all – and we got chatting." I shrugged again. "I dunno, we get along."

Mason nodded. "Cool…"

"But, just friends!" I said quickly, thinking about what Hadley would do. "We're so just friends. God, even Celeste couldn't make Roman boyfriend material."

And, Celeste was known to try to make Gaston boyfriend material. To which Hadley informed her that "You let Gaston have his wicked way with you, then you go home to Beast." I personally wasn't so sure that even being excellent in bed was a good enough reason to go anywhere near the arsehole.

Mason shook himself like he was shaking some thought off. "Nah, it's cool. I mean, kinda weird. But honestly, you seem…"

"What?" Cue panic-mode.

"Dunno. You just seem…brighter since I got back. More…here." He ran his hand through his hair and gave a rough chuckle. "Ah, I don't know what I'm trying to say. But, if you and Roman are friends… Then cool, I guess."

Mason sure did look like it was cool. But, I felt like that might be weird behaviour for the guy who was supposed to want to ask me out. I looked up into those blue eyes and tried to figure out if it was actually cool or not.

"So…you don't care if I'm friends with Roman or not?" I hedged.

And of course, at that moment, Hadley appeared.

"Who else will I use to get into his pants?" she asked with a truly sinful grin.

I shook my head. "Oh, I don't know," I replied sarcastically. "You could not because…no."

Hadley sighed loudly. "Fine. Keep him to yourself."

"It's not about keeping him to myself," I said quickly, throwing a quick, awkward look to Mason. "I don't want him, *comprende*? It's about you not getting hurt Hads."

"Such faith you have in your friend!" Hadley cried dramatically.

"Oh, I'd say the same to him if this conversation were reversed."

Hadley held her hand up. "Fine. Bitch."

"Love you, too!" I yelled at her retreating back and she flipped me the bird.

I laughed and turned back to Mason, the semi-weirdness of the situation making my laughter die a somewhat strangled death.

"It's so not up to me to dictate who your friends are, Pipe," he said with a smile that I was pretty sure was sincere. "I'll tell you what you did miss on Saturday night, though…"

Suddenly, the mood shifted away from weird tensions and it all just felt normal again.

"What?" I asked.

"Hads and Tucker flirting."

"No!"

"Yes," he laughed.

"Proper flirting?"

His grin widened. "I don't think they realised it. But, I think there's definitely potential for something there."

I looked over to where Hadley could have been definitively snubbing Tucker on purpose. In true Tucker form, the guy didn't seem to notice. That is, if Hadley *was* snubbing him. But, my best friend wouldn't possibly be so shallow and childish. Would she?

Well yeah, probably. That was yet another thing about Hadley's flirting technique that I just didn't understand. But, I definitely wanted to know more.

"Tell me *everything*," I demanded with a smile that Mason returned.

There was a knock on my window. Without thinking why there might have been a knock on my window, I rolled my chair away from my desk, my pen hanging from my mouth. I blinked in surprised when I saw Roman crouching on the roof outside in the pouring rain. I cocked my head in question, my smile fading as I saw the dark expression on his face.

I hopped off the chair quickly and opened the window.

"What's—"

He'd climbed inside and was kissing me like the world was about to end before I knew what was happening. His hands slid up my top and he pulled me close. He was soaked and he tasted like alcohol, but that didn't stop him exuding a heat that wasn't just a physical temperature. My heart fluttered in my chest and my stomach tightened.

I pushed him away for a moment. We were both breathing hard. Roman's face was cold and there were new cuts and bruises on him, but his eyes were so full of…just everything. He moved in again and I only just got my head together to put a hand on his chest.

"Roman, what's…? Are you okay?"

231

"No," he growled, his hands tightening on me.

"And, drinking and fucking is going to help that?"

"Old habits die hard," he said, his eyes about as hard as his voice.

"I'm not judging you, Roman," I said softly and I cupped his cheek. He closed his eyes and he leant into my hand.

Suddenly, his eyes flew open and he pulled me to him again. I got entirely distracted for a moment by his kiss and gave him back as good as I got. I was halfway through taking off his shirt – and I was sure one of his buttons ripped off – when my brain stopped me.

I leant my head on his now bare chest. "Roman," I panted, "this isn't– Do you want to talk about it?"

"No."

"Okay. What do you need?"

"I need you to stop talking and kiss me." His voice was still low and rough.

So yeah, a large part of me wanted that, too. But, I wasn't sure that was going to help him. It might, but I had to check.

"Roman...how–"

"Because I need..." He stopped talking and groaned in frustration.

"Honesty, Lombardi."

"Don't make me say it, Barlow. I want to feel better, not worse."

"That makes no sense."

He groaned again and held me close, head bowed against mine. "Why do you always insist on making me sound like a nancy wanker?"

"Well, you just sound like a drunk idiot at the moment. So

232

anything's a step up at this point."

"Why do you have to make everything harder, but easier at the same time?"

"You're still not making sense."

He grunted. "*You're* the only thing that makes sense right now, Barlow. The only thing that makes me feel anything but anger. You're the only fucking thing in my life that makes anything better. And, I need to feel better. I need you, Piper."

"I'm here, Roman. I'm not going anywhere. Just, tell me what happened."

"Nothing."

"Roman," I said sternly.

He sighed as his hand ran absently up and down my arm. "Rio and I found ourselves in a…predicament."

"Are you hurt?"

"I've had worse."

"That's not what I asked.

"I'm fine."

I pulled back to look at him and I hated the sadness in his eyes. They were so vulnerable and deep and I was in serious danger of losing myself in them. I lay a hand on his cheek and I could see the desire swirling with the sadness, the need to just lose himself in something good. Whether I was actually something good, I didn't know. But, he seemed to think so, at least at that moment.

So, I didn't even think about it.

I had the power to make him feel better.

Even if it was only temporary.

And so help me, I wanted to use it.

I was sliding his shirt down his arms before my lips met his again. His arms wrapped around me and lifted me up. He pressed me into the wall and his lips trailed down my neck.

"Roman…my parents are sleeping down the hall," I panted.

"Then, you're going to have to be quiet," he growled softly and kissed me again.

I'd felt his body on numerous occasions now, but I never got sick of the feeling of it under my hands. He was lean and muscular and his skin was oddly soft. I didn't know why that was a surprise; I guessed it was just because everything else about him seemed so rough. I also never got sick of the way he twitched and almost-laughed as my hands ran over certain places because it was a little bit tickly.

Only, that night, there wasn't any almost-laughter. I ran my hand over his abs and he winced.

"Are you sure you're okay?"

He nodded. "Fine."

"Can I do–"

"Barlow?"

"Lombardi?"

"Shut up, love."

He pressed himself against me and kissed me again. I ran my hands through his wet hair and hugged him to me.

For all the light I'd seen in him lately, there was something different about him that night; darker, harder, deeper. I couldn't quite put my finger on it and something about it made me not want to look too closely at it. I wasn't sure if that was because I'd find something I didn't like or something I liked too much.

He grabbed hold of me tightly and swung us around, backing me up to the bed. He knelt on it, keeping a firm hold on me as he lay me down and followed. Before I was lying flat, he pulled away only enough to get my jumper over my head, then pulled me down the bed so my hips were more in line with his.

Roman had never been so dominating and I flushed just realising I didn't hate it. I never thought I'd be in for anything I would consider even semi-rough. But it seemed, when it came to Roman, I was in for anything. A part of me knew that was probably not healthy, but I couldn't help it; I was completely convinced that Roman could do or suggest anything and I'd feel safe with him.

His kiss was like lightning, his touch was like silk, and I felt entirely encircled in protection. It was ridiculous; Roman was in a shit and I was supposed to be making him feel better. But, he soothed every ounce of tension I didn't realise I was holding in.

As he undressed me and I returned the favour, I just stopped thinking and got swept up in the reciprocal comfort we seemed to give each other. The guy knew how to heal me and – as he lost himself in me – he seemed to heal a little too.

Chapter Nineteen
A New John Film?

Roman had got over whatever funk he'd been in by the time he'd left a little later. There had still been a tenseness to his shoulders and that muscle in his jaw twitched, but his eyes were softer as he kissed me goodbye.

A few nights later, we were babysitting Maddy for Carmen. Maddy had asked if I could come and have dinner with them and been a total sweetheart. We'd all had dinner together, played Snakes and Ladders for a while, read her a couple of books and then put her to bed…three times. But, she finally seemed to be asleep.

"What are we watching?" I asked, wriggling in next to Roman to pass the next few hours until Carmen came home.

"You right?" he laughed.

I grinned at him. "Yes. Now, what do you want to watch?"

He grabbed the remote from me. "You'll love this. I found you a new John Cusack movie."

"No!" I breathed, looking at him in awe.

He nodded with a wry smile. "Yes. I did. And Netflix finally has it. So I thought I might, just maybe, suggest we watch that."

"You're not only advocating we watch a John Cusack movie, but you looked it up for me?"

He shrugged nonchalantly and just a little awkwardly. Had he not been Roman, I might have decided I was in love with him. But since it *was* Roman, I was more interested in paying him out.

"Let's not make a big deal out of this, Barlow," he said, noticing the teasing look on my face. "If you don't want to watch it, we don't have to."

He scrolled through, heading for the horror section.

"No!" I cried, grabbing for the remote, but he pulled it out of reach and smiled down at me. Our faces were far too close together and I smiled at him. "No, let's watch that one... Please?"

"You going to beg me, Barlow?" he asked, his eyes dancing.

I gave a mock-huff. "I'll do no such thing. But, I *will* make it worth your while..." I winked at him and his eyebrow quirked as the corner of his mouth did.

"Will you now? And how might you manage that?" he asked. I ran my hand over his crotch and started undoing his jeans. "Oh, Barlow. You think you can tempt me with your body? Babe, you're good, but you're not *that* good."

I smirked at him with complete confidence and I saw a touch of concern creep into his eyes. When I slid off the couch and nestled between his legs he looked at me in question. I shook my head and put a finger to my lips. The question in his eyes burned brighter, but he nodded. I pulled his erection out of his jeans and boxers and ran my hand over it.

"Barlow..."

I put my finger to my lips again and shook my head. Something else burned in his eyes, but he nodded again and seemed to be telling me to proceed. I licked my lips slowly before I placed them over him and he gasped in a totally satisfying way.

I'd never gone down on a guy before. I wasn't sure I had any idea what I was doing, but Roman seemed to enjoy it. If his breathing and the occasional exclamation like 'fuck, Piper...' was anything to go by...

The next thing I knew, he'd picked me up and pulled me onto his lap. He was kissing me fiercely and then he was inside me; skirt and undies be damned. He held me tightly like he couldn't get me close enough. I completely understood that sentiment; I was feeling much the same way about him.

"Fuck, love. Slow down," he panted, resting his forehead to mine and holding my hips tightly so I wouldn't move.

I could feel him pulsing inside me and I smiled. "You going to cum, Lombardi?" I teased, rocking my hips.

He grunted obscenely. "You keep that up, yes."

I trailed my lips to his ear. "And, that's bad how?"

"Because it's been a while since I came before the girl, Barlow. And I'm certainly not doing that to you."

I rocked my hips again.

"Barlow, I am serious here." His tone was certainly hard.

"So, this becomes about whether little Piper Barlow can make the great Roman Lombardi lose his control?"

He scoffed, his hands running up my sides. "I think we've long-since established that as fact, Barlow. Try again."

I rolled my hips slowly and he groaned against my lips. "Tell me, Roman, has any girl managed to make you cum before you were ready?"

I knew the stories of Roman's stamina; he was said to be able to control himself to the point he could get you off as many times as he wanted before he let go. I can't say I'd seen all that much evidence of it, but I was never dissatisfied.

He breathed heavily. "You want the company line or the truth,

Barlow?"

"What do you think, Lombardi?"

He thrust into me deeply, only once, and I wanted more. "Not in a long time. But, this is far from the first time you've been damn close…"

When we looked into each other's eyes, there was something almost vulnerable in his and I stopped for a moment.

"Roman?"

"Piper?"

We were so close to a moment. But, we didn't do moments. I opened my mouth, but didn't really know what I thought I wanted to say. So, I smirked at him and rolled my hips again. His smile went from soft and questioning to rueful.

"You trying to prove something?" he asked.

"Maybe," I said with a smile.

"Babe, you've already come top of everything I keep score of. You've got nothing left to prove. I–" He frowned. "Damn it, not again. Condom," he said in answer to my questioning look.

I moved against him. "You make a habit of forgetting it, Lombardi?"

"Only that once with you…" He frowned again. "Twice now."

"Then, what's the problem?" I asked, undulating my hips. I could have stopped us, but I was happy to take responsibility this time. "Pill, remember?"

He grinned as his hand reached between us. He pressed his thumb against my clit as he started thrusting again. "You're going to kill me, Barlow."

"No, Lombardi. I'm just going to rock your world."

His grin widened before he kissed me. Heat and passion mingled as the pleasure mounted. We came hard together, my name on his lips and his on mine.

"Tell me," he panted, me still on top of him. "Was that my influence, or John's?"

I laughed and batted him as I slid off his lap to standing.

"That, love, is not an answer," he chuckled.

I smirked at him. "It's not, is it?"

We cleaned ourselves up and settled in to watch the movie.

"Oh, fuck! Perfect John's the bad guy!" Roman hissed part way in as he squeezed my shoulders and I swatted him.

It was a weird film and was probably one of the easiest acting gigs John had taken thus far – she says like she has any idea about acting! By the end of it, all I could do was blink in confusion.

"What did you think?" Roman asked me, the arm around my shoulder stretching out.

I was still blinking.

"Piper?"

"I'm not convinced that was worth my first blow job…" I muttered to myself.

Roman snorted. "Well if it makes you feel any better, love, no one was going to think it was your first time."

I stared at him open mouthed. "I'm not sure that's a compliment, Lombardi."

"No, me either."

We looked at each other for a second, then both burst into laughter.

I let my heart flutter happily as I looked at him. I'd long stopped reminding myself we were just friends. Because, that was all we were. And quite honestly, I didn't need to put a label on what we were because whatever it was, it was perfect the way it was.

Roman had snuck me out of his house and into mine at around four in the morning, which hadn't given me a lot of sleep before I was supposed to meet Hadley and Celeste at *Lacey's* at eleven and look somewhat respectable.

Hadley had a whole day of shopping planned – because we had so many options! – and Celeste and I were always told that required plenty of prior caffeinating. Plus, the boys had their out of school sports on Sunday mornings and we usually quite enjoyed having a bit of a perve as they went by.

But that Sunday, I was just sleep deprived and not interested in perving on the boys as I dropped into the seat at our usual Sunday morning seat outside *Lacey's*.

"There she is. On time, as usual," Hadley scoffed with a smile.

"Yeah, hi," I breathed.

"So, how was your *boring* night in?" Hadley asked, giving me a very unimpressed glare.

I nodded. "Fine. Found a new John movie–"

"I can't 'til next weekend." Hadley got her phone out and started scrolling through it.

I blinked for a moment, then realised she meant the same thing she always did and it was just me who wasn't up with anything just then. "Right! No. I don't think you'd like it."

Hadley's hand dropped to the table and her phone with it. "What?"

"You mean we don't have to watch this one?" Celeste asked in mock-awe.

I looked at them both. "Firstly, no. It was…weird. Secondly,

241

does it actually feel like I *make* you watch his movies?"

Celeste shrugged. "No more than Hads makes us go shopping. You know, it's something we do together."

I nodded. "Okay, great. Sure."

I wasn't sure if that was a good thing or not, given I wasn't enamoured by Hadley dragging me around the shops. Although, I did like spending time with my girls.

"Besides, it's not like we weren't at home either," Celeste added, throwing me a smile.

"Yes, but *my* night wasn't boring," Hadley said.

"Uh huh. Remind the class what you did again?" I asked.

Hadley shifted in her seat. "I at least watched a movie from this century."

I spluttered a laugh as I looked at the menu. "Some of John's movies are from this century! And I watch other movies, too."

"Sure, you do," Hadley said disbelievingly. "Remind us again, what was the last movie you watched without your perfect John?"

"*Drive Me Crazy*."

"Not a Rom-Com."

I thought back. "*The Lodgers*."

"You what?" Celeste asked.

I shrugged. "It's a horror."

There was silence and I looked up again.

"What?" I asked.

"Horror?" Hadley asked, her eyebrows drawing together.

I nodded. "Yeah. That okay?"

Celeste and Hadley shared a look then both leant towards me.

"Babes, *Mason* wouldn't make you watch horror movies…" Hadley said slowly, like it was a defence in and of itself, and I knew to what she was referring.

I rolled my eyes. "Roman and I are just friends. Just. Friends. Or, do you two always have hot sex when you watch a movie together?"

I was going to ignore the part where Roman and I were known to have hot sex when we watched movies together.

"Well, I know horror always puts me in the mood," Hadley said, matter-of-fact but also completely tongue-in-cheek.

"What?" Celeste and I laughed.

Hadley shrugged. "I dunno, something about the blood. Reminds me of being a woman."

I snorted in a completely undignified manner and all three of us dissolved into giggles.

Talk shifted and moved between topics ranging from periods to school to clothes to makeup to food, littered with talk about boys, uni in Melbourne or Sydney, too many waffles, and a steady stream of caffeine.

So when Mason walked past and we realised it was something like almost two, it was less surprising that Mason was clean and wearing normal clothes as opposed to his sport uniform.

"Mason! Mason!" Hadley yelled through her most recent giggle fit.

He turned and found us, throwing a huge smile and wave our way. "Hey!"

"Come join!" Celeste said and I nudged her under the table.

"Ow," Hadley said pointedly and nudged me back as Mason walked over.

"What are you girls up to?"

"Oh, just girl time. You know how it is," Hadley said pleasantly.

Mason's eye shone. "Oh, sure. Yeah, we have girl time all the time. Face masks are important, you know. And, Simon does a great pedicure."

We all laughed.

"Cute. We can do girl time without the face masks and the sexy pillow fights, thank you." Hadley shook a finger at him. "We watched sport once."

"Oh, the cliché, Hads," I snorted as I shook my head in my hands.

"Did you *intend* to watch sport?" Mason asked as he did a piss-poor job of hiding his smile.

"At first, no," Celeste admitted. "But, then we realised how hot they were and decided we could suffer through watching half-naked men for a little while."

"Oh, and it gets better," I muttered and Mason laughed.

"What were you watching with half-naked men?"

"Some kind of wrestling?" Celeste guessed, totally clueless.

"I think it was the gymnastics at the last Olympics," I offered. "So, not quite half-naked–"

"But, gorgeous." I'm not sure if Hadley's words counted as a purr, a breath, or an obscene grunt to be honest.

Mason pressed his lips together as he nodded.

"Don't you dare laugh," I said, barely containing it myself.

He shook his head. "No, I wouldn't dare," he spluttered.

"Why don't you sit down and tell us what real sport is, then?" I asked him, pushing the last chair towards him with my foot.

He dropped into the chair and slid into the conversation seamlessly. Nothing was different than it had been a few minutes before just because he was sitting there. It was simple and easy. I mean, I still had to keep a lock on my filter and think about what I said before I said it. But I actually managed some half decent conversation with Mason, curtesy mainly of Hadley and Celeste and their ability to just constantly talk.

Sure it might have annoyed me sometimes and made me feel more claustrophobic than I already was in my own skin, but I actually admired that about them most days. I certainly considered it a flaw that I couldn't easily make conversation with people when it was necessary, let alone when I wanted to.

"…and then… And, then, Piper sent him an email!" Hadley giggled.

I shook my head. "Yeah, it was a bit sad."

"A *bit* sad? Major sad. Did we actually think we were going to make it onto *Big Time Rush*?" she asked as Celeste giggled and I avoided looking at Mason.

I shrugged noncommittally. "No, I s'pose not."

I looked up and saw Roman across the road with Rio and Steve. Rio was the first one to see me and he gave me a curt nod and salute with his cigarette. I saw him mouth something and Roman turned around.

But, whatever humour Rio's words had put on Roman's face was gone as he looked at me. I waved and he gave me an even more curt nod than Rio had. I watched Rio smirk and elbow Roman as he said something. Roman replied to him tersely, threw me a stony look, and turned around.

Hadley's foot connected with my shin and I jumped.

"What?" I asked, taking my eyes off Roman and turning to her.

"I asked what was up his arse."

I shrugged. "Who knows? Time of the month, probably," I muttered.

"What?" Celeste asked, completely confused.

"You mean he's regular or…?" Hadley petered off.

"Regular. Sure."

"Why don't you go see what's up?" Mason asked.

I shook my head. "I'm sure he's fine."

"If it was Hads or Celeste, would you check on them?"

I looked at Mason and sighed. "Yes."

"Good. Then, go."

"I'll see you guys later," I grumbled with a wave and jogged across the street. "Roman!"

He looked at me just long enough for me to know he'd heard me and was purposefully ignoring me.

"You and your lady had a falling out, Lombardi?" Rio teased.

"Always a pleasure, Rio." I smiled, sardonically.

He threw me a wink. As usual, he seemed to be looking at me like he didn't trust me, but found me amusing all at the same time. "Best see what she wants, mate. You can catch us up."

Steve jutted his chin towards me in goodbye and Rio gave me another smoky salute before they dropped their boards and skated off.

"Lombardi!" I warned as he dropped his board.

"What?" he spat.

"Well, aren't you pleasant today?"

"How's your *girls'* day going?"

"Fine. We never actually got to the shopping part, but that's fine by me."

"Carter one of the girls now? You going to braid each other's hair and tell each other secrets."

"Have I ever braided your hair?"

His anger fell as he looked at me in complete confusion. "What?"

"You're the only person I've told any secrets to lately. Have I

246

been braiding your hair? What makes you think I'd possibly be into braiding while I'm baring my soul?"

His confusion vanished and that hard anger was back. "I've got to go. You should get back to Carter."

"Roman."

"Piper?"

He looked me over, the epitome of nonchalance and arrogant defiance. I frowned at him.

"Do you want to talk about it?"

"Talk about what?"

"This funk."

He shrugged. "Just a funk. Nothing to talk about." His eyes slid behind me and then back to his board.

"Are you sure? Can I do anything?"

"Nah. I'll be peachy."

I hadn't seen him be just this dark, blustery Roman in a while and I wondered why he was making a reappearance now. Maybe there'd been more repercussions than I'd seen for his fight earlier in the week? The bruises were still fading even if he'd seemed more relaxed until now.

He shrugged. "It's just a funk. We get funky. Carter's waiting on you."

"Well, he can wait. I'm waiting on you to talk to me. You were fine this morning. Did something happen?"

His eyes slid away again and when they found my face he was giving me his best smirk. "You know me, Barlow. Like clockwork. Haven't had a good brood in a while. Probably shouldn't go ruining my image and whatnot."

"Uh huh. Okay. Well, when you've decided you don't want to be an arsehole anymore, we can not talk about it if you want?"

247

"I said I'm fucking fine, Barlow! Look, I've gotta go. I'll see you in the morning."

He huffed a breath, jumped onto his board and took off after Rio and Steve. I shook my head, wishing there was some way I could read his mind like he seemed to be able to read mine.

With a sigh, I headed back over to Hadley, Celeste and Mason. Thankfully, they were busy arguing about whether Zac Efron or Ezra Miller was more attractive.

"Piper?" Mason asked as I pulled my seat out. "Zac or Ezra?"

I smiled, more than happy to take my mind off Roman's funk. "That's a hard one."

Chapter Twenty
Two Bruises, One Date and Zero Sleep.

"I've noticed Roman's been going to school a lot more lately," Mum called from the dining table where she was on her laptop.

Sure, Roman found himself on the school premises a lot more lately. I wasn't sure that totally classified as going to school, though.

I grinned as I finished cutting the carrots, remembering the rendition of 'Bleeding Love' he'd done on the way home that afternoon. Whatever had been bugging him on Sunday, he'd seemed okay again since Monday morning. Although, he'd seemed tired and his car hadn't been in the driveway next door the last couple of nights.

"Is there a question you wanted to ask in that statement, Mum?"

"I just wondered what kind of time you two were spending together?" she answered with a smile in her voice.

"The friendly kind," I told her as I started peeling the potatoes. "That's all."

"That's all?"

Why did we have to keep going through this? "Yes, Mum. Roman and I are just friends. Nothing more."

"You spend a lot of time with a guy you're *just friends* with."

"I spend a lot of time with Hadley, too. Should I be dating her?"

"If you wanted to, yes."

I smiled. "Right. Well I don't want to date Roman, Mum. But, thanks."

"How about Hadley?"

I snorted, "No. Thanks. I'm not really her type."

I heard Mum laugh. "All right. Well, as long as Roman's not stringing you along or going to hurt you."

"Mum, I know Roman *far* too well. There is no stringing and no hurting going on, I assure you. I expect nothing from him." *Nothing than I've already found myself with.*

"Well, you've certainly had a good influence on him, honey."

"You make it sound like I'm working on a charity case."

Mum chuckled. "Carmen said he's so much better. He's happier, he's out less, he drinks less, he's a love with Maddy."

"It sounds like you two talk more than I'd like."

"Well, that's quite possible."

"Hang on," I said, putting my potato down for a second. "How much do you actually talk about Roman with her?"

"A fair amount, I suppose."

"And about Roman and me?"

"Less."

"But, Carmen *does* talk about Roman and me with you?"

She made an affirmative noise. "And, she says every improvement has been since you two started hanging out."

I smiled to myself, knowing any attempt to tell her there was nothing to talk about would give her more reason to think there was something to talk about.

"Well, isn't that nice. But, I doubt it's got anything to do with me, Mum. Roman's not that bad really, he's just a little lost…"

"Well, that was the impression I'd had for years. But, Carmen seems to think you found him, hon."

"Sure, I did," I replied sarcastically, throwing the vegetables in the slowcooker pot with the meat so it was ready to turn on the next morning. Although, that explained why Mum had been so chilled about Roman and I hanging out. "What are you doing in there anyway?"

"Looking on the real estate website."

A chill entered my veins, but I acted nonchalant; it might not be what I thought it was. "Really?"

"Yep. I thought I'd see what sort of places there were for next year."

"I'll have a look later, okay?"

Mum was silent for a while, just the occasional typing or mouse click. I was just starting to hope she'd moved on to bigger and better things when I heard her make a little triumphant noise.

"Oh, here's a nice little place. Central. Looks clean." A pause. "Honey?" Mum finally called when it was obvious I wasn't going to reply.

I mentally sighed, so over everything. I had Hadley in one ear nattering about applying to Melbourne and Sydney universities as well as Adelaide because, in her words, "if we're moving away, anyway…" I had Mum in my other trying to get me to look at places to live when I didn't even know what uni I was going to get into. If any!

"Piper?" Mum called.

I finished washing my hands in the kitchen sink and leant on the bench, "Yeah, I… I heard you. Can we not–?"

"Sweetie, they're designed for students! And, you want to get somewhere nice. The sooner, the better!"

My heart raced, my breathing was shallow and my head was

just raucous static noise. I looked out the back window and could almost see the lake. I could feel the calm that that elicited in me at the edge of myself as though it were waves lapping the shore. I threw a look back to where Mum was still talking, not really paying me and my lack of attention much mind at all. Back out the window. Back to Mum. Back out the window.

I was out the back door while Mum was still saying something about two bedrooms. I was averse to running at the best of times – I was averse to exercise in general, which was humorous given how often I felt the urge to run – but I needed to leave my problems behind. So, I ran. I ran down to the lake, the closest thing I had that could bring me comfort.

It was dark, but I didn't really notice.

My leg hit something, but the sting didn't slow me down and I hoped I wasn't going to regret that later. A branch caught my arm as I rushed past, moving quite spectacularly for me and my usual level of fitness or lack thereof.

I broke free from the last few trees and over the rise, coming to a sudden stop just shy of the water, and took a deep breath as I fought to keep my balance. My heart pounded and it wasn't just from exertion. Tears were in my eyes, but it wasn't just from smacking into wayward tree branches.

I was so unprepared for the next year and I really didn't want to think about it. I knew I couldn't really put the whole thing off for all that much longer. But for now, I was going to keep avoiding it.

I started pacing, trying to calm the noisy static in my head, and trying to steady my racing heart and my shallow breath. But, my mind whirred; the stress of the next year pushed up incessantly against the static wall in my mind, making the panic ebb and flow on the edges of my soul. I needed distracting. I needed something to take my mind off it completely.

I was pulling my phone out and it was to my ear before I noticed what I was doing. I didn't even know whose number I'd called until I heard the familiar voice yelling over loud music.

"Yeah?" He sounded like he'd been drinking and there were the familiar sounds of a party in the background.

"Roman…"

"Piper?" he yelled, sounding like he was sobering up a little.

"I… Uh, hi…"

"Babe, you okay?" His voice alone soothed my racing heart a little and the concern made me feel more than just the weird numbness that was threatening to overwhelm me.

"I… No? I don't know. Sorry, you're busy. I'll talk to you later."

"No apolo–"

"Fuckin' let's go, Lombardi!" someone called to him.

"Give me a minute," Roman yelled back.

"Dude! Come on!" someone else said.

"Fucking wait!" Roman snapped. The sounds of the party faded and I heard a door close. "What's up?"

"I don't know. Mum was just… And, then I…" I took a deep breath, trying to keep the tears at bay.

"Where are you?"

"It's fine. I'll talk to you later. I didn't mean to get in the way."

"Piper, you could never get in the way. Where are you? I'm coming to you."

"You're busy."

"I'm never busy for you, you know that."

"Roman, I don't want you driving if you've been drinking."

"Fuck that. I'm fine. You need me? I'll be there."

"You're not driving now. Your safety is priority, Roman." My voice was becoming more forceful with the concern he was going to crash or get picked up and it would be all my fault.

"No. You are my priority, Piper." His voice was hard and I recognised the beeping sound of his ute unlocking. "Now, you tell me where you are or you're going to regret it."

"How will I regret it if you can't find me?" I asked, a little playfully.

"Piper…" His voice was a warning, but he sounded humorously exasperated with me.

"I'm at the lake."

"I'll be there in twenty minutes."

I was going to argue, but he'd hung up.

The time passed with me worrying more that he was never going to make it than worrying about the next year. So, there was one slight plus about the whole situation at least. I was pacing when lights flashed over me, were suddenly cut and he slammed the door shut.

"Piper!" he yelled, moving towards me purposefully.

I turned to face him and could do nothing more than shake my head. He wrapped me in his arms and held me tightly. Nothing had ever been more comforting than his arms felt at that moment. I knew he shouldn't have driven after drinking – and I planned to berate him fully later – but, just then, I was so grateful he was there.

"I didn't mean to interrupt your party," I mumbled into his jacket.

"You didn't interrupt anything. I was out, but something more important came up."

I pulled away from him quickly. "Crap! Is Maddy okay?" I asked. A thousand things tore through my head, but all too fast for me to catch.

He chuckled and kissed my hair. "You, you idiot. You're the something more important."

I let out a huge breath and shook my head. "No. Not if Maddy needed you."

Roman let out a tremendously exasperated sigh and held me at arm's length. "Honestly, Barlow – if you'll allow me to indulge in some nancy wank for a moment – you are the most important thing in my world, all right? You need me, I'm here. It's just not a fucking negotiation, love."

I felt like a complete tool for putting him out and for putting him in a position where he felt like he had to get all sincere on me. "I'll concede only so you don't have to be all wanky and emotional anymore, okay?"

He grinned. "Okay. Thank you. Now, did you want to talk about what's up, or are we going to sit here and say nothing for a while?"

I shrugged. "I just… Can we sit?"

Without hesitation, he dropped to the ground and held out his arms. "Come on, then."

I gave him a thankful smile and sat myself between his legs. I leant back against him and he put his arms around me. He kissed the side of my head and leant his chin on my shoulder.

"Where were you?" I asked, having nothing else to say to him. I didn't really care where he was, I was just curious; he might have gone out less these days, but going to a party on a Tuesday wasn't unheard of for him.

I felt him shrug. "At a mate's. He found himself with a bit of a gathering and invited me over."

"You could have stayed," I said without thinking.

He huffed a laugh. "No. We've been through this."

I nodded. "Right, my bad."

"You want to talk about it?"

"I have no idea where to start," I admitted.

"That's okay," he said, rubbing my arm where it lay over my stomach. "Just say whatever you want."

"What if I want to say nothing? What if I want to tell you I'm in love with you? What if I want to say I feel like walking into that water and never coming out?"

He squeezed me tighter. "You can say everything. You can say nothing at all. You know that."

I leant my head back against him and sighed. "I'm just so over it. Why can't we just sit here in this moment forever?"

Roman kissed my shoulder. "Well we're certainly not in any hurry to go anywhere, are we?"

"We can't stay here forever."

"Maybe not. But, we can stay here as long as you like."

"We have to go to school tomorrow."

"Do we?"

I smiled. "Well, I do."

"But, you won't have to deal with next year if you don't pass this year," he teased, hugging me close and dipping his nose in my neck.

I giggled. "I am successfully avoiding my current issues, thank you. I don't need to add to them."

"Can I do anything?" he asked me, his nose running up my neck and sending goose bumps across my arms.

"Just be you."

"Always, Barlow." He rubbed my arm again, then stopped when I jumped at an unexpected sting. "What have you done to yourself?" he asked.

I looked down as saw a dark splotch on my arm. "Ah. I had a battle with a tree and apparently I lost." I stuck my leg out and saw a dark splotch on my shin as well.

Roman sighed and hugged me close. "What the hell am I going to do with you? Honestly. Babe, I can't leave you alone for five minutes."

"I guess you'll have to stay by my side forever."

"I think I could manage that," he said so softly I almost missed it. It was the sort of thing I shouldn't answer because then he could pretend he hadn't said anything.

We sat in silence for a while.

"Lombardi?"

"Barlow?"

"Thanks."

"For what, love?"

"For being here for me."

He scoffed. "The day I'm not here for you, Piper, you can look for my body in the morgue."

"That's rather morbid," I chuckled.

I felt him shrug again. "What can I say, Barlow? Only death will part me from you."

"That's straying into romantic territory there, Lombardi," I warned.

"Well, I guess you can call me a romantic, then."

I snorted. "I don't think anyone would be stupid enough to call you that."

"I might be," he answered, completely seriously for a second.

But, then he tickled me and that totally distracted me from his words.

It was starting to feel like for every step closer I got to Roman, Mason was there taking a step closer as well.

And I mean that was the goal, wasn't it? Sweet, kind, good, friend-and-family-approved,   actually-wanted-a-relationship Mason was the goal, wasn't it?

It just always seemed weirdly coincidental and made things with Roman feel a little bit weird. After the closeness of that night on the lakeshore, Mason was waiting for me at my locker first thing on Wednesday morning. I was tired and grumpy from a lack of sleep, I had bruises on my arm and leg, and the parents had given me a talking to for leaving and not coming back the night before.

In their defence, it was a half-hearted talking to; they'd expected I'd not gone far and they'd expected I'd been safe. When they'd heard I'd been with Roman at the lake, they didn't bat an eyelid, just told me to let them know next time and asked if I needed a ride to school. But, Roman had been waiting at his ute for me and I told them I'd be fine. Mum had turned the slowcooker on, kissed my head, and swanned out of the house cooing a goodbye to Roman.

So, I was in a mood. It wasn't a particularly foul mood, I was just irritable and stressed. So Roman walked me to my locker, pausing when we saw Mason.

"What does he want?" I hissed to Roman, sub-consciously leaning against him as though he needed to keep me safe from something.

I felt Roman's hand against my back lightly. "I don't know, Barlow," he answered sarcastically. "I imagine the same thing he's wanted for the last couple of months. Maybe now he's finally sacked up."

"I am so not in the mood for this today," I muttered and Roman nudged me forward.

"Barlow, you've been waiting for him to ask you out for months. You want to tell him now is inconvenient and ask if he can call back later?"

I wanted to say that yes I did want to tell Mason all that. I wanted to say that, if it had been Roman, I could have done that easily and it would have made no difference to him; Roman would have understood and given me the space I needed. But, Mason wasn't Roman. I wanted to say a damned lot of things, but we were too close to my locker now and Mason might have heard.

Mason eyed Roman warily. "Morning," he said slowly.

Roman nudged me in the back.

"Morning," I said quickly, trying to smile.

"I'll see you back at the car, Barlow," Roman said softly.

For some reason, I really didn't want him to go. But, I had to be a big girl and face my problems. A nice Roman-shaped safety blanket would have made it all better, but we don't always get what we want now do we?

So, I nodded and started unlocking the padlock on my locker. "Yep, I'll see you later."

"Carter."

"Lombardi."

It felt like all the air around me chilled when Roman stepped away. But, that was completely ridiculous and I told myself it was completely ridiculous. I was so busy telling myself that it was completely ridiculous that I almost missed Mason's next words.

"...you wanted to go out with me sometime?" he was asking

and I turned to look at him quickly.

"Uh…" *Come on brain, catch up.* "Yes, sure." I broke into the widest, most sincere smile I owned and hoped it would cover my terribly hesitant answer.

"Don't feel you have to," he chuckled self-consciously.

"No, no. I'd love to," I answered quickly. "Sorry. I'm not with it today. I slept terribly last night. Just ask Roman."

"Ask him how you slept?" he asked slowly.

I blanched; *well, he would know.* I laughed awkwardly. "Uh, no. How not with it I am. I basically ignored him the whole way to school."

Mason smiled, but it didn't quite reach his eyes. "Well, I was thinking we could go to a movie and get something to eat. You know," *oh, great, he was asking me on a group outing again*, "just us."

My heart stuttered and I wasn't sure if it was in a good way or a bad way. "Yes," I squeaked. "Yes. That would be great."

Yet again, I sounded more insincere the more sincere I tried to sound. I mentally rolled my eyes and wanted to slap myself.

Mason's smile finally started to reach his eyes and they dropped to the floor as he shuffled a little awkwardly. I was starkly reminded that Roman would never have shuffled awkwardly after he asked a girl out. Not that Roman would ever ask a girl out.

"Great. Okay. So, uh… It's a date."

I smiled and looked around the corridor. "It is."

Mason and I looked at each other at the same time and smiled. This time, it fully reached those gorgeous blue eyes and he looked a crazy amount of happy. I couldn't believe it was all because I'd agreed to go out with him. Maybe it wasn't. That made more sense; why would anyone look that happy just because I'd agreed to go out with them?

Mason nodded, looking like I'd made his day. "Great," he repeated. "Well, we'll fix a time and that later, yeah?"

I nodded as well. "Yeah, sounds good."

"Sweet." He looked at me, nodded once more, and strutted off.

I wasn't sure how to feel. I wasn't sure how I was supposed to feel.

Were we dating now? Or, were we one of those couples who went out on a few dates before they decided they were officially dating? Why didn't I know? Why was I not on the same wavelength as my guy? Everyone else just seemed to know these things. Why didn't I know?

I got my books ready in a bit of a daze and wandered to first lesson to find Hadley. I dropped down into my chair beside her and only paid attention when she nudged me.

"What?" I jumped.

"What happened? Roman whip it out on the way to school?" Hadley chuckled, sliding a look over to said resident underachiever who apparently had decided to go to class that day.

I choked on an inconveniently placed glob of spit and Hadley smacked me on the back as I gathered my composure. "No," I wheezed. "No, Mason just asked me out."

Hadley squealed so high that it was almost something only dogs could hear. I winced and hit her as everyone who was already in the classroom turned and looked at her with interest. Roman looked at us a little longer before Rio distracted him again.

"Oh. My. God. Finally!" Hadley breathed. "Tell me everything!"

I blinked. "I just did…"

Hadley sighed like I was a little bit of an idiot. "No. What did he say? Where are you going? Details, bitch! Come on!"

I blinked some more. "Uh. Well, he asked if I wanted to go out with him sometime. A movie and food. That was… That was it. What does it mean?" I hissed, panic gripping me.

Hadley frowned like she thought I'd been replaced with an alien. "What do you mean, what does it mean?"

"Well, are we dating? What does it mean?"

Hadley chuckled. "It means you get to say no to Roman more easily."

"I don't need to say no to Roman, Hads," I huffed. And, look, it wasn't entirely a lie. I didn't need to say no to Roman because he never asked for anything I wasn't willing to give him; he just always knew what I wanted and what I needed and when. "But, I mean… Am I his girlfriend? How does this work?"

"You won't have to catch the bus, if that's what you're worried about. Everyone knows Piper Barlow is too sweet and innocent to hook up with the brooding bad boy. Mind you, you're wasting a *very* decent opportunity there."

I frowned at her. "Hads, I'm serious. How does this all work? What do I do? What does he expect?"

The teacher walked in and Hadley just looked at me like I was a foreign breed as she laughed, shook her head and got ready for the lesson.

But, I was panicking; I had no answers to my questions and no idea where I was supposed to sit with Mason. So, I barely paid attention through the whole of class. I made about half a page – if that – of useless, illegible notes while my mind wandered around in ever shrinking circles.

By the end of class, Hadley had to hit me to get me to pack up my stuff and stand up. I followed her vaguely out of the classroom and through the rest of the day in a slightly embarrassing blur. Hadley was constantly elbowing me to get me to pay attention and I was constantly apologising to people and telling them how badly I'd slept.

So, when I heard my name and an arm pulled me to face them at Lunch, my automatic reaction was, "Sorry. Didn't sleep well last night. Bit out of it."

I vaguely registered narrowed eyebrows. "Yeah, I remember. I was there. What's with the apology? What's the matter? You've looked out of it all day."

I blinked and focussed on the comforting image of Roman's face; even defiant, he was a comfort. I shook my head and looked around, feeling that weird antsy feeling I hadn't had in a long time. "I don't know."

"What did he do?" Roman looked up quickly and my focus was drawn back by the movement. He was looking around the oval, scowling a fury.

"No. He didn't…" I sighed. "He asked me out."

Roman's head snapped back to me so quickly I thought *I* got whiplash. "What?" His voice was dead cold.

I was surprised by his reaction and it sent an uncomfortable chill through me. "Mason asked me out."

"Another group outing, then?" Was that a hint of hope amid the condescending mockery in Roman's voice? Surely not.

I looked down and didn't answer until he'd tipped my chin back up to face him, something very akin to panic in his eyes even though the rest of his face was stony. I knew I had to be imagining it, but something about it called to me. But, I either refused to understand what it meant or I just didn't understand it.

"Uh, no. Movie. Food. Just him and me."

Roman snatched his hand back as though I'd stung it, took a noticeable step backwards and cleared his throat. "Right, well. About time, too. Fucker should have manned up weeks ago." He ran a hand through his hair as his other hand dug around in his blazer pocket in that familiar motion that was him looking for his cigarette packet.

He pulled one out and lit it. For some reason, I looked around to check if any teachers were around to see. But, they were rarely on the oval and they even more rarely tried to tell Roman off for smoking anymore. I'd started to think that, as long as he showed up and didn't cause a ruckus, they were happy to leave him be. So I didn't know why I did then, because I'd never worried about it before.

"I… Uh…" I cleared my throat, not sure why it was suddenly so awkward. "So, I um have no idea what it means, of course. And Hads is being no help, naturally. But, well… Yay. A date!" I don't know how sincere I sounded to him. To me, I sounded like I was heading for an execution or something.

Which wasn't fair and I didn't know why I was reacting like that.

I liked Mason, a lot. He was nice and kind and hot, he was funny and smart and good at sport. There was no reason not to be totally ecstatic that he'd finally asked me out. It meant no more waiting, it meant no more wondering. I wanted to go out with him…

Didn't I?

"Piper," Roman snapped and I looked at him. "I get that the fantasy of your date with Carter is totally dreamy, but I asked if you needed a ride home."

My skin crawled at his tone, but I wasn't offended by it. It wasn't the first time he'd snapped at me and it wouldn't be the last;

I wasn't going to judge or blame him for whatever had put him in a bad mood.

"I wasn't daydreaming about my date, thank you," I snapped back, surprising myself. "I just don't know where this leaves me. I don't do this whole dating thing well, all right?"

Roman blew out a stream of smoke, frowning. "How can you be bad at it? You get asked out, you go on a date, you hook up. It's really not that hard, Barlow."

I frowned right back at him. "It is, actually. Are we dating now? Girlfriend-boyfriend? Are we one of those couples that just go on some dates? What do I do?"

"Well, *we're* nothing," Roman answered smoothly and I felt kicked in the gut. "Seriously, Barlow, you worry about everything."

"We're nothing?" I repeated, that empty feeling creeping in.

Roman shrugged. "We're nothing more than what we are."

"What?"

"I'm not seeing the problem here. We're nothing and Carter's your John Cusack."

I blinked. "But, how do I know?"

"That he's your John Cusack? Haven't you been telling me for weeks?"

"No. What we're doing! Is it just a date? It is *dating*? How am I supposed to know? Everyone else seems to know, but I don't know!" My brain was moving too fast but too slowly at the same time and I had trouble working out what I was saying and what he was saying.

His eyes softened, but his tone and his mouth were still hard. "Well, do you know what we are?"

"You just told me we were nothing."

He rolled his eyes. "When I'm not being a dick, do you know what we are?"

I nodded. "Of course I do."

"How?"

I shrugged. "I don't know. I just do."

"Exactly. You have no trouble knowing what we are. Look at it this way, you look at Carter and you apply the same logic. Right?"

I blinked. "How? I'm trying. But, I don't see it."

He flicked his cigarette butt away, his eyes cold now. "Well seems to me, Barlow, that's not my problem. You let me know if you work it out, huh?" he asked shortly.

I bristled. "You can be in a shit all you want, but you don't need to take it out on me."

He shrugged. "I'm not taking anything out on you, Barlow. Now, you need a ride this afternoon or not?"

I frowned at him. "You know what, Lombardi? Don't worry about it."

"Your precious Carter going to drive you home?" he asked, looking genuinely surprised.

"No."

"What? You walking?" he scoffed.

"Anything is preferable right now to being stuck with you being a dick," I snapped.

His face broke into surprise for a moment, then shut down blank. "Fine. Have a nice life."

"Thanks, I will."

I turned on my heel and headed for the library, not having the energy to talk to anyone after that weird encounter.

I was supposed to feel happy, wasn't I? Excited that the guy I liked had asked me out, that we were going on a proper date?

Hadley was certainly excited. I'd thought Roman would… I don't know.

We talked about everything. We shared everything. I'd thought, if Hadley wasn't going to help me work out what the hell Mason and I were doing, then Roman and his vast store of hookup knowledge would have some idea. Sure, the guy didn't date, but it wasn't for lack of knowing how – how else could he avoid it so well?

But, no. He'd decided to be in a mood when I really needed him.

Chapter Twenty One
Roman is <u>NOT</u> Jealous of Mason.

Roman still waited for me at his ute in his driveway every morning and in the carpark every afternoon. But, we barely spoke. The air around us had that sizzle of tension, but it wasn't the good kind. Roman scowled and smoked, but any time he touched me it was soft.

Things with Mason were likewise going swimmingly.

I had no idea what I was doing. I tried – as Roman had suggested – putting the same logic I used to understand Roman and me into understanding Mason and me. But, I couldn't work it out.

Around Mason, I was just a mess. I giggled too much. I blushed too much. I got awkward – and not in a cute way. I actually snorted quite disastrously on multiple occasions while trying to laugh in a way that showed him I was interested.

All it got me was a weird look from Hadley and an awkward smile from Mason like maybe he was rethinking dating me.

So, by Friday – as Hadley and I wandered to the oval – I was already extremely uncomfortable when she brought up the whole uni thing again. Somehow though, I managed to keep *some* composure.

"All I'm saying is that distance could be good. You know, FREEDOM!" Hadley shouted in her best Mel-Gibson-Scottish accent as she flung her arms in the air and I was worried she was about to bare her arse. So yeah, maybe we'd watched *Braveheart* one too many times…

I nodded. "Okay. But, Sydney and Melbourne are so expensive to live in, Hads."

"But, the shopping, babes!"

"But, the lack of money, babes!"

She shrugged. "Mum and Dad said they'd pay for me to go wherever I want."

I rolled my eyes. It wasn't like my parents weren't keen to help me out either. But, that was hardly the point. And, if I wasn't going to tell her the real reason I didn't want to go to Melbourne or Sydney, then I was going to have to come up with some damned good arguments.

"Adelaide is still hours away from the parents. Is that not enough?"

"Hours by car, babes. By. Car. The parents could still drop in unannounced. What if I'm riding some handsome man on our couch and my Mum walks in?"

I snorted despite the rate at which my heart was beating. "Okay, that is one visual I did not need. Besides, two things wrong with that. Firstly, I'm going to need serious prior warning if you're going to be doing guys on our couch. And, maybe a large store of plastic wrap. And secondly, our parents are more than capable of not telling us that they're getting on a plane if they really wanted."

She sighed. "But, plastic gets so hot and sticky. Plus, the way it squeaks? Babes, it's just not sexy. Unless he's into the donkey thing."

I broke into a huge laugh completely unintentionally. "That? That is what you take away from that?"

269

Hadley and I pulled up short as something went whizzing past our faces. But, it was just a football a bunch of the other guys in our year were throwing around. As I looked around at who was playing, my eyes fell on Roman across the oval.

He was with Steve, Rio and Jake as usual. The four of them looking like some poster for juvenile delinquency. Which wasn't fair, and I knew it. Roman wasn't really a delinquent. Well, I mean... Yes, he was. In so many respects, he was. But, that was so not *all* he was. And, I'd bet that wasn't all Rio, Steve and Jake were either when you actually got to know them.

"Seriously, it should be a crime to be that good looking," Hadley muttered.

"What?" I asked.

She laughed. "Like you hadn't noticed in all the hours you two must have spent together lately."

I jumped. "What?"

I took my eyes off Roman to find her watching me carefully. "Are you okay? You're being really weird at the moment."

I shrugged. "I'm fine. Why would I not be fine?"

Hadley's eyes slid behind me to Roman and back again. "Did he try to kiss you and you had to shut him down?"

"Did he what?" I scoffed, totally convincingly (not). "No."

Hadley frowned. "Then, what is up with you two lately? Seriously, the amount of time you spend staring at each other when the other one isn't looking is depressing." She rolled her eyes and waved an arm at him. "Case in point."

I spun and my eyes found Roman just as he was looking down at his board.

"Seriously, what happened? If he didn't make a move on you, what– Oh, I know..." she said, getting that tone she got when she thought she'd discovered something juicy. "He's like properly into you and now he's annoyed you're dating Mason!"

I huffed and started walking over to our friends. "Hads, for the last time, Roman isn't into anyone, let alone me. He's just... In a mood. He gets that way."

"You do seem to know a lot about him..." she teased.

"We're friends... Sort of..." I blinked and shook my head. "I don't know, Hadley. We're friends, he drives me to school so I don't have to get the bus, and he gets super moody sometimes. It's like his thing. I thought you used to like that about him?"

"Oh, I still like that about him. But, I like the timing of his mood more."

I turned to glare at her and she gave me a wink. "Hads, there is nothing significant about the timing. Maddy's just being...awkward, I'm sure."

Hadley grabbed my arm to stop me getting too close to the group and pulled me to face her. "Maddy?" she asked, far too interested. "Jilted ex-lover? Threatened by you?"

I huffed. "No. Niece."

She opened her mouth and paused, obviously needing a moment to digest that. "He has a niece?" she asked finally, then she smirked at me. "Paris got *biz-ay* did she?"

I tried to school my smile, but failed. "That is usually how these things work, yes."

"A niece?"

"She's five."

"And, he what? Looks after her?"

I nodded. "Yeah. Carmen works really hard, so he does what he can. Plays with her, cooks for her, looks after her."

"Oh. My. God." Hadley breathed out heavily and clutched her

lower stomach. "My ovaries, babes!" She made little explosions with her hands.

I snorted. "I know, though, right?"

"Holy shit! Did you just admit you think he's beautiful?" Hadley looked at me like I'd suddenly grown two heads but she was simultaneously proud of me.

I shrugged nonchalantly. "Maybe."

"Progress, babes. Progress."

"Just don't go spreading it around."

"Trust me, the only thing spreading will be my legs to give that gorgeous creature children he will look adorable with."

I burst into laughter and Hadley dissolved into giggles with me. We held onto each other for support as we closed the distance to our friends.

As soon as he saw us laughing our heads off, Mason jumped up and came over to me. I swapped Hadley's arm for Mason's around my shoulders and he kissed my temple.

"What's so funny?" he asked.

My laughter sort of choked off in my throat. "Hads is just being vulgar again."

She shrugged unapologetically. "I can't help it if I'm honest about my feelings."

I giggled. "Yeah, but when your feelings are leading you to shag *unsavoury* characters, I don't need quite *all* the sordid plans."

"You're my best friend. Of course you'll get all the sordid plans. *And*, all the details after. Every. Single. Debased. Detail." She winked and I shook my head with a smile. It was fine for Hadley to corrupt me of course, just no one else.

"You girls often talk sex?" Mason chuckled and I felt my cheeks go bright red.

"Only always," Hadley answered. "We like to compare and contrast, make sure *someone's* doing it right." She gave him her sultriest grin and another wink.

He laughed. "I'll remember that in future."

"Really?" Hadley asked in what I'd coined her 'detective tone'.

He nodded and his arm dropped from my shoulder to my waist, tightening his hold on me a little. "You can be assured my performance won't be lacking. I always bring out my best when I'm being marked."

Hadley slid me an impressed look and I gave her my best smile back. "Is that so?" she answered. "Good to hear. I expect reports of toe curling, name screaming, and marathons."

Mason held me tighter. "Only the best for our Piper," he replied, his tone halfway between teasing and sexy.

Hysterical laughter burst out of me and I winced. "Ha! Good. That's good. The best is…good." My chuckle thankfully died and Hadley gave me the most sympathetic look ever.

Mason chuckled, put his other arm around me so my back was against his front and kissed my cheek.

"What are your plans for the weekend, Hads?" he asked her, resting his cheek against mine.

She flicked her hair over her shoulder in that semi-sarcastic way she had. "Oh, you know. Desperately trying to get Tucker to take me out." She leant forward conspiratorially. "You don't think his best mate could talk to him?" She batted her eyelids and I supressed a grin.

Mason leant over my shoulder towards her. "His best mate could… But, Craig's been a little busy with his own stuff."

I did smile then as Hadley laughed. Then, she cut it short and glared at him, and my smile widened.

"Cut the bullshit, buddy. Is Tucker interested or not?"

I felt Mason smile against my cheek; like me, he knew she wasn't being serious. "You know, Hads. I get the feeling guys don't talk about this stuff as much as you girls do."

"I know for a fact that's shit," she replied, trying to supress her smile.

I felt him shake his head. "Not at all."

"All that time you spend in the locker room and you talk about, what? The size of your dicks?" she laughed.

"Well, in the safety of a man-only environment, it's really just caveman grunts. We get the general feel of a thing rather than the flowery words so desired by you women."

"You think you're terribly funny, don't you?" Hadley asked, her eyes narrowing.

"I'm hilarious. Why else would Piper be interested in me?" he chuckled.

Why else, indeed.

My eyes slid to the other side of the oval of their own accord while Hadley and Mason kept talking. Anyone would be forgiven for thinking Hadley was blindly hitting on my…was he even my actual boyfriend? But, I knew her well enough to know she wasn't. Hell, she spent most of her time sounding like she was flirting with me if you didn't know any better. Hadley was a comfortable, relaxed, flirt. That's just who she was and I was in no way threatened by the fact it could be inferred that Mason was flirting back.

Because, flirty-sounding banter didn't always have to be more, it didn't mean you were accepting anything other than trading words. Unfortunately, some people have yet to accept that when their advances get shut down.

Mason's arms were warm and strong and sure around my waist. Every now and then, he'd lift one to point somewhere or just gesture as he talked in his usual animated way. He was always full of laughter, always happy, carefree.

I felt like I should be calm and comfortable in his arms. And, it wasn't like my heart was about to explode from stress or I was uncomfortable. I just felt constantly…on. Like I had to make sure I wasn't letting my thoughts show on my face, or make sure I was ready to reply with the right thing, or just make sure I didn't explode in ridiculous laughter like I apparently kept doing. My brain was running a hundred miles a minute and I felt like I could never keep up, always worried Mason would think I wasn't interested or I was an idiot or he'd be disappointed in me somehow.

It was tiring.

It felt like it shouldn't be that hard.

It felt like I was the absolutely worst human being on the planet.

As my mind was tumbling in frenzied circles, I realised I was staring at Roman again.

When he looked up at me, my hand rose to him.

I managed to take a deep, relaxing breath.

And another one.

He stared back at me for a moment longer, gave me a curt nod, and went back to whatever it was Roman Lombardi did.

And, my next breath was slightly more tense.

Things were weird between us.

I didn't know how to make it right and he didn't seem inclined to make any effort.

I guess I wasn't surprised really. I mean we'd gone from hanging out almost constantly, sleeping together, some weird sort of friendship I didn't know what I'd do without, to me dating

Mason. We'd always known that our relationship would have to change if or when Mason asked me out. I just hadn't realised it would be quite so difficult to actually do.

"You okay?" I heard Mason's voice in my ear and I had to force myself not to jump at the unexpectedness of it.

I nodded. "Yep."

He wrapped me up, his nose against my neck. "Where did you go?"

I felt myself twitch weirdly again. "Uh, nowhere. I'm here."

Which I just noticed is not where Hadley was as she was over talking to Celeste.

I spun in Mason's arms and gave him what I hoped was a sincere smile. "I'm here."

It was painfully obvious to me that I wouldn't have to be present with Roman. Or that I could have told Roman I'd just wandered off for a moment without worrying about what he'd ask or how serious the conversation would get or what he'd think of me.

But, Mason wasn't Roman.

Mason wanted more.

I wanted more.

With Mason.

It would just take time for Mason and me to get to that comfortable point.

I mean, it had taken Roman and me time.

Hadn't it?

We ambled through the rest of Lunch. When the bell rang, we dispersed as usual. Celeste and I were heading down the hallway to our classroom when I heard Roman's name.

I looked up and saw a girl in the year below us smiling at him in a way that told anyone watching that she was yet another girl who wanted something from him. And, it wasn't anything pure.

Roman looked her over in that bored way he had, that lazy disinterest practically branding her.

My heart flipped and I wasn't completely sure why.

Rio bent his lips to Roman's ear. Whatever Rio said made Roman's lip tip into that crooked mocking smirk. Roman's expression changed to that dark charm as he looked her up and down once more and he gave her a slight nod. I watched as she smiled at him sweetly, ducked her head and hurried off.

My heart went from flip to flop and my breath hitched.

Roman turned and his eyes had just met mine when Mr Dunbridge yelled his name down the hallway.

"Roman! Let's talk about what you were up to last lesson." Mr Dunbridge waved a hand at him. "Rio, why don't you come, too?"

Rio looked to Roman then he followed Roman's gaze to me. His eyes were harder even than Roman's and he gave me a mocking smirk that gave Roman a run for his money.

"Boys!" Mr Dunbridge said forcefully.

"Keep your knickers on, sir," Rio called back. He threw me on of his salutes and dragged Roman away.

Roman's eyes didn't leave mine until Rio whacked him, clearly annoyed, and he turned around. The two of them were quite obviously arguing about something as they stopped in front of the Vice Principal, to the point that I very clearly heard Mr Dunbridge ask, "Am I interrupting something, boys?" as he waited for them to pay him the appropriate attention.

Roman looked at him as Rio threw me a quick look over his shoulder. Then Mr Dunbridge waved them into his office and closed the door behind them.

"Isn't Rio cute?" Celeste asked me with a sigh and I gave her a disbelieving look.

"Rio's about as cute as period death cramps," I snapped.

"Oh!" Celeste chuckled. "Hello, Period Piper."

I couldn't be bothered correcting her. If I corrected her, then I'd probably have to come up with some other explanation as to why I wasn't my usual sweet, polite self.

And I didn't know why I was in such a mood, so I sure as hell wasn't going to be able to come up with any decent excuse.

Chapter Twenty Two

Adjusting, Puzzling and Dating à la Piper.

I'd told myself, 'no more'; Roman and I were going to manage this weird little speed bump and we'd be proper friends again in no time.

Roman had managed to avoid detention on Friday afternoon after whatever it was he and Rio had done to be dragged into Mr Dunbridge's office after Lunch. He'd driven me home and then disappeared.

We hadn't really seen each other all weekend – and his messages had been a little of the brush-off variety – but I was making the effort. I was going to fight for some kind of normalcy between us. Because friends fought for each other. Right?

But come Monday morning, Roman wasn't at his ute.

I was outside a little early in my nervous excitement of re-stabilising whatever we had, true. So, I decided to just lean on his car and scroll through my phone as I waited for him.

But, twenty minutes went by and he still wasn't there.

When his back door opened, I jumped up and felt my smile unbidden. But, no Roman.

Maddy ran out, giving me a huge wave with the book in her hand as she veered towards Carmen's car. Carmen followed her, looking a little bit frazzled as she tried to lock up the house, not drop her bag, *and* keep an eye on Maddy.

I took one look between them and wandered over to Maddy at the car. Carmen spared me a quick smile and went back to shuffling in her bag.

"Hey," I said to Maddy.

She looked up at me, squinting against the sun. "Hi."

"How are the cartwheels going?"

She grinned. "I'm getting *so* good."

I nodded. "I bet you are. Maybe you can show me on the weekend?"

The smile she gave me with her eyes open wide melted my damned heart strings. "Really?"

"Yeah. I'd love to."

Carmen hurried over. "Morning, Piper. Thanks. Sorry. Running so far behind today!"

I shrugged. "No problem. How are things?"

She waggled her head noncommittally. "They go." She looked back at the house. "Sorry, love. Roman's still in bed. He told me to…" she looked down at Maddy and gave me a knowing look as she raised her eyebrows, "when I knocked on his door. So, I don't know how long he'll be."

I shrugged, pretending I didn't care. "No worries."

She rubbed my arm. "I don't know what's up with him at the moment. He was so…good. And, now?"

I didn't know what his problem was either.

Carmen looked like she wanted to say more. But, I had the feeling that whatever she'd been thinking was highly inappropriate to mention in front of a five-year-old.

I shrugged again. "It's fine. He's just him. I'm sure it won't last long."

She gave me a sympathetic look and I wondered what she and Mum had been talking about now at book club – I was starting to think it was more like gossip club. Carmen's expression screamed she thought Roman and I were dating and fighting. I had the distinct impression that both our mums thought that and discussed it with alarming regularity.

"Can I drop you at the bus stop or anything?"

I shook my head. "Thanks. The walk will do me good."

I felt a hand on my sleeve and Maddy was looking up at me expectantly.

"What have you got there?" I asked her, leaning towards her.

She held up the book and showed me the cover; *There's a Monster Under my Bed Who Farts*. I smiled.

"That looks good."

She nodded. "It's my favourite. Miss Buckley lets me take it out of the class library on the weekends."

I grinned. "That's pretty neat. Who do you read it with? Grandma?" I smiled up at Carmen.

"Uncie Roman usually," she answered and my eyes snapped back to her in surprise. "He always does the funny voices, too."

God, her little smile was so infectious. It managed to fight off whatever weird feeling I got at hearing Roman read with her. The times we'd babysat, I'd read to her. Maddy had sat snuggled up to me on one side and Roman had had his arm around me from my other.

"That's great. Hey, maybe after cartwheels on the weekend we can read it together?" I asked.

Her eyes did that thing where she looked ecstatically surprised again and she nodded so enthusiastically I thought her head might fall off. "Can we?" She looked up at Carmen.

Carmen gave me a wry smile as she opened the back door of the car. "If Piper hasn't got anything better to do, sure."

Maddy grinned and started climbing into the car. Halfway, she stopped and ran back to throw her arms around my waist. "Bye, Piper!"

"Bye, Maddy!" I replied as she clambered into the car.

Carmen shut the door and smile at me warmly.

"You don't have to dote on her so." She said it the way people do when they think the world of you for something, hope you'll keep doing it, but also don't want to be putting you out.

I shrugged. "It's not like it's a hardship."

Carmen hugged me.

"Mum, I thought you guys had left?" came a hard, angry voice from behind me.

Carmen pulled away and looked over my shoulder. I followed her gaze to see a mightily pissed off Roman walking towards us. He was straightening his blazer collar like he'd just haphazardly thrown the offending garment on.

"Yes! We're leaving now!" Carmen chuckled and I felt like maybe she was forcing some of that joviality. She patted me on the arm and went to her side of the car. "Oh, Roman. Wednesday. Are you free?"

His gaze narrowed. "Why…?"

"I have a meeting and need you to look after Maddy."

He nodded slowly. "Sure…"

"Great. Thank you, love. Bye, Piper!" She swung into the car and started the engine.

"Bye, Uncie Roman!" came a very muffled scream accompanied by a thump on the window from inside the car.

I watched as Roman looked at Maddy and his face softened. He

282

waved at her and gave her a nod. "I'll see you tonight, trouble!" He kept waving as Carmen pulled away, then turned a significant frown on me. "What are you doing?"

I blinked. "What do you mean what am I doing?"

He sighed and ran a hand over his unusually stubbled face. "Nothing. Just. Fucking. Nothing. Come on. We're already late."

"I didn't think you cared," I answered, walking to the passenger door.

He followed me and opened the door for me like he always did. "I don't. But, you do."

"What's up?" I pleaded, needing to know what I could do to pull him out of whatever funk he was in.

I turned to look up at him. Our faces weren't necessarily inappropriately close. But, they were close. His eyes finally softened and he brushed away a piece of hair that had got stuck to my lip-gloss. He left his hand resting against my cheek.

"I'm adjusting, Barlow."

"You're doing a stellar job of it," I huffed sarcastically.

His eyes hardened again. "I know. Okay? I'm just… I'm trying here, Barlow. What did you expect? We'd have all this figured out straight away?"

I shook my head. "No. I guess not."

He nodded. "Okay. Just… Give us some time, love. We'll find our way back to each other."

"How do you know?"

His thumb brushed over my cheek. "Because we're friends, Piper. And I kind of love you, remember? That doesn't just go away because Carter found his sack."

"Those are some pretty nancy wanker words there, Lombardi," I said, hoping to dispel some of the seriousness of the situation.

He gave me a grin almost as sincere as his old one. "I know, love. But, sometimes I need to say them."

"And sometimes, I need to hear them."

"Hey! You're not the only one."

"I kind of love you, too, you know," I whispered.

We moved forward out of habit and we both only just moved our faces in time so I kissed his cheek. My lips lingered against his skin too long and I mentally kicked and berated myself for my complete idiocy.

We pulled apart – both clearing our throats and both tense – and it felt like we were back at square one. I flushed and looked down while he pulled the door wider.

"Come on. We've got to get going."

He moved off to his side quickly and I climbed into the car by myself, no less awkwardly than I had the very first time.

As we drove along, he kept flexing his hands and rubbing his chin.

But, we didn't talk.

Finally, he shifted in his seat and cleared his throat. "So, being normal?"

I looked over at him. "What about it?"

He shifted again. "Well, Wednesday. Plans?"

I shook my head. "Other than school, no."

"You want to help me tame the trouble, then?" he asked. "You know she'd love to misbehave for you."

I looked away before he saw me smile. "Sure."

He nodded. "Okay. Good. Normal."

"Normal," I replied with a smile, totally believing we could do this being normal thing.

My belief in our ability to do this being normal thing didn't last long.

Tuesday was as stilted and awkward as Monday had been. Not helped by the fact that Hadley took a moment while I was talking to Roman to hit on Rio from behind me. Which then pulled me into a longer than necessary conversation with Roman and his buddies that had the boys hinting all sorts of things about Roman and me which Hadley really didn't need to hear.

Things that made me wonder what Roman told them about me. Things that made me think there was something more behind those weird looks from Rio than just Rio being Rio – I just couldn't put my finger on what it was.

Things like; "he's been totally spaced for months, now" complete with knowing look in my direction; "he left Derek's to meet her last week" with accompanying wink; "the girls have missed him" as Rio waggled his eyebrows; "he's gone soft, with her good influence" as Steve gave me a winning smile. This last one was intended as a friendly dig, but I saw the way Hadley looked between Roman and me like there was more puzzling out to do.

When I finally had us excused – having to quite literally drag Hadley away – she thankfully said nothing. She continued saying nothing as she watched Mason ask me if I wanted to go to the movies that Saturday. If she noticed the way my eyes slid to Roman before I said yes, she kept right on saying nothing.

A real date would change everything for good. Wouldn't it? No more being uncertain of what Mason and I were. Right? No more wondering if holding Roman's hand counted as cheating (because it probably was). And, certainly no more almost-kisses like the day before. I was presumably properly with Mason now; the only lips I kissed would be his.

Wednesday was strained and awkward with Roman in the morning, but got steadily more relaxed as we got closer to school. Roman even smiled at me almost completely normally at Lunch. Well, normal for Roman at school anyway. After school, we went to pick up Maddy. She ran into his arms far more adorably than was absolutely necessary – *see how Hadley's ovaries like that when I tell her!* – and he swung her around with a huge smile on his face.

I noted the way the younger mums looked at him. Kind of that leery way older women looked at younger men like they knew they shouldn't, but they just can't help themselves. I grinned, but didn't say anything to him until later – where I was informed that more than one young mum had hit on him before.

When we got home, Maddy insisted on coming in to see my room while I changed. Roman started to make a joke about coming too, then stopped quickly enough and with a look on his face that I didn't think Maddy was to blame. He went to their place and Maddy followed me up to my room. She had a good nosey around, but that at least gave me some time to make sure I wasn't flashing her anything she shouldn't be flashed. She chattered away as she looked over my stuff until she got to a picture of Roman and me that I'd printed and stuck on the headboard of my bed with all the other pictures of people close to me.

"Why is there a picture of Uncie Roman here?" she asked.

So, I explained, "I put pictures up of all my friends."

"What about me?" she asked, turning to me with a frown.

I smiled. "I don't have a picture of you."

"Why not?"

I shrugged. "Don't know. Shall we take one now?"

She threw me one of those huge smiles and we took position in front of the picture of me and Roman; we took a sensible and a silly – like all good photo shoots should be.

When we were done and I'd assured her that I'd print it out as soon as possible and put it up with the one of Roman, we went back over to Carmen's and found Roman in the kitchen. While Roman cooked dinner, I shepherded Maddy upstairs and got her changed then took her outside to practise cartwheels. After that, it was dinner time, bath time, and bed time for small children. As per usual, it took at least three goes to get her to stay in bed.

Roman and I dropped onto the couch with a heavy sigh. And, from there things got awkward again. He put his arm around my shoulder while I found something to watch and we fell into old habits. We were laughing about something when he started tickling me and I looked up at him.

My heart fluttered and I got that old familiar feeling in my stomach as we looked into each other's eyes. It was too familiar and my body felt like it was on autopilot. Thank God my brain was still working before one of us moved forward.

"I should go…" I said as I stood up faster than I'd ever stood up before.

He shot up with a single nod and ended up on the other side of the room. "Yeah, probably."

"Okay. Okay. So, I'll see you tomorrow?"

He nodded once again. "Yep. Bright and early. At the ute."

"Okay. Yep. Morning. Good. Night."

I grabbed my jumper and let myself out. I paused at my back door and could just see an orange spark pacing outside his in obvious agitation.

"God, you cannot do that," I chastised myself, feeling even worse than the most horrible human in the world.

Thursday we were even further behind square one than we had been on Monday, but we both seemed to be suffering a pretty good case of denial. He smiled and hugged me and chatted about what Maddy had been up to all morning – apparently a heavy amount of talking about my finer qualities. But, his eyes were tense and full of something pretty close to that darkness the likes of which I hadn't really seen in months when it was just the two of us.

Friday was no better. Especially when Mason went past us as I got out of Roman's ute and reminded me to pick a movie for our date. I noticed Roman take a step away from me even though he hadn't been standing anywhere near me. I smiled at Mason and nodded, but there was no ignoring the fact that Roman and I had no idea how to behave around each other and it seemed like time might not be able to fix it after all.

Still, Mason.

Mason was the goal and I'd reached it.

I shook off my worries about what Roman and I were and focussed on the blue eyes that always held a smile for me.

Chapter Twenty Three
Nose-First Crash into Awkward-town.

I'd fretted and fidgeted and I'd left my room looking like a bomb full of unwanted clothes had gone off. Even with Hadley's help most of the afternoon, I still didn't trust I'd worn the right thing. Hadley assured me I looked great, but I didn't really feel like myself.

It hadn't helped when I'd had the strong urge to see Roman before I'd left. But, halfway to his house, I realised his ute wasn't in the driveway and I told myself I could deal with the anxiety myself. I took deep, steadying breaths and explained it away as excitement.

Still, I was walking towards the cinema complex just before half past six on Saturday, willing myself to let go of the death grip on my bag and convincing myself I didn't need to check I'd locked the car *again*.

I jumped like a complete git as I felt my phone vibrate in my hands, but ignored it; ten to one said it was Hadley checking I'd reapplied my lippie before getting out of the car. Ten to one also said I hadn't done anything of the sort.

"Piper!" I heard Mason call and looked up to see him walking towards me.

I gave him my best impression of a relaxed, sweet but still a little spicy smile, and hugged him. I even kissed his cheek for good measure and was gratified when he kissed mine.

I got something right, at least.

"Hey," I answered as we pulled away. "How are you?"

He smiled. "Good. You?"

I nodded. "Good."

He looked down at me. "Wow. You look…amazing. I like what you've done with your hair," he finished as he bounced one of the curls Hadley had insisted on putting in it.

I fluffed my hair self-consciously. "Thanks. I wasn't sure it was going to work. But…" I flailed in a terrible attempt at a nonchalant 'here we are' shrug.

"No, it looks great. Super sexy."

I flushed and looked down, which gave me a decent chance to look at him properly.

Of course he *actually* looked amazing – I still wasn't convinced my skirt wasn't slightly too short for the occasion even with tights. But then, Mason sort of just always looked amazing.

He was wearing sandy-brown boots, grey jeans with an olive t-shirt and a dark denim jacket with a sort of fuzzy lining. His blue eyes shone as he looked at me and his light brown hair was swept back in a way that looked far too cool for school.

Honestly, the whole package just made me a little tongue-tied.

"You… Uh… You look great, too."

His grin was super sexy and he flicked his head back for good measure. "Thanks. Thought I'd dress up. Look the part, you know?"

"The part?" I asked, totally not knowing.

"Well, I could hardly be seen with a beautiful girl like you looking like my usual self," he chuckled.

I knew he was joking really, but something about the idea he couldn't be himself around me unsettled me. I smiled, though.

"Well, how about next time we both just wear our trackies and ugg boots and call that done?" I asked, wondering if I sounded as strained as I thought I did.

He grinned. "Next time?"

I nodded. "I assumed that was the idea here?"

"Pretty presumptuous, don't you think?" he teased.

Well, I certainly didn't know what to think now. Boyfriend-girlfriend? One date-done? Few dates, dating? I was so confused!

Don't let it show!

I broke into a smile. "Well, if I shouldn't be expecting anything, should I know now?"

He took my hand and we started walking. "What do you feel like eating?" he asked with a wry smile.

I shrugged. "I don't mind."

"Well, we have the usual on offer."

With a smile, I answered, "How about burgers at *Lacey's*? It's almost warm enough to sit outside." I paused as a thought hit me. "Oh! What about pizza?"

He chuckled. "Let's start with *Lacey's* and see what you feel like when you sit down?"

Our hands swung. "Sounds good."

We walked along in silence. I wasn't sure if it was companionable or not. I mean, *I* felt okay… But, then I started worrying about how he was feeling. Did he think I was feeling awkward? Was he feeling awkward? Did he expect me to talk? Should we be talking? Should I stop swinging his hand? Should I let go? Was I supposed to be walking closer to him? What should I be talking about?

I wracked my brain for things to talk about. But the harder I thought, the further any potential topics seemed to get from reach.

I was pulled out of my crazy mind when I felt a tug on my hand.

"*Lacey's* yeah?" Mason asked, looking a little confused.

I blinked and looked around, realising I'd been about to walk straight past *Lacey's*.

"Uh, yeah," I chuckled self-consciously. "Yes," I tried again with a little more confidence.

"Outside?" he checked as a waitress came over and I nodded.

"Table for two?" she asked and I recognised her as a girl a year or two below us at school.

"Yes, thanks. Outside, please," Mason answered.

She smiled at him the way everyone seemed to smile at Mason. She flicked her hair and batted her eyes a little. But, Mason just put his arm around my shoulder and looked into my eyes.

"Milkshake or soft drink?" he asked me.

"Coke, I think," I answered, my eyes sliding to the waitress.

The waitress gave me a look that clearly told me I'd won that round before giving me the perfect hospitality smile. "This way, please."

Mason and I followed her to a table under a heater that made it quite pleasant out actually. She passed us menus as we sat and took our drink orders before leaving us to decide what to eat.

"So, have you decided between the burger and pizza?" Mason asked.

I looked up at him and pulled my head out of my arse.

The guy looked at me like Tormund looks at Brienne – or, so I was told – and I was sitting there like a complete dick. I was worrying over every little thing, second-guessing myself, looking for issues left, right and centre.

I took a deep breath, told myself to just relax, and gave him a smile that I was actually pretty pleased with.

"I don't know," I replied. "On one hand, it's a burger. On the other, it's pizza."

Mason laughed, his eyes dancing. "I see the dilemma. The question is, can you eat a whole pizza?"

I felt myself relaxing; food was something I could talk about easily and forever. "Well, I *can*. The real question is *should* I? Especially with popcorn and a choc top making an appearance later."

His mouth dropped open in jest. "Popcorn and a choc top? What makes you think there'll be popcorn *and* a choc top?"

I leant over towards him. "The fact that I am quite capable of paying for those sorts of things myself."

He took hold of my hand on the table. "Anything else you need? I thought after we could get ice cream? Maybe cake if anyone's open?"

"Oh, cake?"

"Mud cake, specifically."

"Why, Mr Carter. You do know how to charm a girl," I giggled and movement caught my eye.

My eyes slid sideways and all laughter died on my lips.

Roman was walking down the street with his mates and a few girls, and his eyes were already glued to me. I couldn't stop myself giving him a once over as he passed. He was wearing white sneakers, dark jeans, a white slouched-neck t-shirt and an unbuttoned dark grey shirt. His dark brown hair was longer than Mason's and there was no way he was even thinking about styling it. But somehow, it still managed to look incredible. My fingers twitched like they wanted to do more than just remember what it felt like.

My chest did that weird jump-plummet thing, but I threw on a smile and waved to him. He did not wave back. Rio smirked at me in that hard way he had lately as he said something in Roman's ear, his arm around a girl I didn't know.

Mason turned and I saw the two boys exchange a hard look.

I really didn't know what else I should have expected. Mason said my friendship with Roman was cool. But they'd hated each other before; why would they just start tolerating each other now one was my friend and the other...my boyfriend?

Before I could get back to the burger versus pizza discussion with Mason, one of the girls with Roman pushed through the group and threw herself around him. He lazily draped his arm around her shoulder as he talked to Steve as though he wasn't watching me. For some reason, the sight had me swallowing hard, but I turned to Mason like it didn't bother me.

"So, with all that future eating in mind, eating a whole pizza seems like a rookie mistake," I said with a piss-poor attempt at unfazed as I brushed some hair from my face.

Mason's eyes followed Roman's progress behind me, but I refused to turn around. Finally, he dragged those beautiful blues back to me and smiled.

"Well if you feel like pizza, then I could probably share one with you," he said.

I grinned. "Remember, I love pineapple."

He leant forward and I mimicked him. "I can live with that."

We looked into each other's eyes for a few nervously excited heartbeats. I felt myself lick my lip and Mason's eyes darted down at the movement. My heart rate somehow managed to increase at the look in them when he finally looked back into my eyes.

I didn't know how a guy could look at you like that. Like you were… I didn't even know. Like you were the only thing he was focussed on? Like you were something to be unwrapped carefully until he found out all your secrets. I wasn't sure if it was a good thing or not. I mean, it *had* felt good until I'd gone into over-analysation mode.

"I'm really glad we're doing this, Piper…" he said slowly.

I blinked. "Doing what?" I asked, like an idiot.

His smile was enough to give my heart that little kick. "Going out."

I licked my lip again, more out of nerves than anything. "Me, too," I replied and hoped I wasn't lying.

We moved forward slowly and our lips touched. It was firmer and briefer than I'd expected, but there wasn't anything unpleasant about it. It made my stomach do a bit of a happy dance and I pulled away with a smile on my face. I tucked a piece of hair behind my ear and stared down at my menu.

Mason squeezed my hand and I squeezed his back.

"Barbeque chicken with extra pineapple?" he asked.

I slid my eyes up to look at him and tried to bite my lip against the huge smile growing on my face. I felt like maybe, just maybe, it was all going to be easier than I was making it. Maybe my guy and I *were* on the same wavelength after all. Maybe I could get the hang of this dating thing.

"Sounds good," I answered.

Our drinks arrived and we ordered and I managed to make it through dinner with some semblance of dignity. I didn't snort obscenely or giggle hysterically or blurt out something *too* idiotic – a little idiotic once or twice, but nothing more than my usual adorable self. Mason did most of the talking and I found that I could keep up. During moments of silence, I started panicking a little about what I should say or do next. But, on the whole – while it could have been a little more comfortable and easy – as far as first date dinners went, I think it was okay.

The movie was good; there was hand-holding and a short popcorn fight. He even kissed ice cream off my nose. But there was no need for talking, so I at least didn't have to worry about what I was saying.

After, we strolled around a little bit and Mason held up the conversation.

That was when the panic started creeping back in. I felt antsy and unsure and second-guessed myself totally. I forgot how to flirt and realised I wasn't sure I'd ever known to begin with. And, that dignity? Yeah, I kissed that goodbye well and truly.

Forget cake – even mud cake. I had to get out of there.

"I guess I should call it a night…" I started. "Get home before Mum and Dad send out the search party." I mentally winced at such a stupid thing to say.

But, Mason smiled. "No worries. Where are you parked?" I pointed back up the street. "Can I walk you?"

I nodded. "Yeah, sure. That'd be nice."

Again, I had no idea if the silence was comfortable or not and I overthought it the whole way back to my Mum's car.

Surely I should say something?

No, Mason would totally say something if he was uncomfortable?

Unless, he's rethinking the whole dating thing?

Then, he wouldn't say anything.

Oh, my God, I've made a total dick of myself tonight.

Did I smile properly?

Maybe I looked like a serial killer when I smiled?

Oh, my God! Did I have something in my teeth?

Did I smell?

What the hell is wrong with you?

So much for wavelengths…

I patted the roof of Mum's car awkwardly as I stepped up to it and smiled at Mason. "Thanks for tonight. I had a good time," I said.

He smiled, but something about his eyes was less enthusiastic than before. "Me, too. I'll talk to you later?"

I nodded. "Definitely."

He nodded and stepped forward.

Right. Goodnight kiss. Standard.

I leant up to him and our noses crashed into each other. We both took a step back with a laugh.

"Wow. Well done me," I huffed.

Mason tilted my face up to look at him. "How do you know that wasn't my fault?"

Mason's voice was low and smooth. His eyes were warm and focussed. He was looking at me like Patrick looked at Kat, like Chase looked at Nicole, like Lloyd looked at Diane. It was everything I should have wanted, but I didn't feel like Kat or Nicole or Diane.

"I highly doubt you're that uncoordinated," I answered

His hand slid from my chin around to cup my cheek. "Second time lucky."

He leant down and kissed me.

I should have leant into him and kissed him back…better. But, I was too busy overthinking everything again. When he pulled away, he looked at me like I'd just divulged my biggest secret –

except I didn't know what it was. I suddenly felt rather naked.

"I'll talk to you tomorrow," he said softly.

I nodded. "I'd like that."

His eyes dropped to my lips and back up to my eyes again. Something about him seemed…dull. Not knowing what else to do, I reached up and kissed him again.

It wasn't fireworks. It wasn't slow burn. But, it was nice. It was something I could get used to. Something steadfast and true. Something I knew I could call mine.

Chapter Twenty Four
Perfect Life 2.0.

"Okay, I lied," he said, standing in front of me.

Rain hammered down around us. His dark hair was flattened and his eyes were lost in shadow. But, I knew them well enough to picture the apology and the sheer depth in them. And, it made me shiver from more than just cold.

"What?"

"I lied." He took a step towards me. "We promised honesty, and I broke that promise."

"How?" My heart skipped, tripped, and beat faster.

"Because I never wanted you to go out with Carter."

"Sorry?" I asked, sounding a little more breathless than was ideal.

He shook his head. "No, I didn't care at first. I was like, whatever, she can do whatever the fuck she wants–"

"Oh, good. So pleased," I muttered.

"–but, then we spent every day together for two weeks and you got under my fucking skin, Piper. We went back to school and I just never wanted that day to come. I wanted him to… Fuck!" he yelled, then continued quieter, "I don't even know."

"What, Roman?"

"Anything. *Anything* was preferable to him asking you out. I felt like my life was split into before he asked and after he asked, and after was just going to be full of shit and misery. I saw it coming and I pretended I didn't. Then, it happened and…I lost you…"

God, my heart fell over its own feet and wasn't entirely sure if it should bother getting back up again yet or not. It was a lovely sentiment, but I really didn't know how I felt – except sucker-punched…

Suddenly, I was rethinking this running after him in the dark thing. Sure, he hadn't spoken to me since I'd seen him out on Saturday night. He hadn't been at school that day and his no-show had seen me properly late for the first time in…well, forever. So, when I'd seen the tell-tale spark of one of his cigarettes out my window, I'd run outside and called his name. I'd called his name and asked him how he was as though everything was fine, as though everything was normal.

I was starting to think I really regretted that now.

"It's a bit late for that, don't you think?" I asked.

"I couldn't not tell you."

I nodded. "Okay, well you did." But, what was I going to do with that information?

"You didn't just get under my skin, Piper. You got into my head. Into my heart. And, I can't fucking get you out."

My heart felt like it was going to have no trouble clawing its way out of my chest at this rate. It was torn between running to him and giving up. Running to him was too hard and too painful. It was just going to give up, play dead, and hope no one bothered it for a while.

"I don't…" I took a deep breath. "What do you want me to do with this?" I asked.

He shrugged. I had never seen him look so defeated. I had never seen him look so unsure of anything. "I don't know. I'm no good for you, but I can't stop thinking about you."

"I really don't know what I'm supposed to do about that, Roman! A few months ago, I would have agreed with you. I would have said you were no good for me. Now, I'm not so sure."

"How can you stand there and say that? You know me better than anyone. How can you believe that?"

"What were we doing, Roman? We hung out, we got along, you were there for me every single time I needed you, and we slept together. Apart from the whole monogamy thing, what we had seemed like a pretty good relationship to me."

"Monogamy?"

"Yeah. Nifty concept. I assumed you'd heard of it."

"Of course I've fucking heard of it, Piper," he spat. "And for your information, I wasn't with anyone else between that first Saturday in the holidays and last Saturday when I saw you and Carter...out."

I somehow knew 'out' was not the word he was thinking of. What had he seen? Me kissing Mason? What else–

Wait...

"What?" I barely breathed; it was barely a sound. I sucked in a breath. "You what?"

"Wow. So that's what you think of me? I'm so fucking shit that I was off sleeping around? You think that little of me?"

"No." I shook my head. "No. No, I think that little of me..."

"How– What do you mean?"

I don't know why I pointed to myself. "I just assumed I wasn't enough. I didn't have any reason to think you were with other people. But, I never told myself you weren't. There wasn't a reason for you not to be."

He took a step towards me. "How could you think…?" He ran a hand through his hair and turned around. "Fuck! This isn't happening…"

"What's not happening?"

He whirled around and laughed humourlessly. "You're telling me we may as well have been dating? We may as well have… Fuck! It's all my fault. I had everything I never knew I wanted and I just stupidly let you go."

I crossed my arms. "Roman, what do you want from me?"

"Short of turning back time? Nothing," he scoffed, and I knew he was more pissed with himself than he was with me.

I sighed and blinked back tears. My heart had decided the floor was a perfectly good place to just lie down for a while, so it was going to stay there. "Honestly, Roman?"

"Always, Piper. You know that."

"Yes."

"Yes?"

"Yes, we may as well have been dating. I don't know if it was all your fault. I suspect I'm as much to blame as you. I can't say if you had everything. But, I was *there*, Roman. *Right there* and you did just let me go. And, now I don't know what to do." I shrugged. "I don't even know where Mason and I stand. I don't know if we're actually dating – if he's my boyfriend – or if we're not quite there yet. It's confusing and hard and it's not supposed to be. Then, you tell me all this and I don't know what to do with it! Am I supposed to dump Mason? I don't know what you want from me, Roman!"

"I don't want anything from you, Piper. I just… Whatever we were, we were always honest and I couldn't not be honest with you. Don't break up with Carter. I've got nothing to offer you.

Nothing's changed."

"Nothing's changed?" I yelled. "Oh, so you just selfishly decided to drop this bomb on me and tell me it ultimately changes nothing?"

"Selfishly?" he spat.

"Yes. If you're not asking me to dump Mason for you then this whole thing was for you. I get we do honesty, Roman. And, I appreciate the fact that that extends to everything uncomfortable. But, this? This is beyond uncomfortable. You think telling me I'm in your heart isn't going to change anything? Fuck, Roman! I thought friends put the other one first. This is anything but putting me first."

I whirled, angry and wanting to hit something. Instead, I looked back at him. "God knows I fucking love you Roman. But I'd managed to stop myself falling completely in love with you because we all knew where that would lead. You can't come here and tell me you can't get me out of your heart and expect me to be unaffected by that! It just doesn't work that way."

I could have kept yelling at him for hours – days probably – but it wasn't going to get us to any better a place. It wasn't going to fix anything.

"Piper–"

"You've just ruined everything, Roman! I can't–" My breath hitched and I fought back tears. "Why couldn't you leave well enough alone? Why couldn't we both go on as we were? I can't live in denial when I know the truth. I can't be friends with you knowing we both want more and can't give it. What the hell makes naïve little Piper Barlow so special that the aloof Roman Lombardi just can't help himself to feelings for once? Where is that typical Roman Steel? The brush-off? The cavalier nonchalance? I just don't–"

I stopped, realising I was doing exactly what I'd accused him of doing; I wasn't putting him first, I was putting my anger first. And that wasn't any more fair than I thought he'd been. I took a deep breath.

"That's not fair. I shouldn't have…"

He shook his head. "No, you're right to be angry. I shouldn't have… I'm sorry, Piper–"

Tears choked my throat and I held up a hand. "Don't apologise, Roman. Please."

The dynamic hadn't just shifted; it was broken. We were broken now, but I was going to hang onto something.

His honesty might have made me angry, but that was only because it made me acknowledge a truth I'd stoically refused to admit until now. It was a truth that had the power to hurt me. It was a truth that I felt keenly. And, it had to happen at some point. But, no matter how much I hurt – how angry I was – it gave me no right to invalidate his acknowledgement. Maybe I was angrier at the fact he'd acknowledged it before me but too late for either of us.

"You don't have to apologise for being you, let alone being honest. Neither of us went about this the right way, any of it. But, we are who we are. You know I'll never judge you and I'll always like you for you, Roman. I don't expect you to be anything other than who you are." I took a deep breath. "That's the guy I love. But, I can't do this right now. I… I need some space. *We* need some space."

I wanted nothing more than to walk forward and have him put his arms around me. And, when he reached out to me, I thought he would. His embrace had always been welcoming, it had been comforting. But in it, I'd found far more than I'd expected and I had to learn not to lean on him; it wasn't fair for either of us, or for Mason.

A single step had never felt more wrong, but a step away from Roman was necessary.

His arm fell and I knew that one step symbolised more to either of us than a mere action.

"No," he said slowly, "you're right. I'll, uh… I'll see you later, Barlow…"

He turned on his heel and walked away. I didn't move. I just stared into the space he'd occupied like it could bring him back, bring us back. But he didn't come back and I didn't know when I'd actually see him again, let alone what that would be like.

"Are you sure about this, honey?" Mum asked, her arm around my shoulders.

I nodded. "Yeah. It's time I faced things head on. No more pretending."

Mum gave a weird strangled breath and I looked at her in exasperated adoration. "Sorry, honey."

I rolled my eyes and smiled at her. "Mum, we've talked about this."

And, we had. After talking to Roman on Monday night, I'd sat my parents down and I'd told them everything. Well…almost everything. All the emotional stuff, anyway.

It had been difficult and draining, but they were there for me and they listened and they still loved me even when I wasn't perfect. It made me realise I could have trusted them earlier and I wished I had.

Mum nodded. "I know. I know." She waved her hand at me, holding back tears. "I'm amazing. I reared perfection and I'm amazing," she said as though it was her new mantra.

I chuckled and hugged her. "Not perfection."

"You're perfection to me, honey."

"Okay! Stop, or I *will* be sick."

Mum took hold of my shoulders and steered me inside. So really, I had no choice about how ready I was or not anymore. But, I felt ready.

After I'd explained everything, Mum, Dad and I had spent hours talking about it and I knew it was the right choice.

"Piper Barlow for Dr Freeman," I said as I walked up to the front desk.

The woman behind the desk smiled. "Hi. We've got a few bits of paper for you to fill in. Just bring them back when you're done."

I nodded, took the clipboard she passed me, and Mum and I found a seat.

"How are you feeling?" Mum asked.

I smiled as I started filling in the paperwork. "Fine. Little nervous I guess. But, there's nothing she can tell me that I don't already tell myself. It can only be good news."

Mum hugged me to her one-handedly and I shrugged her off kindly as I finished the paperwork.

Once it was back with the receptionist, we sat and waited. A few minutes passed and a woman in maybe her mid-forties came into the waiting room. She had dark blonde hair and clear-framed glasses perched on her nose.

"Piper?"

I nodded and stood up.

"I'll be right here, honey," Mum said with a pat to my back.

I nodded again and followed Dr Freeman to her office.

"Have a seat, wherever you're comfortable," she said and I sat on the edge of the couch. "It's nice to meet you Piper."

"Uh, you too, Dr Freeman."

She smiled and sat daintily on the chair across from me, picking up a tablet from the table beside her. "I understand it was your idea to come and see me, Piper?"

I nodded. "Uh, yes."

"Why do you think you need therapy?"

I looked down at my hands and found them interlaced in my lap. "I don't really know how to put it."

"That's okay. How about we start with what brought you here? What made you decide?"

I didn't want to admit it. But, I knew I had to. "Roman."

"Roman?" she asked, writing something down.

I nodded. "Roman."

"And, who is Roman to you?"

I sighed. "Uh, that's the problem. I don't know…"

Somehow, I found myself telling her everything. I started something like three months earlier when Roman moved in next door, to the day Hadley and I were sitting on the bleachers in Mason's PE lesson, I went through my relationship with Mason, Hadley, Mum, Dad, Roman, even Celeste. I stumbled in some parts. But, I knew overall that I wasn't going to get anything out of it if I wasn't completely honest.

"…so, when I turned around and realised I only had one person in my life that I was truly honest with… And, I couldn't talk to him anymore… Well, I figured it was time for a change."

I finally looked up and saw her watching me thoughtfully.

307

"Thank you, Piper."

I blinked. "For what?"

"For sharing all that. I see you've been dealing with a lot of…new things lately."

I shrugged. "I guess."

"Piper, have you ever self-diagnosed?"

"No. I don't think so?" *Should I have?*

Dr Freeman nodded, a smile widening on her face. "Good. You know, that is one problem with the internet these days. Everything is so readily available to us. We can type in a bunch of symptoms and get a whole bunch of things back. You said sometimes you feel…funky?"

I nodded. "Roman and I…" I cleared my throat. "It's what we called it. If I felt down or antsy or uncomfortable, he'd say I was in a funk."

"And, what did you call it before?"

I shrugged. "Nothing really. Issues, I guess."

"Issues? And, the negative connotations of that never made you feel worse?"

"No. I guess it was a bit tongue-in-cheek, you know. Sort of downplay how I was feeling because I knew I'd look stupid to other people if they knew. I kind of labelled things the way I thought other people would relate to them better." I shrugged again.

"Why do you think you'd look stupid to other people?"

"Because what does Piper Barlow have to worry about? Really? I live in a nice house. I have great parents. I have wonderful friends. I get good grades. I'm healthy. I'm lucky. And, feeling any other way is…" I slowed to a stop.

"Is what, Piper?"

"Selfish," I said around the lump in my throat.

308

"Why selfish?"

"There are people dying of starvation, of illness, people alone, homeless. The world is full of horrors. And, then I look at my life and there's none of that."

"You think because other people have what you believe is a worse time that you should be happy all the time?"

I huffed a humourless laugh, thinking I knew where she was going with that question. "Roman would say something much the same."

"Those nancy wanker words?"

I looked up at her and smiled. "Yeah."

She smiled back. "We don't have a lot more time for today, Piper. But, I want to ask you this; when you're feeling…funky can you just think of these other people – of their problems – and feel better about your life?"

I shook my head, feeling guilty. "No."

"Piper, no one expects you to," she said kindly. "Anxiety isn't something we just turn on and off. It's real. Sometimes, we feel like it makes no sense. We make excuses for it or for ourselves. We pretend we're okay." Here she looked at me intently and I knew when I was being given a message. "But, we don't have to. Everyone's experiences and emotions are different. What you're going through isn't less difficult for you just because there are people in poverty elsewhere in the world. We are a sum of our experiences – good and bad – and our brains don't work the way we want them to just because we will it.

"I think it would be good if we could catch up again in a couple of weeks. In the meantime, I want you to think about what makes you unhappy and what you need to be happy. It can be people, things, songs, books, movies…John Cusack." We shared a smile.

"But, I want you to think about what makes you happy and what you can do to surround yourself with positives."

I nodded. "I think I can do that."

She gave me an encouraging look. "Good."

"It'll be hard, won't it?"

Dr Freeman smiled sympathetically. "Sometimes, the way we can find our happiest selves can also be the most painful to acknowledge."

Chapter Twenty Five
To Be or Not To Be [Friends].

Okay, things that made me unhappy and things I needed to be happy. That was easy, right?

Right.

Mum. Dad. John Cusack movies. My friends; Hadley, Celeste, Tucker, Craig…

Mason?

Roman?

Why did my brain insist on making the two of them mutually exclusive?

I had Mason. I chose Mason. Mason made me happy.

But, Roman's friendship meant the world to me. Nothing compared to sitting in the comfortable, comforting silence next to him and knowing he was comfortable too.

Mason was my John Cusack.

Roman was my… Carter from *A Cinderella Story*! He's the best friend. Sure, there was a little bit of a banter that could be seen as flirtation. But, we were just meant to be friends. Nothing more.

Yeah, Roman was my Carter.

And, I needed a Carter.

So, I'd won the boy.

Now, I needed to fight for my friend.

And, that was exactly was I was going to do.

So I ran out my front door on Wednesday, riddled with nervous excitement. Piper wasn't hiding anything anymore. She was being truthful and honest and herself. Friends with Roman was doable. It had to be.

I was in the process of heading for his ute to wait for him when he walked out his back door. We both paused then he stalked forward, looking at me like he dared me to come any closer.

God, if only the brooding thing didn't suit him so well...

I cleared my throat. "Roman, I know I said–"

I stopped when he winced as though he'd actually thought we'd been going to get through this without speaking. "Space, Barlow. I thought we were having space?"

"Yeah, I know, Roman. I said I needed space–"

"*We* needed space."

"Roman... Please, just talk to me."

"About what Piper?" he asked, flinging his arms out. "What could there possibly be left to talk about?"

"Everything? Anything–"

"Nothing."

"Nothing is good."

He glared at me. "Barlow, what do you want?"

"I want us to be friends."

"Friends?" he scoffed, looking completely taken aback. "Barlow... Fuck..." He chuckled and sucked his teeth. "Friends? Barlow, what makes you think we can do friends? Last I recall, we both realised we may as well have been accidentally dating and we needed space to work ourselves out."

"Last I recall you had nothing to offer me. But, I don't believe you."

"Piper, we've been through this. I will never be that guy."

"I'm not asking you to be!" I yelled. "I'm not asking you to be anyone but you, and you're my friend–"

"I'm the town degenerate that you happened to fuck. I wouldn't equate that to friends."

"Why are you making this so hard?"

He shrugged. "I'm not doing anything but being honest. You want the truth Barlow? When I said I had nothing to give you, I meant anything. All right? I can't be there for you the way you want me to be–"

"Why? Because we can't keep our hands to ourselves?"

"No. Because I'm not that guy. I don't do feelings and hand-holding bullshit. I drink. I smoke. I fight. I fuck. That's what I know. That's who I am."

"Fine! I can live with that. I keep telling you, Roman. I don't want you to be anyone other than who you are. You say I'm in your soul? Well, you're in mine. You're as much a part of me as Mum, Dad, Hadley, Celeste… Just like them, you've become woven into the very fabric of who I am, Roman, and I don't know how to be Piper without you."

"I'll bet Carter *loves* that."

"Mason can deal with it. I'm friends with Craig and Tucker. He really wants to be with me? Well, he'll just have to accept you're my friend too."

He scoffed. "Piper, he knows."

I blinked as my blood ran cold. "What?"

He gave me a sarcastic frown. "You cannot be stupid enough to think Carter doesn't see the way I look at you."

"How do you look at me?" I whispered.

"I look at you like a lifer looks past the prison walls. I look at you like…like you look at mud cake. Okay? You're that something I need, but I can never have–"

"Roman, I'm standing right here! And, I'm not asking for anything more than you."

"Fuck," he muttered, whirling on his heel. As he turned back to face me, he said, "Piper, I care too much about you to let you hold onto me. I'm not the guy you think I am."

He hiked his bag further up his shoulder and started walking away.

"Fuck that, Lombardi!" I screamed after him and he paused. "You are exactly the guy I think you are! And, I couldn't care less! I'm just sorry I'm not the girl you wanted me to be!"

He moved so quickly I barely saw him turn and then he was standing in front of me again. "Don't do that," he snarled.

Why did that make my heart flutter? Probably some early sign of cardiovascular disease…

"Do what?" I asked, sassing the shit out of him.

"Short-change yourself. You are exactly the girl I wanted. The girl I needed. The girl I knew you were. You're perfect, no matter how much you wear that stupid mask for everyone else because you think you're not enough. You don't apologise for being who you are. Not to me. We don't apologise, Piper."

"Apologies might not be necessary, Lombardi, but they are polite."

His jaw clenched. "Fine. In the spirit of politeness, I'm sorry you can't have what you want, Piper."

He turned and walked away again.

"You can be in a shit all you want, Lombardi! But, I know you. I know you miss me as much as I miss you," I called after him. "We're friends, remember? That doesn't just go away because

Carter found his sack!" I threw his words back at him.

This time though, he didn't stop. He got into his car and sped away.

Hadley suggested we go to the park again after school and that gave me the perfect excuse not to be going anywhere near the direction of home at the same time as Roman, so I threw myself into it with everything I had. And, I had a good time.

There was no Roman at the skate park to distract me. It was just me and my friends and my…boyfriend? We ate chips and the girls watched the boys play football while we talked about the boys. I was less of a dick around Mason and we got seriously called out when the others saw me kiss him, as awkward and chaste as it was.

As I dropped out of the bus after and started walking home, I felt good. Really good. Well, mostly good. I was focussing on the happy things and letting go of the things that made me unhappy.

Like not having Roman.

I hitched my bag onto my shoulder as I tried not to worry about it. Because, Roman got in shits; it's what he was best known for. And to be honest, I got where he was coming from. I did.

Whatever we were now was strained and awkward and dredged up a whole lot of feelings that were super uncomfortable. But if Roman didn't do feelings, why was he being awkward? I mean, I guess lust was a feeling – or was it an emotion? Either way, I got how that could make things weird.

Our admissions over the past week weren't exactly the sort you should have with a guy not your boyfriend. But, we could care deeply about each other and just be friends couldn't we? I mean, it was possible. People were friends with people and their bonds were tight – didn't mean there was anything romantic or sexual in it.

I sighed.

Who the hell was I kidding?

I was just pretending again.

Roman and I had been practically dating, we'd slept together, we'd shared everything. In what universe could we be friends straight away? In the selfish one I'd created in my head, that's what. Because let's be honest, even those first few nights on the lake had been flirty. We'd been flirty and had sex before we really would have called each other friend.

So, patience.

I would be patient.

He said we'd find our way back to each other and I had to believe it. I couldn't force it. I had to trust that our friendship was stronger than this weirdness I was probably solely responsible for.

And, it turned out trust was the right way to go.

Friday morning, Roman was leaning against his ute, cigarette in hand. When he heard my door close, he looked up and gave me a smile I suspected was meant to be welcoming but looked like it needed practise.

"Hey," I said, failing to not be happy to see him.

He nodded. "Hey. You want a lift?"

I slowed. "Sure. Thanks."

He shrugged as he pulled the door open for me. As I climbed in, he helped me with a hand to steady me like old times and we shared a smile. I am pleased to report that I felt no urge to kiss him or climb on top of him in his car – even if my heart did skip a little.

The conversation started stilted. But, by the time we got to school, we were both laughing hard at something ridiculous. We went our separate ways and only interacted via looks and GIFs all day.

"You're in a good mood today," Hadley said as she nudged me.

I looked up to find Roman and smiled. "I am."

"You and Mason going out again?"

I watched as Roman skated across a patch of cement, saluted me and tumbled off his board. Biting my lip against a laugh as I looked down, I shook my head. "No set plans."

"No…set… Okay?" Hadley answered as though her brain was moving too fast. "And, this is cause for celebration?"

I looked up at her quickly. "No! No," I huffed a laugh. "I just…" I shrugged. "I don't know, I'm just in a good mood."

I squealed in surprise as arms went around me and Mason picked me up around the middle and swung me around. I laughed as he put me down and span in his arms.

"Hi," I laughed.

"Hi."

Why were his eyes always so open? So light? So clear? So…free? Untroubled?

"I'm thinking you should probably come and throw the footy around with us."

I scoffed. "I'm thinking not."

Mason gave me that smile. "I think, yes. Hadley, too."

"Oh, no," Hadley grimaced. "Nope. I do not do dirt."

Mason pouted. "Tucker will be devastated."

Hadley pulled herself up straight. "No, no. I mean… I can make an exception. Surely?" She looked around. "Craig!" she yelled, waving at him as she walked over. "Show me how this football thing is done!"

Once again, Hadley's flirting technique confused me.

"You coming?" Mason asked.

I nodded. "Sure."

He pressed a quick kiss to my lips, grabbed my hand and tugged me to the others where the boys tried to teach us how to kick a decent football. There was more falling over, laughing and flirting than actual kicking going around. But, we were all in stitches by the time the bell for the end of Lunch went and we had to traipse back to class.

Roman and I spared a smile for each other and he picked a piece of grass out of my hair as he passed.

"Nature agrees with you, Barlow."

"Shame it doesn't look so good on you, Lombardi."

He gave me a quizzical look and I pointed to the patch of dried mud on his leg.

"Huh," he mused. "You'd think I'd be better by now."

"You do fall off your board a lot these days."

"You smile a lot these days."

I bit my lip against said smile, batted him gently and followed Hadley to class.

And, things seemed only to be getting better from there.

Well, two steps forward, one step back.

On Saturday we had a relatively warm day and Roman and I decided to take Maddy to the lake. With her, he was amazing as always. With me, he was hot and cold. It was like there was something going on in his mind that would suddenly rain down on his parade. But, if he didn't want to share it, I knew better than to push.

He was like a bloody emotional yo-yo. But, I accepted him as he was in the moment; happy, crazy, funky, surly, broody. And, he did the same for me.

Saturday night, I was studying. I have no idea what he was getting up to until I got a call a little before eleven.

"A happy number nineteen, Barlow," he said jovially and I could tell he was putting on the act.

I also knew exactly to what he was referring. "Happy nineteen, Roman. What can I do for you?"

"Well in good news, no charges. But, they won't let me go home by myself and they just can't find anyone to take me."

I nodded to myself and dropped my pen. "So, you need me to pick you up?"

"If you'd be so kind."

"At least cut the crap," I sighed as I pushed away from my desk and started looking for my shoes.

"Cut what crap?" he asked sweetly.

"This perpetuating nonchalant attitude you have going. You can play it with other people, but not me. I'm not in the mood, Lombardi." I picked up my keys and headed downstairs.

"What attitude, Barlow? This is just me."

I could see it was going to be one of those nights. But, this was Roman and I knew how to handle him in whatever mood he was in.

"I'll be there in about fifteen minutes, okay?" I said.

"You going– Oh, sorry, honey," Mum ended in a harsh whisper as she saw the phone to my ear.

Just as I was about to hang up, Roman spoke again, "Be careful,

Barlow. Yeah?" and his voice was nothing but sincere.

I nodded. "I will."

I hung up and looked to where Mum and Dad were curled on the couch.

"What's up, Pipe?" Dad asked, lowering his book.

"Uh, Roman's just asked if I can pick him up. Can I borrow one of your cars, please?"

Mum and Dad shared a look before they nodded.

"Sure, honey. Whichever one you want."

"I'm just picking him up and coming straight back here. So, I shouldn't be long."

They nodded again. "Have a nice time."

I rolled my eyes, figuring there was no point in correcting them. I grabbed Dad's car keys and jogged out to the car.

By the time I got to the police station, whatever Roman had or hadn't done or needed to do had been sorted and he was ready to go.

"Ah, my knight in...furry pants!" he chuckled as he caught sight of my pyjama pants, obviously totally drunk.

"No wonder they wouldn't let you home by yourself," I grumbled, snagging his sleeve and pulling him after me. "Come on, let's get you home."

He stopped and I was forced to stop too. "Ah, but I have it on good authority that there is a raging party. Rio texted me the address. No dress code, therefore furry pants more than welcome."

I shook my head and pulled on his sleeve until he started following me again.

"Fucking and drinking still solving all those problems, Lombardi?" I asked as I opened the passenger door for him.

He smirked down at me, but any and all humour was gone from

his deep dark eyes. This was the Roman Lombardi I remembered; the resident underachiever Hadley accused of making you wet just by looking at another girl. He was all brooding bad boy. But, I wasn't powerless against it.

"Doing wonders. How about you?" He gave me a wink.

I nodded, not sure why that would make my throat hitch. "So pleased. Come on. Get in."

He gave me another of those smirks and a look that could light you on fire before he nodded and got into the car. I shut the door, took a deep breath, and walked back to the driver's door. Before opening it, I needed to take another breath. Because I knew exactly which Roman I was getting into a car with and I knew he was worse than handsy, chatty Piper after two beers.

Finally, I swung in and started the car.

We said nothing the whole way home, no matter how many times I opened my mouth to say something to him. But, that was unexpectedly expected of Roman.

When I pulled into my driveway, I held out my hand to him. "Keys."

"Keys?"

"House keys. I'll walk you in."

"You think I'm too drunk to make it? Little Piper playing hall monitor now? Or maybe it's doctors and nurses you're after?" he said, his tone telling me exactly what he was thinking.

"Keys, Roman," I demanded.

With a rough chuckle that certainly did not make goose bumps spread across my skin, he finally dropped the keys into my hands. We got out of the car and I unlocked his back door for him.

Under the security light, I could see his face clearly. He looked down at me with a heat in his eyes that told me exactly why we were finding it so hard to be friends. He was all dark smoulder and it was all my brain could do to remind my body we were not available. Not to Roman. Especially not this Roman.

"Have some water. Go to bed. Text me in the morning?" I took a step back.

He nodded slowly in that ridiculously seductive way he had. "Sure."

"Good. Night, Roman."

"Night, Piper."

I gave him his keys back, careful not to touch his hand and practically ran back to my house. I paused outside the back door not to look back at him – because I could tell he was still looking at me – but to compose myself before I went inside.

Roman and I couldn't be friends. It's just how it was.

No amount of fighting for it was going to work.

We could be friendly, share car rides, crack jokes, talk to each other. But, we weren't going to be the sort of friends who stayed up all night baring their souls or hung out together on the weekends. We just couldn't. There was too much between us and I had to accept that.

I had to untangle Roman from everything that made me Piper and let Mason be my John Cusack.

I just didn't know how I was supposed to even start doing that.

Chapter Twenty Six
Hadley and the Unhelpful Advice.

"You and Roman totally went out," Hadley said accusingly as we were studying.

I shook my head. "No, we didn't."

"You so did. Don't lie to me."

She was totally teasing. But, sick of the lies and the half-truths, I dropped my pencil. Well, throw was more apt a word as it clattered and bounced across the table.

"No. That was the exact problem, Hads. We didn't date. We hooked up, we had some fun, nothing more. Then Mason finally asked me out and Roman…moved on. The problem is we then realised it hadn't been just a bit of fun, it had been something more. And now we'll never know."

I was staring at my book and she didn't say anything for the longest time. I finally looked at her and she was glaring at me with her mouth open.

"You what?" she finally asked.

I sighed and looked back down. "In the holidays, Roman and I ended up hanging out. Like every night of the holidays. One thing eventually led to another and we had sex. We had sex and we didn't have sex. Then, Mason asked me out and it all became weird and awkward and complicated. Roman and I stopped seeing each other at all, our friendship was strained, and it was all just so fucked up."

She didn't say anything again and I didn't really want to look at her and see the accusation of her face.

"Yeah, okay. I'm sorry I took your guy from you. Hos before bros and all that. But, it just happened, Hads."

"I'm less concerned with the fact you stole my dream man, and more concerned with the fact that you just said 'fuck' without batting an eyelid, and that you popped your cherry without telling me! What did he do to you?"

"Nothing. He didn't do anything to me."

"I mean… Shit, Pipe. You lost it to Roman Lombardi!" She sounded all at once excited and confused.

I nodded. "Yeah, I lost it to Roman Lombardi."

"How was it?"

I couldn't stop my stupid grin. "How do you think it was?"

"Amazing?" she sighed.

I nodded. "Yeah, about that." Although, not for the reasons she'd assume.

"Oh my God!" she squealed. "You lost it to Roman!"

I smiled. "This was not the reaction I expected."

"What sort of reaction did you expect? Oh shit! Is that what all those looks and those *moments* were? Shit, he didn't nail and bail. Double shit! He still wants you! Triple shit! What are you going to do?"

"Hang on…" I looked at her. "Where is the chastising? Where is the telling me I made poor life choices? Where is the comparison between how terrible Roman is for me and how Mason's my John Cusack?"

"Everyone knows Mason's your John Cusack." She waved a hand. "But, I just don't know what to address first, to be honest."

Hadley re-settled herself. "Okay, so… Start at the beginning. You guys hung out?"

So, I did. I ran her through the first few nights at the lakeshore, the night we first slept together, the days and nights after that, and every nuance she'd missed out on. I finally told her how I felt like shit sometimes and didn't know why. I told her all the things I should have been telling her from the beginning but feared she'd judge me for. The things I could just so easily and cavalierly tell Roman, of all people.

"And, I missed all of this?" she asked when I was done.

"I'm sorry, Hads."

She sighed. "No. I'm as much to blame. I totally should have noticed all this. How did you… Are you okay?"

I dropped my head onto the desk. "I don't know," I said honestly.

"Well, I mean you…" She took a deep breath and rubbed my back awkwardly like we were old people or something. "He… You guys…connected?"

I nodded. "If we're going to be so wanky as to call it that, yeah. He was just…" I sighed. "I don't know, Hads. We can just sit in silence for hours and I feel better. He knows when I need to laugh and when I need to talk and when I need to just not say anything. You know he sings at me when I need a laugh?"

"What?"

I nodded again, my forehead rubbing on the desk. "He'll sing me a totally unexpected song. Like, full on girl-power power ballads; Katy Perry, Leona Lewis, Mariah. There was a Steps song at one point."

"Please tell me it was '5, 6, 7, 8' and he did the dance."

I huffed a laugh. "Yes."

"No! Really?"

"Yes, really. Dance and all."

"Piper?"

"Hadley?"

"Marry him, now."

"What?" I huffed a sceptical laugh.

"Do you think maybe you've made a terrible mistake?"

"What do you mean?"

"Well, it seems to me that you've found someone to serve every single function you could want in a human being – I mean, I've obviously been replaced – so…maybe you're with the wrong guy?"

"Really? You think?"

"Okay, no need to be sarcastic."

"It's not like I could be *with* Roman, though."

"Sounds like you already were to me."

Hadn't I told him the exact same thing? And hadn't we both realised in the moment that for all intents and purposes we had been together? I may have not let myself believe he wasn't with other girls, but I'd believed him when he'd said he wasn't. I'd lost my first real boyfriend before I'd even realised that's what I'd had…

"And, you weren't replaced," I changed the subject so I didn't have to think about what I might have had.

"Babes, you really didn't feel good?"

I sighed again. "I can't explain it and it sounds weak and stupid. But, Roman didn't care. I could be in a total shit, I could be happy, we could just *be* around each other and it was so…easy. I didn't question if what I was doing what right or wrong. I didn't feel like I had to pretend because I shouldn't have any problems."

"You really thought I'd judge you?"

"I don't know. I just worried, you know. Like, what does Piper

Barlow have to worry about? But, here I was feeling down and awkward and just…I don't know. It was tiring, pretending I was fine. I didn't have to be like that around Roman. We had a rule, no apologies. We just accepted each other for how we were at the time. There were no expectations, there was no pressure."

"And, he fixed you?"

I didn't know if I should sigh or laugh at that, so I made a weird combination noise. Sometimes, it felt a whole lot like Roman had accidentally fixed a part of me, but in reality that wasn't quite the truth.

"No... Not fixed. No guy – no person, really – just makes all that go away, Hads. But he made it easier to handle, less stressful. Less like I was a whiny bitch, or how I felt was stupid or wrong. With him, it was easier to…breathe, I guess. I could just be me around him and he accepted every me I am."

And, it was true. Roman hadn't made everything better; I wasn't magically healed or whatever because he'd been in my life. I still felt shit sometimes and I still felt lonely in a sea of people sometimes, for no obvious reason at all. But, him making me feel like it was okay – like *I* was okay, like I wasn't abnormal and still a good person – it made it easier for me to accept myself and that lessened some of the intensity. He let me be me, and being me wasn't always so hard anymore.

"Okay, all this is just cementing in my mind that you chose the wrong guy." She pulled me out of my head and I sighed.

"I chose the guy who wanted a relationship with me, Hads. The guy who wasn't convinced he has nothing to give me. The guy who wasn't going to get bored at some point and leave me behind."

"Yeah, except everything you've told me makes me think that Roman wants that, too. Even if he won't acknowledge it," she said avidly and I wondered how much I believed my previous statement. "Piper, it's hard not to notice him, and I've noticed the way he looks at you. I've been telling you for months that he wants you. And, now I'm convinced. Fuck, babes! I bet he didn't even know how much he wanted you. But, all the signs were there. That day on the oval?"

"What day on the oval?"

"Do you remember that day the two of you were having a super serious conversation about something?"

"No."

"It looked to us like he'd just ambushed you, if you hadn't been so accommodating. And the way you two were together? Honestly, it was fucking inspiring. The two of you kept just subconsciously touching each other, like you were just there for each other, like it was second nature. Then, before he left, I could have sworn he kissed your head. Like, looking back, you two were the epitome of old people relationships–"

I pulled my head off the desk enough to look at her. "What?"

"Well, you know how your parents are always touching, right? I mean, not just *your* parents, but everyone's parents. You know how they're just like extensions of each other? You and Roman are like extensions of each other."

"You're insane."

"No. See, this whole Mason mess wouldn't have happened if you'd just trusted me in the first place–"

"It wasn't a lack of trust, Hads."

Although, I guessed it sort of was in a way. I hadn't trusted that I was worth loving enough to not be judged by the people closest to me.

"Okay, wrong word. I should have been there for you, I should have noticed something was up. But if I'd known, I never would have forced Mason on you."

I scoffed. "You didn't force Mason on me. No one forced Mason on me. I like him and he likes me."

"Yeah, but you love Roman."

"Hadley!"

"What?"

"I don't love Roman."

"Don't you? Because it sounds a hell of a lot like you might. I mean, you and I can't even sit for hours in companionable silence–"

"You couldn't sit by yourself for hours in companionable silence."

She laughed. "Okay, yes. But, you get my point. Babes, I hate the fact I was so blind. But, it seems to me that Roman Lombardi gets you in a whole way that no one else does. And, that's special on any level. I mean, that's not even taking into account the fact that you'd both rather just sit in silence together than be with anyone else in the world, or the fact that you have enough sexual chemistry to light the world on fire."

I scoffed.

"He gets you, Piper, and he's obviously a better friend than I could ever be."

"Hads, that's not–"

"No, I'm glad. I dropped the ball. Whether you thought it should make sense or not, your feelings were valid. I didn't see through your bullshit and that's my bad–"

"Hads–"

"I'm serious, Pipe. I love you like a sister and I hate to admit it but I think you're right. I would have been a completely judgemental arse in the moment or I would have laughed in your face because you looked so… Normal is a terrible word for it. But, you tried to tell me you were feeling shit? I would have shrugged it off. I would never have just let you be in a shit and accepted it. I would have tried to change it for me, not you. Roman?" She whistled.

"I fucked up."

"You fucked up."

"He fucked up."

"He fucked up."

"What do I do?" I asked.

"Where did you leave it?"

"He's no good for me and we have no chance."

"Well, that's bullshit!"

"Hads, he said he couldn't give me anything. There's very little I can do if that's what he believes," I sighed.

"Okay… Well, his idiocy aside, can you keep going out with Mason knowing that you're irrevocably in love with Roman?"

"Firstly, I am not irrevocably in love with Roman–"

"Aren't you though?"

"Hadley!" I sighed. God knew I loved her, but she wasn't always the most helpful. "Maybe I could have been, but we never got there okay? At best, he'll be my 'what if'."

"Oh, because that's better," she scoffed.

"Okay, maybe not. But, Mason and I have a real shot here. I do really like him. He's kind, he's smart, he's funny, he's attractive–"

"He gets you. Oh no, wait, that's Roman."

See? Not helpful.

"You are not helping. And you're the one who wanted me to

330

date Mason in the first place."

She sighed. "Look, all I'm saying is that maybe you and Mason both deserve better? You deserve the guy you'd otherwise wonder about and he deserves a girl who's not wondering."

"I thought Mason was my John Cusack? He's the guy voted least likely, but he's the guy who'll win me over in the end, the guy I couldn't live without–"

"By that definition, Roman's your John Cusack."

I glared at her and kept talking. "What do I do if I push away all of Mason's sweetness and kindness and potential for Roman and it blows up in my face? In fact, it's likely to blow up in my face. Roman doesn't do relationships and I'm not going to waste my time trying to convince him. So, I'd have no potential and still have a 'what if'."

"You're fucked."

"I'm fucked."

We sat in silence for a moment; the longest amount of time Hadley had been quiet in the almost life-time I'd known her. And, it felt comfortable. Other than all the Roman bullshit running around my mind, I felt totally at ease. There were no secrets between us and I could breathe easily.

"You don't hate me for lying to you?" I asked finally.

She hugged me. "I'm annoyed, but I'm going to give you a pass since you were going through shit. But, only this once."

"What would you do?"

"God," she whispered, "I don't know. I mean, Roman is instant passion, you know. And, Mason is like lifetime security, if you want it. But, Roman's passion could be lifetime security. That's the unknown. He could wake up and realise that he actually *can* offer you the world. Mason's got the steadfastness down, the big gestures, his heart is on his sleeve. Roman, though?"

"Yes. Thanks. Not helping again."

"Okay, honestly?"

I was painfully reminded of every one of Roman and my exchanges, but I nodded. "Always."

"I'd pick Mason, but I'm a coward."

And, there was the real Hadley; bullshit bluster aside. Her trusting me with the truth just reinforced to me that telling her everything had been the right choice. I just wished I'd been strong enough to do it earlier, that I'd trusted her earlier, that I'd been braver earlier.

"Yeah. But aren't I, too?"

She put an arm around my shoulder. "I don't know, Pipe. Are you really, though?"

"He scares me, Hads," I said. "He's got too much power over me. Without even meaning to. He's already hurt me. I gave him the power to do it again and I don't know how to take it back. Every day only makes it worse. I don't know if I'm strong enough to go through the risk again."

"Can I give you some advice, Piper?"

"I'd love some."

"Tell Mason it's just not working and go and have mad sex with Roman."

"Fuck you, Hadley."

"Love you, too, bitch."

I buried my face in my elbow and laughed. We may have found ourselves on different pages lately. But when it counted, Hadley knew me and she knew I loved her.

The group was sitting on the oval, having lunch and minding their own business. And that's an important point which will make sense soon.

The oval was a place where a lot of the Year Twelves hung out, so the fact that Roman's group and mine both happened to be there most days was purely coincidental; it was something that had been happening for years.

Anyway, I'd had to see my English teacher about something after class, so I was the last one making their way to our lunch spot. I walked out on the oval and Roman pushed himself off the wall to my right, falling into step with me.

"Hey," he said easily.

My eyes fell on the group, but no one was looking our way.

"Hi." I nodded.

"So, how are things?"

I nodded again. "Yeah, fine. You?"

His hands were in his pockets and he scuffed his shoes on the grass. "Yeah, good. I'm sorry I wasn't there this morning…"

"What do we say about apologies, Lombardi?"

"That they're polite, just not necessary."

I nodded yet again. "Okay. Well, good. Look, I need to go."

His hand brushed my arm, then he stopped. "If you want a ride home… I'll be in the carpark."

I sighed. "Sure. I'll…" Why did things have to be so awkward now? Hadley and my conversation the other day hadn't helped at all in that department. "Maybe. I'll see you later."

I could just picture him nodding once and kicking the ground before strolling back to his friends while I hurried to mine. As I sat down, I was convinced everyone knew I had plenty to be guilty about. But, no one looked at me any differently, Mason took my hand and kissed my cheek before turning back to Simon, and the world just went on.

I was having a little trouble reconciling the fact that the world could just go on around me while my world was in slightly more turmoil than was preferable. But, even though it was a little harder than it had been lately, I smiled and nodded and pretended everything was fine.

I don't even remember what we were talking about when there was a commotion on the other side of the oval. We all turned to see two people fighting, and it was fairly epic even for our school's standards.

I recognised one figure easily and so didn't need Hadley's elbow in my ribs or her hissed, "It's Roman!"

I nodded, telling myself to turn around and not worry about it.

"Go over there! It'll look weirder if you don't!" Hadley's lips were practically in my ear. She elbowed me again. "Go!"

"Like I can do anything," I answered her.

"You've got more chance than anyone else," Mason said and I jumped slightly guiltily.

"He doesn't listen to me."

"You guys are friends. He listens to you."

"Okay, okay," I muttered and got up, knowing they'd keep pushing and then that would make it weird. "I'm on it."

I strode over to Roman, yelling at him. It was surely only a matter of minutes before a teacher was going to notice the fight and pull it apart; they might not pay enough attention to the oval to tell him off for smoking, but a fight wasn't going to get past anyone.

Plus, Roman was due for a suspension this time, so the not getting noticed at all thing was a whole lot better.

"Roman!" I snapped.

Which, turned out to be a bad plan. He turned to me as I said his name again and Grant cracked him in the side of the head. Roman shot me a glare and swung back at Grant with gusto.

"Seriously, dude. You cannot afford–"

"Afford what, Piper?" Mr Dunbridge asked from behind me and I grimaced. *Of course it had to be Mr Dunbridge.*

"Exactly what he deserves?" I answered, turning to him with an awkward smile.

Mr Dunbridge nodded. "Gentlemen. Can we get some control over ourselves, please?"

Grant and Roman stopped and turned. Roman's eyebrow was split and blood trickled down the side of his face. He breathed heavily and his expression was like thunder.

I was actually surprised to see him in a fight at school. He got in a lot of fights outside of school, everyone knew that, I'd seen the evidence plenty. But, I guess it just seemed like all the guys at school knew better than to start a fight with him – not counting Rio. Obviously either Grant didn't know better, or something had gone down.

"Is there a reason for this?" Mr Dunbridge asked.

Roman glared in stony silence while Grant shook his head.

Mr Dunbridge sighed. "All right then. Piper, why don't you go back to your friends. There's no need for you to be caught up in this unnecessarily."

Grant scoffed. "Back to Carter, more like."

Roman span, grabbed him by the front of his clothes and shoved his fist in his face. "You don't fucking talk about her!"

335

I'd stepped forward and had my hand on Roman's arm before I could think about it. "Lombardi, stop acting like a tool," I said, only loud enough for him and Grant to hear me.

Grant looked at me in humoured surprise, but neither of them moved.

"For God's sake," I muttered as I grabbed the piercing in the top of Roman's ear and pulled.

He had no choice but to swing his head after my hand or more carnage would ensue. I pulled him around to face me and his face was even darker.

"You right, Barlow?"

"You right, Lombardi?"

"Fucking pussy," Grant whispered.

Roman turned again and I dropped my hand from his ear before grabbing his arm. I wanted to try to keep some control over him but I wasn't going to rip out his piercing for it.

"Gentlemen!" Mr Dunbridge called. "It is perhaps not a good idea to have either of you in the same proximity. Piper, please take Roman to the nurse and keep him there until I've dealt with Grant."

"Of course, sir." I tightened my grip on Roman's arm and pulled him after me.

"Will you slow the fuck down, Barlow?" he whined.

"No. Besides, your legs are well longer than mine. You've got no reason to complain."

"You know, I don't need you intervening in my fights. I *am* a big boy now."

"Big boys don't start fights on the playground with wrestlers."

"You think I can't take him?"

"I think you're an idiot."

"But, a very adorable idiot." I could hear him pouting.

"Not today."

"Oh, but I have a boo-boo."

"And, I'll give you another one if you don't stop talking."

"I can't be talking. I was sure we weren't on speaking terms."

Oh, good. This *Roman...* He was the sarcastic, dark, broody Roman with an unnecessary level of pissed-off sass.

I rolled my eyes. "If that were true, you wouldn't be annoying me now."

He snorted and I turned to find him giving me a very innocent expression. "What? Not talking!" He held his hands up as best he could while I was hanging onto his elbow.

"You are the bane of my existence, Lombardi."

"And, you're the light of mine, Barlow."

"Oh, how sweet," the nurse cooed as I pulled him into her office and pretended my heart hadn't just jump-crumpled.

"He doesn't mean it," I assured her and ignored the way I felt like I'd kicked myself in the gut.

She gave one of those chuckles adults do when they think kids do something cute. "No, of course not." Then, she winked. "What have you got yourself into now, Roman?" she asked him, humorously exasperated like he was a favourite nephew she'd let get away with murder.

"A fight for a lady's honour, ma'am," he replied dramatically.

"Oh, how lovely. Which lady was that?"

"The beautiful Piper here."

"Oh, no!" I scoffed. "You don't drag me into your stupid fights!"

"S'true. He besmirched your good name and I gave him a good what-for."

"Oh, that's a lovely thing to do for your girlfriend. You two

337

make a wonderful couple."

Roman's face shut down as I went red and cleared my throat awkwardly.

"She's not *my* girlfriend," he said, all trace of cheek or humour gone.

"Oh!" the nurse chuckled. "Even better." Then she winked again and went about checking over Roman's minor injuries.

She was just about done when Mr Dunbridge walked in.

"You've got a week, Roman," he said.

Roman nodded. "Sounds about right."

"You've been warned, son," he said, then sighed. "Come on, you've got a couple of months left and then you're outta here. Let's try not to get into any more trouble, hey?"

Roman gave him his best 'I'll behave' look and the nurse fussed over him some more; honestly, the woman was lovely and excellent at her job, but she was a sap for an attractive young man.

"You know the drill, Roman," Mr Dunbridge said as though he knew it was useless trying to help the guy who didn't want to be helped.

"I do. Off school property by end of Lunch and not back until Monday-week. I'm a very good boy at following the rules, sir."

"The ones that suit you, yes," he muttered as he walked out, shaking his head.

Roman threw me his sexiest smirk, but his eyes were cold. "Suffice to say you'll need to get the bus home, Barlow."

I slapped him once for good measure and stormed out.

Chapter Twenty Seven
Perfectly Not Going Out.

In the end, I didn't have to tell Mason anything. Which is not to say I didn't try. Hadley had been right; Mason deserved better and I deserved better. Even if I never had anything with Roman, I couldn't be with Mason anymore. Not when someone else took up more space in my heart and not when I just wasn't into Mason like that.

I cornered him awkwardly the next lunchtime and laughed awkwardly in his face.

"Hi, Mason," I said, nice and awkward-like.

He smiled down at me. "How are you, Piper?"

I grinned and wrung my hands. "Good. No, I'm good. How are you?"

"Piper, I feel like this isn't going to go well for me."

I looked down and felt my cheeks burn. "Uh, well… It depends, I guess."

"Shall I do it?"

I looked up quickly. "What?"

"Well," he said slowly, a smile growing that didn't really reach his eyes. "I do like you, a lot. And, I get that you like me. But, something's…not quite right, is it?"

I sighed. "I just… I'm sorry, Mason. I spent so much time trying to prove I was interested in you like that that I didn't really register that I wasn't... I tried so hard to make it work – to be that perfect couple that people expected – that I didn't really see it wasn't."

He shook his head. "I get it. I won't pretend I'm not disappointed. I really like you, Piper. But, you're right. We're just not each other's perfect. Besides, it's not your fault if you like someone else."

"I don't..." I stopped myself because lying to him wasn't fair. "I do like you, Mason, and I'm sorry. I'm not really girlfriend material at the moment, if I'm honest. At least, I don't feel like girlfriend material. I'd be doing us both an injustice pretending otherwise, I think."

He nodded. "I get that. I'm just sorry I couldn't be what you needed. And, for the record – if I can be so blunt – Roman really couldn't do better. By any stretch. I never thought I'd see anything decent in the guy. But well, if he's fallen for you, he obviously has *some* taste."

God, why did Mason have to be so nice?

I opened my mouth a couple of times and nothing came out. Finally, I managed words. "Mason... He and I... We never..."

He nodded. "I know." I looked at him sceptically. "I assume," he amended with a wry shrug. "You're not that sort of girl."

I smiled, not quite sure that he'd assumed what I'd been trying to say, or that I was sure about what he'd assumed. But, maybe it was just better to leave it in the good place it was.

"Thanks."

"I imagine Roman's man enough to let us still be friends?" he asked with a smile.

I snorted and looked down. "I don't know that it matters. I really don't see the whole Roman and me thing going forward."

"Maybe I was wrong and he is an idiot."

I batted him playfully. "I'd like to still be friends, though."

"Then we will be." He put his arm around my shoulder and we wandered back over to our friends. "So, about Tucker and Hadley…" he started and I laughed.

Nothing changed between me and Mason. Well I mean, we weren't holding hands or kissing, but we actually got along better. We shared more jokes, we talked more, it was just so much more natural to just be friends; it was easy. We were even at a point where I let him use me to deter Shayla's advances.

The next week was, basically, great. There was no stress, no worry. I had my great group of friends around me, I had my school work to finish, I had plenty of things to distract me. Not that I needed distractions. Because, I was okay.

Although, Hadley had taken to checking up on me far too often. I loved that she'd taken the whole I'd kept things from her thing seriously and wanted to do better, but I also could have done with being a better friend. Like maybe not keeping stuff from her in the first place.

But regardless of all that, life was good.

Without Roman.

I missed him like crazy – I'd be constantly thinking of things to text him or look forward to a hug I'd never get – and I wished I could work out how to fix us. But, for the first time in however many weeks it had been, life was good without Roman.

It felt weird all of itself, but I was quite happy to just let it be that way.

I breathed easier. I didn't feel more than necessary panic when I felt down for no reason. Now people knew and knew how I wanted to play it, it was…easy being me. Well, not as difficult. I finally felt like maybe my life could be that vision of perfect that people seemed to have of it.

Roman and I might have been broken – we might have treated each other like little more than that friend from kindy you feel obligated to still be polite to – but he'd given me a true gift; he'd given me the confidence to be myself. He'd taught me how to be myself and to accept myself. He'd taught me that people could still love me even when I felt damaged. He'd taught me that all I had to do was *show* them I trusted them.

And, whether I was *in love* with him or not, I would always love him for that.

Mason insisted I keep playing football with them and I might have been getting slightly better. That, or the boys took pity on me. But really, it wasn't my fault the ball was a stupid shape and didn't bounce the way it was supposed to.

By the end of the week, I still never expected it to go the way it went.

I squealed as the damned ball in question bounced left instead of into my hands and tried to launch myself after it. The boys laughed as I overbalanced and I huffed a piece of hair out of my face. Mason came running over and looked down at me with his blue eyes dancing like they always did.

"You okay?" he chuckled.

I nodded.

He held his hands out to me and I let him help me up. He flicked his hair out of his eyes and I couldn't help but smile at him.

And, there were no flutters. There was no insatiable urge to divulge unnecessary secrets. I didn't feel hysterical laughter threatening to embarrass the crap out of me. I didn't flush awkwardly. I didn't wonder if what I was doing was right or wrong.

I was exactly where I needed to be, how I needed to be.

And, I was pretty sure Mason felt the same.

"I'm fine, thanks. All but my dignity is still intact."

Mason snorted. "Your dignity has never been in question, Piper."

I grinned. "Oh, I think it has."

Suddenly, his eyes slid behind me and went wide.

"Shayla sighting?" I asked, trying not to laugh at his panicked look.

He nodded. "Yeah. She's just not getting the message."

"Maybe she heard we...weren't seeing each other anymore?" I finished slowly; I was never sure how to phrase it.

But, Mason smiled at me. "Something like that."

"Okay. Well, we could do something cute?" I offered.

He shook his head. "You've already helped me once this week. I can't keep relying on you."

I shrugged. "We're friends, Mason. What else are friends for?"

He looked at me dubiously. "For not being used to perpetuate the idea that we're dating?"

I shrugged. "Mase, come on. You're not using me if I offer." A thought suddenly hit me. "Unless it would be...uncomfortable?"

He smiled at me. "No. We're definitely better as friends, Piper." And, I believed him; he was open and easy-going, his smile reaching those beautiful blue eyes.

"I don't know if I should feel insulted or not, Mr Carter!" I chuckled.

Mason grinned widely, picked me up around the middle and swung me around. "Trust me, Miss Barlow. Friends is way better!"

I squealed and giggled as he swung me, finally putting me down and I gave him a huge hug.

"Thanks for being so amazing, friend," I said.

"Right back at you, friend," he replied, giving me one more squeeze before he let me go and we joined back in on the game.

In what was quite possibly the exact opposite of irony, it seemed Mason Carter was my…Carter…after all.

I was walking home from the bus on Friday afternoon, listening to my music and feeling pretty good, when a rumble of a car pulled me from my song.

I looked up to see Roman's ute coming towards me. He didn't slow. In fact, I would have bet that he sped up as he got closer. I moved closer to the shoulder of the road and looked down, fully intending to avoid eye contact with him.

But, my eyes had other plans.

Before he'd gone past, I looked up quickly and our eyes met for the briefest of seconds.

Like some corny movie moment, it felt like time slowed and it hit me just what impact that Roman-shaped hole had on my life.

No more walking home together and him singing me Katy Perry to cheer me up.

No more Roman raking his hand through his hair as neither of us are sure if he's just insulted me or complimented me.

No more of those sarcastic comments.

No more of him just being honest about thinking I was hot.

No more of him accepting Piper Barlow had issues.

No more Roman falling off his board to make me laugh.

No more watching him skipping stones and realising there was more to him.

No more being told to stay out of my box.

No more seeing his expressions of delighted surprise as I let go of that prudish exterior.

No more watching him with Maddy.

No more of that uncharacteristic, adorable, uncomfortable shifting where he looked at me through his hair.

No more teasing each other.

No more pink beanies.

No more tension eased just because he was there.

No more '5, 6, 7, 8'.

No more passion.

No more protection.

No more…whatever made us…us.

My eyes seemed to focus, and Roman's face was still there. It was hard and I wasn't sure why that made me feel guilty. Then, he was gone and I was standing alone on the road home as he was moving about as fast away from me as possible.

I mean, what had I done to feel guilty about really? We'd had a great time together. There'd been a little too much emotion maybe. But honestly, how much emotion can there really have been if he could so easily push me away?

Roman was the guy who never got too close. He was the guy who never promised more than he could offer. He'd said it on multiple occasions; it was the girls who expected more, expected him to change.

A part of me, personally, still thought that he could probably have gone about things differently if it kept happening. But, that was beside the point.

Roman had never promised me more than he could offer and I didn't want more; I didn't want grand declarations, I didn't want a promise of forever, I didn't want anything more than what he'd given. I just wanted what we'd had. I wanted the brooding, angry, dark parts of him. I wanted the laughing, doting uncle, light parts of him. I wanted all the in-between bits. He'd given me everything I could ever ask for and more without even trying; why did he think that wasn't enough? Why did he think he wasn't enough?

I sighed and kept walking.

The pain – which felt eerily like rejection – was lessening with time and I was just going to have to accept that Roman had to do things his way.

"I'm going to accept it. Because that's what we do. We accept each other in the moment. No matter what," I told myself.

Doing was going to be easier said than done. Especially when everything in me told me to run after him and hug him until he relented. But, if this was what Roman wanted – if that's what he needed – then that's what I was going to do.

For him.

"For him."

Chapter Twenty Eight
The Ideas One Has An Idea.

Roman was back at school on Monday.

I passed him getting out of his car as I came in from the bus stop and gave him a smile as he looked up. I watched as he turned to Rio and threw his arm around the shoulder of the girl Rio was with. I'd expected the curt nod brush-off, but I still had to breathe through the impressive kick it gave my stomach. The intense look Rio confused me with helped.

"For him," I reminded myself as I headed for my locker.

"I'll castrate him if you want?" Hadley fell onto the locker next to mine.

I gave her a semi-decent smile. "He's just being him."

"You forgive him too much, babes."

I shook my head. "No. I just know him. And, I don't expect him to be anything other than he is."

"He's still hurting you…"

I huffed a small laugh because I was pretty sure I wasn't the only one he was hurting. "Is that emotion I hear in Hadley Reynolds' voice? Sympathy perhaps?"

She crossed her arms. "Don't get used to it." She paused. "I still say we castrate the arsehole."

I sighed. "Thanks, Hads. I appreciate it. But, let's forego the mutilation for now, yeah?"

"Good morning, lovely ladies!" Mason crowed and I looked up to give him a smile.

"Good morning!" I answered, my enthusiasm completely sincere.

He put his arm around me and kissed my temple. "How was our weekend?"

"Fine, thank you."

"We missed you out," Mason said, hugging me closer. "Well, some of us did. Hadley was a little busy."

I looked up at her to see her roll her eyes. "If Tucker wasn't going to kiss me, I had to kiss him."

I snorted. "Sure. That makes sense. What did you get up to in the end?"

They chattered about *Lacey's* and ice cream while I listened avidly; I might not have felt like going out – and it was amazing that everyone was okay with that – but I still wanted to hear about it. Out of the corner of my eye, I saw Roman walking towards us. He scowled bloody murder at Mason, but there was very little I could do about that. I gave him a half-hearted smile and a nod before turning back to the others.

"…and, Craig got cracked in the nuts," Mason finished.

"Yeah, I can imagine," I laughed.

And, I could. The boys leapfrogging over the poles outside the ice cream place never went well, so I don't know why they always thought it was going to "be fine this time".

I closed my locker and the three of us headed for class.

And, my week continued much the same.

Roman and I basically avoided each other. I gave up trying to spare him smiles in the hopes it would make him feel better. I gave up hoping he'd even look at me. Although – according to Hadley – he did look at me plenty, especially when I wasn't looking. I caught the bus every morning and afternoon, and he drove. I didn't try to get a ride from him. I didn't force my company on him. I gave him the space he quite clearly desired.

But, something niggled at me like it was the wrong choice.

Something that tried to tell me that what Roman needed was confrontation; he needed me to talk to him, to try harder to make him smile. But, I couldn't. My early attempts had been met with the contemptable Roman, the bristly Roman, the dark Roman. He was obviously decided and there was nothing I could do to change his mind. So, I didn't trust what felt weirdly like instincts. And, I treated him the same way I had months ago.

Hadley, Celeste and I hung out with Mason, Craig and Tucker, and sometimes Simon and the others. I could walk away whenever I needed and they all just understood. The girls flirted and the boys flirted, but it was easy and free and fun and open. Although, there was something sizzling under the surface between Tucker and Hadley that she wouldn't hear about.

Mason and I often laughed about it, along with numerous other things. We argued about which John Cusack movie was the best, we argued about mud cake versus angel food cake, we teased Celeste for her crush on Craig, we danced stupid mock-jigs around the oval to take the notice off Hadley and Tucker off in a heated discussion in the corner.

My school work went well, although the idea that exams were so close was not filling me with rainbows.

My parents were still the wonderful people they always were.

I even felt a little better one afternoon – when Celeste was busy trying to flirt with the boys and playing football and Hadley and I were sitting out – when Hadley decided to bring up the uni thing again.

"So… Primary teaching at Uni SA?" she started.

I nodded. "That's my first preference."

"Okay…"

"Babes, what do you actually want to ask?" I chuckled, throwing her a quick look.

She rearranged in her seat. "Sydney or Melbourne?" she hedged.

My heart hitched, but I nodded again. "What about them?"

"Well, I was just wondering if you wanted to tell me the real reason you didn't want to apply there?"

"Fair enough…" I replied slowly.

"If it's Roman, babes–"

"No!" I said too quickly and too loudly, then I put a hand on her knee so she'd let me finish. "No. It's not Roman. I just… I'm stressed enough about moving just to Adelaide. I know it's stupid–"

"It's not stupid!" she said vehemently. It was the way she'd been trying to express her support and I had to love her even more for it.

"Okay, it's not stupid. I get it might be hard for you to understand. But, I just… I can't do it, babes. I'm sorry."

She threw an arm around me and pulled me close. "No, Piper. I think, if there's one thing Roman got right, it was no apologies. I don't have anything against Adelaide and, knowing that's what's going to make you comfortable, then that's fine."

"But, Hads… If you want to go to–"

"Oh, hell no! We've been inseparable since kindergarten. I'm not going anywhere you're not if I don't have to. We've always planned to go to uni together, live together, cause havoc together. Nothing's going to change that."

"Don't you dare do this just for me."

She shook her head against mine. "Never. I'm far too shallow."

I laughed, but it sounded somewhat tense as I tried to keep the tears at bay.

"You okay?" she asked me and I swear the dam almost broke right there.

She sounded so much like Roman had that first night.

"I'm just being an idiot."

"No, babes. Never." She squeezed me tight. "You can't help you fell for him."

Putting it like that made me feel so pathetic. I knew she didn't mean it to, and I knew I wasn't really pathetic. Because, Roman and I...

"It was more than that, Hads..."

"I know. You also can't help that the great idiot enjoys this self-imposed exile he's put himself in."

"Pain is something he understands too well."

"Piper, he'll work it out." I decided not to call her out on the emotion in her voice this time; Hadley could do with some more practise with emotions.

I shook my head. "I don't think he will."

She sighed. "Then help him, babes."

"How?"

"Well, seems to me that Roman's your perfect, accident or not. So I say, we're strong, independent, modern women. Fight for your perfect, Piper. Tell him what he means to you."

"How? We've tried that, it doesn't work. He just tells me that he's got nothing to offer me and he's no good for me. That he can't be the guy I need."

"What do you think about that?"

I huffed. "It's fucking bullshit."

"Why?" Hadley snorted and I knew she was enjoying this more assertive version of me. "Why is it fucking bullshit?"

"Because he's already the guy I need. He's always been there for me. He knows how to make me feel better. We might get pissy with each other, but in the end it's… It used to be fine."

"Until he decided to deny his emotions."

I nodded, conceding that. "Well, yeah." I looked at her. "Wait. You really think he's denying his emotions?"

"Way I see it, babes… The guy's in love with you. This is new for him – presumably, right? So, it's kinda scary. He doesn't know how to do this attachment thing. So, he freaks out and he pushes you away, thinking it's just a matter of time before he hurts you–"

"You seem very knowledgeable about all this…?"

"I *am* the female him, remember?"

I snorted. "Right."

"So, what you need to do is reassure him he's perfect. Remind him he's already the guy you need and make him really realise that you don't need or want him to change."

I nodded as I waved back to Mason. "And, how do you propose I do this? I've tried, Hads. He won't hear me."

She shrugged. "I don't know. Just ask him to meet you and make him listen."

"Still not really seeing the 'how' here…"

"Babes, I'm the ideas one. You're the make things happen one." She indicated Roman on the other side of the oval. "So… Make things happen."

Of course, it wasn't as easy as that.

352

But, I made full use of the Ideas One and bounced things off her erratic, emotionless brain. She was a fantastic Roman, all snide and sarcastic and rude. If I hadn't known any better, I'd almost have thought Roman at his lowest was standing in front of me. And, I knew she was having a marvellous time with it all. Still, it helped me work out exactly what I wanted to say.

Finding the courage to say it to him was another matter.

Hadley helped keep me distracted with study and uni applications and looking for places to rent. Now that I didn't have the threat of Melbourne or Sydney hanging over me, I felt a little better about it all. Being able to tell Hadley the real reason I was apprehensive also made it all better; when it was all getting too much and the panic set in even unexpectedly, I could just ask her for a break and she was more than happy to oblige with no questions asked.

We all went to Mason's last lacrosse game of his school career and cheered him on fantastically. The trophy hinged on that last game and we all knew Mason was a bit nervous about it. So, we piled ourselves into every piece of school paraphernalia we could find and stood on the sidelines waving to him and booing the opposition.

Naturally, Mason was great. He was the perfect captain who took his team to victory for the last time. He was hoisted onto shoulders and paraded around, to be finally dropped in front of me and I hugged him hard.

When I let go of him, I turned to see Hadley and Tucker in a total make out fest. Mason and I shared a comfortable grin, put our arms around each other and gave Hadley and Tucker a little bit of space.

"How're things going?" Mason asked.

"Other than how sweaty and gross you are? They're actually pretty good."

"Roman pulled his head out of his arse yet?"

Hadley had kept everyone informed of every day that Roman continued to be an idiot. I didn't know if it was a testament to the standing I held with my friends, but they didn't care I was into the resident underachiever. They were totally happy to join Hadley in waiting to see when Roman would pull his finger out and be my boyfriend. It was simultaneously a little sad because Roman was – in Hadley's words – still being a fuckwit, but also a little humorous because it was unexpectedly wonderful of them.

I laughed. "No. And, I don't think he will."

We stopped and he turned to face me. "Ah, I'm sorry, Pipe."

I shrugged. "Don't be. It's probably better I get the whole unrequited love thing out of the way before uni. Makes it easier that way. I'll be more experienced and mature and all that."

He nodded. "Yeah, I reckon you're right."

I felt a huge twinge of guilt hit me. "I'm sorry, Mason…"

He gave me a warm smile, all sincere and happy. "Bit arrogant, thinking I meant you."

"Oh, you didn't–"

"I might have, but it's okay."

"How… Is there anyone else?" I asked.

He shook his head. "Nah, seems a bit late to be hoping for anything when we're all moving away next year. Who knows who will end up where, if we'll all stay in touch?"

"Well, you can be sure we'll always stay in touch."

"I hope so. You're a great friend to have."

"So are you."

"I'm glad we did this," he said, mirroring the words he'd said on our one date.

"Did what?" I smiled.

"Not go out."

I reached up to kiss his cheek and hugged him again. "Me, too." And, this time, I knew I was being honest.

So, there I was. I had about three or four facets of my life working out pretty damn well. Looking back, it all seemed too good to be true. But, I was apparently just that lucky.

I still saw Dr Freeman every couple of weeks and she thought I was making pretty decent progress. I found out that once I embraced my funk and my true self, it wasn't so hard to use the coping mechanisms she gave me. My friends and family were a fantastic support system. And, actually, just having them by my side gave me the confidence to keep going on a daily basis and not give in when it all felt too hard and confronting.

I might never have Roman in my life again and I was slowly coming to grips with that. But, I still had a hell of a lot to be thankful for. I still had my own kind of perfect. And, that was pretty perfect in itself.

Chapter Twenty Nine
The. Last. Damned. Time.

All right, so it had taken almost a week after Hadley had first started coaching me in talking to Roman for me to get up the courage to do it. We'd gone over every possible way I could lose my train of thought and keep me to task. Now, all I had to do was see if all that training was going to pay off.

I paced the lakeshore, not knowing if he was going to turn up or not. Things had been strained enough as it was. I'd all-but ignored him, he'd repaid the favour spectacularly. I'd written what felt like hundreds of messages to him only to delete them without sending them.

I had no reason to expect he'd still feel anything for me anymore that would mean he'd meet me just because I'd asked.

"You're going to wear a fucking trench if you keep that up," came the huff and I span to find him, cigarette in mouth and hand in pocket.

I opened my mouth and snapped it shut again as I tried to find the words that had been swimming around in my head since I'd let Hadley talk me into this whole mess. At the sight of him, I couldn't remember a single one. I couldn't remember why we were both there. I couldn't think of anything, feel anything except the way my heart felt lighter whenever I looked at him and my mind seemed to settle.

So much for training...

"What, Piper?" he asked as he flicked ash onto the shore, sounding incredibly bored.

"You came," was all I seemed capable of saying.

"Yeah. Why?"

My heart finally remembered why it had been feeling so heavy lately and it stuttered a little. "I… I don't know. I mean, I know I don't deserve–"

"Why did you message?" he sighed exasperatedly.

"Oh… Uh… Look, I just wanted to say something–"

"I don't need your apologies, Piper. Okay? Save it for your boyfriend when he finds out you wanted to meet me at the lake in the middle of the night." He ground the butt under his heel and lit another straight away.

"My…? What?"

"You've forgotten his name?" he scoffed.

I blinked. "Uh, no… I mean, Mason and I… We haven't been dating for a while…"

He'd been successfully avoiding looking at me like anything else in the world was far more interesting. But, his eyes snapped to my face now, narrowing in what I couldn't decide was anger or confusion.

"What?"

I shrugged. "We're not dating. Haven't been for…a couple of weeks."

His head jerked a little the way it did when he had to force himself to hold his tongue or his fist. "I'm surprised it took you so long to text. Look, I'm flattered. But, I think I've wasted enough time on you." He'd gone back to not looking at me.

If anyone else I really cared about had said that to me, my poor, beaten heart would have crumpled, insecurities would have flooded in, and I would have been totally offended. But, this was Roman. All I felt was angry with him and I pulled myself up.

It wasn't my fault he felt more for me than he wanted.

"Just because your ego was bruised doesn't give you the right to be a dick. All I've done is try here, Roman. We're both well aware we've both messed up on multiple occasions, but we don't lie to each other. Hide behind that bluster all you like, but I know you don't think any time we spent together was a waste–"

"Do you? What are you? Some kind of fucking psychic?" he sneered.

"Do you know what?" I snapped. "I'm going to say something now Roman and you're going to keep your damned mouth shut. You're not going to want to hear it and I don't really want to say it. But, I'm out of options and this is the only way forward–"

"Forward?" he laughed mirthlessly as he pointed at me with the cigarette he held. "I *knew* you'd become one of those girls. I thought you'd be the only one not to. But, you – like all those other idiots – think I can be changed!"

I crossed my arms and waited for him to finish his tirade.

"I don't change, sweetheart. I am who I am. I'm the slacker degenerate the cops pick up for existing because bets are I've done something illegal. I'm the guy that every father dreads around his daughter. I get into so many fights no one bats an eyelid anymore. I'm the guy the school hasn't expelled only because my father pays a shit tonne to keep me enrolled – like that's going to make me pass. I'm the guy stuck raising his niece because his mum has to work harder so she feels like her family isn't a failure, because her son's a criminal and her daughter has zero sense of responsibility for her own mistakes. And still, I don't change. No matter how much I love her. What makes you think I'm going to change for you? Huh?"

I stood silent for a while, until it was obvious he was done.

"You finished?" I asked and he only glared at me. "Good. Okay. I listened to your self-pitying tirade, time for you to listen to mine. I quite frankly don't give a shit about how you see yourself, because I know it's crap. I don't want you to change, Roman. I always loved you for you and nothing will change that. You might be all the things you say. But that's not all you are, you idiot. Sweet little Piper Barlow might be stupidly naïve, but not when it comes to you. I asked you to meet me for... God, a multitude of reasons, to be honest. But the crux of it is this, I always told you that I was woman enough to ask you out if I wanted to date you. And, I am. So, I'm just going to tell you something and let you think about it.

"I don't just love you. I fell in love with *you*. The dark bits and the light bits and everything in the middle. You thinking you're not good enough or you can't give me what I need isn't going to change that, because I know you are and I know you can. You already did. I know I can be what you need and I know you can be what I need. But, none of that matters if you don't believe it. I want you to ask yourself why that is, Roman. What's holding you back from being with me, really? I don't want to change you. I never want you to change. I want you exactly as you are – moody, angry, degenerate criminal that you are who I know cares about me. Because you can hide behind a scowl and flippant words, but I *know*!

"You don't..." My voice conveniently started cracking here. "You don't share what we did and not care. Not someone like you. You can tell me it was all for show, it was all for fun, you were only in it for the sex. Nothing that comes out of your mouth at this

359

point could be unexpected. But, I want to date you, Roman. It's as simple as that. I want you to think long and hard why you believe it's impossible, because I don't. So…" I cleared my throat awkwardly. "So, I didn't plan on ranting quite so long. But, that's it. I want to be with you. You're that something I need, and you offer me something no one else can. So, you let me know if you change your mind. Otherwise, I guess I'll see you around, Lombardi."

I took a step to leave, paused, shook my head, and took another step.

"Piper…"

I stopped again and took a deep breath. "I don't really need to hear how you can't give me anything and I should be with someone else or whatever bullshit excuse it was you used the last time, okay? Ball's in your court now."

I started walking away and almost missed his next words.

"I thought friends put the other first?" His voice was low, it was angry, and it was accusing.

I turned back to him. "Friends?" I huffed a humourless laugh. "Roman, we're in love with each other. We may as well both have admitted it. This? This *is* putting our friendship first. We're broken, Roman. We've been broken since you told me what you felt didn't change anything. We tried just friends and it didn't work because you were jealous of Mason and I was angry you didn't ask me to choose you when you had the chance. You want to be friends? Tell me you don't love me."

I looked at him, waiting for his answer. He threw his cigarette butt down and I knew he was glaring at me. I knew how angry I'd made him and I knew he was just as angry with me as he was with himself. Both of us were to blame here and there was no going back now. But, enemies felt a hell of a lot better than broken just then. I was being a little selfish again, but I'd come to realise that sometimes you had to put you first.

"I don't love you, Piper." His voice was even, but it was thick. Even though my heart hammered on my ribcage – wailing that it was the truth – my head wasn't falling for it.

I shrugged. "Well, we said no lies. So, I guess that's the truth, then."

We stared at each other for a few moments, the air sizzling around us with expectation and unsaid words. But, I wasn't going to keep fighting him now; I'd done all I could. I'd given it one last shot.

"Can I hug you now?" I asked.

"What?" He was genuinely taken aback.

"Well… Friends hug, right?"

He stared at me in shock, then nodded slowly.

I walked forward and reached up to wrap my arms around his neck like I used to. After a moment, his arms slid slowly around my waist and his nose went to my hair. My heart had a mini tantrum at all the feelings it elicited in me; he smelled so comforting and familiar I wondered how the hell I'd managed to live lately without something that seemed so…right. So much like home.

I pulled back to look at him, our noses bumping. There was pain in his eyes and I knew I'd put it there. I knew it was my fault; that I'd pushed when I probably shouldn't. But, I had a chance to get him back and I was going to take it – I had to know I'd done everything I could. It was up to him what he did with that.

"Piper…" he whispered, his eyes searching for something.

"Roman?" I replied.

"I can't…" It sounded like it took him an effort just to say that much…or little.

I nodded, swallowing the urge to tell him again that he was wrong – I couldn't force him to change his mind and to keep trying wouldn't be right. "Okay."

He dropped his forehead to mine, closed his eyes and sighed. I ran my hand down his cheek and he took a deep breath.

"I can't hurt you more than I already have, Piper…" he breathed.

I bit my tongue against what I wanted to say in response. "I… I understand."

His eyes opened and he looked into mine. "Do you?"

I sighed, trying not to lose the tenuous hold I had over my emotions. "I don't know anymore, Roman. Okay? I think I do, then you say things like that and I have no idea."

He held me closer and I snuggled my face into his jumper. God, he smelled so…him and nice and I missed it. I missed him. I'd take his friendship if that's all he could give. But, could he?

"I just…" He sighed. "This is as good an example as any. I can't keep my hands off you when I'm with you. And, that's not fucking fair. What kind of friend constantly thinks about kissing you, or worse–?"

"You."

He gave a rough chuckle, then all the humour was gone. "Fuck. Maybe this isn't a good idea." He held me at arm's length and searched my face.

Now, my head was starting to listen to my still whining heart. "What?" I asked.

He spun away and ran his hand through his hair. "Maybe we shouldn't be friends…" He took a deep breath. "Fuck, when did things get so hard?"

"When we fell in love with each other," I answered, my tone colder than I should have let it get. But, I could only fight so far.

"I told you I don't–"

I grabbed him, pulled him to me and kissed him. He took less than a second to respond. One hand cupped my cheek and the other gripped my hip tightly. I ran my hand through his hair and kissed him with everything I had. I gave him fireworks, slow burn, everything we could have been if things had been different. And his kiss did nothing to convince me his words were true, that he felt anything less than I did. His hand ran up my side, making goose bumps chase across my skin and my heart flutter painfully in my chest.

Before I completely lost my mind and finished reaching for his belt buckle, I pulled away, both of us breathing heavily. I pointed at him, feeling anger bubbling.

"Don't lie to me, Roman," I spat, venom in my tone. "Ever. Again."

I turned and stomped back towards my house, ignoring him calling after me no matter how much I wanted to turn back. It was the last time I'd walk away from him, that I promised myself. I was never putting myself in the position where I'd have to make that choice again.

I could handle him having the stupid delusion that he couldn't be what I needed or telling himself he wasn't in love with me. But, that wasn't the kind of kiss you gave someone you didn't love in some capacity. Maybe we could have found our way back to friends, but it wasn't happening now.

I felt a hand on my arm. "Fuck's sake, Piper!" he said heavily.

I ripped my arm from him and turned around so fast that I almost overbalanced, but I caught myself. "Just leave me be,

Roman. Please."

"Fuck, no. You want no more lies, Piper? Fine! Yes, I love you. I love you more than I knew was even possible. I love you so much it fucking scares the hell out of me. You're the best thing that ever happened to me. You're the only person to accept me for who I am, not who you want me to be or who you think I can be if I just applied myself a little more. But, I can't be with you because I am *so* afraid I'll ruin it and hurt you more than I already have."

"Nothing hurts me more, Roman, than you thinking so little of yourself. You were everything I needed and you weren't even trying. How can you think you'll fail if you do try?" I asked softly.

He shook his head. "Because it's what I do."

"Roman, I'm done trying to convince you otherwise. You want to believe that? It's not up to me to make you believe in yourself when you don't want me to. I fought for us as far as I could. It's your turn now. You decide you can be with me, then you let me know. But, this? This is done. We can't live with less when we both want more. We've tried and we've failed. I miss you. I miss us. But, we both deserve better."

He looked at me carefully, then started shaking his head again slowly. "I... I can't..."

I nodded. "Okay. See you around, Lombardi." I pulled away from him and went home.

"Piper!" he called, but he didn't follow me.

That.

That was going to be the last time I walked away from him.

Chapter Thirty
When You Say Nothing At All.

The holidays were meant to be final study time. We had mock exams when school went back and then the real things. So, it would have been normal for Piper to spend most of her time avoiding people and studying.

But, she didn't.

I mean, I did study. I'm not a complete idiot. But, I promised myself that I was going to live my life no matter what happened.

I'd given Roman the ultimatum, as unfair as that may have seemed. If that was our goodbye, I knew I'd done everything I could to fight for him, to show him I loved every him he was. I couldn't say I liked it – damn, it hurt – but I'd done what Dr Freeman said; I'd worked out what made me unhappy and took steps to let go of it. Unfortunately, it was a more literal let go than I'd hoped for.

Still, I had Hadley and Celeste, Mason, Craig and Tucker, and all the others we'd seemed to have surrounded ourselves with. Even if I wasn't feeling it, I forced myself to go to at least one out of two things they organised and I always enjoyed myself once I was there.

We took to taking over a few of *Lacey's* outdoor tables with our books and empty milkshake glasses as we told ourselves we were studying but in actual fact just got distracted.

I laughed as Mason batted me for stealing one of his chips and he stole one of mine back.

"I can't find my Stats notes!" Celeste cried as she shuffled books and papers around the tables.

Craig helped her look while she made eyes at Simon – yep, she'd moved off Craig and been through Henry and onto Simon – as I went back to my English notes and Mason and I elbowed each other back and forth. Conversation flowed around the table companionably, both study and general chatter.

"Do you think we need to read the *whole* thing?" Mason asked me.

I snorted as I looked at him. "Don't tell me that Mr Perfect didn't read it all when we were doing it?" I gasped.

He gave me a wry nod. "Very cute. But, no. I didn't." He picked up *Heart of Darkness* and waved it around aimlessly. "I just couldn't get into it."

"How did you get that A then?"

His grin turned mischievous. "SparkNotes is a wonderful invention."

I smacked his arm as I laughed. "I cannot believe Mason Carter cruised through with SparkNotes!"

He shrugged nonchalantly. "Yeah, well. Call me James Dean, rebel without a cause."

"Hardly without. Your cause seems to be passing English Lit."

We both laughed. And that was how easy it was with Mason now. We just worked. And thankfully, Shayla seemed to have finally got the hint that Mason wasn't into her.

After a few hushed, heated words with Tucker, Hadley huffed, pushed herself up from the table, and walked off. Tucker hurried after her, calling her name, and Mason and I exchanged a look.

They'd been doing that a bit lately. After a couple of weeks of seemingly perfection of their own, Hadley and Tucker had been… Well, fighting was excessive. But, she got short with him and he wasn't putting up with it. I mean, good on him; even if she was my best friend, she had no right to snap at him for no reason.

Although, I was pretty sure I knew the reason… Which didn't make it any better.

"Has she said anything?" Mason asked me.

I shook my head as I picked up my glass. "I've tried to broach the subject, but she just gets…antsy and short. I know how hard it can be to talk about stuff so I'm the last person who'd push her. But…"

"But, it's Hadley."

I nodded. "She's freaking out."

"It's hardly just her. Tuck's no better at this shit than *the* Hadley Reynolds. When they told us, I was surprised."

"He's had girlfriends."

Mason shrugged. "He's dated girls. I wouldn't call them girlfriends."

"You know, I'd worry he was going to break her heart. But, I'm not sure she's not going to break his first."

Mason sighed. "Maybe they'll realise it's not working before too much damage is done?"

I nodded and looked after them. I couldn't tell if they were still having a heated discussion or if they were exchanging flirty banter.

"I guess it's not up to us to dictate it's not working…" I said more wistfully than I'd intended.

"Pipe…"

I gave a half-hearted laugh. "I'm fine, Mase."

"For what it's worth – and I know you know him better – but I'm pretty sure he's miserable."

My laugh was more a huff this time. "Thanks. But, I'm going to let it go. I made the decision I wanted to be with him. And, he made the decision to not be with me. A relationship takes two and I have to respect his decision even if I don't agree with it."

Mason chuckled. "You sound like you've thought about this a lot."

I sighed. "Oh, I have. By myself, with Hadley –who's still all for castrating him – with Dr Freeman. I've spent too much time thinking about him, really."

My eyes slid back to where Hadley and Tucker were still in close conversation. I knew my best friend and I was wondering how much of the advice she'd had for me in regards to Roman was showing itself now. Was she freaking out about falling for Tucker? Was she just forcing something to work that wasn't supposed to? Was she actually just as inept at the whole dating thing as I was after all?

But, it really didn't matter in the end because she had to make her own paths and her own mistakes. All I could do was be there for her when she needed me the way I'd learnt to let her be there for me.

I picked up my glass again and realised it was empty.

"Right, I need a refill. Who else?"

Celeste put her hand up and I pushed up from the table and headed inside to get us more drinks. More caffeine meant more toilet breaks and a slight increase in the anxious racing of my heart. But, it also kept me oddly focussed and was far too delicious to pass up.

On a night we'd all decided was going to be a night off from study, we went for ice cream. So of course, the boys decided to play leapfrog with the poles outside the shop again.

I winced as Simon leapt over the pole, but he cleared it.

"See, it *is* fine this time!" Tucker crowed and I shook my head and pointed my spoon at him.

"That's what you say until someone loses a nut," I said.

"All right. You've got no nuts. Why don't you show us how it's done?" Simon said.

I nodded. "Fine, then."

"You're too short," Marty laughed.

I held my ice cream cup to Mason, who took it from me with an encouraging wry smile. "I'll show you short!"

I lined myself up as they all called things out; some encouraging, some jokingly disparaging. I flipped off the naysayers and rubbed my hands together.

"That's going to help is it?" Mason laughed.

"Shut up, all good gymnasts do this before a trick."

"I think it's called an apparatus," Henry said.

"And, I think they have chalk," Hadley offered.

"You can both shut it," I laughed.

"Come on then, shorty."

I nodded and prayed that all those stories about being hit in the vagina hurting as much as being kicked in the nuts were all bullshit.

I took a run up and launched. My hands landed on the top of the pole fine. But, the rest of my body didn't seem to think that leaping over the pole was a great idea. I sort of hopped lopsidedly and ended up staggering off to the left of it as I landed without any part of my body going over it.

Thankfully, Tucker was there to catch me before my hip had a rather rude introduction to the pavement.

"Okay!" I conceded amongst the laughter, leaning on Tucker as I tried to control my own laughter. "Okay! I'm too short."

"Well, you gave it a go," Tucker chuckled. "That's more than I can say for some people." He looked pointedly at Hadley, who huffed.

"Fine. I'll try it." I couldn't tell if it was animosity between them or that flirtatious banter that so often masqueraded as animosity.

The closer Hadley got to Tucker, the harder I found her to read. But, I was starting to determine new little nuances that helped me understand. And I could have been wrong, but I thought her eyes looked more banter than anything else.

She lined herself up just as I had. She took a run up just like I had. Her hands landed on the pole just like mine had. But she cleared it easily, just like I hadn't.

A great cheer went up and I threw my hands in the air as I did. I turned in excitement, but I ran smack into someone. With an apologetic smile on my face, I saw I'd run into Rio. He stopped, but Jake and Steve kept walking.

"Oh, hey," I said, stepping away from him which also happened to be inadvertently away from my friends.

He nodded, his mouth a hard line. "Hey."

"How are you?"

His eyes widened in surprise. "We friends?"

I felt my face flush. "Well, I guess not. No."

He gave one nod. He looked between me and my friends as he

took a drag of his cigarette. "You seem to be dealing with…everything."

My heart thudded. "What do you mean, 'everything'?"

Had Roman gone and told his friends all my secrets? Laughed behind my back about stupid Piper Barlow thinking life was *so hard*?

He shrugged. "Lombardi might be an idiot. The rest of us aren't. Look, it's not much coming from me, but I'm sorry he's being a fucking wanker." He looked over to Tucker. "Mind you, you seem to have moved on."

I frowned. "Tucker's dating Hadley actually. And, I haven't–" I stopped abruptly.

I really didn't want to tell Rio I hadn't moved on. Because I was supposed to be moving on. I knew I had to move on. I could move on. I was going to move on.

But, I could tell by the look in Rio's eyes that he'd understood my unspoken words far too well.

He gave that single nod again. "Yeah. He hasn't either, although he's making a good show of it."

My stomach did that jump-plummet thing it seemed so fond of doing lately because I knew how Roman would be making a good show of it.

"I don't really…" My voice strangled itself out.

Rio looked me over with interest. "You don't really what? Could have sworn Lombardi said you'd grown a spine." The corner of his mouth lifted slightly as though he found me amusing.

I cleared my throat, knowing my current speech impediment had more to do with emotion than anything else. "It's got less to do with a spine – or lack of – and more just…" I took a deep breath. "Look, I shouldn't have fallen in love with him, Rio. I get that–"

371

He barked a harsh laugh. "You all say that. How many girls do you think come crawling to me when he's done with them and ask me to get him back for them? I'm actually surprised–"

"I'm not asking you to do anything."

He blinked. "What?"

"I don't want you to get him back for me, or whatever. I don't need you to do anything."

I wasn't sure how much of his expression was surprise and how much was respect. "You just said–"

"Yeah, I did. I love your best mate, Rio. But, I don't want to change him. So," I shrugged, "he doesn't want to be with me? It's hard, yeah. But, I accept it. I told him what I wanted. He didn't want the same. Now, I'm just waiting on that moving on thing."

"You...?" he started.

I looked at him in question.

He found some of his lost bluster. "You're not going to beg me? Tell me you know he's not really that heartless? Tell me you know you're different? You're the one?"

I huffed a humourless laugh. "Rio, I do know he's not that heartless and I do know I'm different. But, that's worth fuck all if he denies it."

"Okay, I was being facetious–"

I snorted. "What?"

"Facetious, it means–"

"No, I know what it means. I'm just surprised you do."

Rio gave me a half-smile that was a whole lot more pronounced in his eyes. "I'm a degenerate, not an idiot."

"You and Lombardi practise that phrase in the mirror?"

The other half of his mouth rose as well and it transformed him. "Something like that. Anyway, before I was so rudely interrupted… I like you, Piper. If he wasn't being such a fucking tool, he'd realise you're perfect for him. I thought you were like the others, that he'd just gone mental. But you're not, are you?"

I shrugged. "I don't know. I mean, I still fell in love with him."

Rio leant towards me conspiratorially. "Yeah, but he fell in love with you, too. Didn't he?"

I swallowed and looked down to hide my blush. "Did he…? Has he said…?"

"Fuck no," he laughed. "But, he doesn't have to. I can see he loves you in every word he doesn't say." Rio tilted my chin up so I was looking at him. "I can try to talk to him?"

I shook my head and he slowly took his hand away. "Thanks. But…" Oh, God, I was tearing up. "He is who he is."

Rio's eyes softened with sympathy. "At the risk of sounding like a nancy wanker, you're fucking incredible Piper Barlow. You're the only chick I've met who even came close to being right for him. And, you smashed that shit right out of the park."

I huffed a teary laugh. "Thanks."

He held his hand out and I knew what he was expecting – I'd seen him and Roman do it on enough occasions. He went slowly so I could keep up, but I got the handshake right.

Rio was smiling hugely at me when we both heard his name called by the guy in question and I could hear he was pissed, in more than one sense of the word.

"What are you doing, you fucker?" Roman yelled.

He walked towards us, his arm around a girl I didn't know and a cigarette in his hand. Yep, he was definitely drunk. He glared daggers between Rio and me and I realised that my friends were doing a piss-poor job of pretending not to be watching the whole thing.

Roman's eyes finally landed on me and a thousand things went unsaid. My heart joined my stomach in the jump-plummet and I swallowed against my suddenly dry mouth.

"Keep your fucking panties on, mate," Rio replied. "I'm coming."

Roman nodded tersely, threw me one more look, and dragged the girl away.

"Everything he doesn't say," Rio said softly.

"I'm moving on."

"He's not."

"Because that helps," I sighed sarcastically.

"The heart wants what the heart wants. No matter what the head tells it, gorgeous." Then his usual swagger was back. He gave me a wink and his typical salute and strode after Roman.

I looked after him, the realisation dawning on me that every person you met was deeper than you ever gave them credit for. Especially when people they cared about were involved.

My friends all gave me a sympathetic smile. But, when I shook my head, they didn't press. I went back to watching the boys leapfrog the poles and reminded myself that moving on didn't mean I had to stop loving Roman, it just meant that I could go on without him.

And, I was going to go on without him.

Chapter Thirty One
A John Cusack Level of Perfection.

So, life went on and I got on.

School went back and the teachers failed at trying not to stress us out even more; as much from their faith in us and us not wanting to let them down as anything else. Rio took to giving me a nod that I suspected was in his mind the definition of friendly. Roman still ignored me and I pretended he didn't look like he was out all night every night.

Mock exams started right alongside our final overview of the year's work and, before I knew it, it was Friday and we had less than a week left before Muck Up Day officially kicked off SWOTVAC.

Sitting in my Biology mock exam was the last place I expected to hear music. But a familiar song was playing, almost as if from really far away.

I looked at Hadley and crooked my eyebrow. She shrugged, but the smile tugging at her lips made me think something was up and she knew all about it. I scanned a quick eye around the classroom and found people in various states of confusion – though, whether that was from the test or the music, who knew.

It was weird, but I went back to my test and tried not to sing along in my head.

From the other side of the classroom, by the window, people started whispering.

"Silence please," Mrs Grady snapped.

There was a pregnant pause, then people started whispering again. Someone even got up and looked out the window.

"Rachel, back in your seat please." She sighed. "You, too, Duncan!"

But, Rachel and Duncan didn't go back to their seats. In fact, more people got up and looked out the window.

"Class, this really is unacceptable! We are in the middle of a test. I need you all to return to your seats, or I will be forced to fail each one of you."

Even with that threat hanging over them, no one returned to their seats.

The song came to a close. Then, weirdly, started from the beginning again, and slightly louder this time. And, more people got up and went to the window.

"Class, I really must insist!" Mrs Grady said, getting up and walking over to the window herself.

I watched in half-interest, really just wanting to focus on my test – Biology was really not my strong point, but they'd wanted a science so I was doing a science.

I really should have done Psych...

"What is...?" Mrs Grady started.

"I think it's for Piper, miss," Rachel said, awestruck.

My head whipped up and I frowned. "What? Nothing's for me. I'm just quite happy doing my test, thanks."

Mrs Grady looked at me. "Good. I'd have thought you'd have more sense that to get caught up with the likes of Roman Lombardi."

"Sorry, what?" I choked.

Mrs Grady clapped her hands. "Class! As amusing as this is, can we get back to our tests now, please?"

The music got louder again.

"I don't think he's going away, miss."

"Yes. Thank you, Duncan."

Hadley snorted and slid out of her chair, going over to the window. She threw me a look like something impressed her and I had no idea what it was.

"John's waiting for you, babes." Hadley grinned.

"Who's what?" I asked.

"Does this mean something to you, Hadley?" Mrs Grady asked.

"Oh, it means nothing to me. But, it means *everything* to Piper."

"Excuse me?" Mrs Grady looked at me and I blinked.

"I have no idea what she's talking about," I assured her.

Hadley gave me that look that told me I was being the adorable idiot again.

"Piper, come over here please," Mrs Grady sighed.

"I'm fine just–"

"Now, please, Piper."

I got up from my desk and the crowd of students parted and let me through. But, my brain totally refused to register what it was seeing. Hadley grinned at me like it was the best joke – or win or something – ever. I looked back out the window and swatted her elbow away from my ribs.

Roman was standing on the oval in the tray of his ute, holding up an old boom box. And, it was blaring Fall Out Boy's 'Honarable Mention'.

Hadley's elbow found my ribs again.

"Told you John was waiting."

"Holy shit," I breathed, my heart thudding painfully.

"Piper," Mrs Grady chastised.

"You have to go out there," Hadley said.

I shook my head. "No. I can't!"

"You have to!" Rachel hissed.

"That's not how it went in the movie!" I hissed back the only thing my frazzled brain could think of.

"It's how it should have gone," Mrs Grady muttered quietly.

We all turned to look at her in surprise. And she gave us a very innocent look while she busily tried to pretend she'd said nothing.

"I have a test to finish," I said, walking back to my desk.

"Piper Barlow, you go out there and let him romance you!" Hadley ordered.

I looked around the room. Some students – mostly girls – were nodding enthusiastically. Some were looking confused by the whole thing. And, some were just looking pleased the test had been interrupted. Mrs Grady looked like she was entirely into the whole thing but the pesky 'being a teacher and having to be responsible' thing was putting a serious cramp on her style.

"I have a test to finish, and so do the rest of you," I said sullenly, my heart beating quickly. *Why now? Did he change his mind? How do I feel about this?*

Hadley got fired up and pointed out the window. "There is a man out there begging to be your John Cusack! A beautiful man, Piper. A man who *gets* you. You need to go to him!"

I looked around the room, feeling now was not the time to remind her he wasn't technically a man. "He can wait…"

"Yes. Piper's right…" Mrs Grady said slowly and completely unconvincingly.

"We have waited weeks for Roman Lombardi to pull his finger

out of his f–" Hadley stopped, looked at Mrs Grady guiltily, and kept going, "freaking arse. And, there he is! You go out there now and you end the movie right, God damn it! Or, I am never watching one of your precious John's movies again!"

I blinked at her. I was resolved not to. It wasn't going to work out. There were a hundred and one things that were standing in our way. Too much had happened. I'd moved on. But, my feet were already carrying me out the door.

"I regret to inform you that, if you leave this classroom Piper, I'll have to fail you on this test," Mrs Grady warned, and she sounded completely apologetic about it while sounding hopeful that's exactly what I was about to do.

I nodded, "I was probably going to fail anyway, to be honest," and I ran out of the room.

In all the classrooms I passed, kids were staring out the windows; there was whispering and teachers trying in vain to get their classes back under control. No doubt they were all expecting some big dramatic finish.

I ran out of the building and Roman was still standing in the same spot he'd been. I was actually fairly impressed with his tenacity; he'd always had a short attention span.

I slowed when he saw me. He dropped onto the grass and lowered the boom box so he was holding it by the handles by his knees. The air was charged around us again and I felt like *my* knees might give out. We stared at each other awkwardly. It was the first time I'd ever felt awkward around him. Sure, there had been plenty of times when I'd felt antsy and nervous, but never completely awkward.

"I didn't–" we started at the same time, then stopped with wry smiles.

"Sorry…" he said.

I shook my head. "No… I just didn't peg you for the big gestures type."

He nodded. "Yeah. Well, I'd like to not have to do it again. It's kind of unnerving not knowing if it's going to be a good ending or a bad ending."

"And, how do you think it will end?"

He shrugged. "That all depends on how badly I fucked up, doesn't it?"

"That sounds an awful lot like an apology, Lombardi," was out of my mouth before I could stop myself.

He nodded and looked away from me. "Yeah, well. I always said, Barlow, some things you have to apologise for."

"Not to me."

"Especially to you."

We stood in awkward silence, not really looking at each other but trying to sneak totally conspicuous looks at each other.

"Piper, I am sorry." God, he sounded so sincere.

"It's not like I didn't mess up, too," I replied.

"Is that an apology?" he chuckled.

I looked out over the oval and bit my lip against a smile. "It might be."

"Can I hug you now?" he asked.

I was torn between giving in and protecting the both of us. "I've moved on, Roman."

"Rio said."

I nodded. "Did he?"

"Yeah. He told me you were adamant but he didn't believe you."

My heart jump-plummeted all by itself. "I can't imagine why

he thought you'd care."

"Because he saw what you saw, what I need you to see again."

My eyes slid back to him. "I don't know exactly what you're asking of me here."

"Do you really not?" I knew he didn't believe me.

"Do *you* know what you're asking?" I looked at him fully, searching his face.

He searched me just as intently. "Honestly?"

"Always, Roman. You know that."

He nodded thoughtfully. "I realised you were right. I'm asking to be your boyfriend, Piper. For real. Legitimately. To be yours and entirely off the market."

"For how long, Roman? How long until you get bored?" Why was I questioning this?

Because, a voice reminded me, *you know him better than he knows himself.*

"You finally think that little of me? Or, you still think that little of you?"

Well played. "First, you thought there was an expiry date on this, then we were just friends, then we had no hope. And, you can't get bored of something you don't have. What's going to stop you getting bored now? Or, deciding you're not good enough after all? We'll presumably hold hands, we might even kiss at school. People will know, people will see, and you're supposed to only be with one person for the foreseeable future. Can you do that?"

"When that one person's you, I could do it forever."

My heart pounded and fluttered and dropped. "Roman, you can't…" I sighed. "What do you expect to get out of this?"

"I expect to spend every day with my best friend. I expect to sit in good moods and bad moods and comfort the only person who's ever truly accepted me for me. I expect to be able to tell everyone that this beautiful, intelligent, amazing girl is mine and I'm hers. I expect to watch cheesy Rom-Coms with you, to sit through hours of your stupid John Cusack movies, to always wonder if you could ever love me as much as you love him–"

"I don't love *him*. I don't know him…"

There was an incredibly pregnant pause and I didn't know if I could finish that sentence. Honesty was one thing. But, if I didn't open my mouth and say anything then I wasn't lying to him. He knew – I'd already told him multiple times – but I couldn't repeat it if this was going sideways.

"I'm not Carter, Piper. I'm certainly not perfect. But, I am totally in love with you and I want to be your John Cusack…" He grinned ruefully as the song was still playing on repeat, echoing that exact sentiment. "If you'll let me…"

Involuntarily, I took a step forward and "you're perfect to me, Roman," was out of my mouth before I really knew what was going through my mind.

Because, Roman Lombardi was perfect. For all his (many) flaws, he was perfect to me. He was perfect for me.

"You might not be the kind of perfect that people see in Mason. But I know you, Roman, and you're a level of perfect that even he couldn't manage. You're only yourself with me. There's no pretence, no lies, no matter how awkward it gets. And, there's a lot to be said for that."

"But, a John Cusack level of perfection?" he asked, a smile tugging at the corner of his lips.

I took a step towards him and he shifted the boom box to one side. I looked up at him and wondered how I'd ever doubted. It was there on his face. It had been there since that first week at the lake.

Stupidly, I'd just accepted what he believed, then I hadn't really fought until it was almost too late. And, now he finally accepted it. I cupped his cheek.

"Yes. You, Roman Lombardi, are a John Cusack level of perfection," I answered with a smile.

"For God's sake, kiss the boy!" I heard Hadley screech from the classroom and my face went hot.

Roman huffed a laugh. His eyes slid behind me to Hadley for a second, then they were back to mine again. "Your best friend's a bit of a dick."

I laughed. "To be fair, so is yours." Although, I had a sneaking feeling I owed Rio more than just another secret handshake.

He kicked his head sideways, conceding the point. "Yeah, true that."

"Can I kiss you now?" I asked.

He grinned. "Yeah, all right, then."

I paused just before our lips met. "Lombardi?"

"Barlow?"

"Do you want to be my boyfriend?"

His grin morphed into a smirk. "I thought we'd covered this already."

"Well, you made an awful lot of grand gestures and said a lot of fancy, nancy wanker words. But, I don't remember you actually asking."

"Stealing my thunder now, are we?"

I smiled as I looked into those rich, deep brown eyes, wondering how I could ever have thought they'd looked like black holes. "I always told you I'd ask you out if I ever actually wanted to date you."

"You're making this a very unromantic start, there, Barlow."

"Shut up and kiss me, boyfriend."

His eyes shone. "With pleasure, girlfriend."

He dropped the boom box and pulled me close. His arms wrapped around my body like he was never going to let me go. Personally, I was fine with that.

A huge cheer went up behind us and we broke apart with a laugh. I buried my face in his shoulder.

"If you bite me again…" he muttered, kissing my hair.

"You kinda love it."

"I kinda love you."

"I kinda love you, too."

He hugged me tight. "Shall we blow this popsicle stand?"

I nodded and he helped me into the ute. "If I get suspended for this…"

"Don't worry, Barlow, they're not going to suspend *you*."

He dropped the boom box into the tray and we did, indeed, blow that popsicle stand.

Accidentally Perfect

Thank you so much for reading this story! Word of mouth is super valuable to authors. So, if you have a few moments to rate/review Roman and Piper's story – or, even just pass it on to a friend – I would be really appreciative.

If you're so inclined, you can email me the link to your review and I'll send you a special epilogue to see what our accidentally perfect couple are up to a little later on.

 You can also access the Spotify playlist for the story using the QR code (for eBooks, the image is also a hyperlink).

If you want to keep up to date with my new releases, rambles and writing progress, sign up to my newsletter here: http://eepurl.com/doBRaX

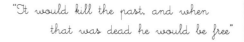

"It would kill the past, and when that was dead he would be free"

Aurora Daniels just wants to get through Year 12 with no distractions.

Then, Cole Fielding comes along.

She is instantly drawn to him but isn't sure he's the sort of guy she should fall for—he smokes, he's unreliable, gets into fights, and just exudes bad boy.

But, Cole hides an intelligence that speaks to her.

As they get closer, so does Cole's harrowing past. Can she believe in someone who can't believe in himself?

Maybe...

Out now.

Thanks

Thanks go out to the usual suspects for this one.

They Who Shall Not Be Named as always for their invaluable support, their brainstorming ideas, and their fantastic cheerleading.

Charny, Josie and Lauren for nattering with me about Roman's finer qualities and all the Chris Evans GIFs (who am I kidding, that one GIF in particular – we all know which one I'm talking about) to cheer me up when I'm down.

To my fur babies for standing on the keyboard, knocking my mouse on the floor, demanding biscuits, drooling over my snacks until I relent (we'll start out diets tomorrow), and sitting with me while I over-caffeinate.

And, my husband, who is always there for me. Without you, I wouldn't remember how to human. Poop jokes aside, you're always a John Cusack level of perfection to me.

About the Author

Born in New Zealand to a Brit and an Australian, I am an emerging writer with a passion for all things storytelling. I love reading, writing, TV and movies, gaming, and spending time with family and friends. I am an avid fan of British comedy, superheroes, and SuperWhoLock. I have too many favourite books, but I fell in love with reading after Isobelle Carmody's *Obernewtyn*. I am obsessed with all things mythological – my current focus being old-style Irish faeries. I live in Adelaide with my long-suffering husband, delirious dog, mad cat, two guinea pigs, two chickens, and a lazy turtle.

Where to find me:
Facebook: https://www.facebook.com/elizabethstevens88/
Twitter: www.twitter.com/writer_iz/
Website: www.elizabethstevens.com.au
Email: elizabeth.stevens@live.com